Tempting Turnabout

Why am I doing this? Emma thought as Lord Ragsdale's arms went around her and held her close. He was incredibly easy to kiss, and once begun, difficult to leave off. Her hands went to his hair then. She had always admired his thick hair, and she wondered if it felt as good as it looked. It did, to her gratification, and to his pleasure obviously, because he sighed and continued kissing her.

We simply must stop this kiss, she thought, and then didn't think anymore, finding herself more occupied with the rapidity of her heartbeat and the pleasant feel of him. *I am being kissed by an expert,* she thought.

Reforming so resourceful and unrepentant a rake as Lord Ragsdale was going to be devilishly difficult for Emma—especially when it would be so sweet and simple to be seduced by him. . . .

SIGNET REGENCY ROMANCE
Coming in November 1995

Elisabeth Fairchild
The Love Knot

Sandra Heath
Lucy's Christmas Angel

Gail Eastwood
The Captain's Dilemma

Reforming
Lord Ragsdale

❧━━◆◆◆━━❧

by

Carla Kelly

A SIGNET BOOK

SIGNET
Published by the Penguin Group
Penguin Books USA Inc., 375 Hudson Street,
New York, New York 10014, U.S.A.
Penguin Books Ltd, 27 Wrights Lane,
London W8 5TZ, England
Penguin Books Australia Ltd, Ringwood,
Victoria, Australia
Penguin Books Canada Ltd, 10 Alcorn Avenue,
Toronto, Ontario, Canada M4V 3B2
Penguin Books (N.Z.) Ltd, 182–190 Wairau Road,
Auckland 10, New Zealand

Penguin Books Ltd, Registered Offices:
Harmondsworth, Middlesex, England

First published by Signet, an imprint of Dutton Signet,
a division of Penguin Books USA Inc.

First Printing, October, 1995
10 9 8 7 6 5 4 3 2 1

To my sisters,
Karen Deo and Lynn Turner—
Family isn't just anything;
it's the only thing.

Keep my counsel lest thou slip.
If love or hate men offer thee,
Hide thy heart and hoard thy lip.
Wed no man. Remember me.
   —from the Irish,
    seventeenth century

Chapter 1

wonder why it is that my mistress is so ignorant, Lord Ragsdale thought as he took a sip of morning brandy and gazed at the evily scented letter spread out before him on the breakfast tray. uld it be that no one ever taught her the difference between ere" and "their"—and what on earth is this word?

He held up the paper closer to his good eye. "H'mmm, it appears that I am either thoughtless, thankless, reckless, or feckless, I don't think Fae knows that word."

He felt a tiny headache beginning from all that scent, so he mpled the letter into a ball and threw it across the room toward wastebasket by his desk, which was overflowing with other respondence. As usual, he was wide of the mark. "Fae, why so ch musk on one letter? Do you think I am an otter?" he asked miniature, which resided, smirking, on his night table.

He took another sip, then slid down to a more comfortable el in the bed. Of course, you didn't take on Fae in the first ce because she was a grammarian, he reminded himself. You quired her services because of her other splendid talents. Fae oullé might not be able to string a coherent sentence across a ge, but she knows her way across a mattress.

It was a thought that only a week ago might have propelled him m his own bed on Curzon Street and into hers only a brisk lk away. As he closed his eye, he asked himself what had anged in so brief an interval. Perhaps it was the rain. That was too much rain always made him restless and dissatisfied, even th the prospect of making love.

Making love. Now there is an odd phrase, he thought as he ened his eye and stared at the ceiling. "Fae Moullé, I do not ve you," he told the plaster swirls overhead. "You provide a easant jolt to my body, but so would another. No, Fae, I do not e you."

Lord Ragsdale sighed and jerked the pillow out from behind head. He lay flat on the bed and almost returned to sleep

again. The room was cool and silent, but some maggot was
rowing about in his brain now and wouldn't let him doze
course, it was well past noon, too.

Perhaps it was time to send a letter to Fae, severing all con
tions. He could sweeten her disappointment with a tidy sum,
offer to provide excellent references. The thought made him g
in spite of his vague discomfort. Any woman who could perf
such magic between sheets ought to have no trouble snaring
other marquess or earl. Lord knows England is full of dilettar
he thought, and we recognize what we like.

He thought back to Fae's letter, and the one the day bef
teasing him for a new wardrobe to peacock about town in. W
he liked the way she looked when she strolled about town v
him, her hand resting lightly—but so possessively—on his a
he was already dreading the mornings that would be taken
with modistes and models. Fae would not buy anything he did
approve of, so he would have to accompany her to the salons.
would coo and simper over each dress trotted out on display, t
look at him with her big blue eyes. "Whatever you want,
dear," she would ask.

"Whatever you want, my dear," he mimicked. She even a
that when they were in bed. Damn, Fae, don't you possess a
gle stray thought of your own? What do *you* like? Do you know

He sat up then and left his bed, thoroughly disgusted with h
self. He glared into the mirror and pointed a finger at his nig
shirted facsimile. "Johnny Staples, you are a spoiled son c
bitch," he told himself. "You pay Fae's bills, and she must ju
through your hoops. You should be ashamed."

He regarded himself another moment, then looked about for
eye patch. No sense in disturbing the maid, who was due in h
any moment with his shaving water. He found it and grinned
himself again, wondering how loud she would scream if she ca
into the room and found him leering at her with his patch over
good eye.

Too bad it was the Season now. He would have happily tra
it all for a week or two on a friend's estate, if he had any frie
left. He could take off that stupid patch and let the cold wi
blow across his dead eye, too, as he rode the land. But this v
London, and really, his eye didn't look too appealing, all mi
white, perpetually half-open, and with that nasty scar. I co
scare myself if I were drunk enough, he observed, as he pulled
robe about his shoulders and gave the coals in the fireplace a li
stir.

Ie grunted when the maid knocked, and she entered with his
water. When she left, he sat at his desk, staring glumly at all
correspondence before him. This was the overflow from the
ok room, too, he considered, wondering again why he had fired
secretary last month. He ruffled through the letters, many of
m invitations that should have been answered weeks ago.
'ell, Johnny, maybe it was because your secretary was robbing
 blind," he reminded himself. Which was true, but Lord, the
n could keep up with my business and knew how to write let-
s that sounded just like I had written them. What a pity the
etched cove could also duplicate my signature.

Ah, well, the little bastard was cooling his heels in Newgate
w, waiting transportation. Maybe if he survived the seven
nths in the reeking hold of a convict ship, he could find some-
e to bamboozle in Botany Bay. Lord Ragsdale sighed and
ked at his frazzled desk. I suppose now if I want to cancel my
son with Fae through the penny post, I'll have to write my own
er.

Nope, no letters to Fae, he reminded himself as he took off the
ch again and lathered up. She thinks I'm thoughtless, thank-
s, reckless, or feckless. And besides that, it's too much exer-
1. I suppose a new wardrobe won't kill me. It's a damned sight
ier than explaining to Fae that I'm tired of her.

Lord Ragsdale was not in a pleasant frame of mind when his
ther knocked on the door. He knew her knock; it was just hesi-
t enough to remind him that he paid her bills, too. He tucked in
 shirttails and buttoned up his pants, wondering at his foul
od. Maybe I should pay Fae a quick visit, he thought. I'd at
st leave her house in a more relaxed frame of mind.

'Come in, Mother," he said, trying not to sound sour. It wasn't
 mother's fault that he was rich and she was bound to him by
late father's stupid will. I really should settle a private income
her, he thought as he reached for his waistcoat. I wonder why
ther didn't? He never did anything wrong. Lord Ragsdale
hed. And death came too suddenly for him to say, "Oh, wait, I
 not ready."

As his mother came into his room on light feet, he felt his
od lifting slightly. How dainty she was, and how utterly unlike
n. She didn't look old enough to have a thirty-year-old son, he
ught as he inclined his head so she could kiss his cheek. True
form, she patted his neck cloth and tugged it to the left a little.

"Am I off center again, madam?" he inquired. "Funny how one

eye gone puts me off, even after . . ." He paused a moment. "L
see, is it ten years now?"

"Eleven, I think, my dear," she replied. "Oh, well. Two e
gone would be worse."

He nodded, wondering at her ability to cheer him up. She
so matter-of-fact. Why couldn't he have inherited that tender
instead of his father's leaning toward melancholy?

"I suppose," he agreed as he allowed her to help him into
coat. "Damn the Irish, anyway."

She frowned at him, and he took her hand.

"Yes, Mama. That was rude of me," he said before she co
"Didn't you teach me not to kick dogs? For so they are. I apo
gize."

He kissed his mother, and she smiled at him. "Accepted. N
hurry up and put on your shoes. They are belowstairs."

He looked at her, then rummaged for his shoes. "Mama, w
are you talking about?"

She sighed loud enough for him to pause in his exertio
"What did I forget this time?" he asked.

"Your American cousins, John. They have arrived."

He paused a moment in thought, embarrassed to have forgot
something that obviously had meaning for his mother. "
cousins," he repeated.

"John, you are the dearest blockhead," she said, and took
arm, pulling him toward the door. "My sister's children from V
ginia! Don't you remember?"

He did now. In fact, he remembered a winter's worth of bills
refurbish the ballroom and downstairs sitting rooms. And was
there something about Oxford? "Let's see if I remember no
Mama," he teased. "Someone is going to Oxford, and someo
else is attempting a come out under your redoubtable aegis."

"Excellent!" she commended him. "Sometimes you are the s
of efficiency."

"Not often, m'dear," he murmured as they descended the sta
"Will you begin reminding me on a regular basis that I must e
gage a secretary, and soon?"

"I have been," she said patiently. "And I've been remind
you about a valet, too, and while we're at it, a wife."

He laughed out loud at the seriousness of her expressio
"Which of the three do I need worse, madam?" he quizzed as s
steered him toward the gold saloon, reserved for unpleasa
events, formal occasions, and, apparently, little-known relatives

"A wife," she replied promptly as she allowed Lasker to op

door for her. "Ah, my dears! Heavens, are you drooping? Let
introduce your cousin, John Staples, Lord Ragsdale. John,
e are Robert and Sally Claridge, your cousins from Richmond,
ginia. Come forward, my dears. He won't bite."

f course I will not bite, he thought as he came forward to
ke cousin Robert's hand. He thought he might kiss Sally's
ek, but she was staring at his eye patch as though she expected
n suddenly to brandish a cutlass and edge her toward a plank.
nodded to her instead. "Delighted to meet you," he murmured
omatically, wondering how soon he could escape to White's
l bury his face in a pint of the finest.

He had to admit that they were a handsome pair, as he stepped
ck and allowed his mother's conversation to fill in any awk-
rd gaps before they had the chance to develop. Sally Claridge
l his own mother's ash blond good looks. If the expression in
· blue eyes was a trifle vacant, perhaps a good night's rest on a
low that did not pitch and yaw with an ocean under it would
ke the difference.

On the other hand, Robert's dark eyes seemed to miss nothing
he gazed about the room, looking for all the world like a solici-
totaling up the sum of each knickknack and trifle. I certainly
pe we measure up, Lord Ragsdale thought as he cast an amused
nce in Robert's direction, indicated a seat on the sofa to Sally,
n turned his attention to the fifth person in the room.

She should have taken up no more than a moment's flick of his
es, because she could only be Sally Claridge's servant, but he
und himself regarding her with some thoroughness, and his own
erest surprised him.

Lord Ragsdale was an admitted breast man. It was the first fea-
e he admired in all classes of women, and this female before
m was no exception to his time-honored tradition. She was still
vered with a rather shabby cloak, but the slope of it told him
at she was nicely, if not excessively, endowed. Ordinarily, his
ance would have lingered there as he contemplated her sus-
cted amplitude, but his attention was drawn to her regal pos-
e. She stood straight and tall, her chin back, her head up, as
ised a lady as ever favored the gold saloon. Her air fascinated
n.

He knew she must be tired. Sally Claridge had sunk herself
to the sofa with the appearance of one destined never to rise
ain, while Robert leaned heavily on a chair back. The servant
fore him made no such concession to exhaustion. She bore her-
f like a queen, and he was intrigued in spite of himself.

"And you are . . ." he began.

Robert threw himself into one of the dainty chairs, and heard his mother suck in her breath as it creaked. "That's Em Sally's waiting woman. Emma, I wish you'd take my cloak. A see here, there's Sally's, too. I don't know why we need to mind you."

Without a word, the woman came forward and took the cloa They were both much heavier than the one she still wore, but draped them gracefully over her arm and retreated into the ba ground again, her back as straight as a duchess.

Lord Ragsdale looked around at his butler, who stood in doorway. "Lasker, take the cloaks. Yours, too . . . Emma, is it?"

She nodded and showed the barest dimple in his direction.

"Lord, Emma, you are such a dunce! Can you not at least s 'Thank you, my lord,'?" Robert burst out.

"Thank you, my lord," the woman whispered, her chee aflame with color.

"That wasn't necessary," Lord Ragsdale replied mildly to cousin.

There was an awkward pause, which his mother filled adroi as he knew she would.

"Robert, Sally, tell me how my sister does. I know you are be tired, but I must know."

With a shy look in Lord Ragsdale's direction, Sally murmu a response to his mother, and Robert rummaged in his waistc for a letter. Lord Ragsdale clasped his hands behind his back a took another look at the waiting woman, as Robert called her.

It was a quaint expression, one he had not heard before, bu fit her exactly. She stood patient and still as his mother forg ahead with conversation, looking like someone used to waitin He thought her eyes were green, and her expression told him th her mind was miles distant. For a brief moment, he wonder what she was thinking, and then he laughed inwardly. Real Johnny, who cares what a servant thinks? he told himself. I a sure you do not.

"Well, son, is it agreed?"

Startled, he glanced at his mother, who was observing him w that combination of exasperation and fondness he was famil with.

"I'm sorry, m'dear, but I was not attending. Say on, pleas Tell me what it is I am to agree to."

It was the merest jest. Out of the corner of his eye, he notic fleeting dimple again. Sally registered nothing on her face, Robert just looked bored.

John, sometimes I think you are certifiable."

ally goggled at that. "Aunt Staples, he is a marquess!" she oed.

A title never gave anyone brains," his mother remarked, her ds crisp. "Bear that in mind, Sally, as you begin your own ad- ture here this Season." She looked at him again. "My dear, I merely suggesting that we all drive down to Oxford to install ert. It will give your cousins the opportunity of seeing their ndmama Whiteacre, whom they have never met."

Then brace yourselves," he murmured, wondering what the ting woman was making of this family talk. "I think it an ex- ent idea. Once you have met the family Gorgon, you will only too grateful for Charon to row you across the River Styx and the quad of Brasenose."

he blank stare that Robert returned made Lord Ragsdale sigh ardly and long for the comforts of his liquor cabinet. Obvi- ly his alma mater would be suffering one more fool gladly.

Provided Mr. Claridge can find the coin necessary for the boat .."

t was said in such a low tone that he doubted Emma's words ried much beyond his own ears. He grinned appreciatively. A hit, a palpable hit,' " he whispered back, and was rewarded h that fleeting dimple again. What have we here? he asked iself. A servant who knows her Greek mythology and Shake- are, too?

3ut there was something else about her softly voiced reply that off a bell in the back of his brain. He knew the lilt in her ce.

Emma, where are you from?" he asked suddenly, his voice too d in the quiet room.

Ie knew his question was inappropriate, and a rude interrup- n to his mother, who was saying something to Sally about andmama Whiteacre. Besides that, he could not think of a time en he had ever asked a servant anything that personal. And e he was at his most strident, demanding an answer.

5he was as startled as he was. The dimple disappeared, and she ked in dismay from Robert to Sally, as though waiting for a rimand.

Come now. It's an easy question," he said, egged on by some non that seemed to be amplifying his voice until he sounded 10st like he commanded troops again. He could see his mother

coming toward him, alarm on her face. He held up a hand to s
her. "I want to know where you are from and what is your nam

The servant's face had drained of all color now. She swallov
several times, then, if anything, her carriage became even m
regal. She looked him right in the eye, something he had ne
seen before in a servant, and spoke quite distinctly.

"My name is Emma Costello, sir, and I am from County Wi
low."

"Well, damn you, then, you and all your bog-trotting relative
he said, turned on his heel, and left the room. In another mom
he slammed out of the house, ignoring his mother, and hurr
down the sidewalk. He was too upset for Fae. It would be Whi
and a bottle of brandy. Maybe two.

Chapter 2

Even the relative serenity of White's in mid-afternoon could not assuage Lord Ragsdale's curious combination of vast ill-usage and shame of the dreariest sort. After a brief appearance in the main hallway, where the billiards players lounged between games and laid outrageous wagers on the evening's activities, he eased himself into the reading room. He sank with a sigh into his favorite old leather chair (wondering all over again why ordinary homes didn't have such simple pleasures), snapped open *The Times,* and burrowed behind it.

There were several articles that should have interested him. Napoleon had left the French Army under the tender mercies of Marshal Soult in Spain, and Soult had cat-and-moused General John Moore all the way to La Coruña in swift retreat.

"Bother it!" John Staples growled as he turned the page. And here was Napoleon in Paris again, enduring another diplomatic minuet by the lame but adroit Talleyrand. "Damn all Frenchmen!" the marquess muttered, and buried his face in the announcements of weddings and engagements. Yes, damn the French, he thought as he perused the closely written lines to read of friends about to succumb to one stage or another of matrimony. If the French had not nosed about the Irish in the last century and given them cause to revolt, he would still be looking at the paper with two eyes, instead of one. And he might still have an army career.

He folded the paper and rested it on his chest, allowing reason—or a close cousin to it—to reclaim him. John, you idiot, you have made a scene in front of a servant, he chided himself. He winced at the memory of the shock on his mother's face, and Robert's frank stare. Like all good butlers, Lasker had developed sudden amnesia, irreversible until the evening meal belowstairs in the servants' dining room, Lord Ragsdale was sure.

Lord Ragsdale knew that once Lasker spread the word belowstairs about the master's rudeness (probably with raised eyebrows and then the sorrowful pronouncement that the late Lord Ragsdale would never have exhibited such rag manners), he would suffer several days from a slowdown in domestic efficiency. Until the staff recovered from this attack on one of their own, the maid who delivered the morning coal while he still slept would rattle it a little louder in the scuttle; his shaving water would be only lukewarm; there would be scorch marks on his neck cloths; and the béarnaise sauce would be soupy. Such were the subtle punishments handed out by powerless people.

He had only managed the barest glance at Emma Costello when he flung himself out of the gold saloon, and was rewarded with a look of bewilderment. If he had suddenly struck her with his fists instead of his words, she could not have looked more surprised. He thought about Emma Costello and County Wicklow, and doubly damned himself for being a fool. He had spent his lifetime upstairs and far from servant gossip, but he knew enough about the hierarchy belowstairs to assure himself that Emma would not be treated well there, either. No one liked the Irish. He should never have shouted at her.

He sighed again and rubbed his forehead above his dead eye. It seldom pained him now, but he massaged the spot out of habit. When his eye was still a raw wound, some imp—was it too much laudanum?—twitted his agonized brain until he began to think that if he rubbed hard enough, his sight would return. It never happened, of course; when the pain lessened, he could only wonder at his foolishness.

So much self-flogging made him restless. With an oath, he got up, listened to the leather chair sigh for him, and moved to the fireplace, where he stood staring down at the flames. Rain scoured the windows again and matched his melancholy.

As soon as the rain let up, he would return to Curzon Street and apologize to his mother and Robert Claridge. An apology to Robert's sister probably wasn't necessary. Sally had watched his brief explosion with the wide-eyed stare of someone destined always to be a fraction late with the news. One didn't have to apologize to servants, of course, so he needn't say anything to Emma.

He returned after dinner at White's and a brief visit to Fae Moullé. She had opened the door to his two-rap knock with her usual cheerful demeanor, and helped him out of his overcoat, chattering half in French and half in English about some neighborhood happening. In the early days of their relationship, her bilingual patter had amused him, excited him even. Now as he allowed her to unwind his muffler and put her hands in familiar places, he felt only a certain irritation that she couldn't confine herself to one language or the other. Hot words rose to his lips, but he forced them back. No sense in tempting another work slowdown among those he paid; one from Fae would be much more uncomfortable than lukewarm shaving water. He kissed her instead, allowed her to lead him toward the bedroom, then changed his mind.

He sat on the bed next to her, but placed her hands carefully in her lap. "No, not now, Fae."

Her lower lip came out in that familiar pout. He looked at her and wondered why he had thought that expression so attractive. *Grow up, you silly widgeon,* he wanted to shout. He took her hand instead, noting how shapely it was, how each nail was filed to a softly rounded tip. Such effort was probably the work of an afternoon for Fae.

He scooted around to face her. "Fae, my love, what do you think about when I am not here?" he asked.

Quite a number of expressions crossed her face, but the one that kept recurring was a vague puzzlement that sank his spirits even lower. She just looked at him, as though wondering what he wanted her to say.

"Really, Fae," he plunged ahead, warming to his topic. "When we're not together, what thoughts cross your mind?"

Again that silence. *I don't pay you enough to think, do I,* he considered, and the realization made him rub his forehead once more.

"Do you ever read?" he asked, his voice gentle.

"Read, John?"

"Yes, Fae. That's when you open a book and examine its contents from beginning to end with the object of interpreting the words on the page. Some do it for enlightenment; others for entertainment," he explained patiently, his insides writhing.

She was silent as she took her hand out of his, and gave him her profile. "I think about what I am going to wear and how I should arrange my hair." She brightened then. "When the delivery boy comes with food, he always jokes a bit and asks what I think about politics."

"And what do you tell him?"

Fae turned back to regard him, her eyes wide in her flawless face. "Oh, I just laugh." She gave him a demonstration, her tinkling laughter as lovely as her features.

He grinned then, pulled her up, and slapped her lightly on the rump. "Fae, well, it was a stupid question, wasn't it?"

Her hands went to his neck cloth then, but he removed them and put on his coat again. "Some other time, m'dear." She was starting in again in her Anglo-Franco babble as he closed the door quietly behind him.

The evening sky was spitting out snow as he hurried along the street. If he didn't feel any worse for his encounter with his mistress, he also felt no better. When he returned home and allowed Lasker this time to help him out of his overcoat, he suddenly realized that it wouldn't take much to send him off to Norfolk finally, to an empty estate and a full wine cellar. I have avoided it too long, he thought. He stood indecisively in the hall, wondering where his mother was.

"She is at cards, my lord," Lasker pronounced.

"Lasker, you are amazing," Lord Ragsdale murmured. "I don't even have to speak to get an answer from you."

"Just so, my lord," Lasker agreed as they walked along together. He opened the door to the morning room and closed it quietly behind him.

Lady Ragsdale looked up from her solitaire and patted the chair beside her. John shook his head and stood over her, looking down at her hand.

"Mother, you're cheating again," he commented.

"Of course I am," she agreed equably. "How do you expect me to win at solitaire unless I cheat?" She took his hand suddenly and kissed it. "My dear, whatever is the matter with you these days?"

He sat down then and, leaning back, stuck his long legs out in front of him. "I don't know, Mother."

She smiled, glanced sideways at him, and then cheated again. "You remind me of someone on the verge of something."

He smiled back and returned the card she had just laid down to her hand. "If I had uttered such a nonsensical bit of illogic back at Brasenose in my Oxford years, my don would have kicked me down the stairs!" He tipped his head back and stared at the ceiling. "As it is, you are probably right."

"Very well, then, son. Go to bed."

"Yes, Mama." Lord Ragsdale stood up and stretched. "By the way, it is snowing again."

While he watched, she put the offending card back in its place before her. "We are still going to Oxford tomorrow."

"Yes, Mama," he repeated, smiling slightly. He may not have apologized in words, but she understood. How dear you are to me, he thought as he admired her calm beauty. Perhaps if I am extremely lucky, one day I will have a daughter who looks like you.

She blew a kiss to him as he stood in the open door. "Son, you have a chance to redeem yourself tomorrow."

"H'mmm?"

"My dresser is not feeling good enough to travel. Emma Costello will travel in her stead and look after Sally and me."

He sighed, started his hand toward his forehead, and then dropped it. "Then I will be on horseback, madam," he replied crisply as he left the room.

Robert Claridge was still up, but only just, when Lord Ragsdale knocked on his cousin's door. When he opened it to Robert's sleepy "Come in," his young cousin sat up quickly in bed, as though trying to appear at attention.

"For God's sake, relax!" John admonished as he closed the door and sat himself down beside his cousin's bed. "I am only your cousin, and by the eternal, I am a stupid one. Forgive me for my outburst this afternoon, Robert," he apologized simply.

Robert scratched his head and lay back down again. He punched his pillow into a comfortable ball and looked at his cousin. "Don't trouble your head about it, my lord," he said. "My Aunt Staples explained why you haven't much love for the Irish."

"No, I haven't," he agreed, grateful to his mother all over again for smoothing his path with his young relative. "But that's no excuse for such rudeness to your servant."

Robert's eyes were closing. "I can't see how it signifies. It's just Emma, and God knows there are times when she would try a saint."

"Of which I am not one," Lord Ragsdale said with no regret, grateful down to his boots to be so easily out of that mess. He crossed his legs and settled back in the chair. "Tell me, cousin, how did you get a servant from Ireland?"

Robert opened his eyes. "I was fourteen or fifteen when Papa bought her in the Norfolk sales."

"Bought her?" Lord Ragsdale sat up straight again. "Surely you don't mean that."

"I do, cousin. She's indentured. I was with him at the wharf when the ship's master led the lot of them into the sale shed."

Lord Ragsdale closed his eyes. He had heard of things like that, but the reality was never closer than a column in *The Times*. "Were they . . . were they chained together?" he asked.

"Lord, no," Robert said. He sat up in bed, wide-awake now. "You've never seen a more harmless lot of lice-ridden, scraggly men and women. Everyone was so thin." He paused. "My lord, that's the way things are in America. We buy and sell, and don't ask too many questions." He reflected a moment, as though groping about in his memory. "There was something about a rising in Dublin. Papa could tell you."

If that's the way things are, good riddance to the colonies, Lord Ragsdale thought. He was spared any comment on the hypocrisies of American government, because Robert was warming to his subject.

"Papa was looking for a clerk who could cipher. He stood there with the other buyers, calling out what he wanted. You know, someone was yelling 'Seamstress,' and someone else, 'Black-smith,' and another, 'Cordwainer.' Quite a racket in that barn," Robert explained. "Anyway, they must have been an ignorant lot of bog-trotters, because no one responded to any trades."

"Were they all Irish?"

"Yes, my lord."

"Then that explains it," Lord Ragsdale said. "You've never seen a more illiterate bunch of popish bead rubbers then the Irish. The only exertion they are capable of is breeding like rabbits."

"Well, I wouldn't know that," Robert said. "Anyway, Papa called out 'clerk,' one more time, hoping for a miracle and Emma stepped forward." Robert smiled at the memory. "I thought she was daft, and Papa even more daft for considering her." He sighed and lay back down again.

"Well?" John prompted.

"She wasn't wearing much more than a shift, her hair was nasty-looking, and her feet were bare, but Papa snapped off a string of figures and she added it all in her head." His cousin's eyes closed again. "Papa wouldn't let her ride in the carriage because she had lice, so she walked behind the carriage all the way home."

Lord Ragsdale shook his head. The Emma in his best sitting room this afternoon was a woman with an unmistakable air of elegance, no matter how shabby her clothes. What a strange day this was. "She was your father's clerk, then?" he prompted.

Robert was a moment replying, and Lord Ragsdale resisted the urge to give his shoulder a shake. "No. Mama wouldn't hear of it. Said it was indecent for any female, servant included, to tote up figures and do bookkeeping in the tobacco barn, and besides, she wanted a maid for Sally. So there you are. She's been with us five years. I could check her papers, but I think she has two years to run on her indenture."

Lord Ragsdale chewed on those facts for only a few moments, but it was long enough for Robert to begin the steady, even breathing of sleep. His questions would have to wait. "How odd," he murmured out loud as he watched his cousin another moment, then snuffed the candle with his fingers. He sat there another moment, then left the room quietly.

Lasker, keys in hand, met him in the hall. He bowed. "Good night, my lord. Is there anything else you will be needing?"

Lord Ragsdale shook his head. He almost asked the butler where they had found room for Emma, but changed his mind. Such a question would seem presumptuous, as though Lasker didn't know his own business well enough to make arrangements, no matter how cramped things were belowstairs. And if Emma ended up sleeping next to the coal shute, what concern was it of his?

He retired to his room, tugged off his boots, and settled on the bed with a full bottle of brandy in his lap and another on the night table. He avoided even a glance at his overflowing desk, hoping that it would go away. The late hour, followed by a swallow or two of brandy, and then another, permitted philosophy to override misanthropy. While he could not overlook entirely the desire to bolt the metropolis, he decided that he could tolerate the remaining few months of this London Season.

There was no question that he owed his mother and cousin the favor of an escort, he thought as he drank steadily. And while he was doing his duty, he could peruse the females that frequented Almack's and other venues of quality, find a lady not wanting in too many particulars, and make her an offer. He had money enough to make Croesus a loan; barring his absent eye, his parts were all present and easy to look upon; he was healthier than most of his acquaintances. "Ah, yes, I will do well enough in the marriage mart," he told the ceiling. "I doubt this will require overmuch exertion."

He took another swig or two from the brandy bottle, then set it carefully on the floor. To his surprise, the bottle fell on its side; to his further surprise, nothing spilled out. He leaned off the bed and regarded the bottle. *I must advise Lasker not to be taken in by the vintner,* he thought. *It seems that he is buying smaller bottles than he used to.*

The next bottle went down faster than the first. Lord Ragsdale considered an expedition down the stairs to the wine cellar for more, but discarded the notion. The room seemed to be shrinking, and he did not think he could get out of the door before it disappeared altogether. Such an odd phenomenon, he considered as he unbuttoned his trousers, loosened his neck cloth, and closed his eye.

Chapter 3

To say that Lord Ragsdale awakened with a big head would be to mince words. His stomach was as queasy as though he was sailing an ocean with mountain-high waves. When he sat up, he whimpered at the pain in his skull. He lay back down again, hoping with all his heart that it had snowed ten feet last night and they would be unable to travel today.

But the gods were not smiling on Lord Ragsdale this morning. When the maid who brought in the coal noticed that he was awake, she screamed a cheery "Good morrow, my lord," that filled the room and echoed back and forth inside the sorely tried empty space between his ears. After she thundered at least a ton of coal onto the grate, she threw open his draperies on runners that shrieked like banshees.

"It's a good morning for a trip, my lord," she offered with the voice of a boatswain in a hurricane.

He could only force his lips into a weak smile, and put his hand over his eye against the glare that threatened to blind his one remaining orb. If you say another word, I will die, he thought. To his relief, she said nothing more, but only slammed the door on her way out so loud that his guts quivered. He gritted his teeth and moaned.

He had progressed to dangling his legs off the bed when his mother banged on the door with a battering ram and opened it a crack.

"John, we want to leave within the hour," she reminded him, then took a closer look. "Oh, John!"

Three hours later, he groped his way downstairs and onto his horse, which waited patiently by the front stoop. Lasker had sent the footman in to help him pack, and also to rescue him from his own razor when he attempted to shave his pale face. A splattering of bay rum was more than he could bear. It sent him lurching back to his washstand, where he vomited his toenails into the basin, vowing, as he gagged and retched, never to drink again.

The cold February air was a relief. He breathed as deep as he
ared of the icy blast, then pulled his hat low and his riding coat
ght around him. He carefully shook his head over his mother's
tempts to get him inside the carriage and waited, reins held in
ack fingers, while Emma Costello carried in the last bandbox.

As she went to climb in, her cloak caught on the door handle.
er hands full, she struggled to free herself, then glanced in his
rection, as if to ask for help.

Embarrassed, he shook his head, knowing that if he dis-
ounted, he would disgrace himself again. To his further chagrin,
e quickly lowered her eyes and turned away as if humiliated,
ntinuing her efforts to free herself until Robert dismounted with
a oath and lent a hand. Lord Ragsdale watched as she hurried in-
de the carriage, closed the door, and made herself small in the
rner.

Oh, Lord, I am off to such a start with this one, he thought as
e regarded Emma another moment, then gently eased Champion
to the street. Please, please let this London Season go by
ickly.

They traveled steadily into a dreary afternoon, the clouds gray
d threatening, the wind coming in puffs of blasting cold from
l directions at the same time. Robert kept him company for part
the journey, and proved to be an amiable companion. He was
e of those persons who, if given free rein to talk, would carry
a a merry discourse that required little comment or addendum
om another. John was content to listen to his cousin. He learned
l he ever wanted to know about tobacco farming, the growing
ave trade, and the trouble with Federalists without having to re-
ond beyond the occasional "H'mm," or "Indeed." Robert's mel-
w voice with its soft drawl was soothing in the extreme. By the
ne Robert succumbed to the weather and begged a seat inside
e coach, John was almost sorry to see him surrender.

As soon as Robert retreated to the relative comfort of the fam-
y carriage, Lord Ragsdale realized that the next few hours of
avel would hang heavy. The day was no warmer, the farther
ey traveled into it, and he felt ill unto death. Had he traveled by
mself, Lord Ragsdale would have stopped at the first hostelry
at appeared to offer clean sheets and quiet premises. His head
gan to throb again.

He was about to stop the coachman, admit defeat, and plead ill-
ss, when Sally Claridge came to his unexpected rescue. He was
vallowing his pride and rising bile when his mother lowered the
ass and rapped on the side of the carriage with her umbrella.

The coachman reined in and peered back at her. Lady Ragsd
opened the door and leaned out to speak to her son.

"John, Sally is experiencing some distress from the motio
know this will irritate you, but could we stop early tonight?"
asked.

It was all he could do to keep from bursting into tears of gr
tude. Dear Sally, can it be that you are as estimable as y
brother? he thought as he faked a frown and then nodded, hop
that he did not appear too eager.

"If we must, Mother," he responded, after a suitable length
time had passed. He sighed heavily for the effect, then wished
hadn't, as his stomach heaved. "Let me ride on ahead and find
nearest inn," he offered, hoping that the inmates of the carri
would see his act as a magnanimous gesture, rather than a desp
ate attempt to get out of their range of vision before he disgra
himself.

Lady Ragsdale nodded and spoke to Sally, who raised her p
face to the window and blew him a kiss. He glanced at Emma,
she studiously ignored him. Ah, well, he thought as he tipped
hat and spurred ahead, eager to outdistance the carriage. I
puke in peace.

When the carriage arrived at the Norman and Saxon, L
Ragsdale was in control of his parts again. The inn was full
other clients who must have had second thoughts about
weather, but he was able to secure a private parlor and two sle
ing rooms. While he waited for the carriage to arrive, he tested
nerve on a pint in the tavern and watched a card game that fr
the unkempt aspect of its patrons, appeared to have been
progress since shortly after Moses brought down stone tabl
from Sinai. The ale went down smoothly, settling what, if a
thing, remained of his stomach's contents. The card ga
tempted him not at all.

He helped his mother from the carriage, quick to notice that
was not in the best of spirits, either. "Poor dear," he murmured
she leaned on his arm. "Too many bumps in the road?"

She nodded. "I always forget what a poor traveler I am. Ple
tell me there is a bed close by, John."

He kissed her cheek, happy to play the competent son. "Th
is even a warming pan between the sheets, m'dear. You and Sa
can keep each other company, snoring to your heart's delight."

He helped her upstairs and then returned to retrieve Sally, w
drooped on Emma's arm in the hallway outside the public room
entrance.

"Can I lend a hand here?" he asked, suddenly shy, and rendered
ore embarrassed when Emma nodded, relinquished her hold,
d tried to disappear against the wall. He took a firm grasp on
lly's shoulder and pointed her toward the stairs, but she sur-
ised him by stiffening up. "Yes, my dear?" he inquired, curious
out her resistance.

She didn't say anything, but he followed her gaze into the tap-
om, where Robert was standing over the gaming table, a pint in
s hand. "I wish you would not let him play," she said.

He laughed. "I am sure it is only a harmless game."

"I mean it," Sally replied, and he could almost feel her gravity.

He took her by both shoulders then. "Sally, I'll get you up-
airs, and Emma can make you and Mama comfortable. I
omise to keep an eye on your brother. I am certain I can keep
m from sitting down at a gaming table. How difficult can that
?" He attempted a joke because her anxiety disturbed him. "I
n certain I outweigh my cousin, if it comes to that."

She regarded him with a wan smile, and allowed him to lead
r up the narrow stairway and into the room where Lady Rags-
le still sat on the bed, the effort to move beyond her. Emma fol-
wed with the luggage. In another moment, the servant was
illfully, quietly in charge. He paused in the doorway until he
as sure that all was well.

"I'll order dinner, Mama," he said. "What would you like?"

"Soup and bread for the ladies, my lord," Emma said firmly.
Nothing more."

"And you?"

She seemed surprised that he would ask. She looked up from
e floor where she was untying his mother's shoes. "Whatever
ou wish, my lord," she replied, still without looking him in the
e, as if she feared she was too much trouble.

He went downstairs to order dinner, and noticed that Robert
d not moved from his position by the gaming table. He watched
e play intently, and Lord Ragsdale had to call his name several
nes to get his attention. Even then, he left the room reluctantly,
ith several backward glances.

"Faro is my favorite game," he confided to his cousin as he al-
wed himself to be led from the room. "But vingt-et-un will do.
ousin, do you play cards?"

"Never," Lord Ragsdale replied firmly. "I hate cards. I thought
night that you and I would discuss your coming matriculation at
rasenose. It's my college, you know." He looked at his cousin

virtuously. "I went to some trouble to arrange your attendance
this juncture in the term, let me assure you."

He could tell that Robert was disappointed to leave the gam
but to his relief, his cousin followed him into the private parl
Lord Ragsdale poured two glasses of sherry, but Robert was pa
ing between the windows. "Do sit down, cousin," he advise
"We still have a half day's drive tomorrow, and you'll need
your constitution to meet your grandmother. Come, come no
Here is dinner."

They ate in silence. Robert was no longer the attractive conv
sationalist of the afternoon, and Lord Ragsdale could only wond
at his cousin's restless air. Well, if I must exert myself, I must,
thought, as he launched into a description of Brasenose and its
lustrious traditions. Through it all, he harbored a very real sus
cion that Robert's mind was elsewhere.

He was interrupted by a soft tap on the door. It was Emm
come to fetch the soup. "Let me help you," he insisted as s
struggled with the heavy tray.

"I can manage," she replied, even as he took it away from h
"Truly I can."

He nodded, feeling oddly useful, even though it was only a di
ner tray. "Well, perhaps you will allow me to redeem myself."

Emma looked at him quickly, and then looked away. "I do
mean to be trouble," she said softly as she opened the door f
him.

He could think of no reply to such honesty so he made no
and was rewarded with a second frightened glance and a percep
ble drawing away from him, even though they stood close t
gether at the room's entrance. As he came through the doorw
first, carrying the tray, he experienced the odd feeling that pe
haps Emma Costello cared no more for the English than he lov
the Irish. It was a leveling thought, and one that he had not co
sidered before.

He left the tray, kissed his mother good night, and started f
the door. He thought Sally was asleep, but she called to him, h
voice hesitant, as though she, like Emma, wondered what
would think.

"Cousin, please. Please make sure that Robert does not pl
cards tonight," she urged.

He smiled at Sally, then bowed elaborately, winking at her
the way up.

"She means it, my lord" came Emma's distinct brogue. H

ice was firm, hard even, as though she spoke to a child, and not bright one, either.

He stood in the doorway, his hand on the knob. "I can't say that care for your impertinence, Emma," he snapped.

"Then I apologize for it," she replied promptly. "But please,
. . ."

He closed the door on whatever else she was going to haver on out and returned to the parlor to find it empty. His mind filled ith odd disquiet, he hurried downstairs in time to prevent Robert om sitting at the gaming table.

"Come, lad, we're off to an early start in the morning, remem-r?" he said, nodding to the other gamesters. "You'll excuse us, am sure."

"Really, cousin, I think that wasn't necessary," Robert otested as Lord Ragsdale followed him up the stairs. "I was ly going to sit for one hand." He stopped on the stairs, and his ice took on a wheedling tone. "I promise to be in bed before u get to sleep if you let me go back down."

"No, and that's final," Lord Ragsdale insisted. His head was ginning to ache again, compounded by the uneasiness that grew him as he regarded his cousin Robert. So you will be no trou-e, he thought as he removed his clothes and pulled on his night-irt. I think I begin to understand your parents' eagerness to get u out of America. How deep in gambling debt were you there? nd why is this my problem now?

It was a subject to ruminate on. Tight-lipped, silent, Robert un-essed and threw himself into bed alongside his cousin. He broke e long silence finally. "I think you are perfectly beastly to deny e one last game before I enroll at Brasenose."

"I think I am nothing of the sort, cousin," John replied. "Go to eep."

He lay in silence then, wondering if Robert would respond. He ared at the ceiling, listening to Robert's breathing turn regular d deep. Relief settled over him, and he relaxed into the mat-ess. He hung on another half hour, listening to Robert, and then lowed sleep to claim him, too.

If he had been under oath in the assizes, he could not have told jury what woke him up early that morning. One moment he was leep, dreaming of nothing, and the next instant he was wide-wake and sitting up in bed. The room was in total darkness and lding his own breath, he listened intently for Robert's breath-g. Nothing.

Cautiously, he reached out his hand and felt the other pillo
"My God," he said out loud as he fumbled for the candle, mo
alert than he had been in years.

He was the room's sole inhabitant. After the moment of par
passed, his next thought was to return to sleep. Robert's spendi
habits were none of his concern. He had promised to accompan
his mother and cousins to Oxford, and surely that charge did n
involve wet-nursing a young man of some twenty years. His ov
mother had assured him that the cousins would be no trouble, a
truly, they would not be if he lay down again and returned
sleep. Besides, he reasoned, half the world's troubles were caus
by people too eager to meddle in others' affairs. So what if Rob
gamed away all his money? How could that possibly conce
him? He blew out the candle.

His eyes were closing again when an ugly thought tunnel
through the fog of sleep. What if it is *your* money he is gamin
you idiot? He sat up again and lit the candle once more, holding
high as he looked around the room. Everything looked as he h
left it. He glanced closer at his overcoat, slung over a chair bac
He was certain he had placed it around the chair before taking c
his clothes.

He was on his feet in a moment, pawing through his overcoa
His hands clutched his wallet, but it was much thinner than he r
membered. "Damn you, cousin," he swore as he opened it an
found nothing beyond a couple directions and a toll chit.

Lord Ragsdale looked at Robert's dressing case. It had been r
fled through, too, as if the owner were looking for somethir
tucked away. He found a leather case containing a variety of leg
papers that looked as though they had been crammed back insi
in a hurry.

This is going to be a nasty scene, he thought as he shoved h
nightshirt into his trousers and pulled on his boots. He didn't sto
to look for his eye patch as he ran his fingers through his hai
then wrenched open the door.

To Lord Ragsdale's surprise, the innkeeper stood before hi
on the landing, breathing hard as though he had taken the flight
stairs two or three at a time.

"What on earth is the matter?" Lord Ragsdale said, wincing
the landlord took one look at his ruined eye and gulped.

"My lord, you had better come downstairs at once. I don't thir
you'll like what's going on. I know I don't, but it's not somethir
I can prevent."

"What can you be so lathered up about?" Lord Ragsdale said

followed the man down the stairs. "I think my young cousin is
ending my money, but that's my business. I intend to give him
ite a scold, rest assured."

The landlord stopped on the stairs and looked him in the eye.
le's gone beyond your money, my lord, 'way beyond. Please
rry."

If anything, the taproom was more crowded than before, even
ough it was hours after midnight. The same group of gamesters
t at the table, with the addition of Robert and the waiting
oman.

Lord Ragsdale barely noticed his cousin, who waved him a
eeting and moved to pull up another chair. His eye went imme-
ately to Emma Costello, who stood in her nightdress behind his
usin's chair. She was as pale as her flannel shift, her auburn
ir flaming around her face, her eyes burning like coals into his
vn. She swallowed once, and he thought she would speak, but
e said nothing and did nothing but stare at the opposite wall.
er face was wiped clean of any hope, or of any expression at all.

He wrenched his glance away from her and stared hard at the
ming table. There was a document on it, with a seal and rib-
ns, and folded in half as though it had just come out of the
ther case upstairs. He looked at Emma again, and back at the
cument, and he was filled with more anger than he would have
ought possible, considering that this whole affair was probably
ne of his business.

He was so angry he could not speak. The man sitting next to
obert nudged him. "Your draw, laddie," he said, and then
nned at Emma and smacked his lips.

"Touch that card, Robert, and I will thrash you until your back-
ne breaks through your skin."

My God, did I say that? Lord Ragsdale thought as he crossed
e room in two steps and stood leaning over his cousin's chair.

To his further amazement, Robert merely looked at him and
rugged his shoulders. "Lord, cousin, I am in debt and nothing
e will do but Emma. I have her papers here, and I can do as I
e. It's legal. Everyone's agreed."

He turned back to the table and reached for the card. Lord
agsdale slammed his fist down on his cousin's hand, shoved him
t of the chair, and sat down in Robert's place, his face inches
om his opponent. "I'll make you a better deal," he said, each
ord distinct in the suddenly silent room. He picked up the inden-
e papers. "Look here, did he show you how this indenture has
s than eighteen months to run?"

The other men at the table crowded close. The smell of ru
breath and tobacco made him want to flee the room, gagging, b
he looked at each man in turn, hoping for a measure of intimic
tion from his unseeing eye. "How much was he going to ask for'

"Two hundred pounds to settle up."

"Against an eighteen-month indenture?" Lord Ragsda
leaned back in his chair to escape the fumes, and laughe
"Well, I have . . ." He paused. Absolutely no money, he thoug!
as he stared daggers at his cousin.

The gambler shrugged. "I can take your money as well as his
he offered.

"I don't have any," Lord Ragsdale said.

"Well, then, we play for the wench," said the gambler. "Y
can go back to bed."

I could, he thought. She is not my chattel. He looked at Robe
And you are not my problem. He started to get up, when he hea
the smallest sound from the servant. He may even have imagin
it, but suddenly he knew he could not leave her there to the merc
of these men, no matter how much he disliked her. He sat ba
down again.

"I have something better than that testy Irish wench." H
leaned forward again, his voice conspiratorial. "Two horses out
the stable. One a chestnut and the other a bay. The chestnut w
at Newport last season. That cuts the debt, and Emma goes bac
upstairs where she belongs."

My God, I am giving away the best two horses a man ev
owned for an Irish bog-trotter who can't stand the sight of me, I
thought as he glared at the other men around the table.

The men looked at each other. The hostler by the bar spoke u
"I curried them two bits of bone and blood this afternoon, an
he's right, lads." He stopped then and looked around, filled wi
the pride that comes from being the expert.

Lord Ragsdale stood up, ignoring his cousin, who still sat c
the floor where he had pushed him. "Does that clear my cousin
debt, then? Two of the best horses in London, and I take back th
paper."

The men nodded. "We'll call it even," the dealer said.

Even, my ass, Lord Ragsdale thought as he watched his cous
get to his feet, sway a moment, and then reach for the paper.

Lord Ragsdale was quicker. He snatched the document fro
Robert so fast that his cousin leaped back in surprise and topple
onto the floor again. "Robert, the only way you can get this pap
back is to pay me the five thousand pounds you now owe me."

mma gasped. Lord Ragsdale looked around in amazement of own. I just bought a woman, he thought, as he took her hand pulled her from the taproom—an Irish woman I don't like too ‍, and who doesn't like me at all.

he sank to her knees in the hall and covered her face with her ds. His first instinct was to leave her there and just go back to . He started up the stairs, then returned to kneel beside her in passageway.

Don't cry, Emma," he said.

I'm not crying," she murmured, even as the tears streamed n her cheeks and she savagely wiped them away.

Thank goodness for that," he replied, keeping his tone light. on my word, Emma, I hope you are worth five thousand nds."

Chapter 4

I wonder what has happened to the simplicity of a good nigh[t] sleep, Lord Ragsdale thought to himself as he fumed in his b[ed] and watched morning gradually overtake the Norman and Saxo[n] Sleep was out of the question; the more he thought about the d[is]aster of the night, the more put-upon he imagined himself.

Never mind that Robert Claridge lay on the floor of the roo[m] noisily sleeping off a prodigious amount of rum. John Stapl[es] rose up on his elbow to give his cousin a particularly malevole[nt] glare. The effort was wasted. Robert slumbered on, wrapped [in] peaceful sleep that he, Lord Ragsdale, could only wish for.

The nerve of his aunt and uncle Claridge, to foist such a pr[ob]lem off onto an English relative they had never met. Lord Ra[gs]dale punched his pillow savagely, trying to find a spot withou[t a] lump, and considered that the whole affair must be yet anoth[er] way for Americans to wreak vengeance on their late antagonists[. I] have done nothing to deserve this cousin, he reflected.

He thought of Emma Costello, standing so quiet as Robert p[re]pared to sell her on the drawing of a card. He groaned and stuff[ed] his pillow over his face, as if to shut out her calm face th[at] seemed to stare at him still. He had never seen anyone so tota[lly] without hope, and yet so brave in the face of it. He removed t[he] pillow and sat up, so he could stare daggers at his sleeping cous[in.]

"One thing is certain, Robert," he said, making no effort [to] lower his voice. "Only a truly wicked master would try what y[ou] tried. And I don't care if she is Irish. It was a low blow."

Beyond the smacking of his lips and a rude noise, Robert ma[de] no comment. Lord Ragsdale sighed and looked away toward t[he] window, urging dawn to forget that it was February and appe[ar] sooner.

By seven o'clock, he was dressed and pacing the floor, steppi[ng] over Robert on each trip across the room, and resisting the urg[e] each time, to kick him. Finally, his baser instincts triumphed; [he] kicked Robert in the ribs with enough force to waken his cousin.

Or perhaps at that moment, Robert had decided to wake up on own accord. He sat up, making no comment on ill-treatment, regarded his cousin beatifically. "Ah, Cousin John," he said. d you sleep well?"

Cousin John could only stare in amazement at his relative, and n his mouth once or twice like a fish hooked and tossed onto shore. Lord Ragsdale looked down at Robert, certain in his rt of hearts that if he murdered his cousin on the spot, no jury welve men just and true would ever convict him. He sat down he bed and glared at his relative.

Don't you remember anything of last night?" he began, and n stopped. The conversation sounded familiar to his ears, and almost smiled in spite of himself. That hoary question, proba- asked since caveman days, was the preamble to many a morn- 's argument when his father was still alive. This will never do, hought as he stared hard at his cousin. "Robert, you are a cer- ible bastard," he stated firmly. "You have been through your ney, and my money; you nearly sold your servant to a man I ildn't trust a saint with, and forced me to give up five thou- d pounds worth of horse to redeem her and to keep you from a fe in the ribs and a trip to the river, I don't doubt."

Robert burped, winced, and sat up. "All that happened last nt?" he said as he clutched his head with both hands.

It did. We happen to be dead broke now, and if my mother sn't have any yellow dogs on her person, we will be making s and cleaning the *pissoir* to pay for our lodging!" Lord Rags- e gave an unpleasant laugh. "Or rather, you will be doing that we will watch!"

He regarded his cousin a moment more, then stood up. "Wash r face and come to the parlor. I think you and Sally owe the oles branch of the family some enlightenment."

He slammed the door behind him, and was rewarded with a an from Robert. Lord Ragsdale smiled in satisfaction and re- ed the desire to slam the door again. Lord, life was suddenly of exertions, he thought to himself as he rapped lightly on his her's door.

The inmates were dressed already, and two out of three were arding him with some anxiety. Sally Claridge was easily the e agitated of the two. She gave a start when he came in, and wondered for a second if he had forgotten to put on his eye h. No, it was carefully in place. As he watched, Sally's face ed bright red as she reached for her handkerchief and began to . The marquess groaned.

"Sally, it is much too early for tears," he assured her. Sa
sobbed louder into the already soaking scrap of lace in her ha
In desperation, he gestured to Emma. "Tell her that nothing v
ever solved with tears," he pleaded.

"I have always found tears to be singularly valueless," s
agreed, and handed her mistress a more substantial rag. "Dry
now, miss, or your eyes will swell and you will look quite twent

Lord Ragsdale smiled in spite of himself, charmed—if agai
his will—by the lilt of Emma's brogue, and her common sen
Lord Ragsdale was grateful. One woman in tears would suffi
especially before breakfast. He regarded his mother, who smi
back at him from her seat by the window.

"Troubles, John?" she asked, her voice hearty enough to ma
him suspect that she was enjoying this domestic tempest.

"You needn't appear so cheerful, Mama," he insisted. "I th
my cousins are a great lot of trouble."

Sally burst into louder tears, edging on the hysterical. He
the hairs rise on the back of his neck and his temper shorten p
ceptibly. He looked to Emma Costello for help, and to his ama
ment, she glared back at him.

"Must you make a situation more difficult, Lord Ragsdal
she asked.

No servant had ever addressed him like that. Hot words rose
his lips, but to his further astonishment, he stopped them. She w
absolutely right; there was no sense in tossing another log o
the blaze. He bit his tongue, glared back, and turned his attent
to his mother again.

It may have been his imagination, but Lady Ragsdale seem
to be enjoying the whole affair. "You needn't take such pleas
in all this," he snapped, coming as close to pouting as he cared
admit. "It may put some sand in your eye when I tell you t
Beau Rascal in the other room gambled away all my money, t
My dear, unless you have some pounds sterling tucked son
where to pay the innkeeper, we're going to have a hard ti
avoiding the constable. Oh, Sally, cut line!" he ordered, when
cousin increased the volume of her misery.

Lady Ragsdale blew a kiss to her sorely tried niece. "Jo
dear, you know I always travel with cash. I have enough to p
our receipt here."

"Well, thank the Lord for one piece of good news this morni
Now if you could only produce enough for me to reclaim
horses."

"That I cannot do," she said, and gave her head a sorrowful wa e sighed, the martyr again. "Mama, they were prime goers," began, then stopped himself, because it sounded like he was ning.

"I'm sure they were, my dear," she agreed as she reached out to p his hand. "But I want you to tell me something, son."

"What?" he asked in irritation when she continued to look at him.

"Tell me if all this will matter in even a week or two."

"Of course it will!" he shot back.

"Why?" she asked softly.

He had no answer. Of course it mattered, he wanted to shout, for the life of him, he couldn't think why. He had plenty of ney, and there would be other horses. He looked at Sally, who hiccupping through her tears now, and then at Emma. Why deuce do I wonder what you are thinking? he asked himself.

He was spared the pain of further analysis by the arrival of ert. It was a soft tap on the door, as though sound was painful his cousin. I can appreciate that, John thought grimly. He ned the door quickly, hoping that his cousin might be leaning t to support himself.

"Robert!" he exclaimed, noting with a certain malicious plea- that his cousin winced at his loud greeting. "Grand of you to us. Sit down, please."

obert sat, after looking around at Sally, as though for help. sister was deep in a handkerchief, and unlikely to be of any stance. No one spoke. To Lord Ragsdale's supreme annoy- e, everyone looked at him as though expecting leadership. He ld have told them that was a waste of time, but since they ned to expect him to take charge, he did.

ord Ragsdale clasped his hands behind his back and strolled he window. He stood there a moment, rocking back and forth is heels, then regarded his cousins. "I would like one of you ll me exactly what is going on, please."

ally tunneled deeper into her handkerchief; Robert merely ked around. Lord Ragsdale sighed and tried again. "Your par- have solicited us to see that you, Robert, are located at Oxford, that you, Sally, participate in some part of the London Season."

either relative said anything. Lord Ragsdale paced away from window, and then back again. "I know there are several excel- , if provincial, colleges in America." He looked at Sally. "And spect that Virginia society is lively enough to provide for a ng's entertainment. I must ask myself, then, why you have in- ed yourself upon us."

"Really, John," his mother murmured as Sally began to sni
again.

"Yes, really," he insisted, then paced some more. "Can i
possible that you are no longer welcome at home, Robert?" L
Ragsdale asked. "Could it be that you have ruined your family"

A long silence followed, but Lord Ragsdale did not leap i
the void. He walked back to the window and looked out, wai
for an answer. And I will wait until hell freezes over, he thou
grimly. We may all grow old in this room.

"I really don't think it is as bad as all that," Robert said at l
his tone sulky. His mouth opened to say more, but Sally leape
her feet and hurried to the window to face her cousin.

"It is worse than that," she said, her voice low and fie
"Robert's gaming debts have mortgaged our home right to the
tics. Papa has had to sell half his slaves, and the next two toba
crops are already lost to repay Robert's creditors."

Lord Ragsdale whistled in spite of himself. "Good L
Robert," he exclaimed. "Can't you resist a wager?"

Once started, Sally was ready to contribute in abundance. '
cannot!" she exclaimed, deeply in earnest, tears forgotten n
"There are whole counties where Robert dare not show his fac
Her own face clouded over again. "And no one will even consi
a marriage arrangement for me, with Robert ready to sponge."

She looked so sad that Lord Ragsdale put his arm around
shoulders, drew her close to him, and provided her with his ha
kerchief. "I appreciate your candor, Sally," he said when he co
be heard over her tears.

Sally looked at him, her wide blue eyes so like his mothe
"What will you do to us?" she asked.

He smiled at her. "Exactly what your parents wished, my de
He leveled a less pleasant look in Robert's direction. "You, cou
will go to Oxford. And if I hear of a single card being turned,
will be on your way to Spain, to serve in the ranks. I kno
colonel of foot who will have you flogged regularly, if I ask
to."

"Oh, cousin!" Robert exclaimed, getting slowly to his feet
am sure that if you will let me bargain with Emma's indent
one more time I can . . ."

"Don't you ever learn?" Lord Ragsdale shouted, oblivious
what the other clients of the Norman and Saxon might think. "
belongs to me now, and I am more careful of my property! Sa
we will attempt to provide you with a come out of some s
There must be someone of my acquaintance who prefers a pr

e to a large income." He released Sally, and turned to his
ther. "And now, my dear, if you will fork over some of the
dy, I will spring us from this inn."

She handed him some money, then patted his arm. "Well done,
n," Lady Ragsdale said in a low voice.

"Someone had to do something," he said pointedly. He started
the door, then turned suddenly and shook his finger at Robert.
mean what I say about serving in the ranks, you hell-born
e!" He yanked open the door, looked at Emma standing there
quietly beside it, and pulled her out into the hall with him,
mming the door behind him.

"I want a word with you, Emma Costello," he snapped.

She said nothing, but pulled her hand from his and clasped
m in front of her. She looked him directly in the eye, some-
ng servants never did, and he found himself unable to bear her
el scrutiny.

"Dash it, Emma," he whispered furiously. "Why in hell did you
ow Robert to take you downstairs last night? Why didn't you
ke my mother, or pound on my door? My God, he could have
d you to one of those ugly customers. Don't you care?"

She was a long time answering him. The servant looked down
er hands, her eyes lowered, and he noticed how absurdly long
eyelashes were. He was standing close enough to see that her
n was as beautiful up close as across a room, and with the most
arming freckles on her nose. She wore no scent but the honest
r of soap. Finally she looked at him.

"I did not dream that you would raise a hand to stop him, my
d," she replied.

Almost bereft of speech, he stared back. "You . . . you think I
uld have allowed him to *sell* you?" he demanded, his voice ris-
to a higher pitch not heard since his younger years.

"I was sure of it," she said, her voice soft.

f she had calculated for six months or more to devise a way to
him to the marrow, she could not have hit upon a better plan. He
red at her another moment, and felt shame wash over him like a
den cold spray. It was the most damning thing anyone had ever
d to him, and it came from a servant. He regarded her another
ment, and the thought struck him that she was probably right.

"Oh, Emma" was all he could say.

"With your permission, sir, I'll go back inside and help the
ies pack."

He nodded and walked down the hall to his own room. He
ned at the door, his hand on the knob, and glanced back at the

servant, who had not moved. She regarded him in silence ano
moment, then went back into his mother's room, closing the d
quietly behind her.

Lord Ragsdale thought the ride to Oxford would never end.
felt the loss of his horse sorely. A restless person by nature,
chafed at the inactivity of sitting still in a carriage. If he could h
paced inside, he would have. As it was, he was forced to end
Sally's snufflings into a long succession of handkerchiefs, and
occasional frightened glances in his direction. Robert sulked in
corner, suffering a hangover of monstrous proportions, brought
by bad rum, drunk in immoderate quantities. He opened his mo
several times to speak, but nothing ever came out.

Lady Ragsdale seemed to enjoy the ride. She settled comfo
ably into the opposite corner, her nose deep in a novel. The o
sound in the carriage beyond Sally's sniffles was the regular s
ting and turning of pages. Emma Costello stared out the windo
occupied with her own thoughts. Her face was blank of all
pression, the perfect servant's face.

Except that I know you have not always been a servant,
thought as he watched her. As the miles and hours dragged by,
remembered a fairy tale from the nursery about a princess for
into servitude by a wicked maid. Absurd, he thought, wishing t
he could fling open the carriage door and trot alongside. Irela
has nothing but a cursed population that stinks and breeds. I w
der how soon I can get rid of her, he thought.

As they approached Oxford, Emma Costello claimed his att
tion again. Sally and Robert were both asleep, leaning agai
each other, but Emma sat forward and grasped a strap by the w
dow, surprised into exclamation. He glanced over idly to see w
was capturing her notice.

"It is Magdalen Tower," he said, following her gaze. Co
come, John, he thought, try for a little conversation, even if sh
Irish. "You should see it in high summer, with the trees all lea
out." There. That was a respectable volley of dialogue. I ca
have her thinking I am a dog of a fellow.

Emma nodded, her eyes still on the scene before her. "I thou
it would look like that," she murmured.

He smiled at her, feeling the hypocrite because of his disli
and unable to resist the vantage point of superiority. "I had no i
that Magdalen was a subject for the servants' hall in America."

It was a shabby remark, and he knew it. She looked him in
eye, and he felt the urge to squirm again under her scrutiny.

"My father went there," she commented, and directed her gaze to the window again, effectively shutting him out of all further conversation.

Lord Ragsdale felt himself blushing. My God, I have been set down, he thought in amazement. His embarrassment worsened when he noticed that his mother watched him over the top of her spectacles, her eyes merry. He glared at her, and to his further discomfort, she winked at him.

"That's enough," he said, his voice too loud. He rolled down the glass and leaned out the window. "Stop the coach."

The carriage stopped. His mother watched in amusement, her finger marking the place in the book. Emma's emerald green eyes measured him up and down, and found him wanting.

He flung himself out of the carriage. "I will walk to Grandmama's," he told his mother.

"Very well, John," she said. "Take your time."

He swore out loud as the carriage left him, and stood there a moment, wondering why he was walking, and not Emma.

Lord Ragsdale took his time getting to his grandmother's house. At first he walked fast in his anger, but as his rapid stride carried him along through narrow, favorite streets, he found himself slowing down, glancing about even, as though his friends from former years might reappear to walk with him, to commiserate, to cajole, to suggest alternatives to duty, to demand that he share notes or a pint. He sighed and stood still, staring up at Magdalen Tower, almost like Emma. "To remind me that life had a purpose once," he said out loud.

Others were passing by. He reminded himself also that at Oxford, no one stared at people who talked out loud to themselves. The colleges cherished their eccentrics, and even after ten years and more, he felt himself under that same protective umbrella. It was a pleasant thought, and oddly soothing. He strolled along more slowly now. True, he could not recall what the purpose of life was anymore, but at least it was a comfort to be there.

He thought about lifting a pint at Walsingham's again, but the moment passed. Instead, he let himself into the Brasenose Quadrangle and walked about until he pronounced himself ready to face his grandmother. I wonder that anyone ever leaves Oxford, he thought as he sauntered along the outer corridor, his eyes on the dark beams close overhead. He stopped, the first smile of the day on his face. There it was. He reached up and traced "John Staples," carved at the end of his second year. The smile left his face. I was different then, he considered. I was better.

Chapter 5

Dusk was approaching when Lord Ragsdale arrived at his Grandmama Whiteacre's house. He stood for a long time outside the building, admiring the stonework as he always did. The facade had been quarried from the same rock works as many of Oxford's buildings, and it glowed with that same otherworldly honey color of late afternoon. But the ivy was dead on the stones now, drooping in the drizzle that had begun as he crossed the Isis and hurried past her neighbor's homes.

He never could think of the place as a home, no matter how hard he tried. There was none of the rest within that he ever associated with his own home. "And precious little of that on Curzon Street either, nowadays," he mused out loud. He wished he understood what had happened to his own home. True, Lady Ragsdale kept it beautiful and timely as always, but he felt no peace there anymore. And there was none here.

As he stood in the rain, several lights came on. He didn't want to go in. Grandmama would be there to pounce on him, and scold him. Lord knows she probably had plenty of charges in her arsenal. Sally would probably cry some more, and there would be Robert, pouting and looking ill-used. Mama would smile at him, as though she knew something he didn't. And Emma? Oh, Lord.

At what point did I lose control of my life? he thought as he started toward the front door. When did everything become an exertion? He rubbed his forehead and wished that the rain did not slither down his clothes and onto his back. He knew that he could not face his grandmother.

He stared hard at the house again, and there was Emma standing in the window. She stood as he was already used to seeing her, with her hands folded in front of her, the very stillness of her impressive to him, for all that he disliked her. He could not make out any of her features, but he knew it was Emma.

As he watched, he thought she raised her hand to him in a small gesture of greeting. He could not be sure, because the light was so dim, so he did not return the gesture. Besides all that, she was his servant.

My servant! he chided himself as he lifted his hand to the knocker, and Applegate—grayer but supercilious-looking as ever—allowed him to enter. Why on earth didn't I just let Robert lose her at the turn of the card? He might even have won, and either road, I would still have my horses. "Yes, what?" he asked in annoyance.

"I merely wished you good evening, my lord," Applegate repeated, sounding, if anything, even more disdainful than Lord Ragsdale remembered.

"Oh, very well," Lord Ragsdale snapped. "Applegate, am I in my usual room?"

"Of course, my lord," the butler replied, as though he addressed a dim-witted child. "My mistress wishes to see you first, however. If you will follow me, my lord?"

"I'd rather not," John said honestly as the footman grasped the back of his coat and helped him out of the wet garment.

It was Emma. "She especially requested that you visit her in the blue room, my lord," she reinforced as she held out her hand for his hat.

He handed it to her. "No relief for the wicked, eh, Emma?" he asked, no humor in his voice.

"Not in your case, my lord," she replied promptly.

Applegate coughed and looked away, as Lord Ragsdale nailed Emma with a frown. John slapped his gloves in her hand. "I should have left you at the Norman and Saxon," he murmured.

"It's a mystery to me why you did not," she responded, the lilt in her voice so prominent.

He shook his finger at her, ready to give her a share of what remained of his frazzled mind. Applegate coughed again, so he swallowed his angry words and followed the butler down the hall. He looked back at Emma once to give her another evil stare, but there she stood again, as calm as usual. Damn me, but you are irritating, he thought.

To his infinite relief, only Grandmama waited to pounce on him in the blue room; he was spared more of Sally's tears and Robert's distemper. He would have liked a pitcher of whiskey, but his grandmother handed him a cup of tea.

"Well, John, what do you have to say for yourself?" she demanded after the maid fled the room.

He took a sip of the tea and pronounced it insipid. In silence for a moment, he gazed back at his relative, wondering what imp was suddenly at work in his brain. "Grandmama, why do you always greet me that way?" he asked, determined not to be afraid of her this trip. "I cannot remember a time since I was out of short pants that you addressed me otherwise." He sat down beside her. "It is not my fault that our American relatives are sadly wanting."

There, he thought, I have counterattacked. He took another sip and regarded his relative, noting that all the females of the Whiteacre side of the family were blessed with pretty faces, from Grandmama to Sally. I wonder why I never saw that before, he thought, as he took another sip, winked at the old lady and set down the cup. Of course, they don't have Emma's high looks, but—hell, *what* is in this tea? I must be losing my mind. Emma has put an Irish curse on me. He stared into the tea, his hastily acquired aplomb in serious danger already.

If he was going insane right there in the blue room, Grandmama did not appear to notice. She choked over her tea and glared at him. "It is ill-bred to wink, John," she reminded him.

Recovering, he smiled to himself, happy to have set her off guard. "Tell me what you think of the Claridges, my love," delighted to watch her choke again at his unexpected endearment.

She scowled at him. "Pathetic!" She wagged a heavily ringed finger in front of his face. "And so I told my daughter it would be when she insisted on marrying that American." She snorted in disgust. "Sally cried until my ankles started getting wet, and Robert could only say how ill you had treated him."

"Silly of me, wasn't it?" he commented. "I wouldn't let him gamble his servant away to a lecher." He paused, and took a thorough, if covert, look at his grandparent. It was always hard to measure her mellowness, but Lord Ragsdale turned on his most blinding smile and ventured. "By the way, Grandmama, how would you like another maid around the place?"

Grandmama let out a crack of laughter. "Not so easy! She's all yours, John! I hear from my daughter that you spent a fortune in horseflesh for her."

"I didn't have any choice!" he shouted, his desperation returning. "Grandmama, what am I going to do with Emma Costello?"

"Buck up, John," she retorted. "I never would have taken you for a whiner."

She finished her tea, refilled it half full from the pot at her elbow, then handed the cup to him, gesturing with her head to the cherrywood cabinet against the far wall. "Put in a drop of brandy before your mother returns," she ordered. "I expect you'll think of mething to use Emma for, if you're any grandson of Lord Whiteacre. Besides all that, she's prettier than your mistress."

He stopped at the sideboard, his hand on the brandy, then poured in more than a drop. "Madam, pigs will fly before I get in bed with Emma Costello!" He doused his own tea with enough brandy to cause a blaze, if he sat too close to the fire.

She took the tea, and nodded at him, triumphant to have the upper hand again. "It doesn't surprise me that you should mention work when you think of your light-skirt."

He glared at her in exasperation, wondering why he could not ever win an argument with this feeble old woman. "Fae is a fine-looking woman," he said, trying to inject the proper amount of injury into his voice, and avoid any suggestion that he was getting a little tired of her. "I *prefer* women with a little *avoirdupois*," he stated. That was true enough. Not for him slender women like Emma Costello, with nothing to hold onto. However, the Irish woman did have a pleasant shape, even if she was a trifle thin.

But this was no time to allow the mind to wander, and his cause was not being served by the fumes that rose from his teacup. "If you will not help me, m'dear," he said after a long, thoughtful sip, "give me some suggestions. Mama has already arranged to have a lady's maid waiting for Sally when we return. You know, someone who knows the ins and outs of life here better than Emma would. And I assure you I will not leave Emma within ten miles of Robert Claridge, no matter how she irritates me."

"You could put her in the kitchen, John," Grandmama said, taking another sip of her brandied tea, and held out the cup for more. "That's a good place for the Irish." She giggled.

"Not Emma," he said, wondering how she would fare belowstairs with the servants he employed. Besides that, as much as he disliked her, he couldn't ignore Emma's obvious intelligence any more than he could overlook her trim shape. The kitchen was no place for Emma, no matter how much she richly deserved to be sentenced there.

"This becomes difficult," he told his grandmother as he laced their tea with a little more brandy. "I don't want her in my bed, Mama and Sally don't really need her, the kitchen would be better off without her . . ." He went to the window and grasped the frame as the room wobbled. "Maybe she can clust and dean. I mean, dust and clean."

Grandmama made no reply. He looked over his shoulder and smiled. Her head drooped on her chest, and she was beginning to

snore. He sighed and rested his head against the window frame
What was he going to do with Emma?

To Lord Ragsdale's infinite relief, Robert Claridge allowe
himself to be taken quietly to Brasenose College in the morning
The two of them rode in silence through the narrow streets of Ox
ford, which already bustled with scholastic purpose. Lord Rags
dale introduced his sullen cousin to the warden, and gave him hi
back without a qualm. After Robert had been ushered away, h
spent more time with the warden, urging that worthy to let hin
know of any infractions.

"He's a worthless young man, sir," Lord Ragsdale concluded
"Had I known the extent of his worthlessness, I would never hav
moved heaven and earth to foist him upon you at this juncture o
the term. But here he is, sir."

The warden regarded him with some amusement. "Do you
have any sons of your own yet, Lord Ragsdale?"

"I do not, sir."

The warden smiled at him. "You cannot imagine then, how
many variations of your conversation I have heard before."

He paused and Lord Ragsdale understood. "My own father
eh?" he asked, with just a ghost of a smile playing around his lips

"Yes, my lord. Somehow we managed to turn you into some
one acceptable to the world at large. I suspect we will succeed
with this American, too."

Lord Ragsdale managed a reluctant smile. "The Brasenose
touch, sir?"

"Exactly, my lord. I think we can render him sufficiently busy
to keep him from the gaming table." The warden rose and held
out his hand. "I will attempt to warn him with the perils of serving in the ranks, should he choose to indulge in a gaming caree
within our walls. Good day, my lord."

His Grandmama Whiteacre kindly loaned him a horse and saddle for the return to London, so it was not necessary to stifle himself inside the family carriage this time. The day was no warmer
than before, but at least it did not snow. His horse, serviceable if
somewhat elderly, plodded sedately alongside the carriage, where
Mama read, Sally slept, and Emma continued her everlasting stare
out the window. He watched her and resolved to turn her over to
his butler. Emma Costello could polish silver, or clean out drains,
for all he cared.

London was already foggy with the light of many street lamps
when the carriage turned onto Curzon Street and released its

ateful occupants. Lord Ragsdale remained on his horse. "Mama, m off to White's," he told her. Lady Ragsdale, shaky and pale m a day's travel, nodded to him as Emma helped her from the rriage. The front door opened then, and Lasker stood there, with footman behind him and Mama's dresser, too.

He left them without another qualm, praying that traffic would t be so terrible on St. James that he would be kept long from brandy he had been thinking about all day. He would sink into s favorite leather chair, a full bottle near his hand, and pro-unce himself liberated from all further exertions. Fae would be ad enough to see him later, he was sure. In her own practiced shion, she would remove any rough edges that remained from day. That was what he paid her for.

As he was dismounting in front of White's, he was struck by thought that this was what he had done the day before yester-y, and the day before that. Barring any unforeseen eventuali-s, he would do it all again tomorrow, and the day after, and the y after that. The thought dug him in the stomach, and he utched the reins tighter, ignoring the porter who stood by to re-ive them.

Something of his unexpected agony must have crossed his face. a moment, he heard the porter asking, "My lord, my lord, are u all right?"

He looked down at the little man, and after another long mo-ent, handed him the reins. "I am fine," he said, fully aware for first time that he was lying. He had never been worse. As he ent slowly up the steps and into the main hall, he realized that would probably never be better, either. This was his life. Oh, d, he thought to himself, oh, God.

The milkmen were already making their rounds when he re-rned to Curzon Street. His head was large as usual. He had unk too much brandy at White's, and then compounded the lony at Fae's by attempting exercise far beyond his capacity. he results had left him embarrassed and Fae irritated, muttering mething she refused to repeat.

The house was dark and silent. In another hour or so, the tchen staff, with yawns and eye rubs, would gird itself for an-her day of cooking, and the upstairs maids would answer tugs the bellpulls with tea and hot water. Lord Ragsdale listed owly down the hall toward the stairs, which loomed, insur-ountable, before him. I think I will sit down here until they rink, he thought as he grasped the banister to keep it from leap-g about, and started to lower himself to the second tread. To his

relief, it did not disappear. He sank down gratefully, leane
against the railing, and closed his eyes.

He opened them a moment later. He was not alone on th
stairs. Someone else sat nearby. He turned his head slowly, won
dering what he would do if it was a sneak thief or cut purse, com
to rob and murder them all. Lord Ragsdale sighed philosophi
cally, and sat back to wait for the knife between his ribs. At leas
when they found his sprawled corpse at the foot of the stairs, th
constable would think that he had died there defending his family
It would be rather like Thermopylae, he thought, and giggled.

"All right, do your worst," he managed finally, looking around

In another moment, his eyes adjusted to the gloom. A woman
sat near the top of the stairs, asleep and leaning against the rail
ing. He looked closer and sighed again. My God, it is Emma
Costello, he thought, the plague of my life. As he watched her, hi
mind began to clear and he wondered what she was doing there
Surely she was not waiting up for him.

Suddenly it occurred to him that she had no place to sleep. He
remembered his mother mentioning something about hiring a
proper lady's maid for Sally. The woman must have arrived and
usurped Emma's place in the dressing room. He stared at Emma
and wondered why his mother had not done anything about the
situation, until he remembered her exhausted face as her own
maid helped her from the carriage. Mama must have gone directly
to bed, too tired for a thought about Emma.

And here she was now, at the mercy of his staff, and asleep on
the stairs. He felt an unexpected twinge of remorse, remembering
his own disparaging words about her to his butler. The staff knew
how he felt about the Irish.

"Emma," he called out softly, not wishing to startle her into a
plunge down the stairs.

He called her name several times before she straightened up
moving her head slowly as though her neck hurt. She was silent a
moment, and then, "My lord?" she asked, not sure of her answer.

"The very same," he replied. "Emma, what are you doing
sleeping on my stairs?"

She was silent a long moment, and he wondered if she still
slept. "I am sorry, my lord," she said finally. "It seems that all I
do is apologize to you. I don't have a place to sleep."

He didn't say anything. After another small silence, she rose
and shook out her skirts. "I'll find the back stairs, my lord,"
she mumbled.

Without quite knowing why, he put out his hand to stop her. Just a moment, Emma," he said. "Help me up, will you?"

She could have left him there, and by morning's light, he probably would have put the whole thing down to an imaginary alcoholic haze. Someone else would find him and help him to bed, and wouldn't be the first time. Emma would sleep on the stairs for a few more nights until his mother got wind of the situation and straightened things out belowstairs. It didn't have to be his worry.

He was about to withdraw his hand when she clasped it firmly in her own and with one swift movement, tugged him to his feet. He swayed on the stairs, and she quickly grasped him around the waist and commanded him to take up his bed and walk. It was a voice of command, resounding inside his head, crashing around from ear to ear until he wanted to whimper and crawl into a corner. Instead, he did as she ordered, putting one foot in front of the other until he was outside the door to his own room.

"I'll be all right now," he gasped. "You can let go."

Other servants had helped him to his room before. Practice told him that he could negotiate the distance from the door to his bed, and throw himself down on it, not to rise until afternoon or the resurrection, whichever came first. He tried to turn her loose, but she would not budge. Suddenly he realized, in spite of his weakened state, that the rules had changed.

"I'll see you to your bed," she insisted, her voice low but carrying into his brain, where her earlier words still careened off his skull. "I'll not give you the satisfaction of telling someone tomorrow that your shanty Irish servant did you an injury, no matter how richly you deserve one," she assured him.

She lowered him to his bed, and he flopped there. In another moment his shoes were off, and she was covering him with a blanket.

"That should hold you until morning," she said.

His head throbbing beyond belief, he waited like a wounded animal for her to hurry up and leave. To his chagrin, she stared around his room until her vision rested on his untidy desk. He watched studiedly as she shook her head in amazement at the ruin of his life.

Then the whole thing made him giggle. He tried to raise up on one elbow, but he seemed to have misplaced his arm. He remained where he was, content to watch the two of her. "Reform me, Emma," he said, and then hiccupped.

"You are disgusting, Lord Ragsdale," she said at last, each word so distinct and penetrating as a bell. She shook her head. "I never saw a more worthless man, much less served one." Her words boomed about in his skull some more. She went to his desk and rummaged about for a moment. He raised up his head to watch her sit down at his desk, clear off a spot, and put ink to paper.

She sat there quite awhile, crumpling two sheets of paper, then resting her elbows on the desk as she contemplated him lying helpless and drunk on his bed. In another moment, she dipped the quill in the inkwell again and wrote swiftly, pausing at last to read over what she had written in the dim light. She nodded, picked up the paper and the ink, and came back to the bed.

"My God, Emma, would you get out of my room?" he insisted, wishing he did not sound so feeble.

"Not until you sign this," she replied, sitting down next to him. "Here." She thrust the paper under his nose.

He tried to wave away the paper, but she would not relent. "What is it?" he asked finally. "At least tell me that."

"It has to do with what you just said, my lord," she said. "You have given me such an idea. Now, sign, and then I will leave you."

Said? Said? What did I say? he thought wildly. I really must stop drinking so much. He closed his eyes, but she rattled the paper at his ear.

As drunk as he was, Lord Ragsdale knew that he could leave the paper alone, roll over, and go to sleep. She would go away eventually, and he would be in peace. Nothing would change; by evening he would be at White's again, and drunk, or at Fae's and miserable. He was on the verge of sleep when Emma Costello touched his hair. She smoothed it back from his sweaty face and rested her hand for a moment on his head. "Sign, my lord," she ordered, her voice softer now, and held out the quill to him.

He grasped the pen and managed to scrawl out his name. He closed his eyes then and relaxed as she stood up. He reached for her hand. "Emma, please tell me that I have just released you from that damnable indenture. Then you can go away, and I will be happy," he said. It was his longest speech of the evening, and his head lolled to one side.

I should worry, he thought when she started to laugh. My God, have I signed away my fortune to this Irish harpy? But she was speaking now, and he strained to listen.

"Lord Ragsdale, I owe you five thousand pounds, and I will pay this debt," she was saying.

"How?" he managed at last, wondering at the effort it took to form the word.

"By reforming you, my lord, now that I have your written consent. It was your idea. Good night."

Chapter 6

Emma's neck was aching in good earnest by the time the scullery maid nearly tripped over her on the way down the back stairs to begin another long day in the kitchen. She grabbed onto the banister, scowled at Emma, and then snickered.

"Can't find a place to sleep, can we?" she mocked. "Find a peat bog." The maid hurried on down the stairs, tying her apron as she went and laughing at her own cleverness.

Emma drew her knees up to her chin and watched the maid's progress. "No, but I will find a place someday," she said, too quiet for anyone to hear.

Not that anyone was listening to her. As Emma sat on the back stairs, she heard the butler giving his orders. Soon the upstairs maids would be coming up the stairs, staggering under the weight of cans of hot water, and then teapots. Another day has come to the Ragsdale household, she thought as she looked down at the paper still clutched in her hand. She spread it out on the landing and wondered for a moment at her audacity. She shook her head over the document containing Lord Ragsdale's shaky signature. I must be crazy, she thought.

She made herself small in the corner—something she was good at—as the first maid hurried upstairs with hot water. Five years ago—or is it six now?—she never would have done something that outrageous. There was a time when I cared what happened to me, she thought as she carefully folded the paper. I wonder which room is Lady Ragsdale's?

The problem was solved for her as she quietly moved up the stairs in the wake of the upstairs maids. The first closed door she identified from last night. No one went in there; she knew it would be hours before anyone stumbled out. Two doors down was Sally Claridge's room, if she remembered right. Ah, yes. The woman who opened the door was the dresser who had made herself quite at home in the little space that Emma had carved out of the dressing room before the trip to Oxford. Robert had slept in

the room next, but now the maid was tapping softly on the doc
beyond. The tall, thin woman with the sneer who opened the doc
was Lady Ragsdale's dresser.

Emma thought at first that she would wait until the maid le
and then knock, but hurriedly discarded that idea. The dresse
probably would not let her in. She took a deep breath and fol
lowed in after the maid, who looked around in surprise and glare
at her.

"I am sure you do not belong in here," the dresser said. Th
cold glint in her eyes told Emma that if Lady Ragsdale's servar
had not been occupied with the tea tray, she would have throw
her out. As it was, the dresser could only sputter and protest a
Emma hurried to the bed where Lady Ragsdale sat awaiting he
first cup of the day.

"Emma, whatever are you doing in here? And for heaven'
sake, why are you so rumpled?" Lady Ragsdale asked, staring a
her unexpected morning visitor.

"I slept on the stairs because no one provided a room for me,
she explained. She spread out her hands in front of her. "I know
that you would have, my lady, but you were so tired from yester
day's journey." She flashed her most brilliant smile at the lady i
the bed, and was rewarded with a smile in return.

"Thank you, Acton," Lady Ragsdale said to her dresser, wh
handed her a cup of tea and stood glowering at Emma. "That wi
be all for the moment. Sit down, Emma. And do excuse this ram
shackle household. I will instruct Lasker to find you a place t
sleep tonight."

Emma perched herself on the edge of a chair close to Lad
Ragsdale's bed. She sat in silence for a brief moment, willing he
heart to stop jumping about in her chest, then held out the pape
to Lady Ragsdale.

The other woman took it and read the few words on the page a
Emma held her breath. To her vast relief, Lady Ragsdale began t
laugh. She set down the teacup on her lap tray and leaned bac
against the pillows, indulging herself until she had to wipe he
eyes with the corner of the sheet. "Emma, you are a shrewd one
Why on earth do you want to attempt this Promethean task?" sh
asked as she handed back the document.

Emma chose her words carefully. "I owe your son a hefty det
and mean to pay him back. It was his idea, by the way."

To her chagrin, Lady Ragsdale regarded her in silence. Emm
returned her stare, pleading in silence for the woman before her t

derstand. I must have an ally, or this will not work, she ought. Oh, please, Lady Ragsdale.

She leaned forward, testing the waters. "Lady Ragsdale, esn't it bother you that he is frittering away his life?"

"It bothers me," the widow replied quietly, after another subntial pause. She took a sip of tea. "John is a stubborn man. I nnot control him alone. Since his father's death . . ." She used again, then visibly gathered herself together. "I'm afraid / guidance is not to his liking." She sighed. "He's bitter about ₂ loss of his eye, and he can't seem to settle down. What he eds is a good wife, and so I have told him." She took another . "Naturally, he does not listen to his mother."

Emma settled back a little in the chair. "What I propose is this, dy Ragsdale. Since he told me last night to reform him, I intend do just that. When he is organized, dried out, and hopefully rried, I think he will agree to ending my indenture. I will feel ₂ debt is paid."

"*If* he will go along with any of this," Lady Ragsdale warned. ohn sober is different from John drunk. What will you do if he nies all knowledge of this pledge of his and refuses to listen to u?"

Emma looked Lady Ragsdale right in the eye. "Then I will gue his life until he does."

How, she did not know. She knew as well as John Staples's other that there was nothing she could do, if Lord Ragsdale de-ed to ignore her. But Lady Ragsdale was looking at her with nething close to hope in her face, and she knew she had an y. She took a deep breath.

"The first thing I want to do is lock up the liquor supply in this use."

Lady Ragsdale opened her eyes wide. "I do believe you are se-us."

Emma stood up and went to the window. The rain thundered wn. It was perfect weather for reformation, she decided. "I ve never been more serious. I truly intend to tidy up your son, d receive my release papers from him in exchange." She hesi-ed, then plunged on. "I have business of my own in London, d now that I am here, I need the liberty to carry it out."

The two women regarded each other for a long moment, then dy Ragsdale held out her hand. After another slight pause, ama extended her own and they shook hands. Lady Ragsdale iled and called for Acton, who came out of the dressing room fast that Emma knew she had been listening at the door.

"Acton, I want Lasker up here right away. We have a matter
a lock and key to discuss."

When the dresser left the room, Emma returned to the chair. "
is perfectly obvious that for some reason, Lord Ragsdale cann
stand the sight of me," she said. "Why? I never did anything
him."

Lady Ragsdale indicated that she remove the tea tray, and s
did. The widow settled more comfortably in bed as the stor
raged outside. "It is not you, my dear, but the Irish that
loathes."

"Why?"

It was a simple question, but it seemed to hang on the a
Emma watched as Lady Ragsdale's face grew as bleak as t
morning outside. I have to know, she thought, as Lady Ragsd
touched the corner of the sheet to her eyes again. She folded h
hands in her lap and looked at Emma again.

"My husband commanded a regiment of East Anglia Foot—c
family seat is located near Medford. He was sent to Ireland
1798, to serve under Lord Cornwallis." She paused and looked
Emma. "Do you remember the '98?" she asked.

It was Emma's turn to look away. Oh, how I remember it, s
thought. "Yes, I remember," she said, her voice low.

Lady Ragsdale looked at her, a question in her eyes, and Emm
was grateful for once to be a servant. The woman in the bed kne
better than to bother with the affairs of a servant, so she did not as

"John had finished his second year at Oxford, or nearly so. H
father purchased him a captaincy in the regiment, and they we
posted together in County Wexford. They were very clos
Emma."

Lady Ragsdale was silent then. Emma sat back in her cha
And somehow I know what follows, she thought. "Did your hu
band die at Vinegar Hill, my lady?" she asked, her voice soft.

Lady Ragsdale nodded, and then waited a long moment to c
lect herself. "He was captured by that rabble and piked to dea
John watched."

Oh, merciful Mary, this is worse than I thought, Emma tc
herself. "And John was injured," she said, when Lady Ragsd
could not continue.

The widow nodded, her eyes staring into the paisley pattern
her bedcovers. "His men managed to drag him away before th
killed him, too, but he lost an eye. And my husband . . ." H
voice trailed away, and she began to weep. "Emma, they nev
found enough of him to bury."

Emma sat in silence as Lady Ragsdale sobbed into the sheet. "My husband was dead, and John was so gravely injured," she managed to say at last. "I despaired of his living, and then when he finally recovered, I knew that my son was gone, too, to some private hell I cannot reach."

"Lady Ragsdale, I am so sorry to have asked you," Emma said, her own eyes filling with tears.

To her surprise, the widow reached out again and grasped Emma by the arm, her grip strong. "You needed to know. John has never allowed an Irish servant into this house. He is moody, and bitter, and drinks too much for his own good. He engages in frivolous pursuits, and cares for no one. He uses people." She released her grip on Emma. "He may say some terrible things to you."

I am sure it will be nothing I have not heard before from the English, Emma thought, and I doubt he will resort to torture. "Words, my lady, only words. Will you help me, then?"

"Most emphatically," Lady Ragsdale said as she dabbed at her eyes and looked up as the door opened. "Ah, Lasker. How good of you to come to me. We have some work to do. Tell me, can we lock up the wine cellar?"

Well, thought Emma, as she stood outside Lord Ragsdale's door, this certainly can't be any worse than other indignities I have suffered at the hands of the British, damn them. She crossed herself, said a little prayer, and opened the door. She took a step back as the odor of stale liquor assaulted her nostrils. Courage, Emma, she thought as she entered the room and closed the door firmly behind her.

The room was still shaded into darkness, so she hurried to the windows and pulled back the draperies. To her relief, the rain had stopped. Letting out her breath, she threw open the windows and the cold air blew in like a declaration. Emma looked back at the bed where Lord Ragsdale lay sprawled on top of the covers, in much the same pose as she had left him.

"Johnny boy, you are a disaster," she whispered as she tiptoed closer. She looked down at him, his face pale, his eyelid flickering now as the light streamed across the bed. His dead eye was half-open, staring whitely at her. He groaned and then belched, and Emma stepped back again. His breath was foul with stale liquor. At some point during the night, he had been sick all over himself.

She shook her head. By all the saints, I am going to earn this release from my indenture, she thought grimly as she squeezed out a washcloth in the warm water she had brought with her. She

sat gingerly on the edge of the bed and wiped his face, brushi
the hair back from his forehead as he tried to pull away from he

"Not so fast, my lord," she muttered, pinning him down u
his face was wiped clean. "I wish you would open your eye. I
morning." She smiled, in spite of her extreme revulsion. "Mo
ing is probably a phenomenon you have not experienced in so
years, my lord."

She did not expect an answer, and she did not receive one. S
refreshed the cloth and continued to wipe his face and neck u
the evidence of his evening of excess was gone. Emma watch
him, grateful right down to her shoes that none of the men in I
family were drinkers beyond an evening sherry or an eggnog
Christmas. "It is a vile business, Lord Ragsdale."

To her amazement, he opened his eye. "Yes, ain't it?"
agreed. He lay there watching her, as if trying to rally those pa
of his brain necessary for rational thought. The attempt was u
successful, because he burped and closed his eye again.

She should have been revolted; he was a disgusting sight.
she sat looking at him, he sighed and rested his head against I
leg, and she found herself resting her hand on his shoulder. In a
other moment she brushed at his hair again. "So you are an o
who uses people?" she whispered. "Well, I am an ogre, too, an
intend to use you, sir."

Her thoughts were interrupted by a scratch on the door. "
come in," she said, and the door opened on the footman and s
eral housemaids, who carried buckets of water. The footman w
into the dressing room and pulled out a washtub, setting it in fr
of the fireplace. Emma nodded to the maids, who stood on
threshold, appalled at the messy room. "Pour it in there. Is it g
and hot, Hanley?"

The footman nodded, and then grinned in spite of himself.
disremember when he ever got up before noon."

Emma smiled back, grateful there was one person in the hou
hold who didn't regard her with indifference or disdain. S
looked at the maids. "We'll need more water."

They left and Emma looked down at Lord Ragsdale again. I
eye was open, and he was watching her warily.

"I don't recall inviting you into my room," he said.

"You didn't," she agreed as she unbuttoned his shirt. "But I
tend to hold you to your word, my lord."

He stared at her, and she nearly laughed out loud to watch a
riety of expressions cross his face. He finally settled on irritati

and clamped his hands over hers. "Leave my shirt alone, Emma Costello," he ordered.

She brushed his hands aside and kept unbuttoning. "As to that, if you wish to take a bath with your shirt on, you may, but it seems a little ramshackle, even for an Englishman."

He tried to glare at her, but the effort of squinting must have hurt his tender head. "Who said I was going to take a bath?" he asked, and began to rub his forehead.

"I did, my lord," she stated firmly. "You are disgusting, and we have things to do today. Now, take off your shirt."

"I won't."

"You will."

He did, to her surprise. The maids returned with more water, which they poured into the tub, and then beat a hasty retreat for the door, their eyes wide with amazement. The footman stood there with a towel draped over his arm, grinning from ear to ear. "Come on, my lord," he wheedled. "It's not so bad."

Lord Ragsdale lay back down again and stared up at Emma. "I seem to recall something last night. I signed a paper. Emma! What are you doing?"

"If you won't unbutton your trousers, then I will," she said, hoping that her voice sounded firm and that her hands did not shake. "You asked me to reform you, and even signed a statement to that effect. Hold still, my lord, or do it yourself."

He leaped up from the bed, nearly toppled over, and sank down, his head in his hands. "Emma, this is insane."

"I have it in writing, my lord," she stated. "Once you are reformed, I am released from my indenture. Now take off your pants and get in that tub." Emma rose and went to the door. "Hanley here said that he would fill in as your valet, my lord."

"I want a drink first," Lord Ragsdale said, and looked toward the dressing room. The longing in his eyes was unmistakable.

He looked at her, his eyes pleading with her, and she had a moment's pause. Such Turkish treatment is a lot to thrust on a fellow, she thought. I shall enjoy this part especially.

"So that's where you keep it," she exclaimed, and hurried into the dressing room, stepping over dirty laundry and nearly tripping over his boots by the door. She found two brandy bottles and a quart of wine, which she tucked under her arm.

Lord Ragsdale watched her from the bed, and smiled as she came back into his room. He held out his hand. "Give it here, Emma," he ordered.

Emma took a deep breath and went to the open window. She

looked down to make sure that no one was passing below, and dropped each bottle out of the window, listening with satisfaction to the crash and tinkle on the pavement below.

She did not think it was possible for Lord Ragsdale to go any paler than he already was, but he did. He whimpered something disjointed and flopped back on his bed as though she had shot him. He lay there in silence for a long moment, and then he waved his hand toward the footman.

"Hanley, go to the cellar and get me some more brandy."

The footman grinned and shook his head. "Oh, I can't, my lord. It's been sealed up, according to your orders."

"What?" he shrieked.

"Just so, my lord," Emma chimed in. "You signed a paper last night. I am to reform you."

"Never!"

Emma returned to the bed and started on his pants. "If I have to serve an indenture with you, my lord, one of us is going to change. And it's not going to be me."

"I," he corrected automatically. "Don't you shanty Irish know anything?"

Emma resisted the urge to smile. "Well, sir, do you continue with your trousers, or must I?"

"Dare you, Emma," he said as he stood up again, clutching his half-unbuttoned pants with one hand and the bedpost with the other.

Emma sighed, reminded of her little brother. "Lord Ragsdale, you are the worst kind of whiner. Hold still." She unbuttoned his trousers and held them down until he had no choice but to stagger out of them.

"Very good, my lord," she said as he leaned against the bedpost, clad only in his small clothes. "I am sure that Hanley can carry on from here."

Lord Ragsdale shook his head, then clutched it with an oath. "Oh, no, Emma Costello," he said, and there was a little bite to his voice this time. "You started it, you finish it. I like my back scrubbed first."

She watched in surprise, and then amusement as he stepped out of his small clothes, made a rude gesture to her, and staggered toward the tub.

He turned to look at her, injury all over his face. "You could at least close the windows," he said. "I have goose bumps all over my ass."

"I'm sure that it will not prove fatal, my lord," she said, wishing she could rush into the hall and laugh herself into a coma.

He stared at her a moment longer, then had the delicacy to cover his parts with the washcloth. "Emma, you're no lady," he said. "Shouldn't you be fainting, or something?"

"And you are most certainly no gentleman," she said. "I wouldn't dream of fainting, and miss all this high drama."

He sat down slowly as the steam rose from the water.

"If I drown, you're to blame," he said, his voice virtuous.

"It won't come to that, I'm sure," she told him as she picked up the scrub brush and bar of soap. "Now bend forward." She lathered up his back and scrubbed away, ignoring his protests of harsh ill-treatment. When she finished, she took a washcloth to his face, making sure there was plenty of soap on the cloth.

"Goodness, did I get soap in your eye?" she asked when he began to squirm and tried to grab her wrist. "How careless of me. Perhaps you'd rather do this yourself after all, my lord. Here, push your head down in the water. That should help."

She shoved his head under the water and held it there as long as she dared. When he came up sputtering and swearing, Hanley had to stuff the end of the towel in his mouth to contain himself.

"I'll see you in Newgate Prison!" Lord Ragsdale roared, quite sober now.

Emma leaped to her feet and moved quickly away from Lord Ragsdale's reach. "Excellent, my lord. I was planning to go there myself this afternoon," she said as Hanley gave up and roared with laughter. "Really, Hanley! Your mother tells me that your secretary is incarcerated there, and I mean to ask his advice."

"You can't be serious," Lord Ragsdale said, standing up and reaching for a towel.

"Oh, I am so serious, my lord. If I am to be your secretary, too, I had better learn the business from a master." She smiled back at Lord Ragsdale as he stared hard at her and wrapped the towel around his waist. "Only I promise not to cheat you. I think it will be much more diverting to reform you. After luncheon, then, Lord Ragsdale?"

"I wouldn't follow you across the street, you presumptuous parcel of Irish baggage."

"Oooh, sticks and stones, my lord," she replied. "Then I'll go by myself. If you want anything before this afternoon, I'll be in your book room, sorting out your bills."

"You can't do this!" he shouted, shaking his finger at her.

"Watch me."

Chapter 7

Emma spent the rest of the morning in the book room, sorting through the clutter of bills, many of them unopened, that resided in dusty piles on the desk. As she arranged them chronologically, oldest first, she found herself wondering how Lord Ragsdale had managed to keep himself out of Newgate. Does this man ever pay a bill? she thought, as she frowned over requests for payment from liquor wholesalers, procurers of livestock feed, and mantua makers.

Mantua makers? She scrutinized the bill at arm's length, and then remembered that Lady Whiteacre in Oxford had mentioned a mistress. Well, at least she is stylish, Emma thought as she created a separate pile for bills from modistes, milliners, cobblers, and sellers of silk stockings and perfumes. I had a pair of silk stockings once, she thought, as she picked up the bill. I will not think about that.

But she did think about it, leaning back in the chair as she sniffed at the faintly scented paper. I wonder who is living in our house now, she thought. I hope they have not made too many changes. Mama had such exquisite taste.

"Now, Emma, you know you cannot think about her," she said out loud, and put down the paper. She knew she had to think of something else, so she concentrated on the house again. The china was gone, of course. The last sound she remembered as they were dragged from the front door was the crash and tinkle of china as the soldiers rampaged through.

Ah, well, the view is still the same, she reminded herself. Even British soldiers cannot move the Wicklow Mountains. She closed her eyes, thinking of the green loveliness of it all, and knowing that she would never see her home again. True, Virginia had been a reasonable substitute, and she knew that she could return there with some peace of mind when this onerous indenture was fulfilled. Emma rested her chin on her hand. Springs could be soft there, with redbud, flowering dogwood, and azalea, but she knew in her heart that there would never be the shades of green from home, no matter how hard Virginia tried.

And so I must forget, she thought, and picked up another stack of bills. There is an Englishman here, damn him, who should keep me sufficiently occupied. He is utterly without merit and ought to occupy my mind to such a degree that I do not have time to remember.

"Seriously, Hanley, how *does* Lord Ragsdale keep himself from debtor's prison?" she asked the footman, who stuck his head in the room an hour later to see how she did. She indicated the neat piles on the desk and in her lap. "He hasn't paid a bill in at least three months. I can't find any posting books with accounts. Do you know where they would be kept?"

The footman looked around at the order she was creating out of catastrophe, his eyes appreciative. "Gor, miss, there's wood on that desk after all!" he joked.

Emma smiled and indicated a chair beside the desk. "What is his secret, Hanley?"

"Simple, miss. He's richer than Croesus, and all these trades-people know that he will pay eventually. If they get tired of waiting, they petition his banker."

"I call that a pretty ramshackle way to live," Emma grumbled.

The footman shrugged. "If you or I were to forget a bill, now that would not be a pretty sight."

Emma nodded in agreement. "Too true." She placed her hands down on the desk. "Hanley, how did you manage with Lord Ragsdale?"

"Oh, he cleaned up pretty well after you left, miss." The footman laughed. "I think he's not your best friend, though."

Emma shook her head. "And he never will be! I suppose that radical reformation must always exact its own price." She changed the subject. "Hanley, do you know how to get to Newgate Prison from here?"

"Gor, miss, you can't be thinking of going there on *purpose*?" the footman demanded. "I won't tell you!"

She was about to reply when she noticed he was staring at her left hand. She put her hand in her lap, coloring slightly. "I have to, Hanley," she explained, hoping he would not ask any questions. "David Breedlow—I believe that is his name—is imprisoned there awaiting transportation, and I need to know something about Lord Ragsdale's account books, if I am to acquit myself as his secretary."

Hanley's eyes opened wide at that piece of information.

"*You're* going to be the master's new secretary? I never heard of such a thing!"

Emma blushed again. "It's part of my indenture agreement, and you needn't frown about it. Do you know who Lord Ragsdale banks with, or the name and direction of his solicitor? I need to speak to someone about his accounts."

The footman stood up, tugging at his waistcoat. "I wouldn't know, miss."

Emma sighed and deposited the papers on her lap onto the desk. "Perhaps I had better ask Lord Ragsdale, though I would almost rather ingest ground glass than do that."

The footman laughed out loud. "I don't think he'll cooperate with you today." He went to the door and peered out, obviously on the alert. "He told me to tell you that pigs would fly before he lifted another finger on your behalf."

"Oh, he did?" she said as she looked about for a pencil and tablet. "Well, then, this mountain will obviously have to go to Muhammad."

"Miss?"

"If the Almighty upstairs is in a twit, I will just have to visit his former secretary, won't I? Please tell me how to get to Newgate," she asked again.

The footman stared at her and shook his head. "Miss, didn't you hear me? You can't go there!"

Silently, she agreed with him. I have had my fill of prisons, she thought. I hope the walls are thicker at Newgate than they were at Prevot. I don't want to hear anything. "Of course I have to go," she said out loud. "How else am I going to find out how to straighten out His Excellency's books?"

"I don't know, miss," said the footman, his voice doubtful.

She could have left it at that, admitted defeat, and returned to pushing around papers into neater piles. It was on the tip of her tongue to say so, but as she regarded the footman, she knew she had to go ahead. If Lord Ragsdale knew he had the upper hand by refusing to help her, she would never be able to reform him. And I will not stay in this indenture one more moment than I have to, she thought grimly.

"Well, then, Hanley, if you won't help me, I'll just start out walking and ask the first person I meet."

The footman blanched. "You can't do that, either. Oh, very well."

Armed with Hanley's directions, she left the house on Curzon Street before the noon hour. The footman had suggested that she

ide the distance into the City, but she had no money. I've walked
arther, she thought as she tugged her cloak tighter about her and
et off at a brisk pace. I've walked from County Wicklow to
Dublin, most of the time carrying my little brother. This will be a
troll.

The day was cold, and she kept her head down, wishing for the
uxury of a warmer cloak and a muffler for her neck. Pedestrians
ll around her were dressed for the weather, with fur-trimmed
loaks, muffs, and stout shoes. She hurried along, knowing how
ut of place she must appear in that elegant neighborhood, and
oping that her shabbiness would not attract the attention of a
onstable. Well-groomed horses minced by on dainty hooves,
ulling curricles and phaetons of the latest fashion. She wanted to
dmire the bonnets of the ladies who passed, but she kept her eyes
efore her on the pavement, looking up at each curb to make sure
he was following the footman's directions.

The broad streets of Mayfair, with its stylish row houses, gave
vay to the business end of Picadilly. She paid closer attention to
er surroundings, knowing she had to watch for the streets that
vould eventually lead to the Strand, and then Fleet Street. The
old clamped down, bringing with it a whiff of sewage from the
iver. She wished she had not come.

"So help me, Emma Costello, if I have to call your name one
nore time, I'll leave you here to freeze your Irish bones."

Surprised, she looked over her shoulder, then back down at the
idewalk. Calm, calm, she told herself. No one knows you in Lon-
lon. It must be a mistake. She started walking faster.

"Emma!"

There was no mistaking that peremptory voice. She stopped
ind looked into the street this time.

Lord Ragsdale, wearing a heavy overcoat and sitting under a
ap robe, walked his horse and curricle beside her on the street. A
iger, fashionably dressed in the family livery, shivered behind the
eat. When his master reined in his horse, the little Negro leaped
lown and indicated that she should allow him to help her into the
urricle.

Emma stared in amazement, then allowed herself to be seated.
The tiger smoothed the lap robe over her, too, then resumed his
hilly position behind the seat. Lord Ragsdale snapped his whip
ver the horse, and they entered the stream of traffic again.

They passed several blocks in silence before Emma worked up
he courage to speak. "I am going to Newgate, my lord."

To her further surprise, Lord Ragsdale smiled. "If only they would keep you, Emma," he murmured, before his voice became firm again. "Hanley told me. Tell me, Emma, and don't be shy. Is your head filled with porridge instead of brains? Have you not a single clue that you were walking into a neighborhood that not even a gypsy is safe in?"

As she listened to his bracing scold, she realized the idiocy of her plan. When he finished, she raised her chin and looked him in the eye.

"I only want information that will help me straighten out your bills and receipts, my lord." It seemed foolish now, and she stared back down at her hands.

"Your energy continues to astound me, Emma," he said dryly. "But why on earth did you leave my house with no gloves, no bonnet, and no muffler? I call that damned silly."

"I don't have any of those things, my lord," she replied, trying to keep the embarrassment from her voice. It was his turn to be silent for several blocks.

"Well, you should have waited for warmer weather, then," he muttered finally. "Those bills have kept this long; they'll keep until warm weather." He was silent then, his eyes on the traffic.

Emma glanced at him, hoping he was not too angry with her. Somehow I must learn to get along with this man, she thought as she watched his expert hands on the reins guide his horse through city traffic. She was impressed, despite her suspicion.

He spoke to his horse, pulled back slightly on the reins, and looked over his shoulder. "Are we going back?" she asked.

"Oh, no, Emma," he replied as he turned the corner onto Bailey. "Actually, I'm looking forward to the opportunity to give David Breedlow a piece of my mind."

Are you sure you can spare that much? she thought, and smiled in spite of herself.

Lord Ragsdale glanced at her, and then pulled his horse to a stop. "I don't know what you find so dashed amusing about a prison, Emma Costello," he snapped.

She sobered immediately and tugged her cloak over her cold fingers. "There is nothing funny about prison," she said, her words more distinct than she intended.

He snorted, and nodded to the tiger to help her down. "You say that like an expert, Emma Costello."

She didn't mean to respond, but the words came out anyway. "Oh, I am, Lord Ragsdale," she replied, then turned to the tiger and took his helping hand.

As Emma waited for Lord Ragsdale to join her on the side-

alk, she looked up at the gray pile before her. So this is New-
ate, she thought. I wonder if they are here. The view blurred
ver then, and she found herself in tears. Quickly she dabbed at
em, intensely aware that Lord Ragsdale was watching her, a
uizzical expression on his face. She waited for a jibe or a scold,
ut instead, he took her arm and steered her toward the entrance.

"It's a sooty neighborhood, Emma," he said as he pulled out a
andkerchief and gave it to her.

He nodded to the porter who stood lounging beside the low en-
ance. "Mind your head, Emma," he directed as he ducked his
ead under the gloomy stone portal.

She followed him in, holding her breath against that first whiff
' prison air that she knew was coming. The oak door beyond was
en, and topped with a row of spikes and transverse bars. She
esitated a moment, fearing all over again the sound of such a
oor slamming.

Don't be silly, Emma, she told herself. Another porter stood
ere, glancing out of the corner of his eye at Lord Ragsdale's ele-
ant clothing, and then ogling her own shabbiness. He winked at
er, and when she drew back, surprised, made kissing noises that
opped when Lord Ragsdale turned around and fixed him with a
are that could have melted marble.

"Dreadful place," Lord Ragsdale said as he waited for her to
and beside him. "I don't know why you couldn't have just asked
e to answer your questions, Emma."

She looked at him, her eyes wide. "Hanley told me that you
ad no intention of helping me."

Emma thought he smiled at that, but the antechamber was
oomy with the light of only one lamp, and she could not be
ire.

"He is quite right, of course," Lord Ragsdale said as he mo-
oned the porter forward. "But perhaps I would have given you
e information you needed in a day or two."

She couldn't tell if he was quizzing her, so she made no reply.
he stench of the place was appalling, and she held Lord Rags-
ale's handkerchief to her nose, thinking to herself as she did so
at British prisons smelled much like Irish ones. Spoiled food,
washed bodies, filthy straw, she thought, disease rampant, and I
onder, does despair have an odor? She concluded that it did as
e stood next to Lord Ragsdale.

"Tell the governor of this fine old institution that John Staples,
e Marquess of Ragsdale, wishes an audience with him," the

marquess was telling the porter. He held his hand to his nose
moment.

The man nodded, backed through a doorway, and vanished. H
was back promptly. "It'll be a moment, my lord," he explained
He looked at Emma, then. "Is she with you, me lord?" he asked.

"Regrettably, yes."

The porter smirked at Emma. "Then she'll have to be searche
by the warden over there before she goes any farther."

Emma looked to the left where he pointed, and saw a pale, thi
woman leaning against a door frame who straightened up an
started toward her. Despite herself, Emma found herself crowdin
closer to Lord Ragsdale.

"A search will hardly be necessary," the marquess snappe
stepping slightly in front of Emma.

"My lord, you'd be amazed what females try to smuggle i
here under them skirts," the porter assured him. "Go with her lik
a good girl, miss, or I'll have her lift your skirts right here."

Emma took a deep breath, regretted it instantly, and steele
herself to step forward. It's not that bad, she told herself. You'v
done this before, she thought as the female warden gestured to he
impatiently.

"I hardly think this is necessary" came Lord Ragsdale's smoot
voice. "Emma, be a good girl and open your reticule for the nic
lady."

She did as he said, and he peered inside first. "H'mmm, noth
ing more dangerous than a tablet, pencil, and what appears to be
letter. Are you satisfied, madam?" he asked the matron.

The woman looked inside, too, then stared up at the marques
"I'll still have to look under them skirts."

"I don't think so," Lord Ragsdale said. "Emma is irritating an
three parts lunatic, but I would wager that there is nothing unde
her skirts beyond a pair of legs."

The porter tittered behind his hand, and the matron glared a
him, then cracked him so suddenly on the side of his head that h
dropped to his knees. Emma flinched and leaped back against th
marquess as the little man howled in pain. Lord Ragsdale put hi
hand on her shoulder and moved them both out of the reach of th
matron.

The woman jerked her hand back to strike again when the doc
to the governor's office opened suddenly.

"Mrs. Malfrey, remember yourself!" growled the man wh
stood in the doorway, a napkin tucked under his chin. As he cam

:loser to the marquess, Emma noticed his greasy shirtfront, and wondered why he bothered with the nicety of a napkin.

The matron slunk back to her side of the hallway as the governor of Newgate wiped his hand on equally shiny breeches and held it out to the marquess, who merely nodded at him.

"What can I do for you, my lord?" he asked. "It's a little late or morning callers." He laughed at his own humor.

"We have a matter of business to discuss with David Breedlow," Lord Ragsdale said. "He embezzled from me and is awaitng transportation."

"Breedlow, Breedlow, Breedlow," said the governor as he moioned them into his office. The remains of a leg of mutton and various pastries were jumbled over his desk, mingling with various papers and what looked like an earlier meal. "Ye caught me at able, my lord," he apologized. "I always eats in my office, I do." He leaned forward confidentially. "Do ye know, I was cited by he Lord Mayor himself last year. He called me a model of efficiency, he did."

"I am sure you are," Lord Ragsdale murmured, shaking his head when the governor offered him a chair. "We won't disturb you much longer. Show us to David Breedlow, please."

The governor looked longingly at the mutton again, then aughed. "I'll have to find the bleeder first, won't I?"

"I'm sure he can't have gone far," Lord Ragsdale said, more to her than to the governor, who busied himself with a row of books hat looked old enough to have been in William the Conqueror's ibrary, if that notable had been literate. He opened the newest-ooking ledger on the row and thumbed through it, muttering 'Breedlow, Breedlow."

In another moment he stuck his head out into the antechamber and called to the porter. They conversed a moment while Emma stayed close to Lord Ragsdale, who was looking about him in real distaste. Finally, the governor turned back to them, bowed to the marquess, and indicated the door again.

"Follow this bloke. He'll have Breedlow taken to an assembly oom."

"Come, Emma," Lord Ragsdale said. "Let's see what delights his charming place has for us."

The governor laughed out loud and then winked at the marquess. "Come back anytime, my lord, anytime."

"Not if I can possibly help it," Lord Ragsdale replied as they ollowed the porter down a narrow hallway, lit, almost as an afterthought it seemed, by candles here and there. "Emma, what did I do to deserve this?"

She thought a moment and then smiled in spite of herself as she hurried to keep up. "Well, you will own, my lord, that you have probably not thought about a drink lately."

He laughed out loud, and the porter stopped and looked back startled. The marquess only gazed at him serenely. "That was laughter—a natural eruption of good humor that occurs when people are amused. Do lead on, man. If we stand here much longer, we will use up all the air in this part of this fine old institution, I am sure."

They continued deeper into the building, winding around in narrow passages that made Emma pray that the porter would not abandon them. We would never find our way out, she thought. They passed several gang cells, filled to bursting with men and women jumbled in together. Somewhere she heard a child cry, and her heart sank. She must have sucked in her breath, or said something, because the marquess reached behind him and took hold of her hand. She clung to it gratefully.

They stopped finally before another oak door bound with iron, one of many they had passed through. For all I know, we are back at the entrance, Emma thought, her sense of direction confused by the gloom and the halls. The porter selected a key from the many that dangled at his waist and opened the door.

"In here," he said as he swung the door wider. "Breedlow, you have visitors."

Emma squinted in the gloom as she looked around. There were several other women there, sitting on benches facing a row of prisoners who were chained to the wall by one hand. Most of the men sat on the straw-covered floor, their one chained arm raised over their head as though they had a question.

"That's Breedlow, my lord, standing there on the end."

"I know him," the marquess said.

Emma looked at Lord Ragsdale, surprised at the uncertainty in his voice. She glanced at Breedlow, rail thin and pale as parchment, who gradually sank to the floor as though he had no strength to remain upright. His eyes were on the marquess, and in another instant, he started to sob.

The suddenness of the sound stopped all the low-voiced conversations in the assembly room for a moment. When Breedlow continued to cry, the talking began again, like water washing around a boulder in a stream. All this misery, and no one has any pity, Emma thought to herself as she watched Lord Ragsdale's former secretary. Yes, this is very much like Irish prisons. I shall feel right at home. She moved toward the bench, then looked back at Lord Ragsdale, who had remained by the door.

"My lord? My business will take some time, so perhaps if you wish to give your secretary a piece of your mind, you might go first," she said.

There was no reply. "My lord?" she repeated. It is different, is it not, she thought as she watched Lord Ragsdale's face, to turn someone over to justice in a fit of rage, and then to see the results of it. "Really, my lord, you may go first. I don't mind."

"No, Emma," he said finally. "I will wait for you in the hall." The door closed behind him.

Emma seated herself in front of Breedlow, and handed him the marquess's handkerchief. "It is only a little wet," she said.

He took it, wiped his eyes, then stared at her.

"I am Lord Ragsdale's new secretary," she said. "I believe that you can help me. You see, I am reforming Lord Ragsdale."

Chapter 8

The hour passed quickly. She took notes rapidly, and trusted her memory for the rest of Breedlow's information about how to manage Lord Ragsdale's affairs. "I am certain he will ask you to write his letters for him," Breedlow continued as the guard by the inner door blew a little brass whistle. "He's not that difficult to please." He paused and looked toward the guard. "I only wish he had not been so lazy. Perhaps then I would not have been tempted . . ." His voice trailed away as the women on the benches started to rise.

"How long before you are transported?" Emma asked, wishing there was something she could do for the man.

"Very soon, I fear," he replied. He took a last dab at his eyes, then started to hand back Lord Ragsdale's handkerchief. He hesitated. "May I keep this?"

Mystified, she nodded. "Why would you want to?"

Breedlow bowed his head, and she could tell that her question had humiliated him further. "I can sell it for food." He raised his eyes to hers. "You can't imagine how hungry I am."

"Oh, I can," she said softly as the guard blew the whistle again. "Keep it, by all means. I wish I had some money to give you."

He shook his head, and managed a ragged smile. "Actually, I have enjoyed your company. You are my first visitor. My sister lives too far away to visit." Again he stopped and looked away as the tears came to his eyes. "And now I will never see her again, and it was all for twenty pounds."

They were both silent. Emma leaned forward then and reached into her reticule. "Please, Mr. Breedlow, can you do me a favor?"

He stared at her blankly. "How could I possibly do you a favor?"

"I want to hand you a letter. Please take it to Australia. See if you can deliver it for me." She kept her voice low as the guards began to herd the women together at the other end of the narrow room.

He shook his head. "You daren't hand me anything. The guards ill only tear it up and beat me later."

"It was just a thought," she said then, and withdrew her hand om the reticule. "Mr. Breedlow, good luck."

He started to reply, when one of the women near the door reamed and fainted. As the other women clustered around, jab- ring and gesturing, the guards hurried to that end of the room.

"Quickly now." It was Breedlow, holding his hand out to her.

She grabbed the letter again and thrust it at him, grateful for the expected diversion. It disappeared as soon as she handed it er.

Order returned quickly, and a guard gestured her toward the. or and thrust his key in the lock that chained Breedlow to the all.

"Good luck, Mr. Breedlow," she called again as he was led vay. "Please don't lose that letter," she said softly as the other omen, more of them crying now, hurried from the room. She atched the former secretary until the door clanged behind him, en sighed and stepped into the hall again.

Lord Ragsdale waited for her. He snapped open his pocket atch. "I trust you learned all you need to know, and I hope you n't have anyone else to visit at Newgate. As it is, I am certain I ll never get the stench of this place out of my coat."

"No, my lord, I have no one else to visit," she replied as he arted back down the hall. "But I do want you to stop in the gov- nor's office for a moment."

"Not if my life depended on it," he assured her, and hurried ster.

"I want you to give the governor some money to keep Mr. eedlow from starving," she said, and then held her breath and ited for the storm to break.

She was not disappointed. He stopped, took her by the arm, and ve her a shake. "Emma, he robbed me!" Lord Ragsdale outed.

Why am I doing this, she thought as she nerved herself to look o his eye and stand her ground, even though he was taller than e by a foot at least, and seemed enormously large in that many- ped coat he wore.

"And Mr. Breedlow is going to a lifetime in a penal colony for aling a paltry twenty pounds from you," she continued, sur- sed at her own temerity. I am not afraid of you, she thought, d to her amazement, she meant it.

"So he is," Lord Ragsdale said, calm again. He let go of her

arm and hurried her along the endless passage, past cell
crammed with wretched people, prisoners for whom all time wa
suspended into a continuous, dismal present that she understoo
very well.

Emma did not really expect Lord Ragsdale to stop at the gove
nor's office again, but he did. The governor ushered them into th
office that still smelled of elderly mutton.

"This is for David Breedlow's upkeep," the marquess said a
he slapped a handful of coins down on the desk and then scowle
at Emma.

"Thank you, my lord," she replied, and edged closer to the ro
of ledgers as the governor searched around on his messy desk fo
a receipt book. In another moment she was looking through th
newest ledger, running her finger down the row of names of pri
oners incarcerated in the last five years. There were so many, an
the governor's scribe had such poor handwriting. This will tak
me an hour at least, and I do not have an hour, she thought as th
governor scratched out a receipt and handed it to her employer.

"Come, Emma," Lord Ragsdale said. He stood next to her, an
she jumped at the sudden intrusion on her rapid scramble throug
the ledger. "We have come to the end of this day's philanthropy,
trust."

She closed the book reluctantly.

"Looking up relatives?" the marquess asked. "Close relatives,
would imagine."

He was teasing her; she could tell. "Of course, my lord," sh
responded promptly. He could think what he chose.

Lord Ragsdale nodded to his tiger, who unblanketed his hors
They started out in silence. It was almost dark now, and Newga
was only a hulking shadow. She shivered, hoping that she wou
not dream tonight.

"I trust we needn't repeat a visit to my late secretary."

"No, my lord," she said. "Tomorrow, though, we need to vis
your banker, and find out what bills remain to be paid. Breedlo
tells me that your banker has his ledgers."

"It can wait, Emma," he grumbled.

"It cannot, my lord. The sooner your finances are organize
the less I will bother you."

"Thank God," he replied fervently. "In that case, I am you
this evening, too."

Silence filled the space between them. They might have bee
miles from each other, instead of touching shoulders. She kne

e should be silent, but Breedlow's face was still so vivid in her
mind.

"My lord, did you ever ask Mr. Breedlow why he stole the
money?"

"No. I don't care why."

The marquess spoke with such finality that Emma knew she
d not dare to continue. But she did, as though some demon
shed her onto an empty stage, daring her to perform for a hos-
le audience.

"His sister's husband died, and that twenty pounds was to
over funeral expenses and a year's rent for her."

She could tell he had turned to look at her, but it was dark and
he could not see his face.

"I told you I did not care. Thievery's thievery, Emma."

She looked straight ahead and plunged on, driven by some imp
at she did not recognize. "When I straightened out your desk
is morning, I noticed that you wagered seventy-five pounds that
ord Lander could not push a peanut with his nose down St.
mes Street during the evening rush of traffic."

His reply was quiet, and she knew she should not prod him any
rther. "It's my money, Emma," he said.

"Yes, it is, isn't it?"

"Emma, you are aggravating!" he said, his voice low but in-
nse. "When we get home, I am going to find that stupid paper I
gned and tear it up, and you can spend the next five years clean-
g out my kitchen! To hell with my reformation."

Well, that is that, she thought to herself as she pulled as far
vay from him as she could, and stared into the gathering dusk.
h, why can I not learn patience? I have ruined everything.

When they arrived at the house, Lord Ragsdale flung himself
t of the curricle, snapped his orders at the tiger, and took the
ont steps in two bounds. Emma followed more slowly, drawing
r cloak about her again. She sniffed at the fabric. Lord Ragsdale
as right; the odor of Newgate had permeated the material.

He slammed the door behind him, not quite in her face, but al-
ost. She opened it and forced herself to go inside. I wonder if
dy Ragsdale found me a place to sleep, she thought. I cannot
ar another night on the stairs.

Lady Ragsdale and Sally Claridge, dressed in evening wear,
ood in the front hallway conversing with Lord Ragsdale. The
der woman nodded to Emma, and then made a face as Emma
wly removed her cloak.

"I was telling my son how much Sally and I were looking for-

ward to his escort tonight and during this Season, and what doe
he tell me but you have commanded his appearance in the boo
room this evening?"

Surprised, Emma glanced at Lord Ragsdale, who stood slightl
behind his mother. He stared at her, and gave a slow wink. Sh
understood perfectly, and resisted the urge to cheer as she sighe
and then shook her head at Lady Ragsdale.

"That is how we must get on, my lady," she said, striving fo
that perfect blend of regret and determination. "Until your son
business affairs are regulated, I must claim his attention. I am su₁
that later in the Season he will be delighted to accompany the tw
of you."

To her relief, Lady Ragsdale nodded her head. "I am sure w
understand, Emma. Come, Sally. I don't believe Lord and Lad
Tennant were expecting my son anyway."

Lord Ragsdale kissed his mother's cheek and managed a loo
of rue so counterfeit to Emma that she had to turn away to mai₁
tain her countenance. *I never met a more complicated man,* sh
thought as Lord Ragsdale expressed his profound sorrow at miss
ing an evening with London's finest, and closed the door behin
his mother and cousin. He turned back to her, and she held h₁
breath.

"To the book room, Emma," he said, handing his coat ₁
Lasker, who frowned and held it at arm's length. "Burn i₁
Lasker," he ordered as he started down the hall. "Come along
come along! I suppose that right now, you are the lesser of tw
evils. I would rather suffer an hour or two in the book room wi₁
you than spend even fifteen minutes in the home of London
most prosing windbags. If some latter-day Guy Fawkes were ₁
blow up Lord and Lady Tennant, he would have the thanks of
grateful nation."

"Thank you, I think," she replied dubiously.

"You have your uses, Emma," he murmured as he held ope
the book room door. "Now I suppose you want me to go to m₁
room and gather up all the bills on that desk and bring them ₁
you, as well."

"Precisely, my lord," she said as she seated herself behind th
desk and reached for the inkwell. "We will sort them, and t₁
them in bales and contract a carter to haul them to Fotherby ar
Sons tomorrow morning."

"Emma, you are trying me," he replied, his hand on the doo
knob.

She returned his stare with one of her own. "Of course, if yo

urry, I am sure you can arrive at the Tennants' in time for a ful-
illing evening, my lord."

"And deprive you of my company, Emma? Never that. By
God, you are a cheeky bit of Irish baggage," Lord Ragsdale mur-
nured as he closed the door quietly behind him. To her amaze-
nent, he was whistling as he headed for the stairs.

He is a lunatic, she thought as she put more coal on the fire. If
nly I didn't owe him so much money. She seated herself again
nd folded her hands on the desk, thinking of Mr. Breedlow. If he
urvives the journey, perhaps he will remember the letter. And if
e does, perhaps it will get to my father, or my brother. And if
hey read it, perhaps they will be allowed to write to me. She
ooked down at the distorted fingernails on her left hand. But I
vill not hope, she thought. For all I know, they are buried in a
ime pit in Dublin.

But I will not think of that, she told herself a few minutes later
s she rested her head on the desk and closed her eyes. She raised
er head a moment later as the doorknob turned.

"Caught you, Emma," Lord Ragsdale murmured as he dumped
n armful of bills on the desk. "Which reminds me. Lasker, in his
ondescension, has permitted you to sleep with the scullery maid.
op floor, second door on the right." He sat down next to her.
All right, Emma. I dare you to organize me."

The clock in the hall was chiming midnight when Lord Rags-
ale stood up and stretched. He looked at the neat piles of bills
estooning the room, and wondered all over again how he ever
ound the time for such profligacy. Emma Costello still bent dili-
ently over the tablet, recording each bill in her rather fine hand-
riting. Every now and then she rubbed her eyes and seemed to
ag a bit, but she kept at the work with no complaints.

They had indulged in several lively arguments throughout the
nterminable evening, and rather than resenting it, he found him-
elf enjoying the spirited exchanges. As much as he disliked the
rish, he had to admit that Emma's native wit kept him on his
oes. He came away bruised from at least one sharp encounter, but
nvigorated by the intensity. He realized how few witty people he
new. His mother was charm itself, but her conversation had de-
eloped a predictability that made him yawn. And Fae Moullé?
Ie glanced at Emma, writing and trying to stay awake. Fae
vouldn't recognize a clever turn of phrase if it bit her on the bot-
om.

Their worst argument of the evening had come about because

of Fae. After having sorted out a sizable collection of bills from
modistes, chocolatiers, and glove makers, Emma had finally
stared at him and waved the invoices in his face.

"My lord, are you aware that Miss Moullé must have enough
gloves to outfit a small army?" she burst out, as though each
glove paraded across the desk. "And what can she possibly do
with all this perfume?"

"I hardly think that my mistress is any of your business," he
snapped, perching on the edge of the desk. He thought he had
spoken in the tone that usually quelled servants, but what with the
late hour, he must have been mistaken. Emma rode right over his
comment as if he had remained silent.

"Actually, I believe she is my business, if reformation is our
topic, my lord," Emma replied. "What are you, sir? Twenty-nine?
Thirty?"

"I am thirty," he replied, wondering down what path she was
leading him. "Your age, at least," he added to goad her.

She only grinned at him as though he did not know how to
argue. Since it was the first time she had smiled, he overlooked
the familiarity of it.

"Good try, my lord," she said. "You are thirty, then?"

He nodded, making sure that he did not smile, even though he
wanted to.

"Would you agree with your mother that it is high time you set
up your nursery?"

He nodded again, less eager. "So she tells me."

Emma folded her hands in her lap. "You stand a better chance
of attracting someone proper if you discard your mistress. Just
personally speaking, I would never marry someone with a mistress. It smacks of the grossest hypocrisy."

"My wife wouldn't have to know," he hedged, thinking about
Fae and those charms that she had perfected to a fine art. Of
course, it had been some time, really, since he had truly enjoyed
them. Of late, he had started to find her boring, but there was no
need for Emma to know that. "I would keep Fae a secret."

"Then you must be planning to marry someone really stupid,
Lord Ragsdale," Emma murmured. "And who's to say your children will have any intelligence whatsoever, if there aren't brains
on at least one side of your family?"

"Damn your impertinence, Emma!" he shouted. "Does reformation mean I must give up *everything* that is fun?"

Emma was silent for a moment, contemplating him. He almost
made the mistake of taking her silence for acquiescence, but de-

ded that might be premature. Now what, you baggage? he
ought.

"I am sure you will correct me if I am wrong, my lord, but I
on't really think you are having any fun."

If his Irish servant had been a barrister in a wig and gown, she
ould not have trussed him up more neatly. He stared at her, then
own at the bills in his hand, at a total loss for words. In a mo-
ent, she returned her attention to the list in front of her and con-
nued with the entries, unconscious of the fact that he was
pening and closing his mouth like a fish.

He watched her, noting how her rich auburn hair was coming
ose from the knot she wore it in, and how her eyes closed occa-
onally. You slept on the stairs last night, he thought, and I was
ad. That was a bit churlish of me, no matter how pointed my
islike. And yes, yes, you are quite right, although I will never
ll you. I'm not having much fun these days.

"You think I should give up Fae?" he asked, keeping his voice
ffhand.

Emma nodded and rubbed her eyes.

"I'll consider it," he said. "Go to bed, Emma. You're about
ine-tenths worthless right now."

She left the room without another comment. He sat down in the
hair she had vacated and looked at her neat list, and the column
f money owed. He totted it up in his head, going from page to
age, all the while thinking of David Breedlow, chained to the
all in Newgate. I could have loaned him twenty pounds, he
ought. I could have concerned myself with his family's trials. I
ould have behaved as my father would have behaved. Why
idn't I?

He yanked off his eye patch and threw it on the desk, rubbing
is forehead. "Damn the Irish," he said, remembering his last
iew of his father before he stumbled, fell back, and disappeared
1 a clatter of pikes and swords. "And damn you, Emma Costello,
ou and all your murderous Irish relations."

Lord Ragsdale went to bed, longing for at least a glass of
herry, and determined to throw a boot at Emma if she tried to
other him before noon. To his dismay, he woke up at nine, alert,
ungry, and ready to go another round with Emma Costello. Han-
y, who seemed to have appointed himself valet, brought him tea
nd stayed to help him shave and dress. He smelled ham and
acon and followed his nose to the breakfast room, where his
nother and cousin were just finishing.

Lady Ragsdale looked at him in amazement, then took out her

little pocket watch and tapped it. "Are you just coming in, John?"
she asked finally as he filled a plate from the sideboard.

Lord Ragsdale had the good grace to laugh. "Mama, you know
I am not! I think everyone ought to eat breakfast occasionally."
He peered at the scrambled eggs and found that they did not dis-
gust him. "So chickens still lay eggs?"

Lady Ragsdale laughed. "How clever of them!" She glanced at
Sally. "My dear, perhaps we can importune your cousin into escorting us to the modiste for a male opinion as we attempt a
wardrobe for you."

Oh, God, not that, he thought as he took a bite of scrambled
eggs. He wanted to chew awhile and give himself time to think up
an excuse, but eggs did not require that sort of exertion. To his relief, Emma came to his rescue yet again. He swallowed and
smiled at his mother.

"My dear, you will think me a dreadful put-off, but Emma and
I must visit the bank today. You should see how neatly she has
the bills organized."

To his relief, his mother did not press the matter. "Very well,
son, we will excuse you again." She looked at her niece. "Come,
Sally, let us see what damage we can do by ourselves. Our bills
will be yours, son, so if you wish an opinion on how we spend
your money, this is your last chance."

Lord Ragsdale finished his eggs and waved his hand in a generous gesture. "Just give the bills to Emma when they come in. I'm
sure she will have a file for everything." He took a sip of tea as
his mother rose from the table. "Mama, you can do something for
me at the modiste's."

His mother turned wary eyes in his direction, and he thought
again about Emma's advice that he discard his mistress. "Could
you order a warm cloak for Emma? Make it dark brown and serviceable. No telling when spring will actually arrive this year."

"A fur collar? Silk frogs?" his mama teased.

Mama, if you had seen her shivering in Newgate, you wouldn't
quiz me, he considered thoughtfully. "Oh, no. The key word is
serviceable. Now that I think of it, perhaps a wool dress, too.
Something with a lace collar." He glanced at Sally, who was regarding him with astonishment. "She's about your size, isn't she,
my dear?"

Sally nodded, too surprised at his unexpected generosity to
speak.

"Well, there's your template, Mama. Cousin, if you don't mind
the observation, she's a bit thinner in the waist and shorter by an

nch or two. Make that two dresses, Mama. A secretary ought to
have a change of clothing."

He was still smiling as his mother left the room. I should have
asked her to pick out a bonnet, too, he thought. Careless of me. I
wonder if Fae could be induced to part with some of those gloves
have been buying for her. I mean, a body only has two hands.
He got up for another cinnamon bun and stood eating it by the
sideboard. No, no. Too much at once might make Emma think I
had declared a truce or something. She can do without gloves and
bonnet.

Feeling pleasantly full, Lord Ragsdale strolled to the book
room, where Emma was gathering the bound bills into a satchel.
She looked up and smiled at him.

"Good morning, sir," she said, and continued her business. "If
we get these to the bank and straighten out your affairs, I promise
not to bother you for the rest of the day."

He raised his eyebrows at her and helped pack the bills.
"Emma, why the magnanimity? Can it be that you have a heart?"

"Of course I do," she replied promptly. "I also intend to re-
rieve your balance books from the banker and spend the afternoon making entries." She closed the satchel.

"I have a better idea," he said, taking the satchel from her. "I
want you to visit Fae Moullé and see how the wind blows."

"My lord!" she exclaimed, unable to hide her dismay.

Aha, he thought, I surprised you. He waited a moment until he
was sure he would not smile, then continued. "I have been thinking about what you said. Perhaps it is time she and I ended our
arrangement. I want you to see what terms would be agreeable. It
s your duty as my secretary," he added, when that now-familiar
obstinate expression settled on her face.

"Very well, my lord," Emma said, and the doubt in her voice
made him want to shout, "Got you!" He did not. Just the knowledge that he had ruffled her equanimity was pleasure enough for
he moment.

"I will probably spend this evening at Almack's with my
mother and cousin," he said as they drove to Fotherby and Sons in
his curricle. "I should be an occasional escort, and besides, I must
contemplate this Season's beauties." He nudged her in the side.
"Tell me, Emma, how can I pick out a smart one?"

To his delight, she laughed out loud. She had a hearty laugh,
and it startled him at first, because it was something he was not
used to. It was no drawing-room titter, no giggle behind a fan, but
a full, rich sound as genuine as it was infectious. He laughed, too.

"I have it, Emma," he said. "I will begin reciting a Pythagorean theorem and see if she can complete it."

She laughed again. "Then a canto from *La Divina Commedia,* my lord."

He reined his horse to a stop in front of his banking establishment. "Emma, there's obviously more to you than meets the eye."

He wished he had not said that. He might have slapped her, for all the gaiety left her eyes and that invisible curtain dropped between them again. She looked again like a woman devoid of all hope, the Emma of the taproom, waiting for her future to be decided by the turn of a card. It was a transformation as curious as her good humor only moments ago.

She said nothing more, but stared straight ahead between his horse's ears. As he watched her, she drew her cloak tighter around her, sighed, and then reached for the satchel at her feet. He took it from her.

You could talk to me, Emma, he thought as he followed her into the building and then led the way down the hall to Amos Fotherby's office. While it is a well-documented fact that I have no love for the Irish, you interest me. And while it is also certain that there is less to me than meets the eye, that is not the truth, in your case.

Fotherby quickly recovered from his initial surprise when he introduced Emma, and the banker realized that she knew her way around a double-entry ledger. The banker's reserve melted further when Emma pulled up her chair, pushed up her sleeves in businesslike fashion, and pulled out the bills and her list. Fotherby hardly glanced up as Lord Ragsdale backed out of the room.

"I'll be in the vault, Emma," he said. "Join me there when you're done, as I need an opinion."

She nodded, as preoccupied as the banker. Lord Ragsdale smiled to himself, thanking a generous God that there were people on the earth who actually cared about assets, debits, and accountings. He watched her a moment more, wishing he had asked his mother to get Emma a deep green cloak instead of a brown one, then sauntered down the hall to the vault.

Emma joined him there an hour later, her glorious auburn hair untidy. He noted that it was coming loose again, and chuckled.

"Emma, do you realize that when you concentrate, you tug at your hair?"

She blushed and tucked the stray tendrils under the knot again. "Your accounts were such a mess, my lord. Some tradesmen have

pplied to Mr. Fotherby for payment, and we had to go through
ie whole lot, so as not to pay anyone twice."

"I trust you have me in order now?"

"Oh, yes. From now on, you give all the bills to me, and I forward them to Mr. Fotherby for payment. I cannot get power of at-
orney to pay your bills myself because I am a woman, Catholic,
nd Irish." She ticked off the items on her fingers.

"I call that downright prejudiced," he joked.

"Well, at least it is more misdemeanors than the law allows,"
he agreed. "I am not sure which of the three is the least palat-
ble."

There was no regret in her voice, but only that businesslike
one that gave him the distinct impression that he had cast himself
ito capable hands. She had a relaxed air about her, as though she
ad just come from a hot bath, or an entertaining party. I suppose
is given to some to bask in the toils of finance, he thought. He
idicated a chair.

"Be seated, Emma, and tell me which necklace I should give to
'ae," he ordered. "I thought a peace offering would be in order
vhen you visit her." He looked away and coughed. "A bauble
might make her not suffer so much when I cut the connection."

He held out several necklaces, and placed them in her lap. She
crutinized them with the same intensity she had tackled his bills,
nen picked up a simple chain with an emerald. "This one, by all
neans," she said, her eyes shining with more animation than he
ad seen before.

As Emma held it up to catch the vault's fitful light, he was
truck by how elegant it would look around her neck. The stone
vinked at him as he took it from her hand and replaced it in the
elvet-lined box.

"No, Emma, that one will never do. Think in terms of greed
nd avarice, and then choose between these three," he said, struck
y the knowledge that he was about to come to the end of five
'ears of Fae Moullé's demands. Greed and avarice? Now, why
lid I never see that before, he asked himself as Emma frowned
nd picked up a particularly gaudy chain with diamonds and ru-
nies alternating.

"Excellent!" He put the rest back in the box and returned them
o the teller, who hovered at his elbow. He slid the necklace into a
elvet pouch and handed it to Emma. "Take this to Fae with my
ompliments, and see if you can figure out how the deuce to get
er to let go of my purse strings." He sighed. "I know she is at-
ached to me, but as you say, it is time to reform."

"Very well, my lord," Emma said. As the teller was replacing the jewels, she picked up a plain gold chain. "Is this valuable to you, Lord Ragsdale?" she asked.

"No. Do you want it, Emma?" he teased.

She shook her head, blushed, and took a deep breath. "If you were to send this to the governor at Newgate, he would make David Breedlow's life almost pleasant." She looked at him, as i gauging his mood. "Or you could send it to his sister. He told me her name is Mary Roney, and she lives in Market Quavers."

He snatched the necklace from her and replaced it in the box, wondering at her nerve. "No, and that is final! You have stretched my philanthropy far enough for one day. Now, now, just go home and reconcile my books," he ordered. "You can see Fae in the morning."

She left hurriedly, as though afraid he would turn her impulsive effort into a humiliation. When she was gone, he took out the necklace again, and another one, which he handed to the teller. "Make up two packages. Address this one to the governor of Newgate, and this to Mary Roney," he said. "I will write a note for both in Fotherby's office."

So there, Emma, he thought. I really am a fine fellow. I only hope Fae does not repine too long over the news *you* bring.

Chapter 9

f anything, it was colder the next morning when Emma left the
house on Curzon Street. Where is spring? she wondered as the
nd whipped around her dress and exposed her ankles, much to
e noisy appreciation of a road crew replacing some curbing. She
gged her cloak tighter, grateful at least that the stench of New-
te was fading from the fabric. Even the scullery maid, no stick-
for cleanliness, had insisted that she leave it outside the room
e two of them grudgingly shared.

Emma hurried along, convinced that her earlier visit to New-
te was a pleasant excursion, compared to this task before her.
ord Ragsdale, you should have been drowned at birth, to have
isted this assignment on me," she muttered. It was one thing to
to prison for him; it was quite another to initiate his dirty work
sloughing off a mistress. Duties of a secretary, indeed, she
ought. What it really smacks of is the most monumental bit of
ziness imaginable, and so I should tell you to your face, Lord
agsdale.

She felt in her reticule for the necklace, wondering at the bad
ste of someone to wear such a bauble. Satisfied that no lep-
chaun had spirited away the necklace, she kept her head down
d turned into the wind on Fortnam Street. No, I shall not scold
u, Lord Ragsdale, although you richly deserve it, she thought.
t now, at least, when we seem to have declared a truce of sorts.

Last evening spent with Lord Ragsdale in the book room was
ore pleasant than she had any hope to expect. To begin, when
had requested that Lasker bring him dinner on a tray, the mar-
ess did not eat in front of her, but shared his meal. It had been
long since she had eaten food of that quality that she could
rdly force it down at first. Not until Lord Ragsdale looked at
r and remarked, "Really, Emma, if you're thinking about smug-
ing this rather remarkable loin of beef to my damned secretary
Newgate, I don't think you could get it past the matron."

I suppose I was thinking about Mr. Breedlow, she reflected as

she blushed and took some food on her plate. She chewed the te
derloin thoughtfully, amazed that Lord Ragsdale cared even th
slightest what she was thinking.

He had been silent then, his long legs propped up on the des
the plate resting on his stomach, concentrating on his dinner. A
tually, Emma considered as she watched him, you should dress
a toga and recline. His profile was strong, and while his nose w
not Roman, there was something patrician about the whole effe
that impressed her. She smiled to herself, and looked away, thin
ing, If I can be impressed by Lord Ragsdale, when I have se
him bare and blasted by last night's liquor, I suppose anything
possible.

"Do I amuse you, Emma?" he had asked.

She looked up, startled at first, and then relieved to noti
something approaching a twinkle in his eye. Only candor wou
do, she thought as he waited for her reply.

"In a way, I suppose you do, my lord," she replied, crossing h
fingers and hoping that her own assessment of his character w
not misplaced. "Only think how far you have come from yeste
day morning, my lord. Reformation agrees with you."

There, now, make something of that, she dared, and took a
other bite.

"Perhaps it does," he agreed, setting his plate aside, but n
moving from his relaxed position at the desk. "I have, only th
day, forsaken liquor *and* my club. I have advanced some coins
feed my worthless secretary, and plan to discard my mistress t
morrow. Next you will tell me that I must go to church, stop gar
bling, give up the occasional cigar, and take in stray dogs."

Emma laughed. "All of the above, my lord."

He pulled out his watch and stared at it. "And this time ne
week, we will go to Hyde Park, and you can watch me walk (
water! Come, Emma, to the books. I want to get to bed early so
can be fresh enough in the morning to find more ways to torme
you."

And so you have, Emma thought as she hurried along th
street. I am to go to your mistress and find a way to diplomat
cally ease your useless carcass out of her life. Oh, dear, I hop
there isn't a scene. How does one do this?

She looked at the direction Lord Ragsdale had written down fe
her, and to her dismay, the narrow house—one of a row of el
gant houses—was precisely where he said it would be. Did yo
think it would blow away? she scolded herself as she took on
last look at the address, then raised her hand to the knocker.

The woman who opened the door was obviously the maid. She
arted to curtsy to Emma, then stopped when she took a good
ok at her shabby cloak and broken shoes.

"Servant's entrance is through the alley behind," she said, and
arted to close the door.

Emma stuck her foot in the door. "I come from Lord Rags-
le," she said, leaning into the crack that still remained open. "I
ve something for Fae Moullé."

"Miss Moullé to you," snapped the maid. She left the door, and
turned in a moment. Standing behind her was an overblown
oman with hair of a shade not precisely found in nature. She had
rge blue eyes, and lips of a color that the homely word "red"
ould not do justice to.

Emma moved her foot from the door and suppressed the urge
laugh. Goodness, Lord Ragsdale, she thought, you really are in
ed of reformation if this is your idea of beauty. She touched the
cklace in her reticule again, thinking how well it would suit.

"I am Lord Ragsdale's secretary, and I have something for you
om him," she repeated.

"You cannot possibly be his secretary," said the woman who
ust be Fae. "My lord's secretary is languishing in Newgate, I
lieve."

She smiled and stuck her hand through the narrowing crack in
e door. "Miss Moullé, he won my indenture in a card game, and
e have resolved that I am to straighten out his affairs."

Her choice of words almost sent her into whoops, so she turned
vay and coughed, hoping the hilarity that threatened to consume
r would pass. Now what will appeal to you, Miss Moullé, she
ought as she turned back. She reached into her bag and pulled
t the necklace.

"He has commissioned me to bring this to your notice," she
id, dangling the gaudy bauble just out of reach.

The door swung open, and Emma felt herself practically
cked inside. The necklace was snatched from her hand at the
me moment the maid relieved her of her cloak. In another mo-
ent, she found herself arm in arm with Fae Moullé, being pro-
lled into the sitting room as Lord Ragsdale's mistress issued
ders for tea, cakes, and more coal for the grate.

As she glanced around the sitting room, it occurred to Emma
at Lord Ragsdale did not stint on his mistress. The expensive
aperies complemented the costly furniture, which sumptuously
t off the deep carpet. She had to consciously force herself not to
ck off her shoes and run her bare feet across its softness. Emma

suppressed another smile; the only thing that didn't seem to fit the room was the young man sitting on the sofa.

Fae's rather shrewd eyes turned a shade anxious as she fo lowed the direction of Emma's gaze.

"Miss . . ."

"Costello," Emma offered.

Fae gestured toward the sofa and its occupant, who appeare poised to bolt the room. "This is my . . . brother," she said.

If this is your brother, then I am the Lord Mayor of Londo Emma thought as she nodded to the young man. "Delighted," sl said. "How fortunate for Miss Moullé to have relatives in tl city."

A small silence followed that no one seemed to know how fill. His cheeks flaming the shade of Fae's lip color, the your man leaped to his feet, babbled something about work to do people to see, and fled the room. Fae watched him go, her fac filled with a longing that disappeared as soon as she fingered tl necklace.

"How kind of Lord Ragsdale to take such good care of me she said, her French accent more pronounced. "Do sit down, Mi Costello, and here is the tea."

Emma sat in the chair closest to the fire, accepted the tea, ar leaned back to bask for a moment in the wages of a sinful lif Mama would be shocked if she could see me in the love nest of debaucher, she thought. I wonder where Fae keeps all thos gloves, she considered next as she watched the woman scrutini the necklace with the practiced air of a gem merchant. I wond she does not put a jeweler's loupe to her eye, Emma considere She sighed and reached for a macaroon, and then another. It wi not be easy to pry Fae Moullé away from these particular flesl pots. I know I would not give up such luxury willingly. Sl waited for Fae to speak, hoping to take some cue from her words

"Miss Costello, you say he won your indenture in a cal game?" Fae was asking. "I can't imagine Lord Ragsdale doir anything that smacked of exertion, and card games can be rigo ous affairs."

"It is true," Emma replied, wondering at a female so lazy th she thought cards a challenge. How fitting for Lord Ragsdale, sl concluded. "But really, I think he is not the idle man you believ him to be."

She stopped, macaroon in hand, and wondered why she wa defending Lord Ragsdale. How odd, she thought, as she popped in her mouth.

"Oh, he is lazy," Fae countered, leaping to her feet and taking a quick turn about the room. "He usually comes here to sleep off the exertion of an evening at White's." She paused delicately, then plunged ahead. "At least, that is all he has come for lately. I mean, he won't even exert himself to . . ."

"I think I understand," Emma interrupted hastily, her cheeks red.

Fae Moullé only nodded and took another circuit of the room, looking out the window as though she expected to see the young man outside on the street. "Sometimes he is so neglectful that I have to invite my . . . brother to keep me company."

You know I do not believe you, Emma thought as she nodded. Brothers can be a wonderful diversion," she said, preserving the fiction. She thought of her own brothers then, both the quick and the dead, and pushed aside the remains of the macaroon plate. She took another sip of tea and looked Fae in the eye. "I have come to negotiate with you, Miss Moullé," she began. "Let us first clear up some questions."

She left Miss Moullé's establishment as it was growing dark, a smile on her face and her stomach too full of macaroons. What a turn I have done you, Lord Ragsdale, she thought as she hurried along, hoping to beat the rainstorm that threatened. Indeed, it is a pity that I could never study for the diplomatic corps. With scarcely the smallest difficulty, I have rid "Your Mightiness" of a mistress, and managed to cheat you soundly in the bargain. Who would have thought the day to have had such promise when it began? I know I did not.

It wasn't the sort of deception that would see her to Newgate, irons, and a berth to Australia. She had merely hinted to Fae that Lord Ragsdale was beginning to suspect that his loving light-skirt was playing a deep game. Fae had squeezed out some noisy tears and just the threat of a spasm, until Emma assured her that Lord Ragsdale had nothing more substantial than suspicions.

She knew that she could have told Fae that it was all over, and Lord Ragsdale's mistress would gladly have packed her bags and let it go at that, relieved that he had not discovered her other male visitors, and made an ugly scene. There wasn't any need for Lord Ragsdale to spend another penny. But since he had many such pennies, Emma smiled inwardly and plunged ahead, content to fulfill his request to the letter of the law.

"Miss Moullé, Lord Ragsdale has authorized me to suggest to you that he would not be too unhappy if you left his employ," she

said. "In fact, he is willing to make you an offer . . ." She paused
and coughed slightly. ". . . An offer to make up for the sadness
such a parting will cause you."

Fae was fanning herself vigorously, despite the slight chill in
the room. Her blond curls fluttered from the effort. "Oh, I am not
sorry!" she burst out, then stopped, and considered what Emma
was saying. Her eyes took on a more melancholy expression, her
shoulders drooped, and she assumed such an air of wounded pride
that Emma wanted to applaud the performance. "Perhaps I am a
little sorry," she amended. "After all, two years of my life . . .
What, uh, kind of offer did he have in mind?"

Emma looked beyond Fae, as though studying the wall. "He
told me he felt honor-bound to provide for you in some way, Miss
Moullé." She folded her hands in her lap. "I suppose that is your
decision. He especially wanted me to ask you what would make
you the happiest."

Fae leaned forward and rested her elbows on her knees in a
most unladylike posture. She stared into the grating where the
flames leaped about. Fae was silent so long that Emma wondered
if she had drifted off to sleep. Emma was about to nudge her
when Fae looked at her, her practiced melancholy replaced with
glee.

"I have it!" she exclaimed. "Tell your master that I want to
open my own millinery shop in Bath."

"My, that will be expensive," Emma exclaimed, unable to keep
the admiration from her voice. "Think what the inventory will
cost, and the expense of a shop and probably living quarters."

"Of course I will need living quarters," Fae agreed, getting up
with a decisive motion to stand by the fireplace. "And nothing
paltry. After all, I am used to Half Moon Street, am I not? And
who can make a success of such an establishment unless it is in
the most forward part of town?"

"Oh, indeed," Emma replied. "After all, Bath is not a town for
nipfarthing ways, or so I am told." She shook her head, aiming for
the right degree of doubt. "This is an expensive proposition, indeed."

Fae rose to the bait. "Do you think it is too much?" she asked
anxiously.

"I am sure there is nothing Lord Ragsdale would not do, no
lengths to which he would not go, to make sure that your leaving
is a pleasant experience," Emma said. *Did I actually say that?* she
asked herself, knowing that she was spreading around as much

fiction as Fae herself. And Fae knew it, too. Emma could tell by the unholy look that came into the woman's eyes.

They looked at each other for another moment, then both burst into laughter. The next few moments were taken up with the most delicious merriment. It seemed to swell from the soles of Emma's feet upward. She laughed until her sides ached, and then lay back in the chair, exhausted with the pleasure of such tomfoolery. The maid even stuck her head in the room's entrance, but Fae waved her away, then surrendered to a fresh spasm of jollity at Lord Ragsdale's expense.

Fae was the first to recover her voice. "Miss Costello, that was outrageous."

"Yes, wasn't it?" Emma replied, wiping her eyes with her sleeve. "But now you wish to . . . ah, change professions?" she prompted.

Fae relaxed again, and looked up from the carpet, which she had been contemplating. "I don't see a future in this one, especially if other men are like John Staples," she said simply. "And I fear they are." She met Emma's eyes then. "And I know how to make hats! Let me show you what I can do."

Emma spent the next hour in Fae's chamber, admiring the woman's dash and flair with bonnet trimming. "I buy the best from the shops here."

"I've seen the bills," Emma interjected.

Fae chuckled. "Then I rearrange them to suit myself," she explained. "A ribbon here, a bit of trim there." She placed a high-brimmed chip-straw bonnet on Emma's head and tied the green satin bow under her ear. "There now. See what I mean?"

Emma looked in the mirror, delighted with Fae's efforts. "It makes my eyes so green," she marveled, turning this way and that for the full effect, and trying to remember when she had last worn a hat. She took it off reluctantly. "I know that you will manage very well in Bath, and so I will tell Lord Ragsdale."

Fae hugged her. "Bless you. If Lord Ragsdale had sent that sourpuss David Breedlow, I'm sure I would have gotten my walking papers and nothing more." She frowned at Emma's expression. "But I hear that he is soon to be transported, and one shouldn't speak ill of the dead."

Emma shuddered. "Just because he is going to Australia does not mean that he is numbered among the dead!" she burst out, freeing herself from Fae's embrace. She was immediately ashamed of the ferocity of her outburst. What must you think? she asked herself, embarrassed in turn by the look of surprise on

Fae's well-fed face. I must not cry, she thought next. What will Fae think?

But Fae only looked at her and took her by the shoulders again. "So that's how it is?" she asked softly. "Bah, these English! Sometimes I think the guillotine is more merciful. Oh, Miss Costello, do let us soak this Englishman for all we can. It is a revenge of sorts."

It was easy then to dry her tears on one of Fae's wonderful rose-scented handkerchiefs, eat a few more macaroons, and then put her head together with Lord Ragsdale's mistress to create a list of necessities for the proposed shop. When Emma finally left the house with a kiss and a wave of her hand, she was wearing one of Fae's many pairs of kidskin gloves, and clutching a precise account of Fae's demands. While it will not choke you, Lord Ragsdale, she thought as she hurried along, it will give some satisfaction to two powerless women. Fae will have a future, and I will have . . . what?

The rain began before she reached Curzon Street, but she tucked the list down the front of her dress to keep it dry. She knew that Lord Ragsdale would swallow Fae's demands and count himself lucky to be so easily rid of her. He would buy his horses, spend his money, and probably take another mistress later, after he was married. She stood stock-still in the rain, fully aware that John Staples represented everything that she hated about the English. I cannot go back in that house, she thought. But I must. I owe him at least my services until this indenture is paid off.

She went up the front steps slowly, dreading the people inside, the silence of the servants' hall when she appeared for dinner, the cold room she shared with a most reluctant scullery maid. She stood on the steps, unwilling to raise her hand to the knocker, as she thought again for the thousandth time of the events of that last dreadful day in Wicklow. The weather had been like this, only she had been on the other side of the window glass, watching a solitary figure approaching her father's house. "And I let you in," she said, her hand on the knocker. "Oh, I wish I had not, for all that you were Robert Emmet." She spit out the name as though it was a bad taste. "Ireland's hero. Oh, God, why did I do it? Why?"

The door swung open then and she gasped out loud. Lord Ragsdale stood there in his shirtsleeves, staring back at her. When she did not move, he took her by the arm and pulled her inside.

"I saw you from the upstairs window, you silly nod," he scolded. "Don't you have door knockers in peat bogs? Really, Emma."

She wished her face did not look so bleak. She shook herself free of him, wishing she could just bolt the hallway and leave him standing there. She could only shiver and look him in the eye, daring him to say anything else.

"We had a door knocker," she said simply.

She didn't know what it was about her words, but he touched her arm again. "Emma, what's wrong?" he asked, bending closer to look into her face.

Startled, she looked at him. *Can you possibly care?* she thought first, wild to tell him, wild to tell anyone, wanting to talk out her misery until it didn't hurt anymore. Perhaps when it had all been said, he could help her. She opened her mouth to speak when Lady Ragsdale's voice came lightly from the sitting room.

"Johnny, are you ready yet? You promised."

Emma closed her mouth. *That was close,* she thought. *I almost wasted my breath telling my story to someone who would only shrug when I had finished. Thank you, Lady Ragsdale, for reminding me that this is my burden alone.* She took a deep breath and pulled Fae's list from the front of her dress.

"Miss Moullé offered these conditions, my lord."

Lord Ragsdale took them from her. "That's not what you were about to say," he commented, his voice mild as he scanned the list.

"No, but it will do," she replied candidly. "We had a rational conversation and I presented your offer, and asked her what would make her the happiest."

She started down the hall toward the stairs that would take her belowstairs. The marquess sauntered along beside her. "And she decided that a hat shop would do. Woman are strange, Emma."

"No stranger then men, my lord," she said without thinking.

He laughed. "I have it on good authority that men are simple."

"Whoever told you that has cotton wadding for brains."

"It was Fae, dear Fae, Fae with the round eyes, round bottom, and probably round heels, for all I know," he retorted, and chuckled when she blushed. "Emma, you're too old to blush." He took her arm. "Well, tell me: what would make *you* happy?"

Locating my father and brother, she thought, *but I don't want you to know that.* She thought a moment, standing there with the rain dripping off her. "I would like a bed of my own, and a chance to hear Mass." *There now. Make something of that.*

Lord Ragsdale nodded. "Too bad you were not my mistress, Emma. Think of the savings to me!"

"My lord!"

He laughed and held his hands to his face, as though to ward off a blow. "Just kidding, Emma. I'd as lief kiss the devil as bed an Irish woman."

I doubt one would have you, she thought. "Now remember, sir, you are to become a model of deportment, if we are to proceed with your reformation," she said instead.

"Of course, Emma, how can I forget?" he murmured, and then grimaced. "And now I must gird up my loins—so to speak—and accompany my mother and cousin to Almack's." He sighed.

". . . Where you will find any number of unexceptionable young ladies to choose among," she said. "One of them may even like you."

"Emma, I don't even know what I want in a wife," he protested.

"Johnny! You have progressed no farther than your shirt and breeches?" his mother said, coming from the sitting room and starting purposefully toward him down the hall.

"Emma distracted me," he hedged. "There she was, shivering on the front step, with no idea how to use a door knocker, bless her black Irish heart. What could I do but let her in?"

"Wretch," Emma whispered under her breath. To her amusement, he leaned toward her and cupped his hand around his ear.

"H'mm? H'mm?"

She continued toward the servants' stairs, and so did the marquess. "Emma, get me up by ten tomorrow morning," he ordered. "We need to discuss what I should be looking for in a wife, and I want to sign this list of Fae's over to you so my banker can deal with it."

She curtsied, as Lady Ragsdale bore down on them, and took her son by the arm. She shrieked when he flipped his eye patch up and grinned at her. "Mama, should I leave this off tonight or wear it? It's not fashionable."

Lady Ragsdale looked at Emma, who was struggling not to laugh. "Don't encourage him, Emma," she scolded. "Johnny, you would try a saint! Come along now, before I lose all patience."

Lord Ragsdale shuddered elaborately, and grinned at Emma as his mother tugged him along the hall. "Tomorrow morning at ten, Emma. Find a tablet and pencil. And by the way, nice gloves."

"Yes, aren't they?" she agreed as she started down the stairs for another evening of cold stares and solitude.

Chapter 10

He had not danced in years, so it did not greatly surprise Lord Ragsdale that he dreamed about Almack's. It was a pleasant enough dream, even though the sound was magnified and the events speeded up until he woke up dizzy with too much waltz and tepid conversation. He lay there, his hands behind his head, loitering somewhere between half-asleep and full-awake, reflecting that conversation with women was stupid.

"Do be charitable," he scolded himself as he settled more emphatically in the middle of his bed. He considered charity for a brief moment, then abandoned it. Most of the Season's beauties were uncomfortably young, undeniably lovely, and utterly bereft of idea. He did not require a great deal of conversation while dancing; indeed, country-dancing only permitted the occasional passing comment. The waltz was another matter. While he could not deny that he enjoyed gazing down upon the same beautiful bosom for the duration of one dance, dialogue of at least a semi-intelligent nature rendered the whole event more pleasant. As it was, he learned a great deal about the weather last night.

He stretched his charity a little farther. It is entirely possible that *I* have forgotten the art of conversation. I will have to get Emma's opinion on the matter, he thought as he yawned and rested his eyes again.

He lay there, rubbing his forehead gently, remembering the brief disappointment last night of arriving home and finding the book room dark. There was no Emma, sorting through his correspondence now, throwing away the rags and tatters of his disordered life. He had wanted to tell her about the scene in the card room, when Lady Theodosia Maxwell—she of the red-veined nose and towering turban—had accused her meek little husband of cheating at whist and thrashed him with his own walking cane. The young diamond of the first water he had been waltzing with merely tittered behind her gloved hand. Emma would have done such a scene justice with that full-bodied laugh of hers.

He reached for his watch on the night table, impatient for Emma to appear. The upstairs maid had already delivered the morning coal, and the brass can of hot water. He had already convinced Hanley that he did not need help shaving and dressing. It remained for Emma to deliver his morning tea and furnish him with some good reason to rise.

Ah, there it was. She had a firm knock, which he preferred to the scratching of most servants.

"You're late, Emma," he said to the closed door.

"Your watch is fast," she countered, and opened the door. "Besides that, the postman was late, and I had to sort your mail." She came closer to the bed and set the tea tray across his lap. "Look here, my lord. You are even getting invitations to places that Lady Ragsdale assures me are quite respectable."

He looked at her and grimaced. "Emma, I am already tired of orgeat and bad whist, and that was just my first visit to Almack's!"

She went to the window and flung open the draperies. "What you are is bored, my lord," she said, her tone firm. "I do not know what I can do about that. I would wish that you had an occupation, because you appear—somewhere under your lassitude—to have a great deal of energy."

He grinned and took a sip of tea. Ah. Just the way he liked it. "Emma, you are the only person I know who can compliment and condemn in the same sentence. Is this an Irish characteristic?"

It was her turn to look thoughtful. "I suppose it is, my lord."

He wanted to tease her some more, because he liked the animation that came into her face when he challenged her with words. I wish that I felt clever in the morning, he thought, as her demeanor changed and she became all business again. In fact, she was clearing her throat and demanding his attention again.

"My lord, here are your bills outstanding. Please initial them, and I will see that your banker gets them." She pointed to a smaller pile. "Here are invitations. Your mother has already perused them, and has indicated with a small check in the corner that these would further Sally's ambitions, and probably your own."

He picked up the one on top, and sighed. "Emma, these people are boring, they have an indifferent cook, and their daughter is plain."

Emma was ruffling through the other pile of letters on his tray, ignoring him. Playfully, he slapped her on the wrist with the invitation he held, and she stopped and looked directly at him.

"Then you can study a little patience, not eat so much, and put
ur patch on your good eye." She handed his eye patch to him.
ut this on, by the way."

He set the patch on the tray. "Does my eye bother you?" he
ked, trying to keep his voice casual, and at the same time, won-
red why on earth he even cared what she thought. "It bothers
/ mother."

Emma was pulling out another letter. "Not particularly, my
d," she replied, her voice absentminded. "I've seen worse
hts. See here, I really want you to pay attention to this letter,
` lord."

He took it from her, filled with a strange new charity. I hon-
ly believe that my eye doesn't bother you, he thought. "I think
u just paid me a compliment, Emma," he said.

Mystified, she held out the letter opener. "I cannot imagine
at it was then." And there was her dimple finally, that visible
pression of humor that gave her face even more character. "I'll
ke sure that it does not happen again, my lord. Do open that
er. Lady Ragsdale says it is from your bailiff on the Norfolk
ate."

He did as he was told, and spread out the letter on the tea tray
he took another sip of the cooling drink. It was Manwaring's
ual reminder about the state of the crofters' cottages, and the
cessity for repairs that could not be put off, but which he had
naged to avoid for some three years, mainly because it did not
erest him.

"Something about new roofs for the crofters," he said, tossing
letter aside.

Emma picked up the letter. "Which are three years overdue, ac-
ding to your bailiff," she added, glaring at him over the top of
letter. "And now he writes that some of the floors are rotting,
, because of this neglect. He wants you to come to Norfolk im-
diately, my lord."

"Too much trouble," he snapped. "I do not know why the man
not just attend to it without my presence."

"You landlords are all the same! I am certain Dante intended a
cial rung in hell for you," Emma raged at him, folding the let-
and shoving it in the pocket of her apron.

He stared at her in amazement, then glared back, wondering at
sudden vehemence, more curious than angry. "You think I
uld go there?" he asked. "To Norfolk, I mean, not hell."

"It is your land, my lord. You should attend to the needs of
r people," she said, her voice quieter now, as though she re-

gretted her outburst. She sat down in the chair next to the bed an
pulled out the letter again. "You can visit your estate, approve t
new roofs, and then at your next dinner party, impress the your
lady seated next to you with your benevolence toward your ter
ants."

She said it so calmly, so factually, that it suddenly becam
quite clear that Emma Costello despised him. She did not have
express her loathing for his class in her voice or manners; it w
amply evident in the matter-of-fact way she reduced any good i
tention—had he possessed any—to pure calculation.

"And you are disgusted that you must cajole me into doin
what I should, eh, Emma?" he asked quietly, interpreting t
wooden expression on her face. "I do not need a special rung
hell, because you have already located me there."

He spoke quietly, biting off each word. He did not think sh
would reply, and she did not; she did not need to. In silence h
picked up the eye patch and put it on, feeling strangely as thou
he was attempting to cover his nakedness, and failing utterly. H
had been weighed in the balance and found wanting by a mai
who, had she found him bleeding by the side of an Irish roa
would probably have crossed on the other side. As it was, sh
must serve him, whether she liked to or not. The shame of
bored into his brain like an awl.

"Go away, Emma," he said quietly, rubbing his forehead. "I
be ready in an hour, and we will see my banker."

She left without a word or backward glance.

He picked up the tea tray and pulled back to throw it across t
room, then changed his mind. Such a stupid gesture would on
confirm his unsavory character, he considered as he set it on t
end of the bed, and got up. He shaved and dressed in fifteen mi
utes, then sat at his desk and read through his correspondence th
Emma had separated for him.

Mama had decreed that he would accompany her and Sally t
boring dinner two blocks over, charades and parlor talk fo
blocks beyond, and then to a dance for four or five hundred of
distant relative's closest acquaintances. By God, this is a palt
existence, and Emma is ever so right. I am lazy and bored, a
don't know what to do about it.

Dressed and ready to go, he remained in his room and re
over all his letters, penciling notes to Emma, instructing her
write his bailiff and tell him to proceed with repairs. He set asi
two invitations that interested him, with directions that Emma
spond. He worked his way through the stack, pausing on a lett

h a peer's frank. It was from his father's old friend Sir Augus-
Barney, whose land marched beside his in Norfolk. He would
te a personal letter tonight, and advise the old fellow to expect
isit soon. He spent a few minutes in conversation with Lasker,
used the correspondence in the book room, then made it to the
akfast room before the maid removed the ham and eggs.

He ate standing up, looking out the window, wondering if
ing would ever put in an appearance this year.

"You'll ruin your digestion, son, if you take your meals stand-
up," said his mother from the doorway.

He smiled and turned around. "Mama, will you still be scolding
when I am forty or fifty?"

She stood in the doorway with a cloak draped over her arm,
blew him a kiss. "If you do not marry, I am certain I will. As
s, I hope you will find a wife who can scold you instead of
"

He shook his head. "It's a heavy business, Mama. I don't think
ade much of an impression on anyone last night at Almack's."

She nodded in agreement. "Thank goodness there is an entire
son stretching before you, with ample time for redemption."

He sighed inwardly, dreading the idea. "I am sure you are right,
ma. I am bound to develop a little polish." Perhaps I can even
my secretary to tolerate me, he reflected.

Lady Ragsdale came closer and held out the cloak to him. It
s brown, quite plain, but heavy. "The first few items have ar-
d from the modiste. I believe you wanted this for Emma."

He took it from her, pleased with the weight of it. "This is al-
st warm enough for a London spring that refuses to come." He
sed her cheek. "Thanks, m'dear. Emma and I are off to the
ker's again. She is determined to organize me."

Whether she will speak to me during the ride to the City, I can-
tell, he thought as he went to the book room and peered inside.
Emma sat at the desk now, her head bent over the ledger, copy-
entries. She looked up at his entrance, and rose to stand beside
chair, as Breedlow always used to rise when he came into a
m. He expected such deference from Breedlow, but coming
n Emma, it seemed strangely out of place. You do not wear
vitude well, he thought as he watched her. Emma, what were
before you came here?

He almost asked her outright, but stopped himself before he
mitted that folly. One didn't inquire of servants' personal
s, for it was the one thing they were entitled to keep to them-
es. He chose a less dangerous subject.

"I see you found this morning's correspondence," he said, ind⟨ cating the pile in front of her. "Please be seated, Emma."

"Thank you, my lord," she replied. "I will have a letter to y⟨ bailiff ready for your signature this afternoon," she offered.

He came around the desk to look over her shoulder. She kne⟨ how to write a letter, he had to admit. Her writing displayed j⟨ the proper firmness and tone of command, exceeding even Bree⟨ low's skills. "Sounds about right," he said. "Tell him I'll be the⟨ in a few days."

She looked up at him, surprised, then favored him with a slij⟨ smile. She made a notation about the letter, then finished her ⟨ tries in the ledger as he sat on the edge of the desk and watch⟨ her. When she blotted the book and then closed it, he held out ⟨ cloak to her.

"Here. I can't have my secretary shivering every time the wi⟨ shifts."

He noted with a certain unholy glee that she was at a loss ⟨ words. Feeling bad for ragging on me this morning? he thought⟨ himself as she took the cloak from him. Blushing a tad from gu⟨ are we? he considered as she stood up and draped the cloak o⟨ her shoulders.

"Thank you, my lord," she murmured.

"You're quite welcome. Now, please have Hanley burn that ⟨ of yours," he ordered. "It still stinks of Newgate."

She nodded. "It will be burned at once, my lord." She ran ⟨ finger over the finely textured wool as though it were satin, a⟨ smiled at him.

He searched her face for some sign of irritation with him, ⟨ there was none at the moment. She was a child with a new p⟨ sent, looking for all the world as though she wanted to hunt fo⟨ mirror and twirl herself around in its reflection. How changea⟨ women are, he thought. It's just a cloak, and not a very attract⟨ one, at that, but if it gets me out of the doghouse, God be praise⟨

"Are you ready to go to my banker's?" he asked. "I think ⟨ more trip ought to be enough to familiarize yourself with the bu⟨ ness, and then you can do it alone."

She nodded and put the bills in her reticule, then pulled on ⟨ kidskin gloves that must have come from his mistress's coll⟨ tion. A bonnet would have been nice, too, something to set off ⟨ green eyes, and the attractive way her auburn hair curled arou⟨ her face, but that was beyond his powers of both interest and ph⟨ anthropy at the moment. Too much largess would only make ⟨ suspicious of his intentions, he reckoned.

There was a long silence in the carriage as the horses clopped ong London's busy streets. He managed a glance at Emma out the corner of his eye, and she looked as though she was on the ge of comment several times. He realized she was working up an apology, and chuckled inwardly.

She finally came out with it as the coachman slowed the horses front of the bank. "I am sorry for the way I spoke to you this orning," she said, the words all tumbling out in a breathless sh. "I was inexcusably rude."

He nodded. "You were. It's a bit disconcerting for an Irish chit no consequence to tell me my business with my tenants. And one's wished me to hell lately, except myself. That's not really ur department."

She winced but was silent, looking straight ahead as the coach- an let down the steps and opened the door. "I'm sorry," she re- ated, her voice so low that he had to strain to hear it. "Mama ways told me that I should think before I speak."

"Your mama was a wise woman," he agreed. He touched her n as she leaned forward to take the coachman's hand. "But I ould take better care of what is my own, Emma. Let us leave it that," he finished when they were both on the sidewalk.

She nodded, too shy to speak, then followed him into the bank, ying several steps behind, as a good servant should. He thought heard her sniff back tears as they passed single file down the g hall. An hour ago, he would have been glad to know that she s crying, but now he just wanted to clap his arm around her ulders and tell her to forget it. I can't do that, he thought. A lit- remorse won't hurt the chit. Instead, he reached inside his ercoat, drew out his handkerchief, and handed it to her behind back as the porter hurried them along. She blew her nose loud, d he grinned; not for Emma a dainty dab at the nostrils.

In no time, the matter of Fae Moullé's demands was signed and led, with the banker's promise to deliver the draft that after- on. "Unless you wish to do that in person, my lord," the banker ggested.

"Oh, no!" Lord Ragsdale stated, leaning back in his chair. "I'm ough with that one. When Fae vacates the premises, you may my real estate agent to rent out the property."

"There, Emma, I am on my way to reformation," he told her en they stood outside the bank again. "I have finally done Fae ullé a good turn. Soon I will be a pattern card of respectability. omen will swoon for my good report."

He looked sideways at Emma, wondering how to get a rise out

of her. She almost said something, but changed her mind. "Ye
my lord" was the response she settled on.

"Come, come, Emma," he chided. "You were about to sa
something much more interesting than 'yes, my lord.'"

The coachman held open the door for them, but Lord Ragsdal
stood in front of it. "No ride for you unless you tell me what yo
were about to say," he ordered, a smile playing around his lip
"Come, come, Emma."

They stood there staring at each other, his arms folded acros
his chest. She pursed her lips into a straight line, then sighed.

"Oh, very well! I was merely going to suggest that you loo
rather too piratical ever to be mistaken for a pattern card of re
spectability." She smiled when she said it, and Lord Ragsdal
sighed with relief. Better and better, he thought as he helped he
into the carriage. Emma, we have to get along.

"John, take us to the gallery in Kensington," he said as h
climbed inside.

He returned her questioning gaze with a smile. "Emma, yo
may redeem yourself for all misdemeanors this morning by ac
companying me to the art gallery. I have it in my head to invite
young lady I met at Almack's to tour it with me and my cous
Sally, and I had better know where I am going if I do not wish
appear . . . well, overly piratical and uncouth."

She relaxed at his words and nodded. "You can probably pu
chase a guidebook at the entrance, my lord. If you commit it
memory, then no young lady will ever accuse you of being u
couth, lazy, and bereft of purpose."

He wagged his finger at her, and she blushed. "Emma, mind yo
own manners! If you ever wish to leave my indenture before you a
gray-haired and toothless, you must learn to like me at least a little.

He leaned back in the carriage, satisfied with himself, an
pleased at the embarrassment on Emma's face. Now I will deliv
the ultimate blow, he decided. "Emma, I almost forgot to tell yo
I spoke with Lasker this morning, and he has arranged for you
move into a room of your own."

"What?" Emma exclaimed, her eyes wide.

He nearly laughed out loud at the look of chagrin on Emma
expressive face. "You'll still have to duck the rafters, but you d
say your own bed would make you happy."

He absorbed himself in gazing out the window then, content
let Emma stew in her own juices. He heard her apply herself vi
orously to his handkerchief, and his cup ran over with merrimer
Got you, Emma. I dare you to be rude now.

Chapter 11

There is no logical explanation for my desire to visit the art gallery with Emma, Lord Ragsdale thought as the carriage began to move. I am either a bigger bully than I thought, or I love art beyond my previous recollection. The initial ride had begun with an ardent desire on his part to get the banking business done, and then return Emma to the book room. He never considered himself a man susceptible to female tears, but there was something so oddly touching about Emma's obvious remorse at her mistreatment of him. He hoped she would not mind a visit to the gallery, but he was beginning to find her interesting.

And, he reasoned, there was at least some truth in what he had said to her about wanting to look over the place. He knew he needed to do as his mother and Emma had mandated and find himself a wife. A gallery would be a good place for a quiet tête-à-tête; he would test his theory on Emma. If it proved to be a good place to spark a lady (or at least, in Emma's case, discussion), he would store the knowledge for future reference.

Emma was still struggling with her emotions, so he did not overburden her with conversation. He was content to gaze out the window at the Inns of Court, where several wigged barristers were getting themselves into a carriage for the short ride to the courts of justice. English law, he thought, a noble thing. He glanced at Emma. She was watching the barristers, too, but her expression was a set, hard one, as though she looked upon something distasteful.

"English law," he said out loud, and it sounded inane the moment he uttered it.

"Don't remind me, my lord," she murmured, and directed her gaze out the opposite window.

How singular, he thought. We see the same thing, and yet our estimations are completely different. I wonder if this is because she is a woman, or because she is Irish. I suspect it is both, he concluded.

So much silence, he thought as they rode along. He was not a man accustomed to silence. I have spent too much time in drawing rooms, card rooms, and taverns, where conversation seems obliged. It was different with Emma, he reasoned. Despite her remorse, she still did not wish to speak to him. Or could it be that she is shy, he wondered. I see Emma as a budding good secretary, but perhaps ours is an odd association. After all, she is female. Indeed she is, he thought for no good reason, and smiled to himself.

He wanted to ask a penny for her thoughts, and the realization gave him a start. He had never cared what any woman thought before. During his affair with Fae Moullé, never had it entered his head to inquire what was on her mind, because he suspected that nothing was. My word, how strange this is, he considered as he settled back in the carriage. I want to know what this woman is thinking.

He stared out the window, not seeing anything on the crowded road. If she is thinking of me, it will not be charitable. He glanced her way and rubbed his forehead, wondering why it mattered all of a sudden that she change her opinion of him. She sees me as a dilettante, a drunkard, a rogue, and a wastrel, he thought, and she is right. And I am British. He grinned at his reflection in the glass. That I cannot change, and it may be the only thing that she cares about the most. I wish I understood Emma Costello.

The gallery was bare of sightseers. There was only a cleaning woman, who wasn't dressed much better than Emma. The charwoman looked up from her brush and pail as they skirted around the area she was scrubbing. Lord Ragsdale could tell she was surprised to see someone so obviously a man of consequence with a woman in broken shoes and a plain cloak.

To his chagrin, Emma noticed the look, too. "I really don't belong here, my lord," she whispered to him, her face red. "Oh, please . . . I can wait outside."

Serenity, John, serenity, he told himself as he touched her elbow lightly and steered her into his favorite room of the gallery. "Nonsense, Emma. This is a public place, and we are the public. Remember now: I want to bring a young lady here, and you are my trial effort."

That sounds pretty artificial, he thought as he sat her down on a bench; I wonder if she will buy it. He glanced at her then, gauging her response, and was relieved to see a brief look of approbation cross her expressive face.

"Oh, excellent, my lord! The sooner you are reformed and at least soundly engaged, the sooner you will be rid of me."

He laughed in spite of his own nervousness. "Emma! Am I that much of a trial? Come now, be fair."

To his relief, she smiled. I wish you would laugh, too, he thought as he watched her. Your laughter is almost a balm. Ah, well, not this time. Perhaps another day. He put his hands behind his back and sauntered over to inspect a painting—it must be a Vermeer—he had not remembered from his last visit several years ago.

All was silence in the gallery; he found himself relaxing in the quiet. This *would* be a good place to bring someone special, he decided as he moved from picture to picture. The devil of it is, I cannot imagine any eligible lady of my acquaintance remaining quiet long enough to absorb what is here.

He glanced back at Emma, who remained where she was on the bench, as if afraid to move from where he had put her. He turned to watch her then, folding his arms across his chest and leaning against the wall.

As usual, she paid him no attention. She sat stiff at first, her feet in her poor shoes tucked up under her so they would not show. (I must see to a cobbler, and when are those promised dresses coming?) As she stared at the painting opposite her, her shoulders lost their tenseness and her face seemed to soften. She sighed once, and he could hear it across the gallery. Her eyes grew dreamy, and for the first time in their brief acquaintance, the wariness left her expression.

Emma was looking at one of Raphael's numerous madonnas, mellowed, as all his works, by a caressing brush and sweetness of expression on the face of Mary. She smiled at the painting of mother and child, and as he watched, she got up from the bench and stood directly in front of the work. There was no barrier in front of the painting, and she reached out her hand, outlining the child.

So you like children, Emma? he thought, wondering at the same time if he was going to have to spend the rest of their association guessing about her past. Presumably one didn't ask servants their business. We have already established that you do not like me, he thought. I wonder if there is someone you do like. Or someone you love.

He felt a moment's irrational jealousy, which made him laugh out loud, and broke whatever spell Raphael was weaving on Emma Costello. She jumped away from the painting and put her hands behind her back, retreating to the bench, where she sat down again. Serenity, he told himself again, as he nodded to her and continued his stately pace about the gallery, hoping she would relax enough again to explore the place herself.

She did not. After a half hour, in which he felt his own frustration growing, he returned to the bench and sat down beside her. She edged away from him slightly, and moved forward on the bench, ready to bolt as soon as he said the word. He said nothing, wondering if she would speak first. Finally, she cleared her throat.

"You know, my lord, I could be finishing my perusal of your old correspondence right now, and starting on that letter to Sir Augustus Barney in Norfolk," she reminded him.

"You could," he agreed. "But isn't it nice just to sit here?"

She did not answer, and he sighed and stood up. She was on her feet in an instant, too, but he took her arm before she could move and held her firmly.

"Tell me, Emma. Is this really a good place to squire a young lady?"

He looked into her eyes, and her expression made him drop her arm and step back. He had never seen such terror before, terror that he was responsible for because he had taken her arm. He looked away and gave her time to collect herself, thinking, So, Emma, you do not care to be grabbed, do you?

His own mind in turmoil, he merely nodded to her and started to leave the gallery at a slow pace. In a moment, she was walking at his side and slightly behind him. "I didn't mean to startle you, Emma," he said. "Seriously, what do you think? Should I take a young lady here?"

"No, my lord," she replied, and her voice was smooth and in control. "She will want to chatter, and you will want to admire, and it will not speed any wooing you might attempt."

"How well you know your own sex," he murmured as he climbed into his carriage and made no move to help her. "But, Emma, you were silent as the grave in the gallery," he insisted. "How can it be that any young lady I would bring there would be a gabble box?"

She pulled her cloak tighter about her. "My lord, if it were someone who returned your regard, she would want to talk with you, wouldn't she? I mean, I would."

And so you were silent. Touché, Emma, he thought. He let it go at that, leaned back in the carriage, and closed his eyes.

He did not expect another word from her, and was even dozing off when Emma spoke.

"Begging your pardon, my lord, but could I ask you something?" she was saying. "It is a favor, in fact."

"Only if you promise that it will not cause me any exertion," he teased.

"Oh, it will not," she assured him seriously, and again he was verbally flogged by her reply.

You think I am in earnest, he wondered. "Say on, Emma," he stated finally when she hesitated.

He thought for a moment she would not speak, after all. "Well?" he prompted. "Come, come, Emma, you make me fear that it is an outrageous request."

"Oh, no, my lord," she assured him, her expression worried now. "Nothing of the sort. I was merely wondering if you would permit me a day off once a week."

Is that all? he asked himself, but he did not respond.

"I have some business in London," she said quickly when he did not speak. "Please, my lord. It is only once a week. I can see that everything is left in order before I leave." She was pleading now, and he wanted to know what it was she had to do in London. He almost asked her.

"A half day then, sir? Oh, please," she was asking now, her eyes on his face.

He felt shame then. I am a churl to make you grovel, he thought as he sat up straight.

"A day, Emma," he said firmly. "Mr. Breedlow had a day, and it is only fair." He leaned forward. "And when would you like this day?"

"Tomorrow, my lord, if you please," she responded, a little breathless.

"You'll have that letter to Sir Augustus ready?" he temporized. "And another which I shall dictate tonight to my bailiff in Norfolk? I mean to leave in two days."

"Anything, my lord," she said.

"Tomorrow it is," he said, adding, "although I cannot imagine what it is that you would have to do in London."

It was only the tiniest opening, but she did not take it. Of course she did not, he told himself, feeling the fool, and a bully in the bargain. John, you maggot, did you ever quiz David Breedlow about his day off? God knows you should have, in his case, but here is Emma Costello, and she is powerless, harmless, and poor. London is safe from whatever she could possibly be planning.

"Thank you, my lord," she said, and her gratitude made him wince.

"You're welcome," he grumbled, "although I wonder what evil plans you have afoot." Ah, there. He was rewarded with a smile.

"If you're worried, Lord Ragsdale, you'd better lock up the silverware before I leave your house," she replied, with just the hint of a twinkle in her eye.

"Oh, I do not think it will come to that, Emma," he said as the carriage pulled up in front of the house. He sighed, considering the evening ahead. "Now I must gird my loins for an evening of fine dining and dancing." He helped her from the carriage, careful not to hold her elbow a moment longer than she needed. "I would almost rather stay in the book room with you, and consider ledgers and double entries."

"And we all know what a fiction that is," Emma murmured as they walked up the front steps.

He smiled. "It's less of a stretch than you would suppose," he said as he nodded to Lasker, who must have been watching for them out of the peephole in the door. "Emma, it is somewhat daunting to converse with lovely young things on the right and on the left, and across the table, and try not to be too obvious staring at whatever charms they possess. Thank you, Lasker," he said as he relinquished his overcoat. "And then, in turn, I must suffer their sidelong glances as they try to discover if there is any substance beneath my shallow facade."

Emma laughed, and it was the glorious, heartfelt sound he realized he had been craving all day. "Are you saying, my lord, that there is rather less to you than meets the eye?"

He wanted to laugh out loud at the strangling sounds coming from his unflappable butler, who had turned away and with a shaking hand was rearranging a bouquet of flowers. "Well, as to that, I wonder, Emma. I think you are improving me already," he said as they continued down the hall toward the book room. "I have not been near my club, the wine cellar is locked, and Mama is looking on me with less chagrin than normal." He chuckled. "Now if only the young ladies will follow her lead . . ."

"They will, my lord," Emma assured him as she removed her cloak and sat down at the desk. "You need merely to decide what it is you are looking for in a wife, and follow through."

Follow through, is it? he thought as he watched her rummage for pencil and paper. You are asking that of the man who could not save his own father from a rabble crowd? I wonder if I know how to see anything through to its completion. I was well on the way to my own ruin, but it seems I cannot accomplish even that.

"My lord?" Emma was asking. "You wanted to dictate a letter to your bailiff in Norfolk?"

"Oh! Yes, yes, I did," he said as he clasped his hands behind

back and strolled to the window. "And you'll have the other
e for Sir Augustus ready by the time I return this evening?"
"Of course, my lord."

It was on the tip of his tongue to ask her to call him John, but
son prevailed, and he did not. The letter was too soon dictated,
d then he had no more excuse to linger in the book room, but
st face, instead, the prospect of shaving again, and dressing,
d staring in the mirror and wondering what on earth he was
ng. *It is not that I dislike women,* he considered as he suffered
nley to arrange his neck cloth. *Quite the contrary. It's just that
egrudge the exertion I must expend to find a wife. Too bad
y do not grow on trees, there for the plucking. Or something
e that,* he concluded, grinning to himself.

Sally Claridge looked especially fetching in a pale blue muslin,
 blond hair swept up on her head in a style that earned a sec-
d look. He watched her descend the stairs, admired, from his
wpoint, her trim ankles, and idly considered the prospect of an
ance with his Virginia cousin. The quick glance of terror she
ned his way before her more well-bred demeanor masked it
nvinced him that she would not be much fun to sport with. *And
n if she were,* he thought as he helped his mother with her
ning cape, *sooner or later she would open her mouth and bore
 into drunkenness or opium use, whichever came first.*

His mother also watched with approval as Sally completed her
cent of the stairs. "My dear, how lovely you look tonight!" she
claimed, kissing her niece on the cheek. "John, only consider
w well your guineas look upon Sally's back."

"Yes," he agreed. "Only think how well *we* are spending my
ney." That ill-advised remark earned him another look of ter-
from Sally and a cluck of his mother's tongue. "Glad to do it
 relatives, glad to do it," he amended, hoping that his evening
s not ruined before it started.

Mama was eager to be pleased (perhaps considering her own
ursions into his fortune). "Quite right, John. Sally, do you have
your dancing shoes? I hear Lord Renwick has engaged a par-
larly fine orchestra for tonight."

Shoes. Shoes. That was it. "Excuse me, Mama, Sally. I forgot
ething in the book room," he said as he hurried down the hall.
Emma Costello looked up in surprise when he opened the
k-room door without knocking. "Now, my lord, you are not
ting cold feet . . ." she began, putting down the quill pen.

"No, but you are, Emma," he said. "I need two pieces of paper
 a pencil." He snapped his fingers and held out his hand for

the items, which Emma brought to him. He put the papers on th
floor in front of her. "Take off your shoes, Emma."

She hesitated. "Hurry up, now," he admonished, taking th
pencil from her. "I don't want to miss a minute of what promis
to be an evening of astonishing boredom."

"You are too negative, my lord," she grumbled as she remove
her shoes, poor, cast-off things that should have been in an a
can years ago.

"Raise your skirt," he ordered as he knelt on the floor besi
her and grasped her ankle.

She gave a noticeable start when he touched her stocking
ankle, then rested her hand lightly on his shoulder to steady he
self while he outlined her foot with the pencil.

"Other foot."

She leaned the other way as he held that ankle. Such a shape
foot, he thought, as he carefully traced it. Not small, he consi
ered, half-enjoying the weight of her against his shoulder. H
looked at the papers. "Well, what color do you want?"

"Black or brown; something sensible. And if you please, stoc
ings to match, my lord," she said. She sounded embarrassed at th
intimacy of their association, so he did not look at her while sh
stepped into her shoes again.

"I'm surprised your Virginia indenture holders didn't see th
you were better shod," he said as he took the papers and stood u
He looked at her then, and her cheeks were still pink.

"My lord, I think you will understand the matter more com
pletely when you consider that Robert Claridge's bills general
outran the family's entire quarterly allowance" was her qui
reply as she took her seat at the desk again.

He strolled over to sit on the desk, ignoring his mother's voi
calling to him from the front entrance. "So you were the afte
thought."

"I and the other servants, sir," she said, dipping the quill
into the ink bottle again. She looked at him in that calculated w
of hers, as though gauging his response. "And I have to tell y
that I like going barefoot in the summer, so please don't feel sor
for me, Lord Ragsdale."

She turned again to the letter in front of her, effectively d
missing him from his own book room. He grinned at her imper
nence and left the room.

Lasker hovered outside the door, obviously sent by Lady Rag
dale to tell him to hurry up, but also obviously reluctant to t
him anything. "It's all right, Lasker, I'll go peacefully," he sa

ased with himself to earn one of the butler's rare smiles. "And
take these to wherever it is Lady Ragsdale gets her shoes
de. I want one pair of sturdy brown shoes." He started down
hall, then turned back, grinning broadly. "And another pair of
Morocco dancing slippers. Good night, Lasker. You needn't
t up," he added, knowing that the butler would be sitting ram-
straight in one of the entryway chairs until the last titled
mber of the household was indoors and abed. It was their little
ion.

Truly enough, there was Lasker waiting for them when they re-
ed in that late hour just before the dark yielded to the bland-
ments of another day, careering in from the east. He handed his
ther and cousin their candles, wished them both good night,
went to the book room, hoping that Emma might still be up.
wanted to tell her about the diamond of the first water—a
ghter of Sir Edmund Partridge's—who had flirted with him
dly, and who appeared, when he worked up the nerve to con-
se with her, to have at least some wit. He wanted to tell Emma
t he and Clarissa Partridge were destined to witness a balloon
ension—he whipped out his pocket watch—in eight hours.

But the book room was dark. He held his own candle over the
k, where Emma had arranged the letter she had composed for
to Sir Augustus Barney, and the other to his bailiff. He
ked up the letter to his bailiff and read it, noting that she had
nged some of his dictated wording, and added other passages.
read it again, and had to admit that her changes were salutary.
ally, Emma," he said out loud as he left the room, "you were
posed to be here so I could tell you about Clarissa Partridge.
I have to do *everything* in this courting venture?"

Well, it would keep for the morning, he decided as he mounted
stairs. He stopped halfway up. Emma was taking her day off
orrow, and he would not see her until the evening. Perhaps I
a little hasty with this day off, he thought. He continued up
stairs, putting Emma from his mind and wondering what one
e to a balloon ascension.

While the day could not have been deemed an unqualified suc-
s, at least Emma Costello ought to have the decency to hurry
k from her day off so he could tell her about it, Lord Ragsdale
ided the following evening as he paced back and forth in front
he sitting-room window.

He had decided that he would begin by painting a word picture
Miss Partridge for Emma, describing her delicate features, her

big brown eyes that reminded him of a favorite spaniel, long d[...]
but still remembered, and her little trill of a laugh. Of course,
the time the balloonists had taken themselves up into the atm[...]
phere, he did have the smallest headache, but he couldn't attrib[...]
that to Clarissa's endless stream of questions. He just wasn't [...]
customed to having someone so small and lovely who smelled [...]
rose water hanging on his every word and looking at him w[...]
those spaniel eyes.

"By God, you are certainly taking your time with this day o[...]
he muttered under his breath. He was beginning to feel that w[...]
Emma finally opened the door, a scold was in order. He would [...]
mind her that London was far from safe after dark, and that na[...]
customers liked to prey on unescorted women, especially if t[...]
were pretty.

There wasn't anything else he could scold her about. When [...]
had wakened in the morning, his correspondence was ready [...]
his attention on the smaller table in his bedroom. He had sig[...]
the letters, initialed the morning's bills, and noted with approv[...]
newspaper article about Norfolk that she had circled to catch [...]
attention. A man never had a better secretary than Em[...]
Costello.

But where the deuce was she now? He clapped his hands [...]
gether in frustration, imagining her conked on the head and be[...]
delivered unconscious to a white slaving ship anchored at De[...]
ford Hard, even as he wore a path from window to window. [...]
would think she would have more consideration for his feelin[...]
That was the trouble with the Irish.

And then he saw her coming up the street, moving slowly,
though she dreaded the house and its occupants. As he watch[...]
she stopped several times, as though steeling herself for the ord[...]
of entering into one of London's finest establishments.

"The nerve of you," he grumbled from his view by the parti[...]
screening curtain. "When I think of the legions of servants v[...]
would love to have half so fine a household as this one . . ."

Perhaps I am being unfair, he thought as he kept his eyes [...]
her slow progress. She trudged as though filled with a great [...]
haustion, discouragement evident in the way she held herself. [...]
thought she dabbed at her eyes several times, but he could no[...]
sure. He waited for her knock, which did not come. You idiot,
realized finally, she has gone around to the alley and come [...]
from the belowstairs entrance. He rang for Lasker.

"Tell Emma Costello that I would like a word with her,"
told the butler.

"I was not aware that a day off meant a night off, too," he
ınd himself telling Emma several minutes later when she
ocked on the sitting-room door and he opened it.

She mumbled something about being sorry, and it was a longer
lk from the city than she realized.

She looked so discouraged from her day off that he felt like a
el for chiding her. Her eyes were filled with pain that shocked
n. He wondered briefly if her feet in those dreadful shoes were
rting her, and then he understood that the look in her eyes was
other matter. He stood in front of her, hand behind his back,
:king back and forth on his heels, feeling like a gouty old boyar
astising his serfs.

"I trust this won't happen on your next day off," he ventured,
shing suddenly with all his heart that she would tell him what
s the matter.

If he was expecting a soft agreement from her, he was doomed
disappointment. At his sniping words, Emma seemed to visibly
her herself together, digging deep into some well of resource
1 strength that he knew he did not possess.

"It will probably happen again and again, my lord," she replied,
:h word distinct, her brogue more pronounced than usual. "Un-
e some of us in this room, I do not succumb easily to misfor-
ıe."

"By God, you are impertinent!" he shouted, wondering even as
 voice carried throughout the room why he was yelling at
neone who did his work so well, and who looked so defeated.
serable and furious in turns, he waited for her to speak.

She took her time, and it occurred to him that she was as sur-
sed as he was by his outburst. The wariness returned to her
:s, and he knew that he had erased whatever meager credit he
1 accrued in the last day or two. I am British and you are Irish,
1 that is it, he thought as he stared at her.

When she spoke, her voice was soft, and he felt even worse. "I
 sorry for any inconvenience I have caused you, my lord."

He could think of none, other than the fact that she had not
en there to hear his account of his day with Clarissa Partridge.
d he been a small boy, he would have squirmed.

"Is that all, my lord?" she asked.

Unable to think of anything, he nodded and she went to the
r. She stood there a moment, clutching the handle. "If I were
 impertinent, Lord Ragsdale, I would have died five years ago.
od night, sir."

She was gone, the door closed quietly behind her. Filled with

that familiar self-loathing that he had hoped was behind hi
Lord Ragsdale resumed his pacing at the window. I have hea
this conversation before, he thought, summoning up images
standing before his father when he returned late, and enduring th
familiar scold that his mama assured him only meant that his f
ther cared enough to worry about him.

He stopped walking and looked at the door again, wishing th
Emma would walk back into the room so he could apologiz
Someday when I have sons and daughters, pray God I will r
member how I feel right now, he thought as he leaned against th
window frame. Somehow he must make amends to his servar
even though he knew there was nothing he could do.

I would like to help you, Emma, he thought. How can I co
vince you that I mean it? He shook his head, and smiled ruefull
My God, this whole thing begins to smack of profound exertion
think I am going to be wonderfully ill-used during your tenu
here, Emma Costello, damn your Irish hide. I had better find
wife quickly so I can release you from your indenture and be mi
erable in private.

He went to the window again, wishing that spring would com
I need a change right now, he thought, something that w
sweeten my life. He considered Clarissa again and smiled into h
reflection in the windowpane. "Madam, you are a peach," he sa
out loud, rejoicing in the fact that he had only yawned a few tim
during their hours together at the balloon ascension. Tonight I
was escorting his mother and cousin to Covent Garden Theatr
With scarcely any effort at all, he could train his glasses on th
Partridge box and watch her from a distance.

He resolved to make the Norfolk stay a short one. The pla
only held ghosts and leaky crofters' cottages anyway. He wou
point his secretary toward his bailiff and let them do the wra
gling. He would pay a brief visit to Sir Augustus Barney, th
prop his feet up in front of a comfortable fire and think abo
Clarissa Partridge. That ought to make everybody happy,
thought. Even Emma will approve, he told himself, provided s
is speaking to me. My God. I may even be forced to apologiz
How unlike me.

Chapter 12

think I will murder Lord Ragsdale, Emma thought to herself as she took off her dress and crawled into bed. She shivered in the cold, wishing for once to be still sharing a bed with the scullery maid. She may have snored, but she at least provided a warm spot. As it was, Emma could only lie there and warm herself with past ill-usage.

She knew she should be tired. It had been a long, discouraging day, spent standing in the cold entry of the Office of Criminal Business, wondering when it would finally be her turn to speak to Mr. John Henry Capper, Senior Clerk. She sighed again and thumped her pillow soundly, trying to find a soft spot in the old ticking. The first problem would be getting past that bastard of a porter. Thinking of that dreadful little excuse of a man, she thumped the pillow again.

She thought she had approached his desk with the proper amount of deference that the English seemed to require from the Irish. Her inquiry had been innocent enough; she just wanted a brief interview with Mr. Capper. One of her fellow servants in Virginia had told her that the illustrious John Henry was the man to see, and she had clung to that scrap of information through her own indenture, a dreary return sea voyage, and now incarceration in the household of Lord Ragsdale.

Something in the porter's eye should have warned her that he would stall and stall. Her inquiry had only earned her an elaborate stare, when the porter finally bothered to look up from shuffling the papers in front of him. When he gazed around and saw that no one else was with her, his stare turned into a smirk. " 'Ave a seat," he said. "Ye'll 'ave to wait your turn, like everybody else."

And so she had waited all day in the cheerless anteroom, watching others go in before her to complete their business with Mr. John Henry Capper. She sat and fumed for the morning, and then in the afternoon, despair set in. As the shadows lengthened in the room and the cold deepened, she realized that there would be

no audience with Mr. Capper that day. Her chances of ever g
ting past the porter shrank with every minute that passed, a
every man who secured an appointment before her.

She only left the building because the porter shooed her out a
told her he was locking up. Swallowing her pride, Emma ma
aged her broadest smile—the one Papa declared would melt m
ble—and asked when she might have an audience with M
Capper. The porter had looked at her in elaborate surprise,
though he were not aware that she had been the only inhabitan
the anteroom for the last two hours.

"Oh, miss, you're still here? What a pity Mr. Capper could
see you today."

She forced down the angry words that she wanted to shower
him, and winked back the tears. "Do you think I could see h
next week, sir?" she asked, knowing his answer even before
looked up from his desk many minutes later.

"I am sure you can try," he had replied, and favored her wit
mocking, superior smile.

By all the saints, she thought, in his better days, her own fat
would have had that porter whipped for insolence. And in my b
ter days? she considered ruefully. I would never be here alone a
unprotected, without my brothers around me. I would be ho
with Mama, and there would be suitors, and I would marry one
them, and life would continue the pattern of centuries. She sat
in bed and hugged the pillow to her, thinking of change and t
moil and wishing with all her heart that she knew—really knew
where her brothers and father were.

She lay down again, bunching herself into a little ball to def
the cold. If all her searching led to a certain knowledge of th
deaths, at least she would be sure. She could return to Virgi
when this pesky indenture was up, and with Mr. Claridge's ble
ings probably find some kind of employment in Richmond. Ex
rience had taught her that she could eventually wear down
sorrow until it was a manageable pain.

And if they were alive? She would spare no effort to join the
even if the cold trail, years old, led to a prison in Van Diema
Land, or dismal servitude in Australia. "Perhaps Australia is
as bad as everyone says," she told herself, relaxing gradually
the moon peered through her window, then moved on. At leas
would be warmer than here.

Warmer in many ways. Lord Ragsdale's scold this evening v
almost a fitting culmination to a dreadful day, Emma allow
wondering at the coldness of her reception. She prodded her ti

n, trying to make sense out of his surprising tirade, but gave
as sleep finally overtook her.

Morning brought with it the guilty realization that she had
rslept, and a summons to Lady Ragsdale's chamber. Emma
ssed hurriedly, hoping that Lord Ragsdale was still in bed and
looking about for his mail. She hurried, breathless, down the
rs, hoping to snatch up the mail from the table by the door and
it upstairs after she endured whatever scold Lady Ragsdale
in mind. She scooped up the mail and was hurrying fast for
stairs again when Lord Ragsdale stepped from the breakfast
m. He flattened himself in mock surprise against the wall as
hurried past.

If there is a fire somewhere, Emma, perhaps you should let me
n the secret?" he commented.

he stopped, gritting her teeth and wondering if he was angry
. She looked at him, and to her amazement, he winked. With-
even thinking, she smiled back and held out the mail to him.

Ie took it from her, and stayed where he was, leaning against
wall. "I'm sorry I was so beastly yesterday evening, Emma,"
said simply. "I was worried about you. The streets are dark,
London's full of ugly customers."

With that he nodded to her as she stared at him in wonder, and
ted down the hall, opening a letter as he went. Before she
ld collect herself, he laughed out loud and turned back to her.
uis is too good to keep to myself," he said. "It's from Fae
ullé. She expresses her—it's either gratitude or attitude, or
sibly latitude—and declares that when I marry, she will trim a
net for the new Lady Ragsdale! I defy anyone to come up
a a better offer from a mistress, Emma. What do you think?"

think I am full of gratitude or attitude myself, she thought,
pling at the idea of Fae Moullé presenting Lord Ragsdale's
le with a bonnet and sharing bedroom confidences.

I think you will have to be extremely diplomatic, should this
ntuality arise, my lord," she replied, feeling a slight twinge at
own deception with Fae. "Perhaps it would be best if Fae re-
ned your little secret."

My thought precisely." He paused then and a slight wariness
ot into his eye. "Emma, you won't be needing me today, I trust."

Well, we did need to look over your estate receipts before we
re for Norfolk tomorrow, my lord," she reminded him gently,
wishing to disturb the moment.

Tonight, then, Emma. I am off to Tatt's to buy another horse,"
old her. "When that arduous endeavor is completed, I will tod-

dle over to Whitcomb Street and pay a morning call on Clari
Partridge."

"Very good, my lord," she interrupted, raising her eyebrows.

"And then, with or without your permission, I will descend
White's for lunch, a brief snooze in the reading room, and the
gentlemanly glass of port. Only one, mind you," he assured her
he continued his progress to the book room. "I intend to becom
pattern card of respectability."

She watched him go, shaking her head and wondering w
men were so strange. He must be in love, she concluded as L
Ragsdale took his correspondence into the book room and clo
the door behind him. *This isn't the same tight-lipped man v
greeted me with such a scold last night. Something wonder
must have happened at the theatre,* Emma decided as she climl
the stairs on light feet. *If this romance with Clarissa prospers, p
haps I will be sprung from this indenture faster than I had hope*

And why not love? she mused as she walked down the hall
Lady Ragsdale's room. *He said he was thirty, high time for a
man to be thinking seriously about marriage and a family.* S
knocked on the door, hugely pleased.

Lady Ragsdale was still in bed. She looked up over the new
paper and smiled at Emma. "Ah, my dear. Over there are
dresses John ordered for you. They came yesterday with Sal
things, and we didn't notice it until the afternoon."

"For me?" Emma asked as she approached the dresses drap
over the chair.

"For you, Emma. And don't look so dumbfounded! John ha
very kind streak, once someone calls his attention to a necessit
Lady Ragsdale stated.

"But I never said anything," Emma insisted, picking up
dress on top and admiring the softness of the deep green wo
There were lace collars and cuffs on the chair, too, and a pettic
far better than the ragged thing she wore.

"No? Well, perhaps neither of us gives John credit for the go
he does."

"I am certain you are right, my lady," Emma said. The ot
dress was black, and experience told her how good it would lo
as a background to her auburn hair and pale complexion. "C
please tell him thank you for me."

"Tell him yourself," Lady Ragsdale said with a smile. "A
Emma, I have a paisley shawl inside my dressing room tha
never wear. It's hanging on the closest peg to the door."

In a haze of pleasure, Emma went into the dressing room a

s brought quickly back to earth by Lady Ragsdale's dresser,
10 obviously had been listening at the door. Acton thrust the
awl into her hands and hissed, "Don't think you'll get any more
m my lady."

"I learned long ago not to expect anything," Emma whispered
ck. "I'm certain you'll be quick to tell me if I overstep my
ice here, Acton."

The shawl looked especially fine with the green dress. Emma
nembered to drop a quick curtsy to Lady Ragsdale and another
eathless "Thank you" before closing the door quietly behind
r. She was down the stairs in a moment, and knocking on the
ok-room door.

"Emma, you needn't knock" came Lord Ragsdale's voice from
thin. "I'm not ingesting opium or fondling the upper chamber-
id. At least not presently."

You are so outrageous, she thought with a grin. It almost
iounts to Irish wit. She opened the door and came into the room,
idenly shy. "I just wanted to thank you for the dresses," she said.

He looked up from the desk where he was going over her
atly entered account books. "I hope they fit."

Some sense told her that they would be a perfect fit. "I am sure
·y will, my lord." When he continued looking at her, she hesi-
ed. Why do I dislike being under obligation to this man? she
nsidered as she watched him lean back and continue his perusal
the ledgers. "Sir, you didn't need to go to such expense for me."

He closed the book and indicated the chair next to the desk.
mma, I may have many faults, but dressing poorly is not
iong them. I like the people whom I employ to look at least half
grand as I do."

She laughed out loud, and he joined in her laughter. "Well, I
n't expect you to match my incomparable high looks, Emma,
t you must agree that if we are to do business together, I have
tain standards."

"Yes, my lord," she agreed, a twinkle in her eyes. "I have stan-
rds, too. Does this mean that if I do not approve of your waist-
at or pantaloons, you will change them to oblige me?"

It was the closest she had ever come to a joke with an English-
in, and he seemed to know. He laughed again, reached out and
iched her arm. "By all means, by all means. I have it on unim-
ichable authority that a good wardrobe covers a multitude of
iracter flaws. You are welcome to correct me."

She watched him a moment more, struck by a sudden and
olly unexpected wave of pity. You are so convinced of your

own flaws, she thought, and how sad this is for you. And h
strange that I am feeling sorry for an Englishman.

"Emma, you must have something quite serious on your min
Lord Ragsdale was saying, when she paid attention to him aga
"Can it be that my flaws cannot even be covered by a good tai
and boots from Hobie?"

I am going to be impertinent, she thought as she sat there. "Y
have far fewer flaws than you think, my lord," she said, her wo
coming out in a rush, as though she feared she would not
able to say them if she gave them thoughtful consideratio
"And . . . and thank you for being concerned enough last night
give me the scold I deserved. I promise not to be out past dark
the future on my day off."

There, she told herself, think what you will. I mean every wo
of it. As she sat there in embarrassment, it was as though a gr
stone rolled off her heart. She could not have explained the fe
ing to anyone, because it was new to her. All she suspected v
that it might not be such an onerous chore to serve this man u
her indenture was up.

He regarded her as seriously as she knew she was looking
him. "Why, thank you, Emma," he said finally. "I believe y
mean every word of that."

"I do," she said promptly as she stood up. "Now, tell me wl
you want me to do today while you are out, and I will get at it."

He considered her another moment, a half smile on his fa
then set her some tasks that would keep her soundly busy unti
was time to leave tomorrow for his Norfolk estate. "When I retu
this afternoon, I'll expect you to join me in the stables for a lo
at my new purchase," he finished, making room for her at t
desk and going to the door. "I warn you it will be expensive, so
you want to prune up now, make faces, and act like a secreta
and fiscal adviser, be at liberty."

She smiled. "I have no qualms about what you spend yo
money on, my lord," she assured him, "as long as it will lead
prompt double entries, your continuing reformation, and event
marriage. You know the terms."

"Indeed, yes," he agreed, opening the door and leaning agai
it. "Do wear the green dress first, will you?"

She blushed and busied herself at the desk, murmuring som
thing in reply.

"Don't mumble, Emma," he said. "It's a bad habit."

"Very well, my lord," she said distinctly. "By the way, I mean
ask: Did you have an especially nice time at the theatre last night?

"You mean, why am I so pleasant this morning?" he asked in turn, leaving her to wonder at his prescience. "Actually, I admired Clarissa's charms with my opera glasses from the safety of my own box, and spent the rest of the time trying to figure out how to apologize to you. Good day, Emma."

She sat at the desk and stared at the door. He opened it again. "And Emma," he continued, "if you should ever feel the urge to trust me enough with your own problems, I might even be able to surprise you with useful solutions."

I wonder if he truly means that, she thought several times that morning as she worked in the book room. This reflection was followed by the fact that no Englishman had ever kept his word to her or her family. She dismissed his offer, but noted, to her annoyance, that his words kept popping into her mind as she answered his correspondence.

Such a plethora of invitations, she considered as she looked them over and sent regrets or acceptances, according to his instructions. Now, I would prefer a picnic al fresco to a dinner at the home of some stuffy, gouty duke, she thought. Perhaps Lord Ragsdale prefers old cigar smoke to ants. She wondered what would happen if she arrived at one of these events in his place, chuckling to herself at the imagined expressions on the face of her surprised host. Papa had always assured her—especially on those days when her brothers were more trying than usual—that she had the poise and ability to move in any social circle. Of course, I would have to lose my accent and study the trivial, so I could be sufficiently vacuous.

Her thoughts drifted to Clarissa Partridge. "I hope you are intelligent enough to realize what you might have," she murmured. "Lord Ragsdale is certainly potter's clay for the molding, if you are suitably managing. He could even amount to something, with the proper guidance."

Emma was starting to rub her eyes and wonder where the day had gone when Lord Ragsdale reappeared in the book room, looking none the worse for wear for what must have been a strenuous day for one so indolent. Do be charitable, she thought as she looked up, wincing at the sharp pain between her shoulders.

"Yes, my lord?" she inquired, noting that in their brief acquaintance, seldom had she seen him looking so pleased with himself.

His eye was lively with good humor, and he seemed to throw off that boyish, barely contained energy that she remembered—with a pang—about her own younger brother.

"Emma, you must see my horses!"

"Horses in the plural, my lord?" she inquired.

"Yes; singular, isn't it?" he quizzed. "I found myself in the middle of a wonderful sale, and who can resist a sale?"

"But two horses?" she asked. "I know sales are wonderful but . . ." she stopped. "It *is* only two, isn't it?"

"Yes," he assured her, taking her by the arm and pulling her to her feet. "Sir Bertram Wynswich of Covenden Hall, Devon, periodically finds himself under the hatches, and he is obliged to lighten his stables. How lucky I am today. Emma, the letters can wait!"

She capped the ink bottle and let him lead her out of the house and into the stable yard, amused by his horseman's commentary on the finer points of his fortuitous acquisitions.

"Next you will be telling me they can fly," she grumbled as he hurried her along.

"Very nearly like, Emma," he agreed, and stopped before the largest loose box. "Well, what do you think? Is this not a sound investment?"

She could not disagree. The horse that came to the railing when Lord Ragsdale leaned his arms on it would have charmed the most discriminating gypsy. He was a tall chestnut, taller than she ever could have managed, with a noble Roman profile, deep chest, and legs that went on forever. He looked as well-mannered as a gentleman, with an intelligent face that seemed to broadcast equine good humor.

Emma stepped up on the railing and glided her hand over his nose. "Oh, you are a bonny lad," she whispered. "Lord Ragsdale, this must be your lucky day!"

He nodded. "Indeed. Didn't I say so? Do you know I even won at cards this afternoon? I have discovered that it is much easier to play when I am sober. Then I paid a call on Clarissa Partridge."

"And Miss Clarissa agreed over tea and macaroons to follow you to the ends of the earth?" she teased in turn.

Lord Ragsdale laughed. "Not precisely, you goose, but she did consent to let me escort her to Covent Garden when we return next week."

"Bravo, my lord!" Emma said, clapping her hands.

Lord Ragsdale bowed, then looked over Emma's shoulder. "And here is another beauty."

She turned around to look across the aisle at another horse, a gray mare, smaller, but just as interested in the people in the stables as they were in her. Her ears were cocked forward, almost as though she understood their conversation. Emma reached up to pat the second horse, admiring every inch of her elegant bearing. Lord Ragsdale knows horses, she thought as she found herself nose to nose with the little beauty. She thought of her father's stables then, remembering with a rush of pleasure completely independent of any regret or longing.

"Oh, Lord Ragsdale, I wish you could have seen my father's stable," she said, forgetting where she was. "He had a roan that would have given your hack a run for his . . ." She stopped, acutely aware of Lord Ragsdale's full attention. "But you couldn't be interested in that," she concluded. She stepped away from the mare, embarrassed.

Lord Ragsdale turned his attention back to his horse, sparing her further embarrassment. "Emma, you're no more shanty Irish than I am," he commented, not looking at her. "Something tells me that your father had a whopping good stable."

He cannot possibly be interested in anything I have to say about my family, she thought, suffering the familiar panic she always felt around Englishmen. "Yes, he did," she concluded, "but I needn't tax you with that." She glanced at the gray, desperate to change the subject. "This is a lady's horse, my lord. I hate to tell you, but if you bought this for Miss Claridge, you will be disappointed. She doesn't ride."

She waited as he continued his scrutiny of her, hoping he would ask no questions that would rip her wounds wide-open, leaving her to bleed inside again. Oh, please, my lord, she thought, change the subject.

He turned from his regard of her and fondled the gray's ears. "If you must know, I was looking to the future," he explained, after a moment's hesitancy. "Perhaps Clarissa will enjoy this horse someday."

My, but you are in love, she thought, smiling at him and grateful he had taken another conversational tack. "Perhaps you are right, my lord. And now, if you'll excuse me, I have your work to finish."

He smiled at her and reached in his pocket, pulling out a sale's receipt. "Very well! Enter this and send it to the bank." He grinned at the astonishment on her face as she absorbed the amount. "I can afford it, so don't you dare scold, Emma!"

She shook her head, thinking that Lord Ragsdale's indulgence in two horses could feed small cities. She stared at the amount. Or build new cottages for all his crofters and the neighbors besides. I hope he is so generous in another day, when he's inspecting thatching and rafters.

And so it goes, she thought, as she took a last look at the beautiful horses and started from the stable. Lord Ragsdale fell in step beside her, shortening his stride to hers.

"Of course, I need to exercise both horses. Emma, could I convince you to ride with me tomorrow on our way to Norfolk? I am assuming that you are a rider."

A very good one, my lord, she told herself. There was a time when I could match my brothers mile for mile across the whole of County Wicklow. You'd have thought we owned it, or at least, part of it. And so we did, but that seems like someone else's life, and not my own.

"I would like that, my lord, but I don't have a riding habit," she temporized, grateful for an excuse and wondering why at the same time.

"That's no difficulty," he assured her. "I am certain my mother has a habit you can wear. She doesn't ride anymore, and it may be a trifle outmoded, but I fail to think that would bother you overmuch. Ride with me, Emma?" he asked again.

It wasn't a command. She knew she could say no. Emma hesitated.

"Of course, if you would prefer to ride in the carriage with Mama and Sally and Acton, I will understand," he continued smoothly.

Acton. The thought of riding for a day and a half in a carriage with that harpy glaring at her made her flinch. "No, no," she said hastily. "I'll ride with you, Lord Ragsdale."

Lady Ragsdale's habit was not a perfect fit, but her boots were, Emma decided, as Lord Ragsdale threw her into the sidesaddle the following morning. She settled herself comfortably and accepted a crop from him, enjoying the feel of the saddle, and the particular pleasure of good boots. She tapped the leather with the riding crop, thoroughly satisfied, for all that she would have to think of something to say to Lord Ragsdale through a whole day of riding.

Leading out in front of the carriage, they negotiated London's early-morning traffic and soon left it behind, riding into the morning sun, which struggled to get away from the low clouds and fog that seemed part of London's perennial landscape. They rode steadily to the north and east, and soon the breeze blowing toward the Channel cleared the air of haze, presenting them with a blue sky of surpassing loveliness.

To Emma's relief, Lord Ragsdale chose not to converse. They rode side by side, but he was silent, and she wondered if he was already regretting his decision to go to Norfolk. Lady Ragsdale had confided in her last night as Emma was helping with the packing that he had not been at Staples Hall since his father was laid to rest in the family cemetery there.

"And even then he was brought in to the chapel on a stretcher," she said. "He has never been back since." She sighed and looked down at the petticoat in her hands. "And we do not talk about it."

Emma looked at Lord Ragsdale's profile. *At least you know where your father is buried,* she thought. *You don't lie awake at nights, wondering if he is alive or dead, as I do.*

"Yes, Emma?"

His question came out of the blue, and she glanced at him, startled. "I . . . I didn't say anything, my lord," she stammered.

"But you looked as though you wanted to," he offered.

She shook her head. "You must be mistaken, my lord."

"I must be," he agreed serenely, and said no more.

As they rode along, mile after mile, she discovered it was not an uncomfortable silence. *I could almost like this,* she reflected, *even though I suspect I am boring company. This is a peer used to card rooms, and clubs, and teas, and drawing rooms, and levees, and balls. I hope he will not fall asleep because I am so dull, and dump himself off his horse.* She smiled at the thought.

"Yes?" Lord Ragsdale asked.

She laughed in surprise. "You must have eyes in the back of your head," she protested.

"Nope. Just one on the left, but it does yeoman's duty. What's so amusing?"

Obviously there was no point in holding back. "I was just picturing you ejected from your horse and supine on the ground, bored into sleep because I am a dull conversationalist."

He shook his head. "On the contrary, Emma, I was about to congratulate you on the pleasure of your silence. Do you know that just since the beginning of this interminable Season, I have heard every stupid conversation that people such as myself utter? I am sure that the things we say over and over, thinking ourselves so witty, must be written somewhere on clay tablets." He looked her in the eye then. "You may reform me too completely, Emma. Suppose I become addicted to long silences and rational conversation that leads somewhere? Imagine the shock to my friends."

He joined in her laughter. "Seriously, Emma, we are halfway to luncheon, and you have not made one single remark about the weather, fashion, or the latest gossip."

"What would you like to talk about, my lord?" she asked finally. "Weather, fashion, or gossip?"

He reined in his horse, and she was compelled to stop, too.

"My father, Emma. Please."

Chapter 13

B ut . . . but . . . your mother tells me . . . I thought you did not wish to speak of him," she stammered. The mare sensed her sudden agitation and stepped in a dainty half circle. She patted the animal into control, searching for the right words. "I mean, your mother, your banker, David Breedlow even—they all warned me not to bring up the subject."

He spoke to his horse, and they continued. "They are wrong," he said finally when they were some distance in front of the carriage, and he could slow the pace slightly. "It may have been my choice at one time, but I find now that avoiding the topic breaks my heart."

His words were so simple, and so full of feeling that they went straight to her own heart. As she rode beside Lord Ragsdale, Emma realized that she would never be able to look at him in the same way again. It was powerful knowledge, and left her almost breathless. What do I say to this man? she wondered. He was looking at her, as though expecting something, and as she searched her mind for something to say, she thought of her mother, that woman of few words and much heart.

"Tell me, my lord," she said simply, remembering with an ache those calm words spoken to her so many times.

"I think he must have been the best man who ever lived, Emma," Lord Ragsdale said, with a glance over his shoulder, as though he feared his mother could hear him. The carriage was only a speck in the distance. He cleared his throat and smiled ruefully down at his saddle. "But I suppose that is part of the problem." He reached over and touched her arm. "Have you ever tried to measure up to an impossible ideal?"

She considered his question, and understood him for the first time. She smiled at him and shook her head. "We were all so human in the Costello household, my lord. I . . . I was the only daughter, and my brothers either ignored me, or were happy I was nothing like them."

He nodded. "I imagine it was a lively household, Emma. Per-
s you will tell me about it some time."

"Perhaps," she replied, trying to keep the doubt from her voice.
ut we are speaking of you and your father, sir, are we not?"

"We are. He was all goodness, all manners, impeccable in char-
er and possessing every virtue, I think. I was a younger son for
ch of my early years, thank goodness, so the onus of perfection
ted on my brother. Claude was very much like Father."

He paused then, and she had the good sense not to rush into the
nce. Perhaps I am learning wisdom, she thought as she
ched Lord Ragsdale struggle within himself.

"Claude died when I was at Harrow, and then Father trans-
ed his entire interest to me."

Again there was a long silence. Quiet, Emma, she told herself
hey rode along, side by side. "I don't mean to say he wasn't
rested in me before, Emma, but this was different." He shook
 head. "I am probably not making much sense, but that's how
vas. Claude died of a sudden fever, and overnight, I was the
ily hope."

He looked at her. "There are some things that the heir learns
t I never learned. I suppose it becomes a way of life. Too bad I
 a poor student."

Two weeks ago—a week ago even—she would have agreed
h him. This is odd, she thought as they rode along. I want to
end him from himself, and he is someone I do not even like.
 looked at the sky; it was still overcast. She could not blame
 strange thoughts on too much sun. Her next deliberation came
villingly, but she considered it honestly as Lord Ragsdale rode
ide her in silence. Can it be that I have nourished myself so
g on hatred that I do not recognize an attempt at friendship? I
 not even remember my last friend.

It was a shocking thought, almost, but instead of dismissing it,
she would have done only recently, she allowed herself the
ury of considering it. That is what I will do, she thought. I will
ve myself open to a change of feeling. She nodded. It is a pru-
t measure, taking into allowance the plain fact that I must
ve this man until he considers my debt paid.

"Emma, what on earth are you thinking?"

It was a quiet question, coming almost from nowhere, so
pped up in her own thoughts was she. Emma knew she did not
e to answer it, but as she looked at Lord Ragsdale again, took
is seriousness where earlier there had only been a certain irri-

tating vapidity, she felt that she owed him an answer. She rei
in the mare and turned to face him.

"I am thinking, sir, that I would like to be your friend."

The impudence of her words caught her breath away. Em
you nincompoop, she scolded herself as Lord Ragsdale stare
her. You're hardly in a position to recommend yourself to a m
quess. When will you ever learn to keep your mouth shut?

"I . . . I'm sorry," she apologized when he continued to
nothing. "That was probably not good form, my lord. Forgive i

I will die of embarrassment if he just stares at me, she thou;
her mind in a panic now. Suppose he turns his back and ri
ahead? Or worse yet, makes me dismount and get in the carri
with the others and that witch Acton? "I'm sorry," she mumb
again.

"Well, I'm not," Lord Ragsdale said. "By God, Emma, l
shake on this. It's damned nice to have a friend."

She looked at him in amazement, well aware that her face
flaming red. He was holding out his hand to her, and sidling
horse next to the mare. Instinctively, she held out her hand. T
shook hands, Emma holding her breath and looking him in
eye. She took a deep breath then, and plunged ahead. "Since
are resolved to be friends, my lord, you can rest assured that
matter what you tell me about you and your father, I will
judge."

He smiled, and some of the ravaged look left his face. ");
will not dare, as my friend, will you?" he murmured. "Let us i
ahead a little." He put spurs to his hunter, and she followed jus
nimbly.

When they were a good distance from the carriage, he slov
his horse, then rested his leg across the saddle as they saunte
along. "As a second son, I was supposed to embrace an army
reer. All that changed when Claude died. After Harrow, I fo
myself at Brasenose." He sighed. "I was not a good student. ʾ
warden remembers me well, and probably is not suffering cou
Robert Claridge any better than he did me."

"Did your papa rake you down and rail on?" she asked.
know mine would have."

He shook his head. "Papa was much too kind to do that,"
replied.

I wonder if that was such a kindness, she thought. Sometir
nothing says love like a really good brawl between fathers ;
sons, Emma thought, thinking of some memorable rows. I won
if your father was as good a man as you think, she consider

tucked the thought away. Surely Lord Ragsdale knew his
father better than she, who had never met the man.

He would come to Oxford, and sigh over me, and remind me
the family was depending on me," the marquess said. "He
right, of course."

My lord, did you begin to drink and wench then?" she asked
denly.

e was silent a moment, reflecting on her quietly spoken ques-
. "I suppose I did," he said slowly. "Of course, it seems as
gh I have always engaged in too much gin and the petticoat
." He looked at her without a blush. "At least I do not gamble,

he laughed. He joined in briefly, then put his leg back into the
up and cantered ahead. Again she followed.

Papa commanded the East Anglia regiment, and they were
ed up during the '98," he continued. "I had always wanted an
y career, and I badgered Papa to free me from Brasenose's en-
ns. He did, finally, and I joined him in Cork. Oh, God,
na."

he did not disturb the silence that followed, because she found
elf forced back into the '98 herself. She was fifteen then, al-
t sixteen, and she remembered staying indoors when ragged
s or uniformed soldiers passed the estate, the one slouching
he prowl, the other marching smartly. And Papa would bang
he dinner table, and shake a finger at her brothers, warning
n of the folly in getting involved in a quarrel that was not
rs. And so we did not, she thought, and see where it got us.
na and Tom are dead, and I do not know where the rest of you
Jesus and Mary help me. She looked at the marquess, and
w that sooner or later, he would ask the inevitable question.

Was your family involved, Emma?"

he shook her head, relieved she did not have to lie yet. "We
e not, for all that we lived not far from Ennisworthy
. . . and Vinegar Hill."

Damned place," he commented. "How did you not get in-
ed?"

he stared straight ahead. "My father was a Protestant
owner, my lord. It was not our fight."

Truly, Emma?" he asked quietly.

Truly, sir." It was right enough. If he did not know any more
it Ireland than Vinegar Hill, he would never come up with an-
r connection, and she would not have to relive anything more,
nd that summer of 1798. She was afraid to look at him, and

chose instead to go on the attack. "But we were talking of y[ ]
my lord. Were you glad enough to be in the army at last?"

He shook his head, then motioned his horse off the road. [ ]
followed, wondering what he was doing. He dismounted th[ ]
and helped her down. "Let's sit here, Emma," he said. "When[ ]
carriage arrives, we can wave them on."

She was glad enough to dismount, and only hoped that she [ ]
not grimace as she walked with him to the tree.

"A little stiff, are we?" he asked, a touch of humor in his voi[ ]

"I haven't ridden since 1803," she said, and then wished [ ]
had not.

"Now, why does that year ring a bell?" he asked, more to h[ ]
self than to her.

Emma held her breath.

"Never mind, never mind," he said, and sat under the tree, le[ ]
ing back against the trunk. She threw the reins over her hor[ ]
head and sat down, when both animals were cropping grass by [ ]
road. "Where was I? Ah, yes, the army." He began to rub his f[ ]
head. "I discovered, to my chagrin, that I liked the army no m[ ]
than I liked school." He made a face. "All those stupid rules. P[ ]
had bought me a captaincy, and let me state here that you h[ ]
seldom seen a more inept officer than I was."

"But I thought you wanted to join the army," she said. [ ]
sniffed at the pleasant, earthy aroma of autumn's leaves blend[ ]
into the soil. I could wish it were a sunnier day, she thought, [ ]
that our topic was a cheerful one. This could be a pleasant setti[ ]

"I thought I did want the army, but the fascination did not [ ]
dure long." He turned to regard her. "Emma, has it ever occur[ ]
to you what a stupid system it is for a man to *buy* a commissi[ ]
The most cloth-headed private in the king's East Anglia kn[ ]
more than I did about soldiering." He sighed and picked up [ ]
hand absentmindedly. "And there we were among the sad[ ]
kind of poverty, and people who hated us. War is not all i[ ]
cracked up to be. Uniforms get dirty fast. Everyone start[ ]
stink." He paused. "And people die. Oh, Emma, how they die."

He released her hand and sat in silence again, rubbing his f[ ]
head over his eye patch.

"My father died at Vinegar Hill because I did not have the [ ]
to save him. My God, Emma, for such a good man to die [ ]
way!"

The words burst out of him, and she jumped. He gripped [ ]
hand again, as if unable to go on without her physical prese[ ]

squeezed his hand in return, and in another moment, he re-
sed her, mumbling some apology.

"I wish I could say it was a glorious battle, but it wasn't even
thing important, Emma. Some of the mob had killed a cow not
from the picket line and butchered it for those enormous cop-
pots. You could tell they were hungry devils. I think I felt
re sorry for them than anything else," he said. "I mean, we
re just standing around watching and nothing more."

She could not wait through another silence. "And then what,
lord?"

"I don't know why, but one of my men leaped up from the
ket line, stormed halfway up the hill, and grabbed a hunk of
t wretched beef." Lord Ragsdale's voice had a wondering tone
it, as though the matter still puzzled him. "True, we had been
half rations for several days ourselves, but why that? It was
h an irrational, impulsive gesture."

Emma leaned closer until their shoulders were touching. "I do
understand how this is your fault, my lord."

"Well, it was," he replied, his voice grim. "I was standing right
t to the man, and all I could do as he sprinted up the hill was
k around for my sergeant, to ask *him* what to do! By the time I
nd my sergeant, the mob had swarmed down the hill and
gged Father off his horse where he sat with his back to them.
never know if he was even aware what had happened, so fast
it occur." He slapped his fist in his hand. "I was so inade-
te!"

Emma took his hand this time, but he shook her off and
unted his horse again. She hurried to join him, but he was far
wn the road before she was even in the saddle again. The car-
ge was close now, but she waved to the coachman and hurried
a gallop after Lord Ragsdale, thinking to herself how odd it was
t sometimes the largest events hinged on the smallest actions.
e felt the tears sting her eyelids. Sometimes innocently offering
aveler a bed for the night can lead to complete ruin. But I can-
think about that, she told herself as she dug her heel into the
re's side.

She caught up with Lord Ragsdale in another mile, but only be-
se he had dismounted, his lathered horse following behind him
v like a large dog. She walked her horse alongside him, and
wondered for a moment if he even realized she was there be-
e him, so deep was his concentration on the road in front of
.

"I started up the hill after Father, but there wasn't any point,"

he continued, his eyes on the road ahead, his voice dull. "Fr
the time they grabbed him until I was wounded couldn't h
been more than a minute, but it still seems to go on forever, w
I think about it." He looked at her then. "And Emma, I th
about it all the time. I don't suppose an hour goes by that I do
think about it."

Of course you think about it, she thought, her own heart f
You are idle and have nothing to fill your time. Now, if you w
serving out an indenture, you would discover that probably t
hours would pass before you thought about it. Emma longe
tell him that she understood what he was suffering, but she h
her tongue. For you would only demand to know why I think m
self an authority on this kind of pain; I haven't your courage
tell yet.

He stopped and raised his hands to her in an impotent gestu
"He disappeared into a crowd of men and women with pikes a
clubs. Then I was struck in the eye by a pike, and I was blin
by my own blood. I don't remember anything else."

"Perhaps it's just as well."

"I suppose," he replied, but he did not sound convinced. "C
ers say that, too. They took me by ambulance to Cork, and at le
I was spared the sight of his head on a pike at the top of Vine
Hill." He shuddered. "There wasn't enough left of his body
transport home for burial."

"Oh, God!" she exclaimed, and took him by the arm. He s
denly twined his fingers in hers then, and they strolled along h
in hand. After a few yards, he looked down at their hands.

"Someone would think we were having a pleasant outing,"
commented as he released her. "I do not have many of tho
Emma."

"You will, my lord," she said finally, not so much that she
lieved it herself, but that he needed to hear it. "You will return
London and drink tea in Clarissa Partridge's sitting room, a
take her to the art gallery, and think of other things." She stop
and took his arm again. "It will help if you do not flog yourself
a regular basis, and if you find some suitable employment."

"Up you get, Emma," he said as he cupped his hands a
helped her into the sidesaddle. He mounted the hunter again, a
they set out to overtake the carriage. "There's the rub, Emma. I
obviously not suited for the army, and I only squeaked by at C
ford. I would be a poor vicar, because I do not believe
Almighty is very nice. Mama assures me that I do not need

work ever, but you know, I will go crazy if I do not find something useful to do."

"Perhaps you will find sufficient occupation in managing your estates, my lord," she suggested.

He made a face. "Unlikely, my dear secretary. My land is prodigiously well managed already, and provides me with an obscene revenue."

She cast about for something to say to encourage him. "I suspect that soon enough you will be a husband and then eventually, a father. This can be time-consuming."

He smiled. "Ah, yes, the unexceptionable Clarissa. She is lovely, Emma, and I am eager for you to meet her. But seriously, one cannot breed all the time. Not even I," he added generously. "And Clarissa is probably not likely to . . ." he stopped, and grinned at her. "Yes, Emma, I need to find an occupation that will keep me too busy to think about what a bastard I am."

She could think of nothing else to say. Mama would have scolded him for being so self-absorbed, but Lord Ragsdale's agonies struck too close to the bone for her to offer advice. I am a fine one to suggest personal improvement, when I spend spare moments wishing I could reverse that awful day in 1803 and begin it again. It would end differently, if only I could take it back.

There was no need for further conversation then, or that night during their stay at the inn. After dinner, Lord Ragsdale announced his intention to take a stroll, and something in his tone told them all that he did not wish company. He was still gone when she crawled into bed and pinched out the candle. Walk some miles for me, my lord, she thought drowsily as her eyes closed.

They arrived at Staples Hall the next day around noon. Miracle of miracles, the sun shone on the East Anglia coast. The contrast of blue sky and low chalk cliffs was almost blinding, Emma thought as they rode along the seacoast route. The wind was bracing and reminded her of home more forcefully than anything she had yet experienced in England. I like it here, she thought all at once. There were no soft Wicklow Hills, and the shades of green were even now just struggling out from under winter, but the landscape was promising. She felt her heart rising like a lark.

Lord Ragsdale seemed to read her thoughts. "Most people think it too dramatic for comfort," he commented as he watched her face.

"I think it just right," she replied. "I suppose the wind can really roar through here."

He nodded, a smile of remembrance on his face. "The rain blows sideways so the grass doesn't even get wet."

The manor was much smaller than she expected, with gray stone and white-framed windows. The front lawn was sparse of shrubbery, and the few trees were stunted and permanently bent into the wind. She looked at Lord Ragsdale in some surprise.

"Where is the big house, you are thinking?" he questioned. "Grandfather resisted adding onto it, and Papa couldn't bear to change anything, either. I think it a little small, myself, but Mama would probably be aghast if I changed anything."

The bailiff met them at the door with a short line of servants, who curtsied and bowed as they entered the hall. Emma looked about her in appreciation and allowed the housekeeper to take her cloak. Lord Ragsdale handed over his hat and overcoat, and gestured to the balding man in well-worn leathers.

"Emma, this is Evan Manwaring, my bailiff. Evan, this is . . ."

The bailiff stepped forward and bowed, to Emma's dismay. "You didn't tell me you had married, my lord," he said, before Lord Ragsdale could finish his sentence. "May I say that your exertions have certainly borne fruit."

Emma gasped, and then laughed out loud. "Oh, sir, you do not understand."

"She is my secretary," the marquess said hastily, his face red. "Oh, don't look so startled! It's a long story, to be sure, but permit me to promise you that Emma Costello here has a right understanding of my correspondence and financial affairs. Emma, this is Mr. Manwaring."

They shook hands as the bailiff stammered out his apologies, then had a chuckle on himself. He wiped his hand across his shining baldness and scrutinized Emma. "It's an honest mistake. You seemed so easy-like together." He stepped closer to the marquess, and tried to whisper. "Your secretary?"

"My secretary," Lord Ragsdale replied firmly. "You will own that she is better to look at than David Breedlow, damn his carcass, and she does not cheat me."

Emma thought of Fae Moullé, and their inflated millinery shop figures, and had the good grace to blush. *What he doesn't suspect will certainly not hurt him,* she thought even as she owned to a guilty twinge. She shook hands with Mr. Manwaring, and resolved not to worry about what he was thinking.

Lord Ragsdale clapped one hand on her shoulder and the other on his bailiff's. "In fact, I suggest that you two adjourn to the book room and you acquaint Emma with the sordid details of my estate neglect. She will truss up your figures and admonitions, and present them to me in a more palatable form, I trust."

"We can do that," the bailiff replied dubiously.

"Excellent, then! Mr. Manwaring, I will watch for my mother and cousin, who should be arriving soon. I trust you will inform Mrs. Manwaring to provide luncheon for us."

"I already have, my lord," the bailiff said. "And do you know, Sir Augustus has invited himself over for dinner."

Lord Ragsdale smiled. "Well, if he hadn't, I would have talked my way into his house. Excellent, sir, excellent." He rubbed his hands together and started down the hall to the sitting room, as the bailiff gestured toward the book room.

Mr. Manwaring paused to watch his master go into the sitting room. "Looks better than he did ten years ago when I saw him last," he murmured, "all wan and white, and looking fit for fish bait. I wouldn't have given him one chance in five of surviving a strong wind."

"You mean he truly has not been here in all this time?" Emma asked.

The bailiff shook his head. "Not once, miss. Now, Lady Ragsdale comes every now and again to sit on a bench in the mausoleum, but Lord Ragsdale never has. Here, miss, have a seat, and let me get at the books."

Whatever awkwardness there might have been wore off quickly, as Emma knew it would as soon as the bailiff realized that she understood what he was talking about. In the time before the carriage arrived, they sat with their heads together, poring over the estate records from the past ten years. From what a cursory glance told her, the estate was well run, the figures all in order. The bailiff finally sighed and pushed the books away.

"We look good on paper, miss, but the crofters' cottages are in serious need of repair."

"All of them?"

"Yes. We've been patching and making do, but it's beyond that now. Cottages wear out fast on this rough coast. It could be a prodigious expense," he warned, "and not one I was willing to undertake without his express knowledge and approval. In fact, I would advise new cottages from the foundations up. And what could I do, when he avoids the place?"

"He is here now, Mr. Manwaring," she said, "and he can be brought to do his duty."

Mr. Manwaring leaned back in his chair. "Then, it will be the first time since I can remember that a Marquess of Ragsdale has been inclined to exert himself for the benefit of others."

Emma stared at the bailiff. "But his father . . . he tells me . . . I mean, didn't the late marquess walk on water?"

"Lord, no!" The bailiff laughed as he pulled the books toward him again. "I think our young lad has spent ten years putting together a mythology, Emma." He rubbed his chin, regarding her. "I'm wondering now if that is how he has managed to get through this pesky time. I mean, there were rumors everywhere about how the son had let down the father. I suppose if you hear something long enough, it almost becomes true."

"He would never believe anything ill of his father, even if you told him," Emma murmured.

Mr. Manwaring put on his spectacles and gazed at her over the top of them. "I know that. I'm thinking he might believe you, miss."

Chapter 14

*E*asier said than done, Emma thought as she allowed Lord Ragsdale to help her into the saddle again following luncheon. It had been a quiet meal, what with Lady Ragsdale and Sally Claridge white-faced and exhausted from a day and a half of travel, and capable of managing only a little soup. Weaklings, Emma thought as she watched them. Exertion does not appear to be a strong suit among any of this family.

She regarded Lord Ragsdale, sitting at the head of the table and tucking away a substantial meal. Two weeks ago, I would have thought you would be the first to complain, she reflected as she watched him down his meal with evident gusto. Yet you have not complained about anything.

"Well, Emma, are you up to a ride about the estate?" he asked, when his mother and cousin excused themselves and allowed Acton to help them to their rooms. "Let's see how bad the damage is that I have done."

It will be a thorny issue, Emma thought as they rode toward the first cluster of dwellings just beyond the back lawn of the manor. How does one convince a lazy, care-for-nobody peer that he is not the beast he has painted himself to be? And if he discovers that he is a better man than he thought, will he be comfortable with the feeling? Heaven knows it is easier to live when no one expects anything of you. She resolved to try.

"My lord, I learned something of real interest from Mr. Manwaring," she began, feeling like a circus performer on a tight wire.

"I hope you did, Emma," he replied in a teasing tone of voice. "Heaven knows, that's what I am paying you for."

She laughed in spite of her discomfort, pleased to see a sense of humor surfacing through all the misery of the last day. "Do be serious, my lord," she began.

"Must I?" he interrupted.

"Mr. Manwaring showed me the estate records, my lord." She

hesitated, took a deep breath, and plunged in. "No one has made any improvements to the crofters' cottages since before your grandfather's time."

He let her words sink in, and then rejected them, as she feared he would. "You must be mistaken, Emma," he said, in a tone that wanted no argument. "My father was the best kind of landlord."

"I am certain that he had the best of intentions, my lord," she hedged, wishing she had not tackled the subject at all.

"You don't know what you're talking about," he said, staring straight ahead. "You never even knew the man. I'll thank you to keep your opinions to yourself about something you know so little."

She winced at his tone, wondering why she had ever involved herself in the matter. I shall hold my tongue, she told herself. There is no reason why I need to make a career out of blundering into crises. She glanced at his face, and it was set and hard again. She reined in the mare, and he stopped out of habit.

"John Staples, you have to tell me what is so attractive about thinking the worst of yourself," she declared. "Just because your father never got around to doing the work you're about to begin, doesn't mean he is less of a man. It only means that he was human like the rest of us."

"Shut up, Emma," Lord Ragsdale said, and put spurs to his horse. In another moment he was gone from sight, and she was left to kick herself in solitude and wonder why on earth she even cared what he thought about himself.

It was a new emotion, one she had not felt in years, this curious anger at the stubbornness of others. She rode slowly along, feeling the raw wind that began to blow in suddenly from the sea, but not regarding it beyond hunching down tighter inside her cloak. I have not felt this kind of irritation since those days before 1803 with my family, she finally forced herself to admit. We fought, we brawled, but we loved each other. I had forgotten that special painful anger, and how it can sting. I want something better for this man, even though there is no real reason why I should.

She looked down the road where Lord Ragsdale had ridden. Oh, I would like to grab you by the shoulders and shake some sense into you, she thought. How dare you go through life thinking you are not a good man?

"I have a few more things to say to you, Lord Ragsdale," she said out loud. "Now, where are you?"

She rode in the direction she had last seen Lord Ragsdale, but he was long out of sight. "You're not getting away from a piece f my mind that easily," she said grimly as the wind began to low harder, twirling in odd circles as it seemed to blow both rom the sea and toward it at the same time.

The rain came then, thundering down until she couldn't see the rack in front of her. After a few minutes she was soaked to the kin, and determined to return to the manor house. But where was t? She looked behind her, but she could see nothing in the pelting ain. Oh, dear, she thought as she reined in the mare and squinted nto the storm. Somewhere not far were the cliffs overlooking the cean. She leaned over and patted the mare.

"Well, it wouldn't be any loss to anyone on this miserable is- and if I rode off the edge of England," Emma told the horse, "ex- ept that I refuse to give Lord Ragsdale that pleasure."

"What pleasure, you baggage?"

A gloved hand grabbed her reins, and then brushed her sodden air back from her eyes. Don't show too much relief, Emma, she old herself when Lord Ragsdale, as soaked as she was, led her orse beside his.

"I just don't want you to think I'm not angry with you still," he concluded.

"By God, Emma, you would try a saint," he said, his voice nild. "I wonder the Claridges in Virginia didn't just pay you to ave their indenture, and good riddance."

She laughed, despite her soggy discomfort. "You know they ever had any money. Robert spent it all!"

He chuckled and gathered the reins in closer. "Well, unlike my ousin, I am rich as Croesus. Had I not signed an agreement with ou—under duress, I might add—you would be a free woman ow, and probably plaguing someone else. Let's find some shel- r."

The rain was turning into sleet as Lord Ragsdale stopped be- ore a crofter's cottage and dismounted. "When in Rome, Emma," e said as he helped her from the saddle, then knocked on the oor.

The cottage was warm with the fragrance of both farming peo- le and cows. "Good heavens," Lord Ragsdale said under his reath as the cows stared back at him, moving their jaws in ythm. "I had no idea."

"Hush," Emma said out of the corner of her mouth as she ob- erved the startled looks on the faces of the people within. "Oh, lease, we are so wet," she began, and friendly hands pulled her side.

Only minutes later she sat before the fire, a blanket clutched

around her, a mug of warm milk in her hand, and her clothin
draped demurely by the fireplace. She sipped at the milk, tryin
not to laugh at the sight of the marquess, similarly clad, but wit
more of him to cover. He tugged at the blanket, trying to cove
both his shoulders and his legs at the same time.

"It's a mathematical problem, my lord, which is why you prob
ably cannot resolve it," she commented, and took another sip.

"What are you talking about?" he snapped.

"There are only so many square inches of blanket, and mor
square inches of you, my lord," she explained, her eyes merry
"As I have already seen all of you before, and these good tenan
have not, you might ask them which end they would prefer cov
ered. It's all the same to me."

He gave her a gallows smile, and resolved the matter by cinch
ing the blanket about his waist and moving closer to the fire t
keep his bare shoulders warm.

"All the same to you, eh?" he asked finally as he accepted
cup of milk. "That cuts me to the quick. No preference, Emma?"

"My lord, I am not Fae Moullé," she retorted, swallowing he
laughter when he blushed.

"No, you are not," he replied finally, when he could think o
something to say. "And I say my prayers daily in gratitude fo
that tad of information." He looked up at the older man, obviousl
the head of the house, who stood beside him, as if wonderin
what he should do. "Do be seated, sir, and forgive this frightfu
intrusion. We thank you for your hospitality and promise to leav
as soon as the rain lets up."

The man touched a work-worn hand to his forehead, and sa
down. "My lord, you and Lady Ragsdale may remain as long as
suits you." He looked about the crowded room, and then at th
cows behind the barrier. "After all, sir, it's your property."

Lord Ragsdale looked about him. "Why, so it is," he mur
mured. "Don't let us keep you from your tasks, uh, your name
please?"

"David Larch," said the man. "My father worked here befor
me, and his father before him, my lord." He stood up, and looke
toward the cow bier. "It's time for the milking, my lord, if yo
and your lady will excuse me."

Lord Ragsdale nodded, but Emma wondered why he did no
correct the man. She moved closer to the fire, careful to keep th
blanket well-draped around her. "Why didn't you tell him we ar
not married, my lord?" she whispered to his back.

He set down the cup and grinned at her. "What? After you in

rmed'um that you'd already seen all of me? And then teasing
e like that? They wouldn't believe we weren't married, and I
an't confuse them."

It was her turn to blush. The marquess tugged her wet hair sud-
nly, then turned back to the fire. "It's so refreshing when you're
eechless, Emmie dear," he said, loud enough for the family to
ar him.

In another moment, to her relief, Lord Ragsdale gathered his
anket about his middle and padded on bare feet over to the cow
er, where he tucked in his blanket, leaned across the railing, and
atted in low tones with the crofter.

"Your lordship has a nice touch about him, my lady."

Emma looked around with a smile as the crofter's wife sat
wn beside with her baby, opened her blouse, and began to
rse. Emma looked on in simple delight, reminded of her fa-
er's estate all over again, and the quiet people who inhabited it.
wonder if they were driven out, too, she thought with a pang as
e listened to the baby's soft grunt of satisfaction. She looked
ck at Lord Ragsdale. He has a nice back, she decided. I hope
arissa Partridge will appreciate the fact that I rescued him.

"Yes, he does have a pleasant way with folk," she replied.

The wife leaned against the wall of the hut and admired her
ild, who was kneading at her breast now, his eyes closed.
Jow, his father before him . . . there was a stiff man. I know he
ways meant well, but he just never could *talk* to people like us."

Emma touched the baby's hair, pleasuring in the fineness of it.
ell me, Mrs. Larch. Did my . . . the late Lord Ragsdale ever
ake any repairs on your cottage?"

She shook her head, and smiled, as if amused at such a naive
estion. "I disremember any repairs, but he did come by every
w and again and promise them." She sighed. "I am certain sure
meant well, but promises don't butter any bread, now, do
ey?"

"They do not," Emma agreed, looking at the marquess and
shing he could have heard Mrs. Larch's artless declaration.
ey both watched the marquess then, and Mrs. Larch shifted her
by to the other breast.

"He looks a sight better now than he did ten years ago," she of-
red, her voice low. "We all went to the chapel for the memorial
rvice for poor Lord Ragsdale, him all cut up in tiny pieces by
e damned Irish."

Emma gulped, and wondered why the crofter's wife had made

no mention of her brogue. "Dreadful affair," she agreed. "I d
not know him then."

"I'm sure you didn't, my lady," the woman agreed. "You don
look much older than a baby yourself. Sometimes I wonder wh
men are thinking when they take a wife. Ah, well. The doings
the aristocracy are not my affair, so pay me no mind, Lady Rag
dale. All I remember was the sight of him on that stretcher, h
eye covered in a bandage, and him so quiet." She shivered. "A
then he began to wail. I can hear it yet, if I think about it." Sl
shook her head as she burped her son and handed him to Emm
"He seems better now. Here, my lady. If you'll hold the little'u
I'll see to some supper. You must be fair famished."

Lord Ragsdale was quiet all through the simple meal of po
ridge and milk. Mrs. Larch had found a cloth to drape over h
shoulders, 'So ye'll set a good example for the elder'uns,' sl
teased, and glanced at her older children, who had come indoor
wet and shivering, from evening chores.

"Mind your tongue, mum," the crofter said, even as he smil
and nodded to the marquess. "Women do get uppity, my lord,
you may have noticed."

Lord Ragsdale dragged his attention to the crofter, who
shoulders were shaking in silent laughter over his own brazen w
He smiled at Emma. "Yes, I have noticed. Sometimes they ev
tell us things we don't want to hear."

The rain stopped while they were finishing the last of the po
ridge. Mrs. Larch cast an expert's eye at the variety of pots set k
the smoking fire, filled with rain. "Storm's over, my lord ar
lady," she said. She winked at Emma. "I must say, my lady, wh
with all this ventilation, we always have rainwater for our ha
and the little tyke's bath!"

"And that's why your daughter here has such a fine comple.
ion," Emma said, entering into the spirit of the joke as sl
touched the cheek of the oldest daughter next to her.

"Almost as nice as yours," chimed in another daughter.

"Almost," Lord Ragsdale said as he touched Emma's chee
He winked at her and then looked at the host. "And now, sir,
our clothes are dry, I think it's time we gave you back your p
vacy."

"Dry enough?" he asked her after they had dressed and mac
their good-byes to the Larches. The family lined up outside tl
door, and waved and curtsied them off.

"I think so, my lord," she replied, still embarrassed by the w:
he had buttoned up the back of her dress, as though it were som

ing he did every day. "I think you are a thorough-going
oundrel, my lord, and I cannot fathom why I did not see this
oner. I thought you were merely a drunkard."

He thought about her words for a moment as they picked their
ay carefully along the road, guided by moonlight. "Maybe you
st weren't looking deep enough, Emma," he teased. He touched
r arm. "Or maybe I wasn't much fun, either." He cleared his
roat then. "And, Emma, I owe you an apology."

"Let's see now, which of the myriad wrongs are you going to
ake amends for?" she teased, eager to lighten his tone.

"The one where I insisted that my father would never have ne-
ected these people," he said, his voice so quiet that she had to
an closer to hear him. "You were so right, Emma, so right.
avid Larch told me all that over the milking."

"There's nothing to apologize for, my lord," she said softly.
ou'd have discovered this same as I did, when your bailiff
owed you the books. What matters is that you're going to do
mething about it."

"I certainly am, Emma," he replied. "Wouldn't you say it was
ne I spent some of my money on new homes *and* separate barns
r these people who work my land?"

"I would," she agreed. "And I don't think it will reduce you to
tching your shirts or blacking your own boots to economize."

He smiled at her and then tightened his grip on the reins. "What
relief! I don't know that my indolence could stand that much
ain. Race you to the house, Emma."

Sir Augustus Barney was there when they arrived, pacing up
d down in the sitting room, impatient for his dinner. Lord Rags-
le greeted him with a broad grin, striding across the room and
asping his hand, and then clapping him on the back.

"I believe we are still a little damp, Gus," he said. "Emma,
op a curtsy to Sir Gus like a good girl. He was my father's best
end, and he can tell you any number of horror stories about my
uth. I think he knows me better than I know myself—now there
a frightening thought."

Emma curtsied to Sir Augustus, wondering how soon she could
cuse herself from the room. Lady Ragsdale and Sally Claridge
re seated by the window, looking refreshed after a long after-
on nap. Emma wondered briefly what they would think if they
ew about her afternoon with Lord Ragsdale, wrapped in blan-
ts in a crofter's cottage. With any luck, she could retreat below-
irs to change clothes, and then to the book room to look over
e estate figures.

"Emma, you'll join us at the table," Lord Ragsdale said as s made her curtsy and started to edge toward the door. "M Larch's bread and milk was good enough, but I'd like somethi more substantial." He winked at Emma. "Especially after a tou afternoon of stripping down and drying off by a crofter's fire. G you, Emma."

Emma blushed and glared at him, carefully avoiding a glan in Lady Ragsdale's direction. "Very well, my lord," she said, "t then I must catch up on my work in the book room."

Sir Augustus stared at her, and then at Lord Ragsdale. " 'P my word, John, I thought your bailiff was quizzing me. She real *is* your secretary?"

"She really is," he agreed, taking the older man by the ar "She knows my business better than I do, which, of course, h not been difficult." He steered his guest toward the door. "Emn pay attention during dinner and let us both hang on such pearls wisdom that Sir Gus chooses to drop about duties of landlords tenants."

Emma escaped to the book room after the last course wh Lord Ragsdale called for port and the ladies retired to the sitti room for cards. She sat down at the desk and ruffled through pages of the estate ledgers, thinking to herself how fortunate Lo Ragsdale was to have such a useful bailiff. She thought aga about what he had said yesterday. "But for all that, what a p things are in such order, my lord," she murmured as she ran h finger down the neat columns of debits and assets. "You wo find employment here to occupy your mind and heart."

She thought suddenly of her brothers then, remembering th constant activity about the estate, and their good-natured exhau tion at the end of each day. She thought of her own household d ties, and the work she was learning from her mother. I alwa knew what I would do in life, she considered, resting her chin her palm. I would marry someone like myself, and take care his estate and our children. It would have kept me busy all n life.

"My dear, do you have a moment?"

She looked up in surprise, startled out of her daydream, to s Sir Augustus standing in front of the desk. He smiled down at h

"I knocked, but I don't think you heard me," he said. "Ma sit?" he asked.

She stood up in confusion, and he waved her back to her cha "I want to talk to you a moment, my dear. That is all. John h gone to the sitting room to set up the whist table."

She sat down again, folding her hands in front of her on the desk. "Say on, sir," she said.

He seated himself across from her, and regarded her in silence for so long that she began to get that uneasy feeling in her stomach. She swallowed, praying that her fear of Englishmen was not beginning to creep into her eyes as she sat and returned his gaze.

"I did not think to see John so improved, and something tells me that the credit is yours," he said finally.

She nearly sighed with relief at his calm statement. "I forced him into a silly agreement whereby I would improve his character and he would then release me from a rather expensive indenture."

He chuckled. "Yes, his mother told me about that while we waited for you to return this evening." He leaned forward then. "Good for you, my dear, good for you. John has some wonderful qualities to share with the world."

"I know," she agreed. "I am Irish, as you can plainly tell, and I was prepared to hate him forever. But I can't. I am determined to see him successfully married. Then remains the thorny problem of finding him some occupation to fill his time."

He nodded but said nothing, as though encouraging her to continue.

"He could easily take to the drink again, if he finds time hanging heavy," she went on, "and this I do not wish."

"Why not?" he interjected suddenly.

Why not indeed, she thought. She leaned forward, too, across the desk, drawn to this kind man, now that she knew he meant her no harm. "I like him, Sir Augustus. He's lazy, and bears no resemblance to other people I used to admire, but I like him. I see . . . well . . . potential." She stopped in confusion. "I do not think I can explain it any better, sir."

Sir Augustus leaned back in his chair then, and crossed his legs comfortably. "I think the finest quality about the Irish is their forthrightness, Emma. I like him, too, and would hate it right down to my socks if he continued to throw his life away." He shook his head. "One tragic death was enough."

"Exactly so, my lord," she agreed.

He sat there another moment, then rose to his feet, nodded to her, and went to the door. He paused there and looked back at her.

"My dear, have you ever considered pursuing him yourself? I think he would make you a first-rate husband."

Emma blinked and wondered if she had heard the old man correctly. When she realized she was staring at him with her mouth hanging open, she closed it.

"I wish you would consider it, Emma. Perhaps his friends would be surprised, but I don't recall that John ever cared much what people thought."

"You cannot be serious," she managed to say finally. "He's only now beginning to court an unexceptionable lady in London."

Sir Augustus considered her reply and nodded slowly. "Well, if you say so. I wonder that he did not mention her, but only spent the last few minutes over port, both extolling your abilities and saying how you drive him to the edge of patience on a daily basis."

She leaped on this opening. "See there, sir, you said it yourself. I drive him to distraction!"

"Yes, you do," he agreed. "If you maneuver this correctly, I don't think it would take more than a week or two to turn that into love, my dear, if it isn't already there. Think about it."

"Oh, I could never!" she burst out.

"Never?" he asked, his eyes bright. "That's a long time. Emma, perhaps you should consider how good *you* would be for John. Good night, my dear."

Emma made a point to dismiss thoroughly from her mind Sir Augustus Barney's closing remarks to her. "I think your eccentricity must come from living too long on a fog-bound, windy coast," she said grimly after the man smiled at her and bowed himself out of the room. She shook her head at the closed door, then picked up the outline of the letter she was to compose to Lord Ragsdale's banker.

She bent to the task in front of her, still at it two hours later and wondering why. The floor around the wastebasket was littered with crumpled papers, evidence of her failure to compose a simple letter. That's what comes from using old ink, she thought as she sharpened yet another quill. She looked down at the page before her, crossed out and agitated over. Of course, ancient ink would hardly account for her numerous misspellings.

This is a lost cause, she reflected as she put away the ink and paper finally. I must admit that Sir Augustus's words have put me into a pelter. She folded her hands in front of her and resolved to consider the matter.

"I don't love Lord Ragsdale," she said out loud, and waited for something inside her to deny it. Nothing did; there were no whistles or bells, or fireworks going off inside her, or even in the near vicinity, so it could not possibly be true. "Well, that's a relief," she said, and again, nothing contradicted that sentiment.

I suppose I am just tired, she thought as she surveyed the ruin around her. This letter can wait until tomorrow. She picked up the crumpled remains of her evening's effort and stowed them in the wastebasket, thoroughly irritated with herself. She stood at the window a moment and watched the rain thunder down, then sighed, blew out the lamp, and left the book room.

She closed the door behind her and noticed a paper tacked to the frame. It was in Lord Ragsdale's familiar, scrawling handwriting that by now she could have picked out from a roomful of letters. "Emma, come riding with me in the morning. Be at the stables at seven. John."

She folded the note, amazed that Lord Ragsdale would rise so early. She could hear laughter from the sitting room, so he was still up. I could go in there and remind him that I have his work to do in the book room, she considered, then rejected the idea. Sir Augustus was probably in there, too, and she didn't feel like facing him.

"Very well, sir, I suppose I will go riding," she said to the note as she hurried belowstairs.

She overslept the next morning, waking to the sound of someone rapping on her door with a riding whip. She sat up in bed, clutching the blankets around her when Lord Ragsdale came into the room. He clucked his tongue at her and shook his head.

"Really, Emma, weren't you the one who extolled the virtues of early rising?" He came closer, and her eyes widened. "Need any help pulling the bed off your back? I seem to remember someone forcing me into a tub at an ungodly hour."

She opened her mouth and closed it, bereft of conversation. Lord Ragsdale laughed as he went back to the door. "Emma, you've been away from Ireland too long," he said over his shoulder. "This is the second time in as many days that I have found you speechless."

Impulsively, she grabbed a shoe on the floor by the bed and threw it at him, but it only slammed harmlessly into the closed door.

"And your aim is off," she heard from the other side of the panel. "Ten minutes, Emma, or I'm coming back in to help."

There is such a thing as too much improvement, she decided as she hurried into Lady Ragsdale's riding habit and pulled on her boots. She grinned to herself, reminded suddenly of Paddy Doyle, one of her father's tenants. After years of "the daemon dhrink," as he put it, Paddy reformed, and spent the rest of his life driving his fellow tenants crazy as he extolled the virtues of abstinence.

"Lord Ragsdale, you could become tedious," she told him ten

minutes later as she found him in the stables, giving a little more grain to his hunter. She yanked the brush she had carried with her across the stable yard through her sleep-tangled hair.

"I'll do that," he said, taking the brush from her and handing her the grain bucket. "Here, have some breakfast."

She laughed in spite of herself and looked in the half-filled bucket. "You wretch!" she exclaimed as he brushed her hair. "I mean, you wretch, my lord."

"Well, I would only say it to the least horse-faced woman I know," he replied, brushing her hair. "If you'll move with me over to the fence rail, you will see a biscuit I brought for you, and some ham. Really, Emma, you should practice what you preach about a good breakfast."

She turned around to say something, but he took her hair in a large handful and towed her toward the fence rail. "You are certifiable," she said as she reached for the ham. "I don't know why I didn't see it sooner. Thank you, Lord Ragsdale."

He chuckled as he finished brushing her hair. She handed him a ribbon, and he tied it in a tight bow while she started on the biscuit. He turned her around to admire his handiwork.

"You'll do," he said, setting down the brush. "You know, Emma, that's the trouble with reformation. Sometimes you get more than you bargained for."

She stood there, her mouth full of biscuit as he smiled at her. She noticed then he wasn't wearing his eye patch. I wonder why I didn't notice that sooner, she thought as she swallowed and wiped her hands on her dress. Maybe because it doesn't matter to me.

He did observe the direction of her gaze. "I'd rather leave it off, if you don't mind," he said. "I don't think we'll see anyone, and it's just you."

She smiled at him, reminded of her brothers and similar, offhand remarks. "It's fine with me, my lord," she said. "It doesn't matter one way or the other."

He took her by the shoulders. "You really mean that, don't you?" he asked.

She gently slid from his grasp. "I really do. If you're more comfortable without it, leave it off."

He thought that over and helped her saddle the mare. "I wonder how Clarissa would feel about that," he wondered out loud as he cinched the saddle.

"You could ask her," she said sensibly as she handed him the bridle.

"Emma, do you always reduce everything to black and white?"

he asked, the humor evident in his voice as he put the bit in her horse's mouth.

I thought I used to know right and wrong when I saw it, she reflected. But that was before that man, that damned Robert Emmet, came walking up the lane to our house and I made the worst mistake of all. Since then, nothing has been black and white. "Of course I do," she lied.

He was watching her face, and she turned away to busy herself with the stirrup.

"You're a liar, Emma," he replied, his voice mild. "I wonder when you will finally tell me something true about yourself."

Chapter 15

Her mind froze as he helped her into the saddle. She arranged her leg across the horse and spread her skirts around her, afraid to look at Lord Ragsdale. She said nothing as he watched her for a long moment, his face unreadable now. When she thought she would start to cry if he did not turn away, Lord Ragsdale whistled to his hunter and mounted him.

"I can wait, Emma," he said as she rode beside him, too shocked to look at him. "I am also led to wonder sometimes who we are redeeming here, me or you."

They rode in silence from the stable yard, until she managed to calm herself. "You could not possibly be interested in anything about me," she said finally, knowing it was her turn to speak, but not knowing what to say to this man beside her.

"And why not?" he asked.

She looked at him then for the first time since his quiet declaration. "Because I am just your servant."

He smiled then, reached over and tugged her horse's mane. "Emma, you've never been *just* a servant. I doubt the Claridges knew what to make of you, all skinny and ragged and covered with lice, from that voyage in the ship's hold. But I know your kind." He touched her arm this time, lightly, briefly. "When you want to talk to someone, I hope it is me."

What good could you do me? she reflected as they rode along. You have to be flogged to do your duty, and you are busy now with wooing. If you are not lazy now, it is only a temporary thing. You will be indolent again, when you are bored. To her relief, Lord Ragsdale changed the subject and began to talk of his plans for the crofters.

"I should think it would be best to build the cottages in a more central location, instead of sprawled here and there across the estate," he said as they rode along. "This area, for instance. It's far enough from the cliffs to cut some of the wind, and close enough to their work for convenience."

They stopped in a pleasant clearing, a small valley tucked be-
ween the series of low, wooded hills that characterized the Nor-
olk coast. Lord Ragsdale dismounted and gestured with his
ding whip. "See, Emma? Plenty of good water, and still some
mber. We could erect barns close by for those who have their
wn livestock."

He held out his arms to help her down, but she shook her head
nd settled herself more firmly in the saddle. He leaned against
er mare, absently fingering the horse's mane. "You don't like
ne idea," he said finally. He looked, to her mind, rather like a lit-
e boy in the throes of disappointment, too well mannered to
how all his irritation, but not averse to a wry expression.

Diplomacy, Emma Costello, diplomacy, she told herself. You
ave already ruined the morning for yourself; see what you can
o to give these people what they really want. "My lord, may I
uggest that you ask your tenants what *they* want?"

She could tell by the look on his face that he had never before
ntertained the novelty of inquiry among those who worked his
nd. Oh, dear, she thought, this is probably more democracy than
n Englishman can stand. She looked beyond his expression of
lack surprise and smiled to herself, thinking of the Claridges and
neir Virginia neighbors, rich and poor alike, gathering to make
ecisions for their county. She remembered the noise, the hot
ords, the voices raised in clamorous agreement or disagreement,
nd then the rational calm that settled on the assembly when the
najority spoke. True, not everyone went home satisfied, not even
ne major landowners, but there was harmony, because all had
ired their opinion.

"It works in America, my lord," she said, warming to the idea,
eeling animation rise in her own heart. "You can hear some fear-
al rows at Hundred meetings, but most come away satisfied, be-
ause they have had their say."

She watched him for signs of resistance, but could see none. He
abbed his forehead thoughtfully and then mounted his hunter
gain. "It's a lovely spot, Emma," he said, drawing close to her.
Why would they object?"

She took a deep breath, at the same time wondering why she
elt the inclination to fight for these people she hardly knew. Am I
ghting for them, or am I concerned that they understand that you
ke an interest? she asked herself, and had no ready answer. "Sir,
eople do not like to be forced from their homes, no matter how
nabby or inconvenient those cottages are."

"Like you, Emma?" he asked softly, a smile of understandin[...] playing around his lips.

"You will not let me forget, will you?" she considered. "Ye[...] my lord, like me," she replied, her voice equally soft. "Prese[...] your argument for removal, but let them decide."

"Won't they think me a weak landlord if I succumb to their d[...] cision?" he persisted, and his interest sounded genuine to her.

"Of course not," she responded promptly. "They will think th[...] you care about them, and they will follow you anywhere."

He mulled that one over, riding in silence for several minute[...] "I doubt even Sir Augustus has ever done anything that radical[...] he said. "My neighbors will think I am daft, and count it a ce[...] tainty that my father left a weak heir."

"Who cares what your neighbors think, John?" she said, blur[...] ing out his name before she even realized it. "They don't work f[...] you, and you don't have to answer to them." She blushed the[...] aware of her social blunder. "Excuse me, my lord," she apol[...] gized. "I was forward."

He smiled at her. "Nonsense! Emma, you are a flaming radica[...] don't you know."

She nodded, relieved at his light tone. "Aye, my lord. But on[...] think: there are so many ways to solve problems. Why limit you[...] self to what's been done over and over? Try something new."

She held her breath as he regarded her thoughtfully. "Ver[...] well, Emma," he said finally, when she thought she would bur[...] with waiting. "I'll do it your way. Let's return to the manor. I[...] make it Manwaring's task to gather my estate workers tonight [...] the old barn by the threshing floor. You'll take notes of the pr[...] ceedings, of course."

Emma grinned at him and clapped her hands, even as h[...] wagged his finger at her. "See here, Emma, I'm going to the en[...] of the plank for you on this one!"

"You won't be disappointed, sir," she replied happily.

"I wouldn't dare be," he said. He looked at her. "Well, spea[...] Emma. You obviously have something else on your mind. I a[...] sure it is radical."

She nodded, wondering if this was going too far, but willing [...] chance it. "My lord, let the women come to the meeting, too, an[...] let them speak."

"Oh, that is radical," he agreed, half teasing, half serious. "Wh[...] ever would I want to do such a thing?"

"The women will know better than the men what they want in[...]

w cottage," she said decisively. "Encourage them to speak, and
y will defend you and serve you to their last breath."

They were in sight of the manor house again. "I'll do it," Lord
gsdale said. They rode into the stables, ducking through the
en doorway. He dismounted and held his arms out for her. She
owed him to help her down. He did not release her immedi-
ly, but put his hands on her shoulders for a brief moment.

"What about you, Emma?" he asked, his voice quiet as Man-
ring approached. "Will you ever speak your mind to me?"

She forced herself to meet his glance, and felt an enormous
ge to unburden herself completely, to tell him the whole, miser-
le story and her dreadful part in it, until she was stripped right
wn to the bone. She hesitated, teetering on the edge, before she
led herself back with a shake of her head. He released her and
ned away.

"Maybe someday, Emma" was all he said as he left the stables
th Manwaring.

Maybe never, she thought as she watched him go.

It was well after midnight before the last tenant left the barn,
l of enthusiasms and new ideas. A smile on her face, Emma
thered together the sheaf of notes at the table where she had sat
r four hours, carefully recording the evening's events, and
tching with delight as Lord Ragsdale mingled so gracefully
th his crofters. She looked through the open doors where the
ants still gathered together in little groups, reliving the give
d take of the evening, and then looking back at the barn with
pressions of real respect.

Lord Ragsdale seemed unmindful of what was going on outside
barn. He yawned and stretched, then took off his coat, reveal-
g a shirt and waistcoat drenched in sweat. He tossed his coat on
table and threw himself into the chair provided for him, which
had not sat in once throughout the night.

"Emma, this kind of exertion is difficult, indeed." He leaned
ck in his chair and propped his booted feet on the table, his
nds behind his head. "I feel as though I have been pummeled,
ung out, and hung out to dry." He looked over at her and took
f his eye patch, rubbing the rim of his eye socket gently.
verything aches."

She merely smiled at him and continued sorting through the pa-
rs. "It's all here, my lord," she said, waving the papers at him.
ou can look it over in the morning and decide what to do."

"It *is* morning," he corrected, "and I have already decided." He

closed his eye and let out a pleased sigh. "We will build the c[...]
tages for the shepherds in that area I suggested this morning, a[...]
which they agreed to. The agricultural workers will remain th[...]
by the cliff road." He opened his eye and looked at her. "I thou[...]
David Larch was particularly eloquent in arguing the virtues [...]
remaining by the main road, didn't you?"

She nodded. "And the women certainly knew what they want[...]
in cottage improvements, didn't they?"

"Most emphatically," he agreed, and reached over to touch [...]
hand. "A good idea of yours, by the way, Miss Secretary. Gi[...]
that information to Manwaring in the morning. The constructi[...]
will be his task." He sat up then, as if energized all over aga[...]
"How does this sound, Emma? I will appoint Larch to be Ma[...]
waring's assistant."

"Bravo, my lord!" she replied, genuinely impressed. "He[...]
never fail you."

Manwaring rejoined them in the barn after separating hims[...]
from one of the groups that had continued the discussion outsi[...]
Lord Ragsdale informed him of his idea for David Larch, and t[...]
bailiff nodded in agreement. "He'll do fine, sir," Manwari[...]
replied, then smiled. "And if you don't mind me saying so, [...]
lord, you'll do, too." He leaned closer. "That's what your tena[...]
are saying, my lord."

Emma looked at Lord Ragsdale in delight, and he winked at h[...]

"And can I tell you something more, my lord?" Manwari[...]
continued. "They're saying how nice it is to know that you ca[...]
about their problems, and do more than just nod and smile a[...]
clear your throat." He stood up and nodded to Emma. "Go[...]
night, my lord. We've a lot to busy us in the morning, no[...]
haven't we?"

"Indeed we have," Lord Ragsdale agreed as he got to his f[...]
and pulled Emma up after him. "My dear, I expect you in the bo[...]
room at seven to begin making order out of this pile of notes. C[...]
ganize it and have it ready for my perusal. I promised a brief vi[...]
to Sir Augustus, and then my nose will be to the grindstone, too."

He draped his coat around his shoulders and waited for her [...]
gather the papers, then nodded to the steward to douse the lam[...]
They started across the barnyard together, Lord Ragsdale walki[...]
slowly enough for her to keep up with him.

"It feels good, Emma," he said finally as they approached [...]
manor house. "I can return to London with a clear conscience th[...]
I have done some good at last." He paused a moment. "There [...]
mains one hurdle."

She looked at him, a question in her eyes.

"My mother," he said as he continued to walk. "She will not be ppy when I tell her tomorrow that I plan to add a wing onto the nor house." He sighed. "She would prefer that I left everything Father had left it, but I want a better bedchamber, one that erlooks the ocean."

"More room, my lord?" she asked, her voice light.

"I think I will be spending more time here in future, Emma, and I bt I'll be alone. Mama will have to live with change, I suppose."

He put a hand on her shoulder, and she was again reminded of brothers. "And now you will recommend that I devote my e to wooing the lovely Clarissa Partridge, especially if I am to on bedrooms to this ungainly old pile."

"Most emphatically," she agreed, enjoying, despite her exhaus- n, the comfort of his arm so casually about her shoulder. "Then en you are thoroughly redeemed, we will reconsider my inden- e."

"Ah, yes. It always comes back to that," he commented, draw- her closer. "Those horses were expensive, Emma," he re- nded her. "Suppose I insist on ten or twenty years more?"

She knew he was teasing, but she realized with a start that a cade in service to Lord Ragsdale would not be an onerous duty. ey were expensive horses, she thought and smiled to herself. ou would never do that, Lord Ragsdale," she said out loud.

He merely shrugged. "How am I to get rational advice and sen- le counsel if you leave me? I might revert to my foolish ways. en how would you feel?"

How would I feel? she considered as they strolled slowly ng. She stopped and looked at him. "I would consider it a terri- waste, my lord, a shocking waste, a tragic waste. Don't you e throw your life away. I could not deal with it."

She was silent then, embarrassed that her voice was shaking. stood so close, and had not released his grip on her shoulder, ich tightened as she regarded him, sweaty and tired, but tri- phant, there in the moonlight of the barnyard. She started lking again, faster now, and he released his grip.

Besides all that, my lord, I have enough death on my con- ence, she thought. Don't make me responsible for the loss of e more life.

I must know more, but how? Lord Ragsdale asked himself sev- l times a day during the next few days. I could just come right t and demand that she tell me, he thought as he watched her at work in the book room, her face a mask of calm again. She ▮ gone from friend to servant again, assuming that unobtrus▮ manner he was familiar with in his other household servants. ▮ work was excellent as always, and innovative as usual, as ▮ speeded up with the demands placed on her by the flurry of ac▮ ity at the manor. She worked long hours with Manwaring, prep▮ ing drafts, itemizing invoices, even speaking with the contract▮ masons, and sawyers, acquainting them with the task ahead. ▮ knew that he could relax and visit his friends in the vicinity, ▮ pay some much-needed attention to Sally Claridge and ▮ mother, because his affairs were in capable hands.

"I have to know, I just have to," he found himself telling ▮ Augustus one night at the Barney estate. They sat together▮ front of a roaring fire, brandy in hand, watching the flames.

"I could ask why, John," Sir Augustus interjected as he reac▮ for the bottle.

Ragsdale shook his head when the baronet offered him more ▮ know that prison was involved. My God, you should have s▮ her face when we made that trip to Newgate! The only thing ▮ got her to put one foot in front of another in that dreadful pl▮ was her single-minded determination to do my business for me▮

"A rare quality in a woman," Sir Augustus commented, fill▮ his own glass and leaning back again to stare at the flames.

"I suspect you are right." Lord Ragsdale leaned forward. "I co▮ make her tell me more, but I honestly think that she would begin▮ bleed before my eyes. There is something here so terrible . . ."

"Then why do you not just leave it alone?" the other man as▮ quietly. "You don't have a reputation as someone who ta▮ much interest in others, John."

Lord Ragsdale leaned back, finished his brandy, and threw ▮ glass into the fireplace, where it shattered and sparked. "I'n▮ damned fool, Gus, why not just say so?" He touched his comp▮ ion's arm. "But do you know something? I am changing."

Sir Augustus downed his own drink. "I think I see, John. S▮ dragged you into reformation, and it seems to be taking."

Ragsdale nodded. "Yes. I expect I will be engaged and marr▮ before the season is out, and living here again by summer."

"Bravo for Emma Costello, then," the baronet murmur▮ "Two words of advice, my friend, neither of which you have ▮ licited, but which I offer because I loved your father and m▮ him, too, and want the best for you."

Lord Ragsdale swallowed, and felt unfamiliar tears behind ▮ eye. "Say on, sir."

"In your zeal at reformation, make sure you do not injure beyond repair what you seek to heal."

Ragsdale nodded. Sir Augustus stared into the flames and sighed. "There is another bit of advice?" he asked finally, when the baronet appeared to be on the verge of drifting off.

The older man smiled at the flames. "I don't know, John."

"Oh, now, you must tell me. I am a big boy now, and can probably take it."

The baronet stood up and stretched. "Well then, chew on this for your ride home. Just make damned sure you marry the right woman. The wrong one will ruin you."

He chewed on that for the remainder of the week in Norfolk, chafing at first that he knew he was becoming remote again, and then relaxing in the knowledge that Emma was relieved. *She does not want to talk about anything right now, and I am considering Clarissa and have nothing to say either,* he realized as they began the return trip to London. *She can have her mood and I can have mine, and we won't bother each other.*

It seemed a fair exchange, except that he found himself wondering, as they rode along, just how he might know if Clarissa returned his regard. He glanced at Emma, who was admiring the wildflowers by the side of the road. Spring had come while they were in Norfolk, creating a path of daffodils along the highway. True, the wind was cutting, but the flowers were there, with a ragged determination to stay, no matter what the North Sea threw at them.

"Emma, tell me something," he asked suddenly. "How will I know if I'm in love?"

She looked at him in surprise, disturbed out of her contemplation. "Well, I don't know," she said.

"Come on, Emma," he teased. "Surely you've been in love before. If I'm to redeem myself, and Clarissa seems a likely repository for my affections, I should have some idea, shouldn't I? What's it like? I cannot imagine that a pretty woman like you has never fallen in love."

She blushed becomingly, and he had to admire the way the color in her cheeks brought out the green in her eyes. *Emma, you're a rare one,* he thought. *Any other man would envy me right down to my socks, riding along with you.*

"Confess, Emma," he said.

She laughed then, and he felt a momentary relief. *So this is a safe topic,* he told himself and waited for her to speak.

"I suppose I fell in love two years ago in Richmond," she said finally.

"And?" he prompted.

"He was another of the Claridges' indentured servants," she said, her voice soft with remembrance. "A Scot, my lord, a cobbler by trade." She patted her horse, not looking at him.

"What made you think you were in love?" he persisted.

She flashed her eyes at him then, and it was a look that made his stomach tingle a little. My God, Emma, those eyes are a dangerous weapon, he thought as he felt the sweat prickle his back. Take a care on whom you use them.

"If you must know—and I think you are nosy past all bearing—I felt comfortable around him, at peace, and not at all afraid that anything would ever hurt me." She returned her gaze to the flowers by the road's edge. "Things were always more fun when he was around."

He considered Clarissa Partridge, and sighed. "I suppose it must be a different feeling for men, then. Ah, well, I was curious."

"You don't feel that way around Miss Partridge?" she asked.

He shook his head. "Not yet."

"Well, it's still early days with you and her, isn't it?" Emma asked.

"I suppose." He looked behind him. They had been riding slower and slower, and the carriage would have to slow down. He picked up the pace of their travel, and they cantered ahead for a good distance.

"Well, what happened?" he asked finally when they slowed the pace again, and Emma still did not say anything. "I mean, between you and the Scot."

"Oh, well," she said, "it came to nothing. His indenture ended three years before mine would have."

"And?" he prompted. "Emma, you are so tight with information sometimes that I find you singularly exasperating!"

"It might not be your business," she responded tartly, then repented. "He was going beyond the mountains to take up some land in the Carolinas. He needed a wife then, so he married one of the other servants who was not under an indenture."

"The cad," Lord Ragsdale said with some feeling.

Emma laughed. "I was probably well out of that, my lord. If he could be so expedient, then he probably wouldn't have been too concerned about my welfare."

"I suppose not," Lord Ragsdale agreed. "I mean, he might have shot you, if you had broken your leg, or something."

And so they were on good terms again as they rode into London. If I keep a light touch, and do not poke and prod about her family, we seem to rub along all right, he considered as they entered the house on Curzon Street again. But dash it, that gets me no closer to finding out anything, and I still don't know if I love Clarissa Partridge.

He paid Clarissa a morning visit the next day, armed with a pot of violets because Emma assured him that ladies loved violets, his eye patch on straight, and his clothes as orderly as Hanley could make them. He was not disappointed in his reception.

Clarissa cooed over the violets, just teetering, to his mind, on the edge of excess, then redeeming herself by sitting close to him on the sofa. Their knees touched once or twice, and he realized that it had been a long time since he had made love to a woman. Well, a long time for him. He dragged his mind along more appropriate lines then, and thought he faked an impressive interest in her needlework. It was good, he had to admit, when she rose to put it away, affording him a particularly fine glimpse of her shapely hips and delicate walk.

I am being diddled, he thought and grinned to himself. By God, it is fine.

"Clarissa—may I call you Clarissa?"

Blush, blush. Titter. "Why certainly, my lord." She had a breathless voice, and he wondered if her corsets were too tight.

"You may call me John," he offered.

Another titter. Another blush. "Very well . . . John."

Take a deep breath, my dear, he thought, or you may have to summon your dresser to loosen your stays. Of course, if you like to it so close, I might want to do that myself. "Clarissa, if I may be so bold, would you care to tour Hampton Court with me tomorrow?"

She cared to, and he left happily, feeling pleasantly randy and wishing that Fae Moullé had not moved to Bath to set up her millinery establishment. Emma would not approve, he thought. I will take a brisk walk home and behave myself.

She was busy in the book room, catching up on his correspondence, when he returned and stood lounging in the doorway. "Yes, my lord?" she asked, her eyes still on the paper before her.

"Congratulate me, Miss Costello," he said as he came in and dropped into a chair. "We are Clarissa and John now, and she will go riding to Hampton Court with me tomorrow."

Emma put down the pen and clasped her hands in front of her. "Bravo, my lord!" She twinkled her eyes at him then, and his stomach did another tingle. "I think Manwaring will not be finished with that addition on your manor a moment too soon."

He nodded, not altogether satisfied with her reply and wonder-

ing why not. He also wished she would not waste those fine eyes
on him. You should get out more, Emma, he wanted to tell her,
and meet some young men. He regarded her a moment more, reminded himself that she couldn't because she was in his indenture, and felt vaguely silly.

She appeared not to notice, but cleared her throat. "My lord, tomorrow is my day off . . ." she began.

He made an expansive gesture, grateful to cover his stupid
thoughts. "Of course, of course. Just don't come home so late this
time, and I will not scold you."

"I won't." She was brief, to the point, withdrawn again, and
looking at the correspondence in front of her. He eased himself
out of the room, hoping that she would return in a better mood
this time from her day off.

She was gone in the morning before he left, leaving neat piles
of his correspondence in the book room, with directions on what
to sign, and what to tell Lasker to set out for the post. He initialed
the little receipt for yesterday's violets, and on impulse, added a
note for another pot and directed it to the florist. This one's for
you, Emma, he thought as he tucked that receipt with the others in
the envelope for his banker, and folded the note to the florist.

The weather was fine so he drove his curricle, leaving his tiger
behind this time to fret. Since traffic was light, he turned toward
the city first, thinking to drop off the note to the florist himself.
Emma would probably enjoy a little surprise when she returned
that evening.

He hurried through his errand and was moving into traffic again
when he noticed Emma, her eyes straight ahead, moving swiftly
along the sidewalk not fifty feet in front of him. He almost hailed
her, thinking to invite her to ride with him to her destination, then
thought better of it. I will follow her instead, he considered.

It was an easy matter to travel behind her, moving slowly with
the traffic, always keeping her in sight, but not dogging her heels
either. She had no notion she was being followed, but hurried
along with that purposeful, swinging gait of hers that he had admired on occasion. She walked like someone used to walking,
someone who was going somewhere. It was a healthy walk, and
one that stirred him, somehow.

She led him deep into the City to a row of government buildings not far from the Admiralty. The traffic was thinning out now
so he drove to the curb and left his horse and curricle under the
watchful eye of a street urchin and his little sister. "Mind that

othing happens, and you will have a crown," he admonished as e tied the reins and continued after Emma on foot.

He recognized the Home Office and waited on the sidewalk ntil she was inside. He sprinted across the road then, determined ot to lose her in the building, and remembering it, from a visit ears ago, as a regular rabbit warren of offices and cubbyholes.

There she was, walking slower now, almost reluctantly, as she ad during their visit to Newgate. She appeared to hesitate before n open door. As he watched, she squared her shoulders, appeared) take a deep breath, and held her head up as she walked into the oom. The gallant gesture went right to his heart.

He knew he dared not follow any farther, some instinct telling im that she would be unhappy to see him there. She appeared to e in a lobby or antechamber, and there were others standing and aiting. He turned to go, and collided with a clerk, his sleeves olled up, his expression harried, carrying stacks of papers that ew out of his hands and slid across the cold marble floor.

"I beg your pardon, sir," the clerk gasped, going down on all urs to retrieve his papers.

"Oh, my fault, my fault," Lord Ragsdale insisted, and dropped) his knees to help. They gathered up papers in silence for a mo-ent, then he sat back on his heels. "Tell me, what is that office?" e asked, gesturing toward the door where Emma had disappeared.

The clerk, his face red from exertion, took the documents from im. "It's the Office of Criminal Business," he said. "Mr. John enry Capper is chief clerk, sir."

Lord Ragsdale thanked him, got to his feet, and brushed off his ousers. He strolled toward the entrance, his mind in a ferment. mma, what is your business with that band of thieves?

He stood outside the building a moment, wondering what mma would do if he joined her in the anteroom. This is none of y business, he argued with himself. If she wanted to tell me, she ould. I have given her plenty of openings. He thought again of r Augustus's advice. Do I dare poke at your wounds, Emma? ou prodded mine, but then, I agreed to it. I have no right to do e same to you.

And Clarissa was waiting. "Damn!" he said out loud, and arted running toward his curricle. He looked back once at the ilding, then tried to put it out of his mind.

Chapter 16

Lord Ragsdale had always liked Hampton Court, even from h
earliest days, when his mother and father took him walkir
there on one of their infrequent trips to London. He loved tl
sound that a pair of firm footsteps could make in the great ha
and never objected, no matter what the weather, to a perambul
tion about the whole building to gaze at the medallions on tl
walls and wonder about the arrogance of kings. As he grew olde
he occasionally thought how nice it would be to bring a lady
Hampton Court. He couldn't imagine a better place for a little s
rious wooing.

But not today, not even with one of the Season's loveliest di
monds hanging on his arm and looking at him with those cryst
blue eyes. On another day, perhaps he could have appreciated tl
way her bosom brushed his arm, and the way she had of runnir
her tongue along her lips that had probably reduced other peers
blancmange. As it was, he entertained as best he could with tal
of headless ghosts, thinking of Emma in that anteroom of the O
fice of Criminal Business.

By God, criminal business. But Clarissa was tugging at h
sleeve and pouting her prettiest pout, one that surely should ha
earned her a quick kiss at least. He swallowed, fighting dov
words of irritation that he knew he would regret, and resisted tl
urge to brush her off.

"You're not listening to a thing I am saying, John," she said.

She was right. He hadn't heard one word in ten of her babbl
What *was* she carrying on about? Could it be even half as impo
tant as what Emma was doing, even now as he dawdled through
musty old hall with England's prettiest woman on his arm. The
were other tourists about, and he looked up occasionally from h
contemplation of the parquet flooring to notice the envio
glances other men were giving him. I am a fool, he thought, a
the idea cheered him immensely. But I was already a fool, so th
is nothing to repine about.

"I'm sorry, my dear Clarissa," he said, hoping he sounded con-
te. He stopped and faced her, taking both her hands in his. "I do
ve a little business on my mind." He kissed her nose. "Let me
solve to forget it."

But he couldn't, no matter how hard he tried to devote his
hole attention to the beauty he squired about. His head was be-
nning to ache. His scalp began to itch where the ties to his eye
tch knotted at the back of his head. He found himself walking
ster, as though trying to hurry up the afternoon so he could re-
n to the Home Office. He could not fathom why he had ever
nsidered Hampton Court such a favorite of his.

Clarissa, Clarissa, what the hell am I going to do with you, he
ked himself. You are beautiful, and it could very well be that I
ve you, but right now, I wish we were anywhere but here. He
ught a moment, considering his options, and then decided that
ly the honorable thing would do; he would lie.

"Clarissa, I do have some pressing business in the City," he
nfessed. "It involves some . . . some charitable work I am doing
Newgate." Lord, what a corker that is, he thought. The Lord
y strike me dead. Why couldn't I have mentioned orphans at
Paul's or the deserving poor under some bridge?

"Newgate?" she echoed, her voice reaching a distinctly un-
easant pitch. "You?"

"Well, yes," he said, piqued that his reputation was so lacklus-
that she considered philanthropy out of the question, and then
named of himself for the lie. "They are wretched creatures."

That was no prevarication. He could testify to their wretched-
ss. He took her hand and strolled along, resisting the urge to
ip out his pocket watch and begrudge each second that crawled
. "I have a transaction I must perform on their behalf at the Of-
e of Criminal Business, and I really should not put it off." He
ced his hand on his chest. "They need me."

He tried not to wince, waiting for Almighty God to smite him
ad. Nothing happened, except that Clarissa clung to his hand
en more tightly, and gazed up into his face with an expression
sely resembling adoration.

"What a wonderful man you are," she breathed, and again he
ndered about the stress to her corset strings. "I am sure I never
ew anyone as considerate as you."

Her statement was so ludicrous that only by force of will did he
ep from laughter. He lowered his head and bit his lip, and man-
ed somehow to appear so modest that Clarissa rested her glori-
s blond hair against his arm for a long moment.

"You must tell Papa all about your philanthropic work amo[ng]
the felons when we see him in Bath in three days."

My God, what have I promised? he asked himself wild[ly].
When did I ever say I would go to Bath? Could that have b[een]
when I was admiring her bosom during the interval at the op[era]
and nodded? He quickened his pace toward the entrance.

"I don't precisely remember Bath," he began cautiously as [he]
directed the porter to bring his curricle. He staved off the beg[in]-
nings of a pout by a quick kiss on her forehead, wondering w[hat]
else he had promised Clarissa Partridge. "Perhaps you could [re]-
fresh my memory."

"Silly boy," she began, generous in her scold. "I'm sure y[ou]
have so much more on your mind than little me."

You can't imagine, he thought and kissed her hand. "Oh, y[ou]
are a dear one," he mumbled. It made no sense, but Clari[ssa]
would never know.

"Papa is in Bath because of his gout, and you promised Ma[ma]
and me that you would accompany us there on Thursday," she [re]-
minded him.

Did I? He slapped his forehead. "Oh, of course, my love," [he]
said. "Silly me."

She dimpled prettily and let him help her into the curri[cle].
"You said you wanted to talk to Papa about something." S[he]
blushed and fluttered her eyelashes at him. "I can't imag[ine]
what . . ."

Oh, God, I am to be married, he thought wildly. It was a c[old]
day, but he could feel sweat forming on his spinal column. [He]
took his time going around to the other side of the curricle. Ca[lm],
calm, John, he told himself. You know this is what you want.

"Oh, I am certain Sir Cecil and I will think of something to [say]
to one another," he teased, feeling as though someone else w[as]
speaking through his mouth and he was standing outside his s[kin]
watching. "My dear, if it chances that my business should t[ake]
another day, would Friday be amenable to your plans?"

"I am sure Mama and I would be only too happy to delay [our]
departure and give you one more day to do good. Oh, John, [I]
cannot imagine how I feel."

Nor I, he agreed, starting his horse off at a sedate pace, w[hen]
he really longed to snap the whip and leap hedgerows. I know [this]
is what I want, and I will make Emma ever so proud. Why are [my]
hands shaking?

He was able to convince her to come to the Home Office w[ith]
him, assuring her that he would only be a minute. He left

nding in the entrance and sprinted toward the Office of Crimi-
l Business. He would go to the porter and ask for an appoint-
ent with Mr. Capper on the morrow; perhaps he could learn
nma's business that way.

He hurried to the anteroom door and stopped. Emma stood
ere alone in the room, her back to the door. He looked around in
rprise. No one else was there except the porter, who was busy-
g himself with papers on his desk. How strange, he thought;
rely Emma arrived early enough this morning for an audience.
tiptoed quietly away from the office and met Clarissa at the
ain lobby.

"This is a dreadful place," she whispered to him as she grabbed
s arm. "I have never seen so many sinister-looking fellows."

"And those are just the solicitors," he joked. She looked at him
ankly, and he knew then that his future would involve explain-
g witticisms to his wife. "Well, never mind, my dear. Let me
ive you home now."

He resisted her invitation to dinner, assuring her that he would
t faint from hunger between Whitcomb and Curzon Streets, and
omising her that he would take her driving tomorrow afternoon.
Ve will discuss this delightful expedition to Bath, my dear," he
d as he blew a kiss in her general vicinity, leaped into his curri-
 as soon as the door closed, and sprang his horse back to the
y.

Emma was not in the anteroom when he returned, out of breath
m running through emptying corridors. The porter was gather-
g up his papers and climbing down from his stool by the inner
or.

"We're closed now, sir," he said, nodding to Lord Ragsdale.
ome again in the morning."

"I am sure that won't be necessary now," he said as he ap-
oached the porter. "That pretty woman who was here a moment
o . . . did she finally get in to see Mr. Capper?"

The porter laughed and shook his head. "Oh, Gawd, but I love
diddle the Irish!" He winked at Lord Ragsdale. "She can keep
ming back week after week until she wears out, and she'll
ver get through that door."

Lord Ragsdale stared at him. "What are you saying?"

The porter grinned back. "I'm saying that I have no use for the
sh. I think they should all be transported, and not just a select
v."

And so I thought, too, he considered, pausing to catch his
ath. I hated them all, but now I just worry. He tried again.

"Was she asking for information about someone transported
Australia?"

"Well, laddie, America's out now. Where else do we send the
felons?"

"I'm Lord Ragsdale to you," he snapped, suddenly furious, a
fighting down the strong inclination to grab the man by his ne
cloth and do him damage. "Give me a straight answer, or it's yo
job tomorrow."

The porter obviously believed him. His eyes widened, and
hurried to straighten his coat and run a hand through his thinni
hair. "I means no disrespect, my lord," he gasped. "She . . . s
said something about wanting to know the whereabouts of son
prisoners transported after the Castle Hill Revolt in 1803."

Lord Ragsdale nodded. Castle Hill. He remembered readi
about it in the London papers over his morning brandy. The
were hangings, which only pleased him at the time, and a m
who declared that no one would write his epitaph until Irela
took her rightful place among the nations. He remembered laug
ing over that bit of high Irish drama.

"And you won't let her in to see Mr. Capper?" he asked q
etly, turning his attention back to the porter. "What gives you t
right? You are a bastard, and I don't mind telling you."

"Y . . . y—yes, my lord," the porter stuttered, retreating behi
his desk again.

"How dare you humiliate that lady," he said, warming to
cause and coming around the desk.

The little man scrambled over the desk and darted for the do
"But she's Irish! She's fair game!" he shouted as he tripped ov
the doorsill, leaped to his feet, and ran down the hall, leavi
Lord Ragsdale in possession of an empty anteroom.

It was dark out now. Lord Ragsdale shoved his hands in
pockets and walked slowly from the building, nodding to
night watchman. Outside, he leaned against the wall and collec
himself. How can we be so cruel? he asked himself. What gi
us the arrogance to treat our own kind like the meanest vege
tion? She has family somewhere, and no one will help her fi
them. I make her do my stupid business, when I should be do
everything in my power to help her find those she loves.

He drove slowly back to Curzon Street, ignoring the curses
other drivers in more of a hurry. I do not know that I could e
apologize enough, he thought as he rode along, hunched down
the seat, the reins loose in his hands. And if I were to try, I wo
probably be trading on her dignity yet again.

He arrived in time for dinner, or so Lasker informed him as he ame into the main hall, feeling as though he had just climbed one ndred steps instead of ten.

"I am certain Lady Ragsdale and Miss Claridge will understand you do not dress, my lord," Lasker offered as he took Lord agsdale's overcoat.

He paused then and took a serious look at Lasker. "Did you er think how silly that expression sounds?" he asked his sur-ised butler. "I mean, 'dressing for dinner.' I am already dressed. nd who the hell cares whether I address a roast of beef in proper tire?"

"My lord?" Lasker inquired.

"Nothing, Lasker," he said, waving his hand wearily. "I am just nazed at myself, and people like me."

"Very well, then, my lord, but are you coming to dinner?" the tler asked, persistent to the end.

"I'm not hungry, Lasker, and I am not going to Almack's, or e opera, or any other damned nonsense selected for me tonight." e wanted to say more, to remind his butler that there were peo-e on the streets of London who were hungry, and cold, and who eded help, while people like him dressed for dinner and put eir rumps in chairs at the opera. "I'm not going out tonight, sker," he said instead.

"Very well, my lord," Lasker replied, his face wooden.

Lord Ragsdale looked at his butler and took a deep breath. "I ll be in the book room. I want you to send Emma Costello there mediately. We are not to be disturbed."

He turned on his heel and left his dumbfounded butler standing the hall, holding his overcoat. He stood for a long moment in e book-room doorway, acutely aware that this was no place to od at someone's wounds until they bled again, but he could nk of no other place. He closed the door behind him and lit a e, noting with some surprise that his hands were shaking.

He was seated at the desk, looking at nothing, when Emma ocked on the door.

"Come in," he said, wishing that his voice did not sound so ntry. It was not her fault that he and his countrymen were ighed every day in the balance and found wanting. "Please," he ded.

Emma came into the room, and stood before him at the desk. e looked up at her, noting her red eyes, and the defeat evident in e way she held herself. He pulled up a chair beside his at the sk. "Sit down, Emma."

She sat, leaning ever so slightly away from him, as though sh
feared the look on his face. He sighed and began to rub his for
head. He took off his eye patch and leaned forward, his hand
clasped in front of him.

"Emma, I've just come from the Office of Criminal Business
He heard her little gasp, but spared her his scrutiny. "The port
there assured me that you would never get in to see Mr. Capp
because you are Irish. I will have his job in the morning, my dea
and I promise you we will see Mr. Capper."

She began to cry then, a helpless sound more painful to his ea
than any he could remember, including his own agony at th
death of his father. She bowed her head and wept, and he cou
only sit there and watch her. In a moment, he handed her h
handkerchief, and she hid her face in it, sobbing the deep, wrac
ing tears of someone in the worst kind of misery. He let her cry
peace, wondering what to say. I think I shall be wise and keep m
mouth shut, he decided finally.

Emma stopped crying and blew her nose vigorously. Sh
dabbed at her eyes, and glanced in his direction. "I am so sorr
my lord."

"No, it is I who am sorry. I want you to tell me everythin
Don't leave out a detail. How can I help you if I do not know?"

She stared at him then, her face red, her eyes swollen. "Yo
would help me?" she asked, her voice filled with disbelief.

"Oh, Emma" was all he could say.

She took a deep breath and leaned back in the chair. "My fath
was a landowner in County Wicklow. He was a Presbyterian, an
his family had been in Ireland for generations. Mama w
Catholic, but he loved her and married her anyway. There we
four of us, two older brothers, me, and a younger brother."

She paused then, as though even that much was difficult. "I r
member you told me once that your father went to Magdalen Co
lege," he said, trying to keep his tone conversational, hoping
relax her.

She nodded, and gave him the ghost of a smile. It vanished a
most before he was sure he had seen it. "Eamon was headed the
in the fall." She shook her head and began to wail this time. Th
hair rose on the back of his neck as he remembered that kee
from his days of trouble in Ireland. He wanted to leap from h
chair, but he forced himself to stay where he was. He took h
hand, and she squeezed it so tight that he almost winced.

"What happened, Emma?" he asked, feeling like a brute in t
face of her torment. "Why didn't Eamon go to Oxford?"

"Because he was dead by fall, or I think he was. Oh, John, I n't know! I have spent over five years not knowing, and it is ling me." Her words came out in a rush, as though they had en dammed up years ago.

She loosened her grip on his hand, but did not let go. He put his er hand over hers, too.

"Then tell me, Emma."

She nodded. "We never involved ourselves in Irish troubles, lord," she said. "Da always said it was not our fight. After the , he severed any connections any of us had to the Society of United Irish. Some of our neighbors belonged, but Da said to ve it alone, and we did."

"Are you Catholic, Emma?" he asked.

"Aye, me and two of my brothers. Eamon and Da were Presby- ian." She released his hand then, and wiped her eyes again with soaking handkerchief. He looked in his drawer for another, l handed it to her. She accepted it with a brief smile.

"I suppose he thought we could rub along and not get in- ved," she continued, and her voice took on an edge. "And we uld have, except that I blundered. What happened then is all fault."

She bowed her head, as though the weight of her pain was too at. He moved closer, and touched her hair, his hand going to back of her neck and then her shoulder. She leaned her cheek inst his hand for a moment, as if seeking strength. Strength m me, he thought in wonder. Emma, this does reveal the mea- e of your desperation.

"Tell me," he urged.

She straightened up then, but would not look at him. He could se the shame in her, the godly sorrow that went beyond bone p, and it touched him as nothing ever had. "Emma," he said.

"Timothy—my younger brother—was ill with a cold. Da, non and Sam were away on estate business. I was in charge ause Mama was asleep from tending Tim all night. Oh, John, I 't," she said. "Don't make me."

"You have to, Emma," he insisted, feeling like a churl.

She rose and went to the window, looking out for the longest e. He turned to watch her profile, and he knew that the view saw was not the one he was familiar with out that same win- v.

"He came walking to the house at dusk. I remember the time, ause I had just lit the lamps, and told the cook to wait dinner il Da and my brothers returned."

"Who, Emma?" he asked.

She turned to look at him then. "Robert Emmet, my lord."

Suddenly he remembered. "Castle Hill," he said.

Emma nodded. "He told me his carriage had broken down o the road from Cash, and asked if he could stay the night. I . . . I [him in."

She turned back to the window and raised her fist as though strike the glass. He leaped to his feet and grabbed her hand befo she did herself an injury. She began to weep again, and he pull her onto his lap, holding her so tight that he could almost feel h sobs before they came. He listened to her sorrow, and began understand. He kissed her hair and kept her close.

"Of course you did, Emma. I am sure your mother alwa taught you to help those in trouble. But you didn't have any id who he was, did you?"

She shook her head. "No. It was just a name to me then. I to him he could stay and be welcome, too. He said it would only for the night."

He searched his mind, trying to recall the Castle Hill revolt j outside of Dublin, and Robert Emmet's attempt to stage a risin If he remembered right, it had fizzled and come to nothing.

"How old were you?" he asked, marking time, and trying help her calm down.

"I was nineteen, my lord. My little brother Tim was five." S was silent a moment more, and he could feel her relax slightl He loosened his grip on her, but kept his arm about her waist.

"When your father returned . . ." he prompted.

"Oh, he and my brothers welcomed him, too, and they sat long time over port when dinner was done." She laughed bitter] "Papa told me later they talked about hunting and fishing, and h fiancée who lived close by. He said he was on his way there wh his carriage broke down. Of course, Papa never saw a broken ca riage on the Cash road, but he didn't think of it at the time."

She realized then that she was sitting on his lap, and put h hands to her cheeks. "I am sorry, my lord. Please forgive me f being so forward!"

He smiled at her. "I put you there, Emma, and I believe I w keep you there."

He thought she would leap off his lap then, but she did not. S settled herself against him like a puppy seeking warmth. "I stayed the night, and then he was gone by morning light." S stared straight ahead then. "He was arrested by governme troops at the entrance to our estate. I think they must ha

atched us all night." She shook her head and made an impotent
esture with her hand.

It was so clear to him what had happened then that his own
ind recoiled from speech. How could they? he thought. If the
ns of nations must be atoned for at some distant judgment bar,
ngland will pay for this one.

"And they arrested your family for complicity," he whispered,
hen he could speak. "Oh, God, Emma."

She spoke then in a monotone voice, so low and chilling that he
as reminded of tales of zombies his Caribbean nursemaid told in
e nursery years and years ago. "They yanked Tim out of his
ckbed and ordered me to carry him. Da, Eamon, and Sam were
und together. Mama and I carried Tim ten miles that day to-
ard Dublin." She paused then, and her voice because wistful. "I
member that it was raining, and I lost a shoe in the mud."

"You walked all the way to Dublin?"

"Aye. Tim died on the way." She made another odd gesture
ith her hand, as though to wipe away the memory. "At least, I
n sure he did. He was burning with fever, and the captain of the
ard forced us to leave him in Diggtown with a family named
olladay." She burrowed closer to him. "His eyes were sinking
ck in his head, and there was a fearsome gurgle in his throat."

He chewed that over, letting her sit in silence until the coals
ttled in the fireplace and she sat up, startled. He pulled her back
gainst his chest again.

"The rest of you made it to Dublin?"

"Aye. Mama and I were taken to the Marlborough Street Rid-
g School where they were holding women involved in Castle
ill. The others went to Prevot Prison." She shuddered, and he
nderstood why. He had been to Prevot himself in 1798, when he
d escorted prisoners there from Cork before his own injury.

"Were they tortured?" he asked as gently as he could.

She nodded. "But they wouldn't say anything." She looked at
m, her eyes huge. "What could they say? They knew nothing!"
e pounded on his chest in her rage, then threw her arms around
m and wept.

He held her close, murmuring softly to her, devastated at the
pth of her sorrow, and understanding her deep shame. And you
ink you brought it on them all, my dear. This is too big a burden
bear alone. "This is tragic, my dear, but hardly your fault."

"I am not through," she interrupted, her voice cold. "When they
uld not speak, the English took me from Marlborough to Pre-
t and tortured me in front of them."

"Oh, God!" he exclaimed, feeling such a measure of horror and revulsion that his stomach writhed. "No, Emma!" he declared, a though his words could take it away.

She held up her left hand to him, holding it with her right to steady it. "You've noticed my fingers, my lord?" she asked, he eyes glittering with a fierce anger that burned into his body al most.

"Yes," he whispered. "They pulled out your fingernails, didn' they?"

"Aye." She looked at her hand, the fingernails grown back, bu with bumpy ridges. "I tried not to scream, but I couldn't help my self. I even bit through my lip."

"Emma, don't," he pleaded.

"You wanted to know," she said calmly. "Well, now you wil know. They told my father they were going to rape me right there That was when Eamon confessed."

"But . . ."

"Confessed to crimes he never committed, to spare me." She stood up, and there was a dignity and majesty about her. "Now you begin to understand something of what drives me, my lord. I is not pretty, is it?"

Chapter 17

No, it is not pretty, he agreed, after a night of twisting and turning in his bed until he was a prisoner of his sheets and weary with no sleep. As dawn was beginning to tinge the sky, he dragged himself to his armchair by the window and propped his bare feet on the ledge. I wonder that she can endure. May the Lord smite me if I ever whine again.

The rest of her story was told in fits and starts. How Eamon had been ripped from them and thrown into a cell for the condemned. They heard gallows under construction for some, and learned from their triumphant jailers of Robert Emmet's death by beheading. They begged, they pleaded, but the authorities did not bother to tell them who else had died, as though Irish grief was as admissible as a gnat before the face.

On his lap again, Emma spoke of her escape, her voice still wondering at the mystery of it all. They had kept her in Prevot for another week, and then suddenly all the prisoners were removed to Marlborough Street Riding School, hurried along through the streets of Dublin as night was falling.

"It was typhus, and they moved everyone," she explained into his soaked waistcoat. "Da and I were not chained together, and I now it must have been an oversight. When we passed a crowd and the guard wasn't looking, he pushed me into the mob and said, 'Indenture,' to the man who caught me."

Her voice lost some of its tightness as she told of being hustled that very night to the Dublin docks and put aboard a ship bound for America and the West Indies. "And so I came to the Clarges," she concluded. "I never thought I would have a chance to look for my family again, but when Mr. Claridge said he was sending Sally and Robert to England, I knew I had to come."

"And you have been treated shabbily," he concluded. "That will change tomorrow, Emma. We are returning to the Office of Criminal Business, and I assure you that Mr. Capper will see you."

"You would do that for me?" she asked in surprise, not realiz
ing how her spontaneous question deepened his own shame.

"Of course, Emma."

"Of course," he repeated at dawn to the window. And the
what? Will there be tidy lists of prisoners bound for Australia, c
am I only letting Emma in for more frustration and heartache? Pi
baldly, is this a kindness?

He decided that it was, as he watched, bleary-eyed an hou
later, as the maid put more coal in the grate and started the fire
He knew he looked worse than usual, because of her dartin
glances and the way she almost ran from his room. Even if Emm
continues to be disappointed at every turn, at least she will kno
that we tried everything we could, he reasoned. This was far be
ter than going through life never knowing.

Dressed and ready for the day, he came downstairs at six, su
prising Lasker. "There is no breakfast yet, my lord," he apolo
gized, even as he hurried to light the candles in the breakfa
room.

Lord Ragsdale shrugged. "Tea then, Lasker," he said, and sa
down at the empty table with the paper. He looked up at his bu
ler, whose face wore a quizzical expression. "Tell Emma to com
here."

"Yes, my lord." The butler hesitated. "I do not believe she slep
last night," he said. "The scullery maid heard her crying in th
next room."

Emma, and I was not there to hold you? he thought. I woul
have. I was sleepless only one floor below you. He considered th
paper a moment, then rejected it, struck by the fact that he was th
best friend she had at the moment. "Well, then she'll be awake
won't she?" he asked, and turned back to the paper. "Bring tw
cups."

She was there in a few minutes, pale and serious in the dee
green wool dress he had commissioned for her. He gestured to
chair, but she did not sit. He looked up.

"My lord, it is not my place to sit here," she reminded him.

"It is if I say so. Sit."

She perched on the edge of the seat, as if ready for flight if ar
other family member were to appear. He filled a teacup ar
pushed it toward her. She sipped it slowly, cradling her hanc
around the cup as though she were cold inside and out.

He read through the paper without comment, then folded it ar
looked at her. "I am remiss in something, Emma," he said.

She looked at him then, curious.

"Do you remember when I asked you what would make you happy?"

Emma nodded. "That seems so long ago, my lord."

"I think it was longer ago than either of us can really appreciate," he murmured. "You have your own bed and your own room, do you not?"

She nodded again, mystified and wondering where he was leading.

He stood up and gestured for her to follow him. "I believe you also wanted to hear Mass. Let us go."

She took him by the arm. "You don't need to do this, my lord," she said.

He took her hand and pulled her after him into the hall. "Of course I do, my dear. I will take you to St. Stephens, where you will have ample time for confession first and then Mass."

"You want me to tell this whole story to a priest," she asked, but it was more of a statement.

"I do, indeed." He allowed Lasker to help him into his overcoat, and then he waited for Emma to retrieve her cloak. "Unless I have been misjudging the Almighty all these years—and I probably have—you are about to discover that you have nothing to be forgiven for."

She said nothing as they rode toward the city, only beginning to stir now with carters and other early risers. She stared straight ahead, but he knew it was not the angry, sullen mistrust of their earlier acquaintance. Again, he had the feeling that she was seeing things out of his vision. He looked down at her hands, and noticed that they were balled into tight fists. He put his hand over hers.

"Don't worry, Emma. Have you ever considered the possibility that the Lord might be on your side?"

He could tell from her expression that she had not, and he wisely gave himself over to silence, too.

There were only a few worshipers in St. Stephen's, a small Catholic church on the outskirts of the financial district that he knew about only from driving by on several occasions. The earlier Mass had just finished, and the smell of wax was strong in the low-ceilinged chapel. Emma took a deep breath of the mingled ecclesiastical odors and sighed.

"It has been so long, my lord," she murmured as she started toward a priest who stood beside the door to a confessional. She looked back at him once, real fear in her eyes, and he longed to follow her, but he only smiled and seated himself in the back of

the church, crossing his fingers and hoping that the Lord was the
kind of fellow Lord Ragsdale thought He was.

She was a long time in the confessional, but he knew it was a
long story and felt no impatience. He was content to breathe deep
himself, and allow the aura of the place to work its way into his
spirits. When she came out, he made room for her on the bench.

He wanted to speak to her, but she dropped immediately to her
knees and began to recite the rosary, murmuring softly. She had no
beads, so she ticked off the litany on her fingers. He watched
Emma and resolved to find a rosary from somewhere for her. What
a paltry gift for someone who has given me so much, he thought.

When she finished, she sat beside him. "You were right," she
whispered.

He leaned closer until their shoulders touched. "I thought so.
Any penance?"

She smiled at him, and his heart flopped. There was nothing in
her smile of reticence, calculation or wariness this time, only a
great relief probably visible to ships at sea or Indians in distant te
pees. "He told me to recite one rosary," she whispered back.

"Small penance, my dear," he said, wishing she would turn her
marvelous, incandescent gaze on some other man.

She grinned even wider. "Faith, my lord, he's an Irish priest."

He burst into laughter, forgetting where he was. Heads turned
parishioners glowered. He rested his long legs on the prayer
bench and sank down lower in the pew, stifling the laughter that
still threatened, and thinking suddenly of Clarissa, who wouldn'
recognize a joke if it said hello.

The Mass began. He nudged her. "You know, Emma, we're
very much alike," he commented.

She digested this, her attention divided between him and the
priest at the altar. "Oh, we are?"

"I drowned myself in bitterness and alcohol, and you let yoursel
be captured by guilt. Such foolish damage we have done ourselves.'

She nodded and sighed. "I probably would have taken to the
bottle, my lord, but I had no money like you."

"Ah, my dear, the toils of the too wealthy . . ."

The parishioner in the pew in front of them turned around and
put a finger to her lips. Lord Ragsdale winked at her, and she
turned back swiftly.

"D'ye know, I think I will seek out the man I hate the most
and give him the contents of my wine cellar," he whispered to
Emma. "And my first choice is the porter at the Office of Crimi
nal Business."

She laughed this time, and the priest paused momentarily, glaring at her. "Hush, my lord," she insisted. "You are a bad influence on me. In another moment, I really will have something to confess, and it will be your fault."

Lord Ragsdale behaved himself for the rest of the Mass, marveling at the prescience of the priest to deliver his homily on forgiveness. He watched, great peace in his heart, as Emma took the sacrament at the altar, then returned to kneel beside him. He knew she was crying, and he kept his hand on her shoulder for the remainder of the service.

"Well, my dear, can we face the porter now?" he asked her in front of the church as he helped her into another hackney.

"I can face anything," she assured him.

"It may be that we learn little or nothing," he warned her. "We may come away feeling worse."

"I know, my lord," she said quietly. "But at least we will know we are trying."

Her hand tight in his, they approached the porter in the Office of Criminal Business, who practically threw himself off his stool and asked in unctuous, kindly tones if they would like to see Mr. Capper.

"Indeed we would," Lord Ragsdale said. "You must want to keep your job." He looked the cowering man in the eye. "Do you know, it probably wouldn't be too hard to get *you* transported."

To his grim amusement, they found themselves hurried into a cluttered office. "Mr. John Henry Capper," the porter announced, and then beat a hasty retreat.

Capper stood and motioned them into chairs in front of the desk. He took a few swipes at the piles of paper surrounding him, gave up, then seated himself.

"I am Lord Ragsdale, and this is my servant, Emma Costello," he began, gesturing to Emma. "She has a story for you." He sat back then, and let Emma tell it all again, leaving nothing out. He watched the clerk's face, wondering if such a man in such a job could be moved by her words. *I wonder if it is possible to become hardened to such wretchedness,* he thought, and then decided it was not. Capper listened intently, asking questions quietly, but not disturbing the flow of her narrative. Several times he passed his hand across his eyes, but his attention never wavered.

When she finished, and blew her nose on the handkerchief Lord Ragsdale kept handy, Capper looked from one to the other, his lips set in a tight line. He asked her the names of all her family members, and scribbled them on the pad in front of him.

"Your mother, Miss Costello. Do you think she is yet alive?"

Emma shook her head, and reached for Lord Ragsdale's hand again. "She was so sick when I was taken out for torture in Prevot."

Capper drew a line through her name, and Emma flinched. Lord Ragsdale tightened his grip. "And here, your little brother Timothy?" he asked, his pencil poised over the next name.

"Oh, no," she whispered. "He is the only one I am certain of."

Lord Ragsdale felt his own nerves tingling at the pencil's brief scratch.

Capper quickly drew a line through Eamon's name. "I suspect he was hanged, as you fear. You say he was separated from you after his confession?"

Emma nodded, her face pale. Capper sighed and drew a circle around the two remaining names. He stared at them a moment, as though wishing the names would turn into information, then reached behind him to pull down a ledger. He searched through the pages, then opened it on his desk.

"Miss Costello, you must be aware of one thing that might render any search futile. A great number of those Irish insurrectionists were never tried, but were sent directly to Australia or Van Diemen's Land. I am telling you this, because there will likely be no record of them in any Home Office or judicial files."

"They just vanish then, as though they had never lived?" Lord Ragsdale asked in amazement.

Capper nodded. "It certainly makes for untidy records," he said.

"Damn your records," Lord Ragsdale said. "These are people we are talking about."

"I know, my lord, I know," Capper said. He directed his attention to Emma. "Miss Costello, I can think of only one way to learn anything, and that is to locate the ship's manifests for those convict voyages. They may or may not contain the information you seek on prisoner rosters."

He turned back to the ledger and ruffled through several more pages before pausing. He pounded on the ledger in triumph. "And here we have the ships, my dear." He leaned closer to the book, then began to write on his pad again. "There were six ships in the 1804 transport." He looked up at them. "And we are only assuming here that they were transported in 1804, and not 1805. It could not have been 1805?"

Emma shook her head. "I think it was almost October when I was taken to Prevot."

"Well, then, here we are. The *Minerva*, the *Lady Penthyn*, the

iendship, the *Marquess Cornwallis*, the *Britannia*, and the *Her-
les*." He wrote down the names of the ships and handed it to
nma. He spoke to Lord Ragsdale. "I will send you with a porter
the Home Office archives. I do not know that they can offer
u any assistance, but the records could be there."

Lord Ragsdale rose and shook hands with Capper. "We appre-
te your efforts."

"It was paltry," he said, nodding to Emma. "And you must also
lize, my dear, that even if you discover they were transported,
t is far from being a guarantee that they are alive."

"I know that," Emma replied, looking at the names on the
per she held. "But I must try."

Capper nodded and walked them to the door. He handed a note
the porter, who led them quickly through the corridors to the
me Office, looking over his shoulder in fear at Lord Ragsdale
eral times. They followed him up a flight of narrow stairs and
o a room filled with file boxes. "Criminal Business there in the
ner," he said, gesturing to a row of boxes stuffed on shelves.

"You are all kindness," Lord Ragsdale murmured. He rubbed
forehead, feeling the beginnings of a headache. "Well,
ma," he began when the porter left. "Shall we start?"

Hours later, his head was pounding in dreadful earnest as he
sed, and looked at the pile of papers that surrounded them. His
od eye was beginning to tear and blur, and he knew he was de-
ted. Emma watched him from the middle of her pile of papers,
l he could see nothing but concern in her eyes.

"You have to stop, Lord Ragsdale," she said, her voice practi-
, as though she admonished him over tea and biscuits. "I am
covering how much I can bear, but I could not bear it if you
the sight in your eye because of this."

"I'm sorry, Emma," he began, but she stopped him with a gesture.
"I'll stay here a little longer," she said. "Why don't you go
ne?"

"I feel like a quitter," he protested. "Perhaps if I just lie down
a while and close my eye . . ."

"I won't hear of it," she insisted as she got to her feet and
led him to his. "You used to tease me about 'too much exer-
, ' but this is truly too much for you. Just leave me a little
ney for hackney fare."

He fished in his pocket for some change and handed it to her.
e can return tomorrow . . ." he began, then sighed in exaspera-
. "Damn! Emma, I am to go to Bath tomorrow with Clarissa
ridge!"

She smiled at him, "That is hardly lover-like, my lord. It good thing I do not intend to tattle to her. I will return here ton row, if I have your permission. And you will go to Bath and your fate."

He wished she would not put it like that, and nearly told her Before he could speak, she stood before him on tiptoe, dabbed at his eye. "Please go right home, and have Lasker you a cold cloth for that. I'll follow soon enough. I promise."

"Oh, very well," he grumbled.

He was still muttering to himself as he descended all th stairs and found himself on the street again. He hailed a hack gave his direction, and sank into it with some relief as the ja cracked his whip and they started off. He closed his eye, won ing if he would be dreaming of ships and lists all night, and p ing that Mama and Sally had no evening plans that would af him beyond a little polite conversation over dinner.

They had traveled several blocks toward Mayfair when he denly realized where they had gone wrong. He sat up, pounded on the side of the cab. "Stop this thing!" he roared.

The jarvey did as he was bid. "Sir?" he asked in frosty surp

"Turn around," Lord Ragsdale said decisively. "Take me to docks."

He sank back into the cab two hours later, just as the sun going down. He could scarcely see out of his good eye, an wondered how much of a peal Emma would ring over him. held the lists tight in his hand and brought them close to his f "Yes!" he said in triumph, and closed his eye for the return tri

His eye had stopped blurring by the time the jarvey let hin at Curzon Street, and he had no trouble negotiating the ste his front door. He knew that Emma would be waiting for hir soon as he opened the door, and she was. He wanted to grab and whirl her about, but the look on her face brought him quickly to his own state.

"Where have you been?" she asked, and she helped him his coat, ignoring Lasker, who hovered nearby. "I have beer side myself."

He knew she was telling the truth. Her own eyes were p from crying, and it touched him to the bone that she care much. He let her help him to the book room, where she pu him down on the sofa and told Lasker to bring a cold cloth fo eye, scolding all the while.

"I am certain your doctors tell you not to strain your eye

d," she said as she took off his shoes and made him swing his
gs onto the sofa. She covered him with a light blanket and gen-
put the cloth to his eye when Lasker returned. The darkness
is soothing, and he almost allowed himself to sleep. The lists.
· sat up, even as she tried to push him down again.
"Emma, don't be a carbuncle," he protested. "Hand me my
ercoat. I have something for you."
She did as he asked. He kept the cloth to his eye as he groped in
inside lining. He held up the sheaf of papers to her. "I was start-
; home when it occurred to me that I should check some ships' of-
es at the docks. Emma, we were looking at this problem from the
ong end!" He handed her the papers and lay back down again.
'My lord, these are three rosters!" she said, her voice filled
th wonder.
He grinned at her. "There they were, languishing on yet an-
er dusty shelf. Mr. Capper didn't stop to consider that some-
es the prisoners were transported in vessels contracted by the
yal Navy, and other times, by commercial carriers arranged by
Colonial Office. I can only conclude that 1804 was a year for
merchants, and not the navy." He paused then, and took the
th off his eye. "Much better, Emma." He raised up on his
ow. "I do have some bad news. The *Lady Penthyn* went down
a gale with all hands."
She considered that information, sitting beside him on the sofa.
intend to believe they were not on that ship," she said quietly.
e looked at the papers in her hands. "Thank you, my lord."
'You're ever so welcome, Emma," he said. "You peruse them,
I then I must see the lists are returned. I have promised half my
gdom and my firstborn son as ransom for those rosters."
he smiled, and looked at the lists. "That leaves the *Hercules*
I the *Minerva* unaccounted for now. No trace of them?"
'None," he agreed, "but they're out there somewhere. They
e to belong to someone."
Emma nodded, then looked up as Lasker came into the room.
es?" she asked. "Lord Ragsdale should not be disturbed, if you
help it, Lasker." She rested her hand on his shoulder, and his
ran over with the pleasure of it all. "He's had such a day."
Then I hate to add to the misery" came a vaguely familiar
ce. "Lord Ragsdale, may I trouble you to take your miserable
sin off my hands before he causes the complete downfall of
ord University?"

Chapter 18

He sat up quickly, despite Emma's protests, and slowly to the compress off his good eye, hoping that when he did his sight would have returned to normal, and it would not Robert Claridge smiling down at him.

But it was Robert, and there was his old warden fr Brasenose, even more grim-lipped than usual, standing bes him. As he stared at his cousin, Robert's grin widened, as thou he had never been so happy to see anyone.

"My God," said Lord Ragsdale. He had long believed the ap rypha that the warden never even left the quadrangle Brasenose, much less ventured to London. And here he is, glar at me, he thought. Oh, the wonder of it all. He sank back down the sofa again, and put the compress over both eyes. "I think I hallucinating, Emma. Please wake me in an hour or two wl both of these gentlemen have disappeared."

It seemed a reasonable request, but in another moment, warden was leaning over the back of the sofa and staring dow him. "Lord Ragsdale, remove that cloth at once and listen to m he uttered in crisp tones, when Lord Ragsdale continued to co behind his compress.

Lord Ragsdale did as he was told. Not for nothing had he s fered through two interminable years at Oxford with this ward He would be compliant; he would grovel, if, indeed, grove were needed. And that appeared to be the case. There was noth remotely pleasant in the gaze that the warden fixed upon him. deftly tossed the compress into a wastebasket, stood up, would have promptly sat down again, if Emma hadn't been th to support him. He opened his mouth to apologize, but he had reckoned on his little secretary.

"Sir, I wish you would leave," she said, addressing the war in tones as stringent as his own. "Lord Ragsdale has had a ra trying day, and he does not need this kind of donnybrook."

I have had a trying day? he asked himself, as his estimatio

nma rose another level. My dear, you must be full to bursting
th anxieties, and you are worried about me? He looked at the
arden, determined not to whine or grovel, after all. If Emma
esn't, I won't, he decided. I'd like to think I have learned some-
ng in these few months.

"Please be seated, sir," he said, indicating a chair. He sat down
ain. "Tell me what my wretched cousin has been up to. I am
ger to know whether we should flog him, place him in irons,
rl him into the ranks, or let some damned bird or other peck out
s liver while we chain him to a rock."

To his gratification, the warden blinked and sat down. "Well, I
not know as it is all that serious . . ." he began, almost put off
Lord Ragsdale's plain speaking. Then the ill-used look came
o his eyes again, and he leaned forward. "Your cousin has per-
trated the most fiendish deed ever to sully the golden stones of
r fair university on the Isis." He sat back in triumph, daring
rd Ragsdale to respond.

"Oh, surely not," he replied easily, with a glance at his cousin.
obert is not intelligent enough to bring down a . . . let me see
w . . . six-hundred-year-old institution. I seem to remember a
ltitude of pranks, especially one involving a number of naked
n and a traveling circus. Please be more specific, warden."

'Was that *you,* sir?" Robert interrupted, his eyes wide. "That is
l talked about in hushed tones."

"Oh, really?" Lord Ragsdale asked, pleased with himself, and
dly overlooking the choking sounds coming from Emma as
e went to the window and stood there with her back to the men.

'It was cards, Lord Ragsdale, cards!" said the warden indig-
tly playing his own trump. "Exactly as you warned him."

Oh, damn, thought Lord Ragsdale wearily. Does this mean I
l actually have to make good on my promise, and send this
less fribble into the army? I feel sorry for our side already. He
sted around to look at his American relative, who was still
nding by the door. "Well, sit down, lad, sit down where I can
 you, and tell me the whole sordid tale."

Robert sat next to him, which Lord Ragsdale thought a bold
ce of impertinence, considering the cloud of ruin that hung
r him. He continued to smile with an expression that Lord
gsdale could only call cherubic. His eyes were even a little
amy.

John, it was the most magnificent opportunity, and I could not
st. I tried, though, I really did. Imagine, if you will, all those
n in each hall and quad. It was, it was . . ." Robert raised his

hands helplessly. "Words fail me," he concluded in a mode
tone.

"They don't fail me!" said the warden, pointing his finger
Robert Claridge. "He organized what he called a floating pok
game that traveled from college to college, until the entire unive
sity was involved. It was scandalous!"

"The whole university?" Lord Ragsdale asked, his voice an o
tave higher than usual. "Even those tight rumps at All Souls? C
pardon, warden, that was *your* school wasn't it?"

"Oh, especially them," Robert said, warming to his subject.
think they were dashed grateful to be asked to join in the fun." I
cast a kindly glance at the warden, who was turning whiter by t
second. "Really, I think they ought to get out more, sir."

The warden leaped to his feet, stabbed the air with his fing
then sank into his chair again, a much older man. Emma snatch
up the ships' rosters and began to fan him, crooning little nonse
sicals until he regained his color and waved her away.

"You should know there were vast sums involved," he co
cluded, enunciating carefully.

Lord Ragsdale sighed. "I was almost certain there were, si
He fixed his blurry eye on his cousin. "What do you have to say

"Only that it will never happen again."

Lord Ragsdale and the warden sighed in unison and then
dulged in a hearty bout of silence, which was broken at last
Robert.

"I suppose you do not wish me to continue at Brasenose,"
said to the warden, his tone hopeful.

"Most emphatically not," the warden stated. "We will be luc
if anyone decides to study again before the end of term." He a
pealed to Lord Ragsdale. "And now, my lord, what are *you* goi
to do with this worthless bit of pond water?"

By God, I wish you would stop grinning in that idiotic fashi
Lord Ragsdale thought, looking at his cousin. "I will think
something terrible," he told the warden. "It will probably be
bad that it will even eclipse the naked men and the circus."

The warden waited expectantly, but Lord Ragsdale only smi
and rose to his feet, extending his hand. "Thank you so much
bringing him here in person, sir," he said.

"I wouldn't have it any other way," the warden replied.
would not for a minute wish this American on an unsuspect
population!"

Lord Ragsdale nodded. "I share your concern. I trust we w
meet again in future under more kindly conditions."

The warden shook his hand, and moved purposefully to the
~~r~~, which opened as if by magic. Lasker, his face utterly un-
~~able~~, stood there to usher him out. The warden looked back at
~~bert~~ and shuddered, then delivered his parting shot.

"We will *not* meet again, my lord. Should you, by some grave
~~chance~~, ever find a consenting female, marry, and reproduce
~~urself~~, do not send your offspring within a mile or two of Ox-
~~d~~."

~~Lord~~ Ragsdale took it all in, and managed to avoid catching
~~ma~~'s eye. If I look at you, I am doomed, he thought. "Very
~~l~~, warden, very well," he said, his voice contrite, and almost
~~hout~~ a quaver. "The lady I am contemplating an alliance with
~~es~~ from a Cambridge family, so we need not ever trouble you
~~in~~." He looked at Lasker, who held the door for the warden.
~~sker~~, because the warden is still so upset with us, you have my
~~mission~~ to slam the door on your way out. Ah. Excellent."

~~How~~ I wish I could laugh, he thought after the slam had fin-
~~d~~ reverberating throughout the main floor. He turned instead
~~Robert~~, then sat down.

Now that I am seated, you can tell me the total of your
~~es~~." He glanced at Emma. "I cannot tell you how delighted I
~~to~~ have a problem that I can solve merely by throwing money
. This will be close to a pleasure, Robert."

~~t~~ was Robert's turn to stare at him. "Cousin, you have
~~nged~~," he exclaimed.

~~I~~ suppose I have," Lord Ragsdale agreed, pleasantly surprised
~~someone~~ noticed. "Come on, tell me what I am to pay, and to
~~m~~."

~~Robert~~ pursed his lips and perused the carpet for some time, as
~~ugh~~ seeking guidance. When he looked up, he still had that
~~grin~~ on his face. It's entirely possible that I could throttle
~~yet~~, Lord Ragsdale thought. I wish he would not chortle over
~~upcoming~~ losses.

~~Cousin~~, I think you do not perfectly understand the situation,"
~~ert~~ began, choosing his words carefully.

~~Oh~~, no?" Lord Ragsdale asked.

~~No~~, sir, you do not." Robert leaned forward, and looked
~~nd~~ as though the warden were within ten or twelve blocks. "I
~~this~~ time." He looked at Emma. "Seven thousand pounds,
~~na~~!"

~~Lord~~ Ragsdale closed his eye. Emma gasped and sank down
~~de~~ him on the sofa. He reached over and patted her. "Tell me

I heard what I heard, Emma. My eyes are gone, my hearing going. Who knows what will go next?"

"You heard me," Robert insisted. "I won fair and square." opened his blue eyes wider. "Of course, I don't think that Br are any great shakes at poker yet. It may take some time." pulled up a chair closer to the sofa. "That's what I want to talk you about."

Lord Ragsdale opened his eye. "You want to pay me back?" asked

"Possibly," Robert temporized. "I could pay you back, and th I could release Emma from her indenture." His voice became co trite, hesitant even. "It's the least I can do, Emma. I know tha has not been a pleasant situation for you."

"It's not that troublesome," she said simply, looking down the unread ships' rosters she still held in her hands.

"You could do that," Lord Ragsdale said, wishing sudder that Robert were still at Oxford, and had never considered pok Couldn't you have waited a week or so, Robert? he wanted to a I'm busy here with something of substance for the first time my life.

But Robert was not through. He looked at Emma until s glanced up and met his eyes. "Emma, may I tell you what I wo rather do with the money?"

She nodded, and set aside the rosters. Lord Ragsdale could f her tension, so he moved closer until their shoulders were tou ing.

"I would rather take all the money and go home, throw mys on my father's mercy, and start repaying him what I owe." looked at Lord Ragsdale soberly. "I truly do not wish to gam again. What would you have me do, John?" he asked.

I would have you take the money and run, Lord Ragsd thought. Go home to Virginia, and leave Emma and me to s through this terrible time. He looked at Emma, who was rega ing the carpet as Robert had earlier, and chewing on her lip.

"I think it should be Emma's decision, Robert," he said fina "She's the one who has suffered the most from all this and—"

"Oh, I have not suffered," she interrupted quickly. She blush and held out her hands to Robert. "I was prepared to, and mayl even wanted to, but I have not suffered. And Robert, you wo believe what I have learned."

Robert smiled at her. "He's right, Emma. What do you w me to do?"

Please, Emma, do not leave me, Lord Ragsdale thought. If

go, I am sure I will not have the courage to propose to Clarissa and "fix my fate," as you so ingenuously expressed it. I might not treat my servants right, or keep away from alcohol, or find anyone half so fine to handle my correspondence.

"Your decision, Emma," he added, determined not to hold his breath and appear like a small boy.

She picked up the rosters again and looked at him, then at Robert. "Take your money and go home, Mr. Claridge," she said quietly. "I know your father will be pleased." She touched Lord Ragsdale's hand. "Lord Ragsdale has promised to release me when he is engaged, and I think he has almost reached that point. I want you to go home, Mr. Claridge."

Robert leaped to his feet, pulled Emma up, too, and swung her round until she protested and told him to let her down. He kissed her on both cheeks, and hugged her until Lord Ragsdale feared for her ribs.

"Emma, you are a game goer!" he said. "I will leave you enough money to pay your passage back to Virginia, if you should choose to rejoin us. I am sure Father will find you a position as a teacher, or nursemaid." He went to the door. "And now I want to find Sally and tell her." He leaned against the door. "Thanks, John and Emma. I wonder why I never noticed before what wonderful people you are."

"Perhaps because we were not so wonderful," Lord Ragsdale commented, after Robert left the room. He looked at Emma. "My dear, I will release you from your indenture anytime you say."

She took that in, and settled herself more comfortably on the sofa, kicking off her shoes. "We have not yet finished the bargain, my lord." She got up suddenly then and went to the desk. "Now I think you should write a note to Miss Partridge and tell her that you will be at her home first thing in the morning, so you can set out for Bath."

He joined her at the desk, sitting down and picking up the quill. "I know she will do terrible things, like make me propose," he grumbled.

"And it will be good for you," Emma insisted. "When you are finished, I will give it to Lasker and tell him to have the footman deliver it tonight."

He did as she said, pausing here and there for advice on lover-like words. He finished and signed his name with a flourish. "I suppose you realize this means that I will be reformed, rehabilitated, married, and will probably turn into someone so dull that my children will wonder what their mother was thinking."

She smiled at him. "Serves you right, my lord," she replied with just a touch of her former acidity. She took the note from him and opened the door upon Lasker, who appeared to be waiting outside. "Please have Hanley deliver this to the Partridges on Whitcomb Street," she instructed.

"And bring us some coffee, Lasker," Lord Ragsdale said as he returned to the sofa. "It's going to be a long night."

"I told you to go to bed and rest your eye," Emma said, then blushed and added, "my lord."

He resumed his former position on the couch. "I won't leave, Emma. Sit down right here and let's start looking."

I am seeing the backside of too many dawns, he reflected several hours later as Emma finally admitted defeat after two readings of the lists. I would have quit after one reading, he thought, closing his eye to the smudged, faint lists, and weary of looking.

Ever mindful of his eye, Emma had done much of the reading, going slowly through the lists, saying each name aloud, and only troubling him when she could not decipher the words before her. He lay with his eye closed, listening to her, holding his breath when she paused, and sitting up once or twice when he heard her sharp intake of breath. But each time was a false alarm. There was no David or Samuel Costello on any of the lists they had searched so hard for.

"Could it be that the political prisoners were not even mentioned?" he speculated at one point. "I mean, if the assizes have no record, why should the ships' manifests?"

It was a discouraging thought, but early morning was a time for discouraging thoughts. Emma considered it a moment, then rejected it. "I cannot see how that would be so," she argued. "A ship would need to know precisely how many were on board concerning matters of space and food."

"I am sure you are right," he said, happy to agree with her.

And so she had read through the manifests two more times, grumbling the second time about ship captains, and bad handwriting. On the third reading, her voice was subdued. Finally, after the clock chimed three, she put down the lists.

"They're not here," she admitted.

She sat on the floor beside the sofa, leaning against it. He reached down and rested his hand on her shoulder. "Emma, do you really think they ever left Ireland?" he asked quietly.

She was silent for a moment as she rested her cheek against his hand. "Yes," she said finally. "They were in good health, and as Eamon"—her voice faltered—"Eamon who confessed to verything." She drew up her knees and rested her chin on them. Do you know, the interrogators pressed him for other names of ccomplices, and he recited the whole family graveyard." She rned her head to regard him. "No. Eamon implicated no one se alive. They had no reason to kill Da and Sam, too. No rea- n."

"Well, then, we must find the *Minerva* and the *Hercules*," he id. "Give me a hand up, Emma."

She stood up, rubbed the small of her back, then helped him to s feet. "I suppose it can keep until you return from Bath," she id as she placed the lists on the desk.

"Emma, you have my permission to return to the docks and eck some more," he said. "Only please take the footman with u, and enough petty cash for bribes. Oh, and return the lists to- orrow."

She nodded. "I'll make sure you have receipts for anything I end."

"It's not necessary, Emma." He opened the door, surprised how rk the hall was, then remembering that everyone else was long bed. "I'm so tired," he said, more to himself than to her. And scouraged, and wondering when this will end for you.

They walked upstairs together, and she said good night to him the landing that led to the servants' quarters on the third floor. mma, stay with me tonight, he thought suddenly. It's only a few urs before dawn, and I'm a little low in spirits.

He shook his head at the thought and wished it would go away. t there it was, dancing about in his head like a little shadow ppet. I do not wish to do anything to you—I'm too tired for at—but I would like to hold you in my arms.

"My lord," Emma said, her hand on the railing.

He looked up expectantly, wondering if by some miracle she uld read his mind, and was not opposed to the idea.

"Yes, my dear?" he asked, his voice soft.

He could hear her chuckle in the gloom, even though he could t see her. "You should know that I made another confession s morning."

Her tone was playful, but not amorous, so he put away his own guish thoughts. "Say on, Emma."

She must have sat down on the stairs, because he heard a rustle skirts, and her voice was lower. "When I went to Fae Moullé, . . . I encouraged her to cheat you. The receipt we compiled her milliner's shop was greatly more than she really needed."

"Emma, you're a rascal," he said, amused where a month ag‍
he would have been angry. "You wanted to cost me money."

"I hated you, my lord," she said simply, her voice coming ‍
him so quiet from the darkness of the stairs. "You were just a‍
other Englishman."

He felt his way to the landing again, and rested his arm on th‍
newel post, not certain of where she was. "Well, what penan‍
did the priest suggest?"

She laughed, and got to her feet, and he could tell that she w‍
farther away than he thought. "Remember, I told you he w‍
Irish, too! He told me to pray for your soul, but only if I thought ‍
wanted to."

He joined in her laughter. "And do you?" he asked finally.

"Oh, I already have," she said quickly, and she seemed almo‍
surprised at his question. "Good night, my lord. I'll be in the boo‍
room for your instructions in the morning."

And then she was gone, hurrying up the stairs to her little cu‍
byhole under the eaves. In another moment he heard a door clo‍
quietly.

Chapter 19

Could it be that this is what the French aristocrats felt like on their way to the guillotine? Lord Ragsdale thought, as the Partridge carriage rumbled on its sedate way to Bath. He could almost imagine the cheering, cockaded crowds milling about and ready for a whiff of blood.

But this is absurd, he thought, as he smiled down at Clarissa Partridge, who had captured his hand so possessively and pressed her thigh against his in a manner that was faintly pleasant. When they clamp me to the board, slide me under the blade, and we are pronounced man and wife, I will be the envy of my generation. Envious males will probably drink my health in clubs all over London, and marvel at my good fortune. The thought sent a shudder through him, which he could only ascribe to feet of the coldest sort.

See here, John, he told himself, it is merely that you are afraid or nothing. Surely every man experiences some little trepidation the loss of liberty, and at the reality of life with a wife. He returned his gaze to Clarissa again, admiring the gold of her hair, and her flawless complexion. Clarissa, if you happened to throw out freckles like Emma Costello, you would probably lock yourself in a dark room and remain there. But there was no danger on that head. Clarissa possessed skin that most women could only dream about.

"Don't you agree, John?"

What? What? Clarissa was gazing at him with something akin adoration, and obviously waiting for an answer. "How could I disagree with you, my dear?" he replied, hoping that would satisfy, and wondering to what he had just put his imprimatur.

She appeared satisfied with his response, if he rightly interpreted the little squeeze she gave his arm. Pay attention, John, he admonished himself, even as her voice rippled on and he thought about his departure that morning.

Sally Claridge had met him in the breakfast room with the star-

tling announcement that she was returning to Virginia wit
Robert. He had sputtered into his tea briefly, reminding her th
there were several young bucks—chaps he had handpicked, min
you, because they did not require a fortune—who were hoverin
on the brink of offering for her. She only treated this magnanim
ity on his part by a smile and a kiss in his general direction as sh
breezed by.

"I would rather go home," she had insisted when Lady Rags
dale added her admonitions to his. Sally smiled at him, then
Robert. "I am mindful of all you have both done for me, but
want to go home."

His pride piqued, Lord Ragsdale appealed to Robert. "Let m
remind you, cousin, that for reasons which you know only to
well, Sally will make a much better marriage over here."

Robert was no help. He only shook his head and dug a litt
deeper into his eggs and ham. "Cousin, you don't really argu
with women, do you?"

"Well, I, no . . ." he stammered.

Clarissa looked at him, her eyes wide, her lips in their read
made pout, and he realized he was talking out loud. "My dear,
don't think I would be a disappointment to you behind a curric
of my own," she was saying. "Papa taught me to handle the ril
bons."

"Oh! I am certain you would not," he agreed. "Whatever cou
I have been thinking?" Pay attention, you cloth wit, he told hir
self, then promptly dismissed Clarissa again.

Sally was not about to change her mind. "I will return home
Virginia," she had stated firmly, after he went through a patente
catalog of reasons why she should remain in England. "Cousin
do not care how poor we Claridges are, or how everyone else
Henrico County laughs at us because of Robert's spendthri
ways." She smiled at her brother. "I know he means to chang
and besides all that, I want to be with my family. It's where I b
long."

Of course she is right, he thought, as the carriage travel
through the spring finery of Berkshire. He listened patiently th
to Clarissa's description of the rest of this year's Season, and t
twin delights of a ball and a presentation next month, which,
knew in his bones, would somehow involve him to an unpleasa
degree. He nodded where he was supposed to, and felt some sm
relief when Clarissa's eyes closed and her adorable head came
rest against his arm. Lady Partridge smiled indulgently at hi
and returned to her tatting.

And so he had given his blessing for a happy journey to both of the Claridges, had finished his breakfast, and had adjourned to the book room, where Emma waited with his correspondence to sign. He signed where she indicated, and was struck by the fact that if Emma found that her father and brother had indeed been transported, she would probably want to join them in Australia.

The thought was distressing in the extreme. He sat on the sofa and watched her as she finished some last-minute paperwork he had requested. She was young and strong and healthy, but the thought of her going to such a place made him want to rise up in protest. He had heard stories at his club from army officers who had returned from duty in the antipodes, and they had nothing kind to say. It would be the worst exile of all for someone so lovely, vibrant—for someone with such promise—as Emma, he decided. And she would be fifteen thousand miles away. She might as well be on the moon.

It was a melancholy reflection; the idea of losing his secretary pained him. I could keep her in the indenture, he told himself as he came closer and looked over her shoulder at the ledger and her careful entries. But that would be heartless, and if I have discovered anything this spring, it is that I have a heart. It is a dashed nuisance, but there you are.

But Emma among convicts? Emma condemned to toil for her bread in such an inhospitable climate? Emma so far away? I will not think about it, he told himself firmly. There is no indication that we are any closer to a solution to her mystery, and for all we know, the Costellos went down with the *Lady Penthyn*. He sighed and kissed the top of Clarissa's head, then leaned back, closed his eyes, and wondered why on earth he had felt compelled to kiss Emma when he left.

They had just finished the most prosaic of conversations in the book room, like many others during the last few months. She had assured him that she would return to the dock for another look, and that she would participate in his banker's upcoming audit. She even promised to go to Norfolk with Lady Ragsdale, if he did not return after two weeks, and check out progress on the construction.

Maybe I shouldn't have put my arm around her shoulder, he considered as the carriage bowled along. He had thought it was a brotherly gesture, perhaps even avuncular. He had not been surprised particularly when her arm went around his waist as they walked together to the book-room door. Truth to tell, they had both been through a lot in the past week.

But why had he kissed her? She had done nothing in particul
to encourage it, other than look at him when he was raving
about being pitchforked into a visit to Bath that was destined
end in his proposal to Clarissa. It wasn't his fault that she got th
twinkle in her eyes when he started to complain about exertic
and ill-usage. And truth to tell, probably nothing would have ha
pened, if she had not stopped, put her hand on his shoulder, a
straightened his neck cloth.

It must have been Emma's fault, he decided, because I w
only falling back on natural instinct. He thought about the matte
concluding that the experience was inevitable, considering th
every time previous to his reformation that he got that close to
woman, he invariably kissed her. You put water in a streambe
and it will flow, he reasoned. If you place Lord Ragsdale
breathless proximity to a female who is not a relative, he will ki
her. It happens ten times out of ten, whether kisses or water. "H
draulics," he murmured, then nodded and smiled at Lady Pa
tridge when she looked up from the intricacies of her tatting wi
a faintly puzzled expression.

A mere few months ago, that would have been enough explana
tion to satisfy him. He would have promptly dismissed the eve
from his mind, and gone on to other conquests. Things are diffe
ent now, he thought. I am now blessed with a modicum of sens
and my sense tells me that I enjoy kissing Emma Costello.

The motion of putting his hand under her chin and his lips
hers had required not an iota of thought, so practiced was h
lovemaking. The part that so unsettled him then, and that w
breaking out sweat on his forehead now, was the way Emma
lips and then her embrace made him feel.

He eased out his pocket watch, so as not to disturb the sleepi
Clarissa, and consulted it. Up until half past seven this morning
kissed females with the idea of what I would get out of the e
change, he thought. Kissing Emma was the first time ever tha
wanted to give more than receive. I wanted to let her know th
someone cared what happens to her. I wanted to share n
strength, I who have never been strong. That one little kiss—we
perhaps it was not so little—made me better than I ever was I
fore.

He looked out the window at the glorious spring, and wish
himself back in the book room. He tried to imagine how he wou
replay that good-bye again, and he could not envision any oth
conclusion. As surely as God made sinners and fools to test
world, he would have kissed Emma Costello. The thought sho

him to his very soul, and he felt tears starting behind his eye. Why did I have to do the most stupid thing of all? he berated himself. Why did I have to fall in love with Emma?

At his insistence, they stopped for the night at Market Quavers. "I do not know why we cannot stop at Reading," Clarissa protested, her pout more pronounced than usual. "I mean we usually stop in Reading."

Well, too bad, he wanted to say, change your blasted routine. Instead, he kissed his love's forehead. "I have a banking transaction to undertake in the morning, my dear," he explained, tucking his arm through hers as he escorted her to the Quail and Covey.

She suffered him to lead her along, pausing only at the doorway for another attempt to reason with him. When it failed, she gave him a searching look. "This quite cuts up my peace," she assured him.

"I trust you will forgive me," he said with a smile, all the while writhing inside and wondering if he had been so vacuous before his reformation. The realization that he had been that petty and more so did nothing to raise his spirits.

He allowed her to tease him into an explanation, partly to placate her for the disruption to her usual itinerary. "I wish to begin an annuity for Mrs. Mary Roney, the sister of my former secretary. That is all, Clarissa."

He paused, knowing that she would fawn over him for his kindness to the downtrodden, and embarrass him with her praise. He waited uneasily for her to laud him for such benevolence to someone who had cheated him. What she said surprised him.

"You cannot be serious," Clarissa said, her voice a trifle flat, the music gone out of it.

"Of course I am," he replied, wondering where this was going.

"You are actually going to *help* the sister of the man who robbed you?"

He nodded. "It seems about the least I can do for David Breedlow, who only thieved from me to help his sister in her great need."

"John, what do you think prisons are for?" she asked, stamping her foot. "A servant should never steal from his master."

"Not even when the master was a stupid lout who should have cared enough to see to his servant's needs?" He heard his voice rising. "Clarissa, there is a man on his way to exile and possible death in a place I wouldn't wish on a dog because I whined about twenty pounds."

Clarissa, her eyes big at his outburst, yanked her arm from h[is]
and hurried to her mother's side. "I can only hope that you do n[o]
dole out too much of your income to gutter rats."

There will still be plenty of it left, and then some, for your rib[-]
bons, hats, and shoes, he thought. "But I thought you wer[e]
pleased when I mentioned my work among the prisons?" h[e]
asked, reminding her of his fiction of several days ago.

"It is one thing to take Bible tracts and jellies to prisoners, b[ut]
it is quite another to give them your money and encourage them,[]
she said. "Come, Mother. I feel a headache coming on."

He ate in solitary splendor in the private dining room tha[t]
night, and the food was excellent. To aid his digestion, he wen[t]
for a long walk that took him through the village, out into the su[r-]
rounding farmland, and back again. On the walk out, he had a[l-]
most convinced himself not to make Clarissa Partridge an offe[r.]
On the way back, he realized that was impossible.

She expects me to propose, he thought, and I would be un[-]
gentlemanly not to. My reformation will be complete, and I wi[ll]
free Emma from her indenture. If she ever finds that her fath[er]
and brother are truly in Australia, she will go to them. He stoo[d]
still in the road and watched the lamps lit in houses on the villag[e]
outskirts. And even if she never leaves England, she has seen m[e]
at my worst, and could not possibly want anything to do with me[.]

No, he would speak to Clarissa's father tomorrow in Bath, pro[-]
pose, present her with a stupefying diamond, and become an un[-]
exceptionable husband. No one would ever know that he was [in]
love with his secretary. How odd it is, he considered, that here [I]
am, trying to help Emma find her relatives. If I succeed, she wi[ll]
certainly leave.

"The old Ragsdale never would have done this," he said o[ut]
loud to a cow by the fence. "The old Ragsdale would hav[e]
dragged his feet and whined, and not lifted a finger to help, esp[e-]
cially if by so doing, he ruined his own chances. I am a fool."

He walked back slowly, trying to figure out at what point h[e]
fell in love with Emma. As he stood outside the tavern, he rea[l-]
ized that he must have felt something that night she stood besi[de]
him with her fate resting on the turn of a card. Is it possible th[at]
what I took for hopeless submissiveness was courage on a sca[le]
so great that my own puny resources could not measure it? he r[e-]
flected. Was that when something in me began to understa[nd]
what Emma Costello meant?

He couldn't go inside. He stood beside the door, wondering [at]
the workings of fate. If things had been different, Emma, perha[ps]

ou could have loved me, too. How tragic for us, this endless war
etween our people. You have been misunderstood, scotched, lied
o, and diddled at every turn. I can only be grateful that at least
ou do not hate me anymore.

Clarissa was in good spirits in the morning. When he returned
rom his errand at the bank, she condescended to take his arm and
llow him to walk with her to the waiting carriage. He helped her
nside, then climbed in after her.

Lady Partridge was still inside the inn, giving a portion of her
nind she could ill spare to the landlord over the damp sheets. He
urned to Clarissa. Now was as good a time as any. He took a
eep breath.

"Clarissa, I am sure you are aware of my pleasure in your com-
any." I should take her hand, he thought, so he did. "I wonder if
ou would do me the honor, the ineffable honor, of consenting to
ecome my wife."

There. That wasn't so difficult. It was words strung together,
nd from Clarissa's reaction, they were the right ones. She
queezed his hand, and he returned the pressure.

"I know a lady ought to turn down a first proposal," she said,
nd his heart rose for a moment. "But I shall not," she continued,
for I fear it would disappoint you, my dear. Yes, I will be your
ife. Nothing would make me happier than to put some regularity
nto your disordered life."

He almost winced at her words, and by the greatest effort
hoked back his own indignation. Regularity? Regularity? he
anted to shout. I am so regular now that Greenwich could set its
lock by me. You will make me boring, and prosy, and stuffy,
nd my children will only suffer me. They'll never know there
as a time when I was fun, and a bit of a rakehell.

"I am so pleased," he said, and kissed her.

It was a test, really, and not a kiss, and he failed. Her lips were
very bit as soft as Emma's, and if anything, her bosom pressing
gainst him was more bountiful than Emma's, but he felt nothing
eyond the usual stirrings of the healthy male. He could have
issed the most veteran doxy at Vauxhall, and felt nothing more.
he wasn't Emma, and he didn't care from his heart.

He was spared from another demonstration by the arrival of his
ture mother-in-law. Clarissa, all blushes and breathless sen-
nces, told her the good news, and he was rewarded with a beam-
g smile from Lady Partridge, and the assurance that she would
evote the remainder of the Season to arranging the most brilliant
edding.

He was content to suffer in silence for the remainder of the trip to Bath. Clarissa and her mother moved with lightning speed from silver patterns to china to damask curtains, and were careening onto the honeymoon itself when Bath appeared like a benediction. He sighed with relief, and called their attention to the city before them, using it like raw meat before wolves to distract them. "Now tell me how I should approach your father," he interrupted, not wishing to think about his honeymoon because Emma would not be the last person he saw when his eyes closed, and his first sight in the morning.

"Papa will be delighted," Clarissa assured him. "Only do not bump his foot, or ask for sherry. The doctor has put Papa on strict regimen of pump water mixed with vinegar and cloves."

"Heavens," he said. Is this to be my future, as well? Gout and pump water?

To his dismay, a tidal wave did not roar in from the Bristol Channel and float them out to sea before they arrived at the Partridge home. Sir Clarence was in the library, with his bandaged foot propped on a footstool, looking at though he could chew through masonry. Lord Ragsdale took a deep breath, blew a kiss in the doorway to Clarissa, and closed it behind him.

"Sir Clarence," he heard himself saying, "how nice to see you again. I believe we have a matter of the heart to discuss."

I refuse to flog myself because I allowed Lord Ragsdale to kiss me, Emma told herself at least one hundred times before noon, laying on the mental lashes as she busied herself with his instructions. That the experience was pleasant beyond all reason only added to her logic that she was getting old now—almost twenty-five—and more susceptible to such things. She considered the matter, and resolved that, when this matter of her father and brother was settled one way or the other, she should give some thought to marriage and a family of her own.

Not that her future husband would be anything like Lord Ragsdale, she told herself, suppressing a small shudder. She allowed herself a smile, wondering what he would say if she told him that he had become her measuring stick of what *not* to look for in husband.

She frowned, aware of the fiction of that statement. While may have been true several months ago, it was not true today. Lord Ragsdale showed great potential now. Emma picked up the quill again and dipped it in the ink. Miss Clarissa, she thought grimly, I hope you appreciate the paragon—well, the improve

erson—that I have helped to fashion. I hope you will have the
wit to scold him where he needs it, and give him plenty of head-
room in matters where he shines. She sighed. I should write a
manual for the care and upkeep of Lord Ragsdale and give it to
you, Miss Clarissa. Why am I afraid that you won't know what to
do with him?

The thought dogged her for several days, but she eventually put
aside as she and the footman made several more trips to Dept-
ord Hard, and the shipping offices. No one had ever heard of the
Minerva or the *Hercules*, not even when she attempted bribery.
When she explained it to him, Robert Claridge took her task to
heart, and traveled to Portsmouth, seeking news of the missing
ships. There was no news, not even any scraps of information in
the dusty boxes at the Home Office, which she returned to during
the remaining days of the week.

"I begin to wonder if they ever existed," she told Robert as he
sat in Sally's room, watching her pack.

"You could return to Virginia with us," he offered. "I do not
think Lord Ragsdale would mind, and didn't you say he is probably engaged by now?"

She nodded, and began to fold the chemise in her hands smaller
and smaller. "I am sure you are right." She looked down at the
garment in her hands and shook it out, to begin again. "Perhaps
Lord Ragsdale will have thought of something else. I should
wait."

And so she did, although it gave her a pang to stand with Lady
Ragsdale and wave good-bye as the Claridges departed for
Portsmouth and a ship to America. Robert had kindly left her
enough passage money to see her to Virginia, "When you decide
you've looked enough," he had told her the night before.

To take Lady Ragsdale's mind off the melancholy of farewell,
Emma saw to it that they traveled to Norfolk to look in on the
progress of construction and renovation. She took notes on the
improvements, pleased to see how well Manwaring and Larch
worked together. The sheepherders had already moved into their
new quarters, and work would begin on the crofters' cottages as
soon as the planting was finished.

"Lady Ragsdale, you can tell your lordship that he has a good
instinct where people are concerned," Mrs. Larch told her as they
walked around the newly dug foundations on her last evening in
Norfolk.

"Mrs. Larch, I am not married to Lord Ragsdale," she said
quickly, before she lost her nerve. "I serve him as his secretary. I

do not know why he didn't correct you during that first visit, an—
then I was too embarrassed to say anything."

Mrs. Larch stared at her in amazement. "I never would hav—
believed it!" She looked at her husband, who was chatting wit—
the bailiff. "And didn't my David remark to me that you tw—
looked like you had been married years and years?"

Oh, my, Emma thought to herself. This is worse than I though—
"It was just Lord Ragsdale and his rather demented sense o—
humor, Mrs. Larch," she apologized. "I trust you will excus—
him."

Mrs. Larch allowed as she could. "Well, you may say all tha—
but I think you would have made a grand Lady Ragsdale."

"Why, thank you," Emma replied. How curious, she thought. *—
few months ago, I would have pokered up and protested at such—
statement. Perhaps I am learning something of toleration.

And something of patience, she told herself early the next wee—
as she shook her head at Lasker's offer of hackney fare an—
started walking to the bank for the monthly audit of Lord Rags—
dale's accounts. I will certainly need it if I am to say more tha—
three or four sentences in my life to Clarissa Partridge.

That morning's interview with Clarissa called for a brisk walk—
she decided. They had returned from Norfolk to a letter fro—
Clarissa. Lady Ragsdale read it, then held it out to Emma, a broa—
smile on her face. "Well, it is about time," she commented.

Emma read the brief note, marveling that Clarissa could wri—
as she spoke, in breathless sentences, little wispy fragments tha—
managed to convey her delight at Lord Ragsdale's proposal, an—
then ping off half a dozen other topics in the brief space of half—
page. She looked on the back, but there was nothing more.

And then only days later, the fiancée herself sat drinking tea i—
Lady Ragsdale's private sitting room, all blond and lovely an—
wearing a diamond that Emma thought vulgar. When Lady Rags—
dale inquired where her son was, if he had not returned with he—
Clarissa only shrugged her shoulders.

"He bolted out of Bath after only three days," she said, her ex—
pression somewhere between a pout and a simper. "He said some—
thing about business that would not wait. Yes, thank you," sh—
said, selecting a macaroon from the tray that Emma held out t—
her. "I will have to speak to him about such precipitate behavior."

"He does his best work on impulse, I think," Emma noted.

"Well, it won't do, and so I will tell him," Clarissa conclude—
speaking with finality. She took a long look at Emma. "And I wi—

so tell him that once he is married, he can find himself a regular ale secretary, like all his friends."

Oh, I like that, Emma thought as she quickened her pace to the nk. Of course, as soon as the wedding—and maybe sooner, if day's conversation were any indication—she would find herself independent woman. There will be nothing for me here in England. There is nothing in Ireland. I suppose I will return to merica.

The banker's audit was the usual ponderous process of reconling ledgers and figures, with occasional reminders this time for r to pay attention. "Emma, this is not like you," the senior clerk olded.

I suppose it is not, she considered as she turned her attention om a perusal of the paneling to the ledger before her. She acpted the Bath receipts, her eyes widening at the cost of the diaond ring that Lord Ragsdale had lavished on his bride-to-be. sus, Mary, and Joseph, he must be dead in love, or monstrously ılgar, she thought as she added the sum to her entries.

She looked up from the next receipt. "Mary Roney in Market uavers?" she asked.

The clerk leaned over the ledger, his spectacles far down on his se. "He has decided to award an annuity to the widowed sister David Breedlow," he announced, then fixed her with that dry ok that clerks reserve for the foolish wealthy.

You dear man, she thought as she finished her accounting and t the ledger under her arm again. Only marry now, and I will nsider your redemption complete. She started the long walk me, then reconsidered. "No. I will celebrate," she told herself, she stepped into the street to hail a hackney.

"Kensington, if you please," she instructed the jarvey, and setd back with a sigh. I will wander among those paintings I was frightened to look at, when he took me to the gallery. Of urse, it would be better if Lord Ragsdale were here, because en he could explain them to me.

She paid the small entrance fee from the few coins she allowed rself from Robert Claridge's passage to Virginia, and strolled wly through the gallery. The peace of the place made her epy, and she found a comfortable bench. I will sit here and nk about my future, she told herself as her eyes closed.

She couldn't have put her finger on what woke her, except that sun was slanting across the gallery floor and telling her it was ıe to go home. She sat up and looked right into Lord Ragse's eye. She gasped and let the ledger drop.

"I wondered how long I would have to stare at you before yo
woke up," he said to her from his seat across the gallery. "And
have only one eye."

Her face red with embarrassment, she fumbled for the ledge
and started to rise. He held up a hand to stop her, and starte
across the gallery.

"Stay where you are, my dear. I have such news, and I'd rathe
you were sitting down.

"Well, did you keep things running smoothly while I wa
away?" he asked as he reached inside his overcoat.

"Of course," she replied promptly. "Probably better than yo
would have, my lord," she teased. Her smile deepened as h
pulled out a small packet and dropped it in her lap.

"From me to you, Emma. It was easy to find where I've been,
he explained.

She unwrapped the package and held up a rosary. "Oh, than
you!"

"You're so welcome, Emma." He reached into his overco
again. "Here's something else."

The smile left her face when he dropped a bundle of papers i
her lap.

He tried to keep his voice casual and offhand, but through h
obvious exhaustion, she could almost feel his excitement.

"Emma, you can correct me if I'm wrong, but you might fin
some familiar names here."

She looked down at the lists in her lap, afraid to touch them.

"My dear, it's silly of me, but I must insist that you breathe i
and out," she heard Lord Ragsdale saying from what seemed lik
a great distance. "I found the *Minerva* and the *Hercules*!"

Chapter 20

mpulsively, she took his face in her hands and touched her forehead to his. "Somehow, I knew you would," she murmured, and
e meant it.

Lord Ragsdale picked up one of the lists and placed it in her
nd. "They were on the *Hercules*," he said, unfolding the papers.
Wouldn't you know I would go through the *Minerva*'s list first."
e scanned the second page, and then ran his finger in practiced
shion down the second column. "There."

She looked where he pointed, read the name, and allowed her-
lf to breathe again. "David Upton Costello," she read out loud.
Ay lord, that is my father."

"I thought as much. And look here," he said, pointing farther
wn the list. "There were several Costellos. Samuel—I cannot
ake out the middle name, but it starts with an A."

"Ainsworth," she said, touching the name. She folded the paper
refully, tenderly, then leaned against Lord Ragsdale's shoulder
d closed her eyes, unable to say anything.

"They sailed in April of 1804," Lord Ragsdale said as he put
; arm around her shoulder. "Now you know, Emma."

She opened her eyes then and sat up, her mind suddenly full of
estions. "But where? How? What magic is this?"

He laughed at her and raised his hands as though to fend her
f. "For two people who think themselves at least more intelli-
nt than dahlias, we were remarkably thickheaded on this one,
ima."

"Tell me!" she demanded, ready to pluck at his sleeve like a
ild.

"During my third night in Bath when I was tossing and turn-
;—oh, by the way, you may congratulate me on my forthcom-
; nuptials," he said, interrupting himself.

"And I do congratulate you," she replied, then looked at him
ewdly. "And why, pray tell me, if you are so happily engaged,
re you 'tossing and turning'?"

He was silent a moment, and she almost wished she had n
asked. "It is merely that I prefer my own bed here in London." H
tugged at her hair under its cap. "That is none of your busines
and has nothing to do with my narrative!"

"Very well, my lord, pray continue."

"It suddenly occurred to me that the most logical place to loo
for a ship bearing Irish convicts was Ireland itself." He smiled a
her openmouthed amazement. "Impressive, ain't I?"

You went all the way to Ireland for me, she thought, eve
though you have sworn to me how seasick you get in a full bath
tub, and I know you really do not care to exert yourself. "Ver
impressive," she said quietly. "Lord Ragsdale, you are a wonder
ful man. Have I ever told you?"

In reply, he took her hand and kissed it. "No, you have not, bu
it's nice to hear. I made up some fancy lie about business tha
could not wait, placated Clarissa with an obscene diamond—"

"I've seen it," Emma interrupted, "and you are right."

"—And caught the next ship to Cork." He pressed his hand t
his stomach. "I can only marvel how anyone survives a sea voy
age. Emma, the things I have done for you . . ."

"I told you I was grateful," she said, twinkling her eyes at hir
and holding the lists closer.

"Well, I combed the docks for any record of our missing ship
but found nothing. It only remained for me to catch the ma
coach to Dublin." He looked up as the gallery clerk motioned t
them, and then tapped his pocket watch. "Emma, we're bein
ejected. Shall we?"

She put her arm through his and strolled with him into the ga
dens. She stopped then, and looked at him. "How did you know
was here?"

He took her arm again and moved her in the direction of h
curricle. "Simple. I went to the bank, and the senior clerk said l
thought he heard you tell the hackney driver to take you to Ken
ington." He looked around him at the flowers. "It's much nic
now than it was the first time I brought you here." He sat her on
bench. "Back to the story."

"But, aren't you in a hurry to get home? This morning Mi
Partridge mentioned something about a party."

"There will always be a party," he said, dismissing his fianc
somewhat callously, she thought. "I want to tell you here."

"Very well, then," she replied, mystified.

"I went to Dublin." He paused then, as if wondering how mu
to tell her.

Her hand went to his cheek. "I want you to tell me everything, my lord," she said simply. "You just said that you would, and I have waited so long."

"Of course." He spoke quickly then, as though the news he bore pained him to the quick. "I checked the records at Prevot. Your mother died of typhus, much as you had thought."

She waited for the news to slap her, but she felt instead a peaceful calm. Mama must not have suffered long then, she thought. Ah, well, she is at rest now, and the soldiers cannot touch her.

"Eamon?" she asked.

He put his arm around her again. "He was hanged in the Prevot prison courtyard in October, about the same time Robert Emmet was beheaded." He twined his fingers in hers, and she clung to his hand gladly. "Emma, the United Irish dead, or Croppies, or whatever you want to call them, were all tumbled into a common grave. Do you know, it's become a shrine of sorts." He smiled at the memory. "Damned if the British don't try and try to keep it from happening, but flowers are forever turning up on that mound."

"I wish I could add mine," she said softly.

He kissed her hand again. "Consider it done, Emma. The guards there are really slow, even though I left a regular florist's shop."

The tears came then, and she clung to him as he patted her back and let her cry. They were cleansing tears, and when she finished and blew her nose vigorously on the handkerchief that Lord Ragsdale always seemed to have ready, she knew she would not cry that way again. She would remember Eamon always, but she could not mourn him anymore, now that she knew a nation in the making held him dear, too.

Lord Ragsdale looked at the sky. "I think we will continue this drive." He stood up and held out his hand for her. "I knew I would find the ships' rosters in Dublin, and I did," he said as he helped her into the curricle. "Both ships had Dublin registries." He spoke to his horse, and they started back to Curzon Street. "I actually spent an evening with the captain of the *Hercules*. He assured me that there was little loss of life on the voyage to Australia." He looked at her. "Of course, you won't know until you get there . . ." His voice trailed off. "Emma, it's a long way."

"I know."

They were both silent for several blocks. "I had to hurry back to Bath," Lord Ragsdale said finally, continuing his narrative. He

nudged her shoulder. "By the way, I stopped in to see Fa
Moullé's millinery shop, and it is a fine one. How pleased I ar
that you both cheated me." He laughed out loud at the look sh
knew was on her face. "She gave me a rather elegant bonnet fc
you, which I was hard put to explain to Clarissa."

Emma joined in his laughter. "You have my permission to giv
it to her as a wedding present."

He nodded. "I expect my wife will wear it," he said enigmat
cally. "But Emma, I have not finished my Irish tale."

"What more can there be?" she wondered. "Everyone is ac
counted for now.

"Not everyone, Emma."

What can he mean? she thought as the traffic claimed his atter
tion. I have no hidden relatives, waiting to give me a fortune so
can travel to Australia.

"I took the mail coach for the return trip to Cork," he continue
when the traffic abated.

He looked at her, and she found the expression unsettlin;
There is such tenderness in your face, she thought. There can t
no more bad news, so it must be good news. "I wish you wou
tell me," she urged.

"I thought I would stop in Diggtown. I remember you said th
was where you left Tim."

She nodded, afraid to speak, and allowing herself the tinie
glimmer of hope, after years of none.

"I thought to find his grave, so I could give you a complete r
port, but Emma, there was no grave for Timothy Costello. I tri
all three cemeteries."

She took his arm. "That's all right," she soothed, worrying
the emotion coming into his voice. "It really isn't necessary f
you to absorb all my troubles, my lord."

"Oh, Emma." He shook his head. "Well, I tried the better pa
of the day to remember the name of that family you said you ha
left him with."

"Holladay," she said automatically.

"Yes. I remembered it just when I was about to climb aboa
another mail coach." He chuckled to himself. "I think the oth
passengers thought me daft when I leaped off that thing and r
back into town."

"Please tell me," she pleaded. "Surely they did not toss hi
into a common grave with no marker. I could not bear su
news."

"Emma, you can bear anything," he murmured. "That is t

vonder of you. I found the house—a nice one, by the way—and
nocked on the door." He paused, then covered her hand with his.
Emma, the young lad who answered the door looked a great deal
ike you."

She stared at him, dumbfounded.

"Tim is alive."

Tim is alive, she repeated in her mind as she clutched Lord
.agsdale's hand. She closed her eyes to let the words sink into
er brain. Tim is alive. She had carried him ten miles through a
riving rainstorm, and him burning with fever. She shuddered, re-
nembering all over again the death rattle in his throat, reverberat-
ng so close to her ear as she staggered along, one shoe on, the
ther lost in the mud, her clothes plastered to her, and soldiers
verywhere to prod and poke if she slowed down with her burden.

"It cannot be," she whispered.

"Then I can't imagine who it was there at the Holladays who
eld open the door and asked would I like to come in," Lord
agsdale said mildly as he pulled up in front of his house. "He
as charming freckles, marvelous green eyes, and an appealing
ay of cocking his head to one side when he listens."

"Tim," she agreed. She folded her hands in her lap, wondering
hy it was so difficult to absorb such news. "Then I must return
 Ireland."

Lord Ragsdale smiled and shook his head as he took her hands
 his again. "I wouldn't, Emma. When I told him who I was, and
hat had happened to his family, he wouldn't settle for less than
ming with me."

She looked up at him and swallowed, wishing for words, but
able to think of any.

"My dear, he's inside." He tightened his grip on her hands. "I
st wanted to break it to you out here before you did something
lly like faint or succumb to hysterics." He smiled into her eyes.
im said he doesn't like girls to make a scene, and I assured him
u would not."

She sat in silence, her senses reeling. How do I put into words
y gratitude, she thought as she looked at Lord Ragsdale. I hated
u at first because you are English, and now I have such pro-
und regard for you. I will never be ignorant of your faults, but
u have borne mine with uncommon grace. I wonder if I will
er be out of your debt, even if you release me from my inden-
re and I travel thousands of miles.

"Emma, I am not handsome enough to stare at for such a
1gth. Is my patch over the wrong eye? Spinach between my

teeth?" he teased. "Come, come. You have some reacquaintanc
to make, and I do believe he is looking out the window right now
wondering about his sister."

She leaped from the curricle, even as he tried to help her down
gathered up her skirts and ran into the house. Tim stood in th
hallway. How tall you are, she thought as she just stood ther
taking in the sight of him, hugging him in her mind and hea
even before she held out her arms.

He walked toward her slowly, as if checking her out with ever
footstep, looking for the sister he remembered when he was fiv
"Emmy?" he asked finally.

Without a word, she grabbed him fiercely into her arms. In
second his arms tightened about her, and she felt his tears on he
neck.

"I waited and waited for you to come for me," he sobbed, eve
as she kissed his neck and clung to him. "I kept hoping."

"Such watering pots," Lord Ragsdale commented as he hande
each of them a handkerchief, then pressed a third to his eye. "Se
here, you have set me a bad example." He grinned at Tim. "But
will practice economy and cry out of only one eye."

Tim laughed and blew his nose, and allowed Lord Ragsdale
give him a hug of his own.

"Good lad," Lord Ragsdale said as he put his arms around bo
of them and steered them toward the book room. "Do you know
Emma, he does not get seasick." He ruffled Tim's hair with a f
miliarity that made Emma smile. "He assured me that I would n
die, and ignored me when I threatened to throw myself overboa
and end it all."

"You did not say that!" Tim declared.

"Hush, lad!" Lord Ragsdale said with mock sobriety. "If yo
and I are to rub along together, you must realize I enjoy giving
tale a good squeeze."

"Like Da," Tim said.

"Why, yes," Emma agreed, wondering why she had never n
ticed that tendency about Lord Ragsdale before.

In the book room, Lord Ragsdale ceremoniously seated himse
at the desk and rummaged about in one of the drawers. "I kno
it's here, unless you have organized the very marrow out of m
bones," he grumbled.

"I would never," she protested as she possessed herself
Tim's hand. "In fact, I think I will advise Clarissa to give y
ample room to maneuver, my lord. You do your best work on
spontaneous basis, I believe."

"So glad you finally recognized it," he murmured as he pulled out a document. "Here we have your indenture paper. Tomorrow it goes to the bank to be signed down here and notarized, and then it goes to you, my dear." He folded his hands on the desk. "I think you should frame it, so you can tell your children someday how you reformed a rather dingy member of the peerage because of a card-game wager." He winked at Tim. "It's a story worthy of the Irish, lad."

She accepted the paper from him, looked at it, and returned it to the desk. "I would like to continue working for you for wages, until I earn enough for passage for two to Australia, my lord."

"I fear that is quite impossible. Clarissa has told me on several occasions that she thinks I need a male secretary," he replied.

Emma nodded, remembering her conversation with Clarissa only that morning. "Well, then, can you give me a character reference?"

He smiled at her. "Before I came looking for you, I wrote this character. Perhaps it will suffice. Take it, Emma, and with my blessings."

She held out her hand for the letter and held it so Tim could read it, too. He can't be serious, she thought. "My lord, this is addressed to Lachlan Macquarie"—she looked closer—"the governor of Australia . . ."

". . . Who said he would be delighted to provide you with employment in the colony. When I went to the trouble of finding out who he was, I was only too delighted to discover that he is sailing on this next supply convoy. Apparently, the Colonial Office thinks Macquarie is just the man to take over from the unfortunate William Bligh," he said. "It seems that Captain Bligh cannot weather mutiny on sea or land, and there has been trouble in Australia."

"But"—she frowned—"that may be, my lord. Don't think you will scare me off from making the journey."

"I would never!" he exclaimed, his voice shocked. He winked at Tim and quite ruined the effect.

"Lord Ragsdale, do be serious!" she said. "This paper is well and good, but I need employment here to pay for passage there. It is quite simple. I cannot swim there!"

"You probably could," he disagreed. "But to spare Tim any possible embarrassment, I intend to pay your passage and his, if I can't talk him into coming with me to Norfolk."

"You can't, my lord," Tim said.

"You sound just like your sister," Lord Ragsdale said mildly. " didn't think I could."

"I never asked you to pay our way," she protested, all the whil knowing that he was going to do what he wanted.

"I know you did not. I want to do it, and I don't want a lot c argument, and please, no pouts. I am already steeling myself for lifetime of those from Clarissa. Don't you do it, too," he con cluded with some finality.

He rose to his feet, as though signifying the end to his audi ence. *Very well, my lord,* she thought. *Our relationship ha changed yet again. Now you are formal and dignified, and in con trol of things. I know this is what I worked for, but I miss the ras cal a little.* She held out her hand to him, and they shook hands.

"Thank you."

"It's nothing, Emma." He looked at Tim. "Lad, go tell Laske not to hold dinner any longer. I want the two of you at my tab tonight."

"Oh, that isn't necessary," she said as Tim grinned at Lor Ragsdale.

"I want to, so don't argue. The convoy leaves in a matter of te days or so. When I visited with the new governor . . ."

"You visited with him?" she interrupted.

"Of course!" he replied, sounding genuinely indignant th time. "You don't seriously think I would just turn you over to th vagaries of life at sea without looking into the matter!"

"Such exertion," she murmured, touched at his interest.

Lord Ragsdale appealed to Tim. "See how she baits me? W she this way at home?"

"I can't quite remember," Tim said, and then brightened. "B my brothers were."

Emma laughed and pulled Tim closer. "Very well! If you mu be solicitous, I suppose there is nothing I can do about it. Go c now, Tim, and speak to Lasker."

"There isn't," Lord Ragsdale agreed after Tim left, his equ nimity restored. "I learned from Governor Macquarie that the lo inspector will sail, too. You will be in quite distinguished cor pany, so you might brush up on your manners."

"You seem determined that I remain firmly in your debt," s protested with a smile.

"Of course," he agreed cheerfully. "I like to have people ov me."

It is more than I could ever repay, she thought, *but a burder* gladly bear. She went to the door, then turned back on impulse and kissed him.

Why am I doing this? she thought as his arms went around her and held her close. He was incredibly easy to kiss, and once begun, difficult to leave off. Her hands went to his hair then. She had always admired his thick hair, and she wondered if it felt as good as it looked. It did, to her gratification, and to his pleasure, obviously, because he sighed and continued kissing her.

We simply must stop this kiss, she thought, and then didn't think anymore, finding herself more occupied with the rapidity of her heartbeat and the pleasant feel of him. I am being kissed by an expert, she thought. It was nice before, but this is infinitely better.

He seemed in no hurry to end the experience, except that someone had the bad timing to knock on the book room door. Lord Ragsdale released her and began to straighten his neck cloth. "Drat!" he muttered, even as she went to the window and stared out, hoping that the intruder did not have intense scrutiny in mind. Her cheeks felt flaming hot, and she stood there, astounded at her own temerity. This indenture is not ending a moment too soon, she thought as Lasker opened the door, announced dinner after a quick look around, then took himself off again.

"Dear me," she murmured when the room seemed awfully silent.

"Dear me, indeed," said Lord Ragsdale, sounding quite as out of breath as she felt. "If I had known how you felt about release from your indenture, I'd have signed that blooming document once each day, maybe twice."

The enormity of her indiscretion nearly removed what breath she had left. I must be losing my reason, she thought, measuring the distance between the window and the door, and wondering why it looked so far away. And there was Lord Ragsdale, his face flushed, his eye decidedly bright.

"I cannot imagine what you think of me," she said, feeling such intense shame that she thought she would melt with it. Is it really shame? she considered. Or am I wishing you would lock that door and continue this event on the sofa? "Dear me," she said again, her voice more faint this time.

To her acute discomfort, Lord Ragsdale came no closer, but continued to regard her, his expression thoughtful. He started to smile then, and her shame deepened. He sat on a corner of his desk.

"How odd, Emma," he commented, not looking at her now, but gazing over her shoulder. "You have worked so hard to redeem me, but I wonder if you have succeeded." He grinned at her st[u]pefied silence. "I suppose that would depend on what your ai[m] were. Did you really plan for me to fall in love with you?"

She shook her head, astounded at his words, wishing he had n[ot] said them. "I was out of order," she said when she thought sh[e] could manage complete sentences.

"Well, no, actually, I thought you followed through in remar[k]ably fine order," he commented as he gave a final tug to his ne[ck]cloth.

She edged toward the door. "You simply have to disregard m[y] behavior."

He shook his head. "I am able to forget a considerable numb[er] of things, but I don't think my amnesia would extend that far."

"I was improper," she said.

"Decidedly. I wonder why I am not bothered by that?" [he] asked, more to himself than to her.

What can I say to this man? she thought miserably. I can on[ly] wish that ship were leaving in fifteen minutes. In another mome[nt] there was no need to decide. Someone knocked on the door.

"Cut line, Lasker," Lord Ragsdale snapped, giving her reas[on] to suspect that he was not so calm as he appeared. "We won't p[er]ish if the peas are cold."

I will if this conversation continues, she thought. She went [to] the door and opened it, not turning around when Lord Ragsda[le] called her name. In another moment, he grabbed her arm.

"Emma, please," he insisted. "We need to talk."

"There is nothing to say, my lord," she replied, retreating b[e]hind her formal exterior again. "I will remind you that you are e[n]gaged to Clarissa and I am bound for Australia. Good night, m[y] lord. I think I would rather eat belowstairs with Tim. We ca[me] somewhat close to forgetting ourselves, didn't we?"

Chapter 21

I am a coward, she thought that evening as she stayed belowstairs with Timothy, and listened to him tell her of his life with the Holladays. She held him close, her arm tight around him, and gradually allowed good sense to reclaim her. After she was sure that Lord Ragsdale had left the house for the evening, she prepared a pallet on the floor of her attic room and took Tim there. They spoke of the coming voyage until she could almost forget what had happened in the book room.

This is the reality of my life, she told herself firmly. We are sailing to an unknown place, and we do not know what we will find. We will be among soldiers and convicts. She sighed and looked down at Tim, whose eyes were closing slowly, even as she watched. She touched his shoulder, then pulled his blanket higher, marveling all over again in the pleasure of seeing him. Am I wrong to take him along to this dreadful place? Lord Ragsdale said he would take him to Norfolk.

"Emma, I wish you would answer me," he was saying.

"What? What?" she asked, guilty at the thousand directions her mind was taking.

"I want to know if you are afraid," he asked in that matter-of-fact voice of his, unchanged by five years of difference between them.

"I used to be," she said honestly, knowing that she could not lie to her brother. "But now that you are to come with me, I don't think there is anything that can frighten the two of us."

"But suppose Da and Sam are dead?" he persisted, closing his eyes against the possibility, but taking her hand.

"We will decide what to do when it comes to that, Tim. Go to sleep now."

He slept peacefully, quietly, but he would not relinquish her hand. She sat on the floor beside him, knowing that sleep was far from her. I wish my conscience were as clear as yours, Tim, she thought as she gazed at his relaxed face. I have labored so hard to

mend a faulty character, not realizing all the while that it wa
mine.

She undressed finally and crawled into bed, only to stare at th
ceiling, and listen to house noises until everyone was asleep. Ol
well, she decided as her eyes began to close, it is better to lov
foolishly than to hate bitterly. I hope I am wiser than I was, an
more kind.

Her resolution was firm, and in the morning she dressed quiet
and tiptoed out of her room, careful not to waken Tim. She wei
to the front hall for the mail, dreading that Lord Ragsdale woul
rise early and demand more conversation.

The mail was gone. She looked around at Lasker.

"Lord Ragsdale has already perused the correspondence an
placed it in the book room," he said. "He has gone to Norfoll
taking Miss Partridge and her mother with him."

She sighed with relief and went to the book room. His usual li
of instructions was on the desk, as well as a folded note. She s:
down and opened the note. "Dear Emma," she read, "Clarissa
eager to see the manor, and figure out more ways to spend n
money constructively. We will return after your ship sails, so l
me wish you happy journey and good news at the end of it. E
cuse my bad manners. John Staples."

There was no need to read it again and search for hidden mear
ings, for there were none. She managed a smile and chided herse
for being an idiot. We are talking of Lord Ragsdale, she told he
self, he who loves to kiss women. It was that and nothing more.
am only chagrined that I caused such a kind man any embarras
ment. I trust he will soon forget it, if he had not already.

His kindness to her continued through the days of his absenc
Her next visit to the bank was more in the way of a command pe
formance, as the custodians of a major portion of Lord Ragsdale
wealth assured her that she was to take the enormous sum of tv
hundred pounds with her. She could not imagine such largess, ar
told them so, but the senior partners only looked at each other ar
chuckled.

"He told us you would say that," they assured her. "Lately, I
is so well-organized and sensible that we do not argue with hi
over paltry sums."

I have created a monster, she thought with amusement. "Ve
well, then, sirs, so it will be. Never let anyone say that I dor
know when to save my breath to cool my porridge."

She also knew better than to argue when Lady Ragsdale i
sisted that they visit the cloth merchants and purchase yards ai

ards of muslin goods, and silk stockings, and bonnets of a practi-
al nature. "I cannot imagine where you will get these things if
e do not buy them now," she said, explaining away her own
enerosity. She paused in front of a bolt of handsome burgundy
ool. "Do you suppose . . ."

"No, my lady," Emma said hurriedly. "I fear it is rather hot in
e antipodes. Let us confine our enthusiasms to muslin."

"It seems so ordinary," said Lady Ragsdale with a sigh. "Do
ou not suppose there will be balls there occasionally, or even
usicales?"

I could never tell this dear lady what I fear I will find, she
ought as Lady Ragsdale cast a longing eye on a nearby bolt of
le yellow silk. We are going to a convict colony, a place of
rsh rule and desperate men. She, who had been coddled so gen-
y, would be horrified if she knew how hard it might be. I shall
ever tell her.

"Do you know, you may be right, my lady," she said, choosing
r words carefully as her own fears returned. "I think that silk
ould be entirely in order."

"I knew it!" Lady Ragsdale declared in triumph. "With that and
pair of Morocco leather slippers to match, I will pronounce you
. You may keep my paisley shawl," she added generously.

"Where can we squeeze it all?" she grumbled to Tim several
nes in as many days when Lady Ragsdale continued to add to
e contents of the sea chest. Her largess spilled over into another
ank and then another, each requiring the strenuous efforts of the
otman to close them, with Lasker sitting on top, dignified to the
d. "This has to be enough," she said firmly on her last night on
urzon Street as Lady Ragsdale met her on the first-floor landing
ith another nightgown.

"Certainly, Emma," Lady Ragsdale agreed. "And if I think of
ything else, I can send it 'round later."

Emma turned away to hide her smile. Lady Ragsdale, you have
concept of geography, she thought. She took the nightgown
om Lady Ragsdale, said good night, and went into the book
om for one last look around. She could hear Tim and the foot-
an bringing the trunks down two flights of stairs. Lasker had
ade arrangements with a carter to pick them up at first light.

And we will follow, she reflected. A penny post from the dock-
rd had informed them of their departure with the tide in the early
ernoon. She went to the window to stare down at the street
low, rain-slicked from a sudden squall and washed clean of the

day's commerce. Soon there would be only months and months
waves and wind, and small ships. "And wormy food, and sea bi
cuit," she said out loud as she opened the window for a deep brea
of flowers in the window box. "And serious uncertainty, as yc
would say, Da. I wonder what I will find at the end of my journey.

She tidied the room, hopeful that Lord Ragsdale would be ab
to discover everything in order when he returned. She was abo
to turn out the lamp, but suddenly she knew it wasn't right
leave without even a farewell note. There can be no harm in e:
pressing myself this last time, she thought, no harm at all. She s
down at the desk.

It was easy to tell Lord Ragsdale thank-you on paper, to thar
him for putting the heart back in her, for making her angry enoug
at times to keep her from melancholy, for finding her family, f
tying up the ragged strings of her life. She labored over the pag
wanting to express her whole heart and mind. "I do not kno
whatever good I may have done you, my lord, but you have give
me back my brother," she wrote, then hesitated. I could tell you
love you, she considered, the quill poised over the inkwell.
would be true, probably the most true thing I ever wrote. She p
down the quill and rested her chin on her hands. There will alwa
be some part of me that longs for you, but should I say that to
man so soon to be tangled in the toils of matrimony?

"How fortunate I will be so far away," she said, and picked
the quill again. "I can be no possible threat, Clarissa Partridg
bless your pouty hide." She wrote swiftly then, telling him of h
love, leaving nothing out, not mincing a single word. Nothi
could be safer; she would be in the middle of the Atlantic befo
he returned from Norfolk. She picked up the letter, still frowni
over it, wondering why even that declaration was not enough.

And then she understood and laughed out loud, sticking t
quill back in the ink. Not only do I love you, Lord Ragsdale, s
told herself as she wrote the words, I also *like* you.

It looked silly on the page, like something you would say to
friend from childhood, or a schoolmate. She almost tore up t
letter. He will think I have lost all reason to say something
childish, she thought. She stared at the note for a long while, th
sighed and tucked it in under the paperweight. She blew out t
lamp, took another look around the room, and closed the door
her career as a secretary.

Leaving the house on Curzon Street was harder than she cou
have imagined. Lady Ragsdale cried, the footman looked dec

ly forlorn, and even Lasker showed a glimmer of some expres-
on besides patient condescension when he helped her into the
ckney, nodded to Tim, and told the driver to take them to the
cks. When she looked back, she even thought she saw him dab
his eyes. She may have been mistaken; it was a blustery day,
d there were cinders in the air.

"We have so much to look forward to," she told Tim, who
inned at her.

"You sound like you're trying to convince yourself," he teased.

I suppose I am, she thought, struck by the truth of his observa-
on. Leave it to a little brother to define my own melancholy. If I
d not know better, I would accuse him of taking lessons from
rd Ragsdale.

They arrived at Deptford Hard in plenty of time to catch the
e that even affected the oily swells of the Thames, far upstream
m the ocean. The *Atlas* rode low in the water, full of supplies
r the seven-month journey, and more victuals for the convict
lony that still needed food from home to take the ragged edge
f hunger. She looked closer, frowning. There was no bustle of
tivity on deck to signify a ship about to sail, no one but the cap-
n, who stared at a long list as he paced the deck.

Tim noticed the strange silence, too. "Emma, was it today or
morrow?"

Before she could add her questions to his, the captain of the
las spotted them and came to the railing. "Miss Costello!" he
outed to them on the dock. "Go home. Something has hap-
ned, and we cannot sail today."

"What?" she shouted back, dreading a return to Curzon Street,
d another round of farewells tomorrow, or the day after.

"The lord inspector died last night. We won't sail until the end
the week."

Trust the lord inspector to be so thoughtless, she told herself as
ey returned to Curzon Street in silence. Now we must go
ough all this again. She leaned back and drummed her fingers
patiently on the seat, too irritated for rational conversation with
m.

By the time they were approaching the turn to Curzon Street,
e acknowledged the hand of providence in this event. At least
e would have time to reclaim the letter from the book room and
place it with something more dignified. That hope crawled up
er throat, and then flopped back into her stomach as they turned
e corner to see the Ragsdale carriage at the front door.

"Jesus, Mary, and Joseph," she gasped.

Tim looked at her in surprise. "Don't you want to have
chance to say good-bye to Lord Ragsdale?" he asked. "I know
do."

"I'm not so sure," she wailed, wanting to leap from the hack
ney, run back to the dock, and hide there.

Tim peered at her. "Don't you like him? After all he's done fo
us?"

She nodded, kicking herself for her own folly, and hoping th
Lord Ragsdale's indolence would lead him to avoid the boo
room altogether, now that she was no longer there. "Of course
do," she muttered.

"Good," Tim said. "He told me he likes you."

Emma groaned and closed her eyes. That word has come bac
to haunt me, she thought, then stared at her little brother. "He sa
what?"

"That he liked you," Tim repeated patiently, with that sly loo
that brothers reserve for especially dense sisters. "I told him o
course he did, and he just laughed."

Well, you won't be laughing now, Lord Ragsdale, she thoug
as she grossly overtipped the jarvey in her confusion. You w
think I am such an idiot.

She contemplated sneaking around to the servants' entranc
but Lasker flung open the door, an actual smile on his face as sh
started to tiptoe away.

"Miss Costello! You have changed your mind! Lord Ragsdal
can you imagine who has returned?"

To her everlasting chagrin, Lord Ragsdale stood in the doo
way, too, his mouth open in amazement. "I thought you would
gone by now . . ." he began.

"I did not know you would return so soon," she started to te
him at the same time.

Tim laughed and hurried inside. Emma came up the ste
slowly. She tried to observe him without being obvious, a
could see no sign of disgust on his face, or exasperation. The
was nothing beyond a deepening of the crease between his eye
and a certain dullness in his expression she had not noticed wh
he left. As she watched, he made a visible effort to appear chee
ful.

"Change your mind, Emma?" he asked as he held open t
door for her. "If it's any consolation, I think I would have." I
shuddered. "All that water moving up and down! I would prob
bly get calluses from kneeling over a bucket for seven mont
Wise of you to reconsider."

She shook her head. He walked with her down the hall. She
lanced at the book-room door, which was closed. His trunk was
till at the foot of the stairs.

"Did you just return, my lord?" she asked, her voice hopeful.

"Only just," he agreed. "But you have not answered my ques-
on."

Good. He cannot possibly have seen the note yet, she thought
ith relief. "The lord inspector has died suddenly, apparently. We
ill sail in a few days, my lord," she explained.

Lord Ragsdale managed a rather mirthless chuckle. "I never
ought he was a man for the rigors of Australia, myself. He prob-
oly is only pretending until the ship leaves without him."

She laughed because she knew he expected it. Go upstairs like
good man, she thought, willing him to move away from the
ook room, where he stood now with his hand on the doorknob.

"If you do not mind, then, my lord, we will remain here a few
ore days until we sail," she said, when he continued just to ob-
rve her. And for heaven's sake, don't go in there, she thought.

"You know I do not mind, Emma," he replied, then opened the
oor and went in, closing it firmly behind him.

I think I will die of embarrassment, she thought as she stared at
e door. She held her breath, expecting any moment for Lord
agsdale to come bounding out, note in hand, to scold her for
ing an idiot. Nothing happened. She let out her breath, and qui-
ly climbed the stairs.

She spent the rest of the afternoon lying on her bed and staring
the wall, Tim curled up beside her, asleep. She dreaded every
und on the stairs, and panicked when darkness came and some-
e knocked.

"It's only me," said the footman.

"Come in then, Hanley," she said, hoping the relief in her voice
as not too obvious. Tim sat up and rubbed his eyes as she
ened the door.

"Lady Ragsdale would like you and Tim to have dinner with
r," he said, then added, when he noticed the hesitancy on her
e. "She does not like to dine alone, Emma."

"But isn't Lord Ragsdale available?" Emma asked.

The footman shook his head. "Oh, my, and didn't he tear out of
re like a man with a mission!"

I wonder what that means, she considered as she ushered Tim
t the door. I only hope he has not returned to his club and his
mer bad habits.

She and Tim followed the footman downstairs, and she sent

them on ahead as she went to the book-room door, listened a moment, opened it quietly, and tiptoed to the desk. Relief washed over her. The note remained exactly where she had left it, tucked under the paperweight. She snatched it up, crumpled it into a tiny ball, and threw the note into the fireplace, where she watched until it flamed and crumbled into ashes.

Her heart ten times lighter, she managed to make herself good company to Lady Ragsdale for the evening, never a difficult task. As much as she disliked cards, she knew she could while away an evening with them, nodding occasionally, making comments here and there as Lady Ragsdale chattered, cheated, and triumphed. She kept her ears open for Lord Ragsdale's return, but when she finally surrendered her cards at midnight, his candle was still waiting for him on the entrance hall table.

She decided the next day that he must have seen the note, after all, and had chosen to avoid her. It was the only conclusion she could make, because he left the house before she woke, and had not returned late that evening.

"I do not understand it," Lady Ragsdale commented as she signaled to Lasker to pour the sherry after another interminable night of cards. "Perhaps he is still with Clarissa. The wedding is planned for early June, after all, and these things take careful planning."

"I am certain you are right," Emma agreed, happy to end the discussion by yawning, stretching, then saying good night. What a sham, she thought as she climbed the stairs again. Now I will toss and turn and pretend to sleep, when I am in a perfect agony over Lord Ragsdale. Suppose he has returned to his former bad habits? she thought again. It seemed unlikely; the footman made no mention of anything out of the ordinary. I am stewing over nothing, she decided, but that thought did nothing to hasten sleep.

I cannot manage another day of sleeplessness, she told herself as she dragged out of bed and sat there until she had the energy to rise. Tim was already gone; in fact, his pallet was neatly folded. She rose, looked at the tangle of her own bed, and shook her head at her folly.

She was straightening the sheets when Tim burst into the room.

"Emma, there is a message from the *Atlas*! We are sailing at noon!"

"Thank goodness," she said, and meant each word. The sooner I am gone, the better.

They arrived at the *Atlas* within the hour, after suffering through another round of farewells. She knew that Lord Ragsdale

as in his chambers, because she heard him walking about as she
ptoed down the hall. There were more tears from Lady Rags-
ale, and then they were safely inside the hackney. She made the
istake of looking back at the house, where, to her horror, she
w Lord Ragsdale standing at his bedroom window. To her fur-
er amazement, he opened it, leaned out, waved, and blew her a
ss.

This is so odd, she thought as she waved back, but omitted the
ss. There have been too many of those to unsettle a rational
ind, she assured herself as she set her heart and mind on the
urney ahead.

The *Atlas* was a swarm of activity this time as she and Tim
ent on board and found their cabin, a tiny cubbyhole crammed
veendecks. They drew straws, and Tim won the top berth. She
t on her berth and looked around her. For six or seven months
is will be our home, she thought, and then we will be in a most
stile place, from which so few return. She considered the mat-
r, and then realized that it did not make a difference where she
as. There was no home anymore in Ireland; Virginia had been a
easant interlude, but only a place to mark time; England was the
emy still.

She lay back and propped her hands behind her head. No, that
as not true, she reasoned, thinking of Norfolk and the good peo-
e there. And Lord Ragsdale is in England. Silent tears rolled
wn to wet her hair. "Oh, Clarissa, please realize what a gem
u have," she whispered. "Do you know that you are the luckiest
ly in England?"

She dried her eyes before Tim noticed, and assured him that
e would join him on deck later. There would be no pleasure
en in watching London recede as they worked their way to the
annel. The familiar numbness that had captured her heart the
y after Robert Emmet walked up the lane to her house was re-
ning again. She closed her eyes against it, knowing that she
d not the strength to resist anymore.

But I must exert myself for Tim, she thought, sitting up. Even
ve arrive in Sydney and find no trace of Da or Sam, I have Tim
think of. She straightened her dress and went into the compan-
way.

t was full of trunks and boxes. She stepped around them and
t the apologetic glance of the ship's steward.

"Sorry, mum," he said. "It's the new lord inspector's stuff, and
ere am I to put it, I ask?"

She shook her head over his dilemma, and hurried on deck,

minding her steps around more luggage and rope, and casks. Ti
had already attached himself to the seamen doing their slow shu
fle around the capstan as the great anchor rose. He grinned at h
in self-conscious delight, and she smiled back. This trip will be
boy's paradise, she thought. I wonder what I will make of it?

The captain and first mate were everywhere, bellowing orde
to the men balanced on the yardarms. She glanced at the sma
knot of men standing forward, chatting by the railing, obvious
the other passengers. There was a lady with them, well-dress
and standing close to the man who must be the colony's new go
ernor. Perhaps she will need a servant, Emma thought. I shou
make myself known to her.

She stayed where she was, shy again. I have seven months
make her acquaintance, she excused herself. It can wait. Sl
turned to go belowdeck once more, but stopped and look
around again. Someone had called her name.

She looked at Tim, who was still pulling up the anchor, his
tention concentrated on the sail above him that was slowly filli
with air now. I must be hearing things, she decided, and mov
toward the companionway again.

"Emma, I wish you would pay attention," Lord Ragsdale call
to her.

She whirled around, and stood in dumbfounded amazement
one of the men separated himself from the group by the raili
and strolled her way. She stared at him, then sank down on
hatch as he came closer, taking his time, ambling along as thou
he owned the ship.

"What a lot of clutter," he said with some distaste as he seat
himself beside her. "The captain tells me that we will stop in F
to take on livestock, and then it really becomes interesting."

Her mind was even more cluttered than the deck. If I look
him, I know he will vanish, she told herself, but could not bri
herself to glance his way. She knew quite forcefully that the l
thing she wanted was for him to disappear. I will just sit here a
pretend another moment, she thought.

It would have worked, except that he took her hand then, a
she knew he was real. She looked down at his fingers twin
through hers and closed her eyes as she sighed and leaned agai
his shoulder, feeling safe again.

"Emma," he said after a moment, and there was nothing of
surance in his voice now. "I hate to admit it, but I've made a r
muddle of your excellent work of redemption."

She smiled, but did not open her eyes. "I suppose you will

e now that there is a ferociously angry lady in London who
ould probably break you on a rack if she ever catches you."

"Well, yes," he said. "You Irish have such a way with a phrase,
d you know?"

She giggled. "What have you done, Lord Ragsdale?"

He raised her fingers to his lips and kissed them. "I think I have
ade it impossible to return to London anytime soon." He paused
moment. "How fortunate then that I have taken on the job of
d inspector for Australia and Van Dieman's Land."

She gasped and looked at him then. "You can't be telling the
th!"

"Why would anyone lie about that? Really, Emma, you disap-
int me."

He kissed her then, and as she let him fold her in his arms, she
ew his disappointment did not extend to his lips. Or his heart,
viously; it was pounding as hard as hers was. She would have
en happy to continue kissing him until they arrived in Sydney,
t he stopped suddenly and looked up at the cheering sailors in
mast overhead.

'We should obviously continue this belowdeck," he com-
nted as he tucked her close under his arm. "I am somewhat
eamish about spectators to my lovemaking. Call me prudish,
there you are."

'I could never call you prudish, Lord Ragsdale," she assured
n.

'Yes, well," he said. "Neither are you, my dear. That was quite
ote you left on my desk."

She blushed. "I had hoped I was able to retrieve it in time."

'So glad you didn't," he murmured. "It sent me out the door
l on my most spontaneous errand ever. Clarissa Partridge—
uld you ever require this information—does not enjoy tumult,
llenge, or change of plans." He kissed her head. "She'd have
n a dead bore in a place like Australia, which will probably
tain generous parts of all three."

It was the note?" she asked.

Well, yes and no," he said. "I had decided several weeks ago
I loved you, but figured that was a lost cause. So I thought it
ild be less painful all around if I stuck with the original plans
married Clarissa. I did not want to return from Norfolk until I
sure you were gone." He chuckled and shook his head. "I
such a debt to the defunct lord inspector."

But I do love you," she assured him. "I didn't think you could

ever be serious about me, so I left that note only because I kne
you would never see it when I was around."

"Of course; makes perfect sense," he said calmly, with only
hint of a smile, then glanced at Tim, who stood beside Emm
"And you, lad, what does your expression tell me?"

"Only that I do not understand adults," he said honestly.

"Nor I," Lord Ragsdale confessed. He kissed Emma again.
had to make some arrangements, obviously, to show you wha
good fellow I am—hardworking, honest, and all that, and fit to
father to your children. I don't think your da would much appro
if I were to arrive unemployed with you in Australia and tell h
what a bargain he was getting for a son-in-law."

"And all this because I wrote, I love you," she marveled. "I :
sure you have heard it before."

"Heavens, yes," he agreed, the picture of serenity. "Fae Mou
used to tell me that on a regular basis, so she couldn't have me:
it." His voice turned serious then, and her heart pounded loud
"Actually, Emma, what no one has ever said before was that th
liked me."

"I do," she said simply, and kissed his cheek.

"Thank you," he said, his voice equally quiet.

"And you are truly lord inspector?" she asked. "How did y
manage that?"

"Simple, really. And let me state here how nice it was of '
former lord inspector to oblige by dropping down dead during
first course of his farewell dinner."

"You are a rascal," she said with some feeling.

"We know that already," he reminded her. "After leav'
Clarissa in strong hysterics and starting to foam, I dashed off
the Office of Criminal Business. Emma, I do not understand v
our favorite porter gets so excited when I come around. Th
how relieved he will be not to see me for a few years."

"Go on, and leave out the dramatics," she warned him.

"He took me right in to see Mr. Capper—imagine that, if '
can—who walked, nay, ran me over to the Colonial Office, wh
they took me to Home Office. Oh, I love bureaucracy, Em
Think what a politician I will make."

"I warned you . . ." she began, but stopped when he kissed
again.

"A kiss or two, and you are so easy to deal with," he m
mured. "Imagine what can happen when we attempt sometl
more strenuous! Well, to my narrative, if you insist."

"Oh, I do."

"Someone thought to check my military record at Horse Guard. must have been sufficiently distinguished—my dearest, lose an e and gain your country's love—because I waited in a few ore anterooms, then was sent back to Home with a recommen- tion."

"Such exertion," she murmured, and held out her arm for Tim, no sat down on her other side. The ship was moving now, the ils filled.

"Actually, it was worth it. Emma, I cannot confirm this, but e of the senior clerks in Home told me that Spencer Perceval— e prime minister, my dear. Don't look so blank—even said, /hat a novelty. Did they finally get someone who might actually the job?' " he concluded modestly.

"They did," she said. "Mrs. Larch always swore that you know w to handle people."

"Let us see if I can deal with felons, murderers, blackguards, sorted lowlife, and touchy Irish. Let me promise you that for ery old idea I use, I will think up two new ones," he said, and ched into his pocket. "Which brings me to my next bit of ef- t. Emma, you see before you a special license. It cost me a ndle, and I would hate to waste it."

She took the writ from her hand and looked it over, then handed it ck. "You've become so frugal, my lord."

'Yes. Economy is the key here, my love. Do call me John, by way. I think our association is shortly to become somewhat imate, and I think too much 'my lording' will quite put me off best conjugal efforts."

'Really, John," she said, and blushed.

'Economy, dear. You see, I need a secretary for my new du- s—if David Breedlow cannot be found—and I need a wife and ther for my children. As I am only allowed so much poundage this voyage, I must economize and combine all that in one."

She smiled at Lord Ragsdale and nudged Tim. "Doesn't he ry on?"

Tim nodded. "I think he is asking you to marry him."

'Smart lad," Lord Ragsdale said with approval. "How about it, ma? Will you marry me? It's an exertion, but I think I can nage."

'Of course I will marry you, John," she said promptly, "but I ght remind you that we have left the dock."

'True," he agreed. "Isn't it our good fortune that the Colonial ice decided to send out a vicar to Australia? He's the one over re looking decidedly seasick already. Granted he is not

Catholic for you, my dear, but he'll make us legal." He looked
Tim. "Will you mind having your cabin to yourself? I plan to
seasick and a devoted husband, in equal parts, and it won't b
pleasant sight for you. Perhaps Emma will be a loving enou
wife to raise my head from the bucket every now and then."

Tim shook his head and grinned. "I won't mind, as long as y
treat her well."

Lord Ragsdale stopped smiling then, and his face became
serious that Emma felt tears in her eyes. She brushed at the
then squeezed his hand tighter.

"I promise, laddie," he said softly. "She'll have no cause to
gret her decision." He released Emma's hand and reached acr
her to take Tim by the shoulder. "And if for some reason we c
not find your father, I would beg the raising of you as my own
that's agreeable."

"Aye," Tim whispered, his face as solemn as Lord Ragsdale'

"Very well, then!" Lord Ragsdale said, and looked at Em
and Tim. "What a couple of long faces!" He slapped his foreh
then in theatrical exasperation. "Oh, Emma, I know why you
so solemn right now! Didn't you once tell me that nothing wo
make you happier than a bed of your own?"

She laughed out loud, wondering at how she would manag
lifetime with the quixotic, outrageous Lord Ragsdale. One l
time will never be enough, she decided, loving him with all
heart. "I did say that. Once."

"You will have to share your bed again, Emma. I'm sorry, b
must insist."